continued . . .

Final Sentence

"Murder, revenge, secrets . . . and cookbooks! *Final Sentence* . . . is a delectable page-turner with a tasty mix of characters, crime, and cookbooks, blended beautifully in a witty, well-plotted whodunit that will leave you hungry for more."
—Kate Carlisle, *New York Times* bestselling author of the Bibliophile Mysteries

"There's a feisty new amateur sleuth in town and her name is Jenna Hart. With a bodacious cast of characters, a wrenching murder, and a collection of cookbooks to die for, Daryl Wood Gerber's *Final Sentence* was a page-turning puzzler of a mystery that I could not put down."
—Jenn McKinlay, *New York Times* bestselling author of the Cupcake Bakery Mysteries, the Library Lover's Mysteries, and the Hat Shop Mysteries

"Daryl Wood Gerber has found the perfect recipe for all of us who love cozy mysteries and food."   —*Lesa's Book Critiques*

"This is a great new series by a very talented author. This was one book that I picked up and could not put down. I just had to know what would happen next."   *MyShelf.com*

"Daryl succeeded in writing a wonderfully crafted whodunit that quickly became a page-turner thanks to a great setting, a feel-good atmosphere, engaging dialogue, and an eclectically quirky cast of characters."   —*The Cozy Chicks*

Stirring the Plot

DARYL WOOD GERBER

BERKLEY PRIME CRIME, NEW YORK

THE BERKLEY PUBLISHING GROUP
Published by the Penguin Group
Penguin Group (USA) LLC
375 Hudson Street, New York, New York 10014

USA • Canada • UK • Ireland • Australia • New Zealand • India • South Africa • China

penguin.com

A Penguin Random House Company

STIRRING THE PLOT

A Berkley Prime Crime Book / published by arrangement with the author

For information, address: The Berkley Publishing Group,
a division of Penguin Group (USA) LLC,
375 Hudson Street, New York, New York 10014.

ISBN: 978-0-425-25806-4

PUBLISHING HISTORY
Berkley Prime Crime mass-market edition / October 2014

PRINTED IN THE UNITED STATES OF AMERICA

10 9 8 7 6 5 4 3 2 1

Cover illustration by Teresa Farolino.
Cover design by Jason Gill.
Interior text design by Kelly Lipovich.

To Avery Aames,
who opened the door for me

Acknowledgments

"Family is not an important thing. It's everything."
—Michael J. Fox

Thank you to my family for loving me and understanding the crazy schedule it takes for me to write a book. Thank you to my sweet lifelong friends for your love and friendship. Thanks to my talented author friends Krista Davis, Janet Bolin, Kate Carlisle, and Hannah Dennison for your words of encouragement and insight. Thanks to my brainstormers at Plothatchers. Thanks to my blog mates on Mystery Lovers Kitchen and Killer Characters. And thanks to SinC Guppies for your enthusiasm for the written word.

Thanks to those who have helped make The Cookbook Nook series a success: my fabulous editor Kate Seaver, Katherine Pelz, Amy Schneider, Kayleigh Clark, and my cover artist, Teresa Fasolino. I am so blessed.

Thank you to my business team. The amount of work it takes to launch a book is amazing to me. You are truly appreciated!

Thank you, librarians, teachers, fans, and readers for sharing the world of The Cookbook Nook in Crystal Cove, California, with your friends. I am learning so much from all of you.

Thank you, Rebecca Marie Hernandez-Gerber, Jill Baker, and Luci Zahray for helping me with my research. The inspired input from all of you has been invaluable. And last but not least, thanks to my culinary bookstore consultant, Christine Myskowski. You have made exploring cookbooks such a joy for me!

"Gossip brews like a roaring cauldron."
—Victoria Abbott

Chapter 1

A CAT YOWLED. Not mine. Tigger was back at The Cookbook Nook. However, I couldn't stand for an animal to be in pain. I leaped out of my chair and scanned the garden of the Crystal Cove Inn. At five eight, I could peer over most of the crowd. I looked from booth to booth. The Cookbook Nook was one of many vendors selling its wares at the Winsome Witches Faire on a gently breezy Sunday, all to benefit the Witches' cause—literacy. I dropped to all fours. I must have looked pretty silly in a black sheath with my rear end in the air and my sandals ready to fall off my water ski–sized feet, but I didn't care. "Here, kitty, kitty."

"Hi, Jenna." Katie, my friend and the head chef at the Nook Café, taller than me and larger all over, arrived with a tray of delectable homemade candies to give away to afternoon customers. "What are you looking for?"

"A cat yowled. Do you see it?"

"No, but don't worry. I'll bet it was a mouser. They're tough. Someone stepped on its tail, that's all."

Then why did a shiver run down my spine?

"C'mon." Katie nudged my knee with her toe. "Lose the frown. Cats are resilient. Remember that litter of six we found when we were kids?"

I'd wanted to bring them all home, but Katie reminded me that my mother was allergic. We put the kittens in a box and went house to house to find them new families.

"You're right," I conceded. Not hearing another screech, I scrambled to my feet and brushed off my hands.

Katie pointed at my head and chuckled; her wildly curly hair shook. "Fix your witch hat. It's lopsided."

I righted the hat, a little gold number I'd crafted together with felt, ribbon, and wire. Though I wasn't much of a cook yet, I was an artist. Oil paints and clay were my preferred mediums, but I wasn't bad with a pair of scissors and hot glue.

"Better." Katie shoved the tray of goodies my way. "Try one. I've brought *Iron Chef*–inspired maple mascarpone brittle."

I downed a crunchy piece and hummed my appreciation. "Wow."

Katie set the tray on the table beside the various Halloween-themed cookbooks, kitchen utensils, and color-ful salt shakers and pepper mills I'd brought from the shop. Each year at Halloween, the Winsome Witches—they weren't really witches—held a number of charity events, culminating in an annual fund-raising luncheon, which was scheduled a few days from now. Throughout the week, the group asked that all attendees open their designer handbags and *give*, *give*, *give*. Prior to the luncheon, the community of Crystal Cove got into the spirit, too. The Cookbook Nook was planning a couple of family events. On one day, Katie would lead a candy-making class. On another, we were fea-turing a potion-making demonstration as well as a magic show to entertain the kiddies. In addition, the local groomer and pet rescue group sponsored the Black Cat Parade, and each shop in town participated in the annual Spookiest Win-dow Display contest, which reminded me: I needed to get cracking on that. One more thing to add to my to-do list. Swell.

Glass shattered.

I gasped. My heart started to chug. "What now? Is it the cat?"

"Nope." Katie pointed toward the candle maker's booth, where a woman was trying to sweep up the remains of an antique mirror. "Poor thing." Katie *tsk*ed. "Like that will do any good. No matter what, she's got seven years of bad luck."

"You don't really believe that, do you?"

"Of course I do. Superstitions aren't conjured out of thin air. Centuries of folklore create them. Do you remember back in eighth grade how we used to dash past the cemetery holding our breath?"

Did I ever. We believed ghosts would follow us home. I shuddered again. Why was I so jumpy? I shook off the bad vibes and squared my shoulders. "Superstitions, like wives' tales, are exactly that, fabricated to instill fear."

Katie lasered me with a cynical look. "Hold on a sec. Aren't you the one who used to wear only white to take tests in your senior year?"

I grinned. "That was just savvy wardrobe sense."

"How do you feel when a black cat crosses your path?"

"Lucky."

"Liar," Katie teased.

"Let's end this discussion, okay?" I eyed our display table, which Katie had rearranged to make room for the goodies tray. She could plate food better than anyone, but her display styling left something to be desired. Gingerly, I regrouped the cookbooks and drew the pumpkin-shaped salt shakers and pepper mills to the front. Voilà. Customers started to flock to us.

"Ooh, how cute," was a common phrase, and, "Wow, I had no idea there were so many cookbook choices."

Neither did I until I opted to leave my advertising job in San Francisco and move home to Crystal Cove to help my aunt open a culinary bookshop and café. Best choice of my life. Especially now, after discovering the truth about

my deceased husband and his dismal business—*life*—
decisions. I needed family, and I needed friends. To remain
in San Francisco, alone with my memories, wouldn't have
been, well, *fun*. I wanted to move upward and onward.
Too-ra-loo, as my aunt would say.

"I love this time of year," Katie said.

"Because we can dress up?"

Katie rarely dressed simply, preferring checkers and
stripes. For the faire, however, she had donned a black dress.
She also wore a silver Wizard of Oz necklace. You know
the one I mean, with the witch riding the broom.

"No, silly," Katie said. "Because making sweets is one
of my favorite things to do. Chocolate witches. Cinnamon-
candied apples. Caramel popcorn balls. Yum." Katie moved
a salt shaker and ogled me, daring me to reposition it. I
controlled the impulse. Hard to do. "How about you?" she
went on. "Do you like Halloween?"

"Of course." I treasured fond memories. My mother had
loved to make costumes. She would choose a theme. My
sister and brother and I were her guinea pigs. One year we
were, indeed, that—the three little pigs. I was the bricklayer.
Another year, we were characters right out of *The Chronicles of Narnia*. I demanded to be Lucy Pevensie, Queen of
Narnia. My brother was Aslan, the sage lion. My sister was
Jadis, the White Witch, which was, I must admit, appropri-
ate. Whitney could be an ice queen.

"What's your favorite costume ever?" Katie asked.

I didn't have to think long. "Glinda, the Good Witch of
the North."

"I remember that one. It was so cool." Katie and I were
lifelong friends, although we took a few years off during
college for bad behavior—mine, for not keeping in touch.
We reconnected a few months ago when I hired her for the
position of chef at the Nook. "You had a crown and wore a
bubble from the top of your head to your waist."

I'd looked a bit like a see-through beach ball. Fortunately,
my mother possessed enough foresight to cut air holes in
the bubble so I could breathe. My crown, which was coveted

by my peers, glistened with *jewels*—stones my mother had gathered on a local hiking trip.

"Don't you love this inn, by the way?" Katie said.

"I do. It's got good vibes."

"Aha. So, you *do* believe in woo-woo stuff."

I cut her a wry look. "No, I don't."

"Do, too."

"Don't."

The Crystal Cove Inn, one of the original establishments in town, was a charming bed-and-breakfast made of stone and wood. The grounds reminded me of an estate right out of a Jane Austen novel. Like many of the buildings in Crystal Cove, the inn was painted white and sported a red-tiled roof. The hillside behind the inn boasted forests of Douglas fir, oak, and maple trees. The inn's gardens were filled with azaleas and hydrangeas, though none were in bloom in October. Nestled beneath the plants were masses of blue asters, autumn crocuses, and assorted wildflowers.

Katie gestured to the crowd. "Don't you adore all the witches' costumes? Everyone looks so festive."

Each participant, whether at the luncheon or the faire, had been asked to wear a decorative witch hat.

A pair of women in matching silver witch hats stopped by our booth to purchase a specialty cookbook we had stocked for Halloween: *The Unofficial Harry Potter Cookbook: From Cauldron Cakes to Knickerbocker Glory— More Than 150 Magical Recipes for Wizards and Muggles.* Who could resist dining on pumpkin pasties and treacle tart?

The larger woman said, "My nephew is going to love this. He's so into Harry Potter."

"Isn't he twenty-five?" her friend asked.

"He wasn't a reader until Harry came on the scene. He bought each book the day it came out. You never outgrow your first love of books."

How true, I thought. I had devoured the Potter books. Spoiler alert, but Ron and Hermione getting married . . . who'd have guessed?

I slipped one of the bookmarks I'd made with a list of

the shop's special events inside the book, offered the ladies a candy from Katie's assortment, and bid them Happy Halloween. The women moved on, giggling like schoolgirls.

An hour later, after I served our three hundredth visitor, I needed a break. Also, I wanted to check in on my aunt, who was giving tarot readings at the far end of the garden. I asked Katie if she would mind tending the booth. She was delighted. The assistant chef that she'd recently hired was working out great. She didn't have to return to the café for at least a half hour.

"You're sure?" I said.

"Absolutely. I can go it alone." She grasped one of the salt shakers and spritzed salt over her left shoulder.

"Why did you do that?"

"For luck. Other than the broken mirror, no other bad things have happened, but"—she winked—"one can never be too careful."

I FOUND AUNT Vera beneath the shade of an elderberry tree, sitting at a table giving tarot card and palm readings. She didn't have ESP, but she loved providing people with possibilities. Though she typically wore a caftan and a turban, my aunt had gotten into the spirit of the event by donning a purple witch costume and purple hat adorned with antique lace and silk flowers. Of course, she was also wearing her phoenix amulet. She never went anywhere without it. Her table looked fabulously exotic, covered with a rich purple cloth, on top of which sat a crystal ball surrounded by an array of polished glass stones and tarot cards.

With her face fixed in concentration, Aunt Vera addressed a woman whose hand she was holding. "He's going to love you forever," she said.

"Really?" Bingo Bedelia was one of my aunt's longtime friends. She got her quirky name in what my aunt described as a lengthy but funny story; her real name was Barbara. "You swear?"

"On the cover of one of your dusty old Bibles."

Bingo was the owner of Aunt Teek's, a popular antiques and collectibles shop near the center of town. She was also the second-in-command for the Winsome Witches' event. With her ruby red hair pulled off her face and her black witch hat pitched back off her forehead, I couldn't help but notice Bingo's very prominent, knobby chin—what many called a lantern jaw.

Bingo frowned. "Don't lie to me."

"You know I wouldn't."

Bingo, like my aunt, had never married. Neither was a spinster, just unlucky in love. I didn't know if Bingo had been jilted as a younger woman or whether she had lost the love of her life. My aunt had suffered a double whammy.

"Look here. Your love line is strong." Aunt Vera drew her finger along Bingo's palm. "I assure you, he knows you are a treasure."

Bingo caught sight of me and flushed the color of her hair. "Hello, Jenna. Are you listening in?"

"Trying to catch some tips," I quipped.

"Whatever you do, cherish your man."

I had, but he died. There was a handsome guy in town I was interested in, a former chef who switched careers and now owned Bait and Switch Fishing and Sport Supply Store. We'd known each other only a short time, but I sizzled with desire whenever I was around him.

"There are so few good ones," Bingo added. "Mine"— recently, Bingo had become engaged to a darling pastor everyone in town referred to as the Reverend—"is such a sweetie pie. I don't know what I'd do without him."

A plump forty-something woman sneaked up behind Bingo and gripped her shoulders. "You'd die."

Bingo shrieked.

The woman, Pearl Thornton, cackled; her black witch hat made her hair appear as white as snow. "Did I scare you, Barbara Bedelia?" Pearl was a therapist in town—mine, as well as others'. I was seeing her to learn coping skills. Being a widow, at any age, isn't easy.

"You know you did, and you'll call me Bingo, if you

know what's good for you." Bingo pulled her hand free from my aunt's grasp and shook a finger at Pearl.

"Or what?" Pearl said.

Bingo popped her finger as if pulling a trigger. "Bang! You're dead."

Pearl laughed heartily. So did Bingo. She wasn't angry. How could she be? She and Pearl were dear friends. Pearl was the High Priestess of the Winsome Witches.

"Do you need me for a prep meeting?" Bingo asked.

"No, relax. Enjoy." Right after Pearl's husband died, she founded the Winsome Witches and wrangled her friends to participate. I don't think anyone had foreseen what a huge success the annual week of events would be.

"Are all of you ready for the"—Pearl rested the tip of her finger to her mouth—"*haunted* walk on Tuesday?" She teetered a bit. "It's going to be *spoo-oo-ooky*." The event planners had scheduled an evening tour to visit Crystal Cove's historic sites. "If you don't watch out, someone might"—she wiggled her fingers in Bingo's face—"scare you."

"Stop it." Bingo batted her friend's hand away. "What's gotten into you?"

"Nothing."

"Have you been drinking?"

"No."

I wasn't so sure. Pearl appeared a little off-balance.

Suddenly, she clutched her chest. Her eyes widened. She gasped for breath. Without warning, she crumpled to the ground. Bingo, who had been a nurse before she moved to Crystal Cove to open her dream shop, crouched beside Pearl. She grabbed her wrist. Just as she pressed two fingers against Pearl's throat, Pearl bolted to a sitting position. Bingo fell backward on her rump.

Pearl roared with laughter. "I'm not dead, you goon."

Bingo's mouth fell open. "Why, you—"

My aunt leaped to a stand and said, "What on earth?"

Pearl continued to laugh. "I'm sorry. It's almost Halloween."

"Pranks are for April Fools' Day," Bingo chided.

"C'mon. Can't anybody take a joke?"

"Dying is no joke!"

"Of course it's not," Pearl stammered. "But you mimed pulling a trigger a second ago, and I thought—"

"You could have given us all a heart attack."

"But I didn't, and it's just . . ." Pearl's mouth drew into a grim line. Her gaze turned serious. "I apologize. I'm a little punch-drunk, that's all. I—" She hesitated.

"Out with it," Bingo demanded.

"I just learned the results of some tests. I've been diagnosed with type 2 diabetes. I know it's not life-threatening. It's all about having the right amount of insulin in my system, but the report sounded so stark. I've never watched my weight. I should have"—she patted her plump stomach—"but I haven't. I simply needed to do something to lighten my day. I didn't mean to frighten you so much. Forgive me?" She reached for Bingo's hand and squeezed.

"Are you going to be okay?" Bingo said.

"Of course. I've started my medication, and I'm taking the advice I give to my patients. Positive thinking." She eyed me. One of her favorite mantras was: *All things level out in time.* She lumbered to her feet and offered a hand to Bingo, who accepted.

Bingo brushed off her dress and said, "Come with me. Let's get a cup of tea, and I'll fill you in on some dietary tips. Number one, remember that stress can raise glucose levels." The pair walked off, arm in arm.

My aunt turned to me and kissed me on both cheeks. "Well, that was fun. *Not.*"

I laughed. "I have to say I was shocked Pearl would do something like that, as rational as she always is."

"Medical surprises can turn a person's world upside down." Aunt Vera glanced at her watch. "My, my. Time flies when you're having a ball. Speaking of which, I've been cleaning up at my table. I've earned over three hundred dollars for the cause." She was charging a dollar per palm or tarot card reading. "How about The Cookbook Nook booth?"

"We're doing great. The Harry Potter cookbook, as

expected, is a bestseller, and we've sold tons of herbal potion books. I think everyone attending the faire is drawn to the mystical."

"Wonderful. Now . . . as long as nothing else goes wrong . . ." Her face, normally radiant with hope, turned grim.

A chill ran through me. "Why would you say that?"

"A moment ago, when Pearl arrived, I got the worst feeling."

My breath caught in my chest. "What kind of feeling?"

"I was all itchy, and the light up here"—she tapped her temple—"went extremely dark."

"Maybe you were sensing Pearl's prank."

Aunt Vera nodded in agreement. "You're right. Silly me." She kissed her fingers and tossed the imaginary kiss to the wind, something I'd seen her do all of my life. She said it was a good way to return bad energy to the universe.

In spite of her gesture, an uneasy feeling surged through me. Desperate to shake it off, I said, "It's a good thing no more mirrors have broken."

My aunt rapped the table. "Knock on wood."

Chapter 2

MONDAYS AT THE Cookbook Nook could be taxing because we had so much to do before taking off Tuesday, like inventory, restocking, and dusting.

However, prior to attacking the mundane, I intended to focus on our Halloween décor. I hadn't finished putting together our window display yet. Time was a-wasting. I was almost done. I had cut out a leafless tree, using brown paper with foam board as backing, and then I'd added a silhouette of a bat hanging upside down and an owl perched on a tree limb. Very spooky. Very cool. Beneath, I had laid a black polka-dot carpet and set out an assortment of pumpkins, each decorated with black felt for the eyes and mouths. In front of a short, white picket fence, I was arranging seasonal cookbooks with lengthy titles like *35 Halloween Recipes for the Faint of Heart: Recipe Ideas for Halloween Parties, Dinner, and Appetizers* and *Hungry Halloween: Featuring Movie Monster Munchies, Bewitched Buffet, and Dead Man's Diner.* I had stumbled upon the cookbooks when I was playfully searching for a make-a-person-nicer potion, the kind of elixir I could sneak into someone's iced tea or lemonade. One of the shop owners at Fisherman's Village, where The Cookbook Nook was located, had it in for my family, but I was determined to win her friendship. Even if I had to coerce her with, ahem, a *spirited* potion. So far, I hadn't found a recipe, and honestly, I didn't believe a potion would work, but I was having fun conjuring up ingredients to include: eye of newt, oil of snakeskin, or essence of Komodo dragon.

"Hey, Jenna, look at this." My lifelong pal Bailey Bird, whom I had hired to be our sales associate, waved to me from the rear of the store. All I could see was her hand. In addition to the walls of bookshelves that were filled with books and culinary giftware, we had movable shelves in the center of the store. Bailey, who measured five feet tall only because of the high heels she always wore, was completely hidden from view.

I abandoned the window display and hurried to where she was setting out more Halloween-themed cookbooks on display tables, like *The Alchemist's Kitchen: Extraordinary Potions & Curious Notions*, which was packed with assorted recipes from ancient glue to herbal tinctures.

"I think I found it." Bailey waggled *The Herbal Alchemist's Handbook: A Grimoire of Philtres, Elixirs, Oils, Incense, and Formulas for Ritual Use*. The dozen bangles on her arm slid to her elbow with a clank. The oversized earrings she wore jangled with enthusiasm. A flash of sun light through the plate-glass window outlined her and made her spiky, copper-colored hair gleam like polished metal.

"Found what?"

"The potion that we need."

"Potion?"

"Something we can use on Pepper to sweeten her up."

Ah, yes. Pepper, the owner of Beaders of Paradise, was the persnickety woman who needed a dash of sugar added to her cynical spice.

Without opening the book, Bailey, who had an eidetic

memory, recited, " 'Steeped in mysticism and magick, alchemy is also an ancient path of spiritual purification and the transformation of the spirit.' You get it, don't you?" Bailey looked at me expectantly. "We'll make a potion and hide it in some kind of charm. It'll be an amulet for Pepper to wear. Hardly anyone says *no* to a present. We'll even use some of Pepper's beads to adorn the necklace. That way we can combine both the plant and mineral sides of alchemy."

I snickered. "I was just kidding when I said we needed to create a potion. Stop worrying. Pepper will come around."

"There's no harm in a little push. What was that campaign you did back at Taylor & Squibb?" Bailey snapped her fingers, trying to summon a memory. She and I had spent a few years at a large advertising agency in San Francisco—I on the creative side, she in the numbers arena. "Oh, I remember! The um . . . um . . . you know which one I mean. I had to hand it to the dancers. They really threw themselves into the routine." She set the book aside and did a Hokey Pokey–style dance. "Give a little push, give a little shove."

"Let them know they're wonderful," I chimed.

"Use a little love." Bailey clapped her hands. "I adored that commercial. What was it for?"

I gawped. "Really, you don't recall?" The whole point of making a catchy commercial was so folks would remember it and either purchase the product or enroll in a plan. If someone who worked at Taylor & Squibb couldn't remember its purpose, I had truly failed at my job. "A Dieter's Dream," I said.

"That's it. It would've come to me. I loved the junk food flying out of the cupboards and being replaced with wholesome foods."

I was proud of the campaign. The outfit that had hired us consisted of a group of dedicated dieters. All had succeeded on the diet, which included a lot of spinach. No fad foods. All natural. Last I'd heard, the sixsome were writing a cookbook.

Bailey set aside the alchemy handbook and offered me a stack of cookbooks. "Help me arrange these."

"Can't. I've got to finish the window display."

"Do that later." Bailey planted her fists on her hips.

"Who could say no to such a lovely offer?" I teased. As I set out books, I said, "How's the new apartment?" When Bailey moved back to Crystal Cove, she settled in above The Pelican Brief Diner, her mother's restaurant that overlooked the bay. Free rent. Free food. What more could a girl want? But Bailey, like me, was nearing her thirtieth birthday and craved to be independent again. I totally understood.

"Superb. No aromas of fried fish making me want to binge-eat." Bailey would never have a problem with weight. She might be short, but she darted around like the Energizer Bunny. "All the furniture I kept in storage in the City fits perfectly."

The City. San Francisco. I missed living downtown. There were restaurants up the wazoo—a gourmet's haven—museums, art galleries, and so much more, but I was happy with my choice to return to Crystal Cove. We had plenty of delicious restaurants from which to choose, lots of shops to browse, and my aunt had offered me the cute cottage beside her seaside home. I relished the sound of the surf.

"I'm going to paint my new place blue and pink," Bailey said.

"Pink? You hate pink."

"Okay, coral. Something very beachy. However, I don't have a view, so I was thinking of commissioning you to do a picture of the ocean for me. I could hang it over the fireplace and imagine I lived in your cottage."

"You know that if I had the room, I'd invite you to move in."

"Are you kidding?" Bailey said. "The two of us living in the same apartment? Ugh. No, thanks. Girlfriends should never do that, if you ask me. It's the little petty things that start building up, and wham, you're no longer friends. All I want is a painting."

I grinned. "I'll paint it for free in my spare time."

Bailey cleared her throat. "Um . . ."

"What?"

"No dancing ballerinas, please."

I gave her a bemused look.

"I know how much you love your Degas period," she added.

My mother used to take me to the beach to paint. I would watch other little girls, like me, dancing across the sand, and I dreamed of becoming the next famous ballerina painter. Didn't happen. I was good, just not great.

"No ballerinas," I agreed.

"Thank you." Bailey clenched me in a hug that took my breath away.

I felt a wisp of warm fur bat my bare leg. Tigger, the ginger kitten I found the week I arrived in Crystal Cove, meowed. I broke free of my ecstatic pal and scooped him up. "Feeling neglected, Tig-Tig?" I'd dubbed him with the same name as the Disney character because the little guy could bounce and pounce with the best of them. I nuzzled his neck and set him back on the floor. "You have treats. Go find them. I'm busy." He meowed again.

A group of mothers and children entered the store. One of the moms held up a cute black cat vase filled with orange gerbera daisies. "Yoo-hoo, Jenna, I found this on the door-step." She offered it to me. "I think it's from a secret admirer."

I checked the note looped to the cat's tail. *From the one who adores you.* Sweet. Rhett, the guy I was occasionally dating, must have left it earlier in the day and I missed seeing it as I entered. Tigger butted my ankle. I crouched down to him. "Hey, pal, fresh humans," I whispered. "Go get 'em." He bounded toward the children. Squeals of delight followed.

"Nice flowers," Bailey said. "Which reminds me, are you ready for the Black Cat Parade?"

"I am. I have Tigger's costume set to go." For the parade, cat owners were encouraged to dress up their furry friends. One would win an award. I had made Tigger a gold witch hat to match my own. I didn't think I could get the squiggle worm into anything more elaborate. I set the flowers on the counter and glanced again at the romantic message. "By the way, how's it going with your Latin lover?" Bailey's boyfriend, a hunky South American aeronautical engineer, was working as a paddleboard instructor while updating his citizenship status.

Bailey screwed up her mouth. "Fine, I think. Do you ever know with men?" She wasn't a commitment-phobe, but she hadn't had a serious relationship for a long time. "We'll talk one day and then three days will pass before we talk again. Weird."

"Give him breathing room."

"That's what Tito said."

"Where did you see him?" Tito Martinez was a reporter for the *Crystal Cove Crier*. He reminded me of a boxer, the middleweight-athlete-of-the-dog-world kind.

"At Latte Luck Café." Bailey had tried to give up caffeine a month ago; she'd lasted only a few days. "You know, the guy isn't half bad when you get to know him." Most often, Tito loved to brag and seemed totally self-absorbed, but recently I'd been hearing other people say good things about him. For example, he volunteered at the high school to teach adults English as a second language. I guess you never know about people until you discover the layer beneath what they present on the surface. Bailey said, "I think he's lost a little weight, and he might be getting smarter."

"Smarter?"

"You know, savvier. Between you and me, I think he's going to therapy."

"Really?"

"He gave me basic psychobabble tips regarding Jorge. He said, get this, 'Be sure to practice good self-care.' That's shrink talk, right?" Bailey eyed the black cat vase. "Enough about my sorry life. I'm assuming it's going well with Rhett if he's sending you flowers."

I nodded. "We're going on a date tomorrow night."

"He's taking you on the haunted historic walk? Ooh, snuggle close, girlfriend. Be daring."

Daring. Right. Rhett and I had kissed. Briefly. I'd cut that short. Not because I wasn't attracted to him. I was. Totally. The man created more heat in me than a steam engine. Whoo-whoo! But I wasn't ready for a deeper relationship. Yet.

I started for the window display and paused. "I almost forgot. Speaking of daring, I'm going to throw a Halloween party."

"Get real," Bailey said.

"And I'm cooking. By myself."

Bailey snorted.

"That's enough out of you." Okay, so I wasn't the world's best cook, but a few weeks ago, I'd added learning to be a good cook to my bucket list. Sure, I needed lessons, and I needed practice. But I adored Halloween. Why not start there? The shop had some wonderful Halloween cookbooks. One, for kids, was called *Our Favorite Halloween Recipes Cookbook: Jack-o'-Lanterns, Hayrides and a Big Harvest Moon . . . It Must Be Halloween! Find Tasty Treats That Aren't Tricky.* It had simple, easy recipes, perfect for the novice like me. One of the recipes was for spider pizza. How hard could that be?

"Costumes required," I said.

"I'll be there with eerie bells on."

Chapter 3

ᗝᏖᏇᏇᎶᎶ

ON TUESDAY EVENING, about fifty of us met in the parking lot of Fisherman's Village to get on a bus for the haunted tour. Winsome Witches board members and their guests planned to visit a number of historic places around the area, including the first graveyard, the first garden, and the first mansion in Crystal Cove.

Our initial stop was to the one and only lighthouse. The building was constructed to ensure that ships didn't hit the prominence of land that jutted out at the northern tip of town. As a kid, I had learned about the shipwreck that occurred in 1890, but to hear my aunt—the leader of the tour—tell the lighthouse's history of treasure and woe gave the place a whole new twist. By the end of the trek, I had to admit my legs were tired; I definitely needed to add some stair climbing to my exercise routine. Perhaps I should have worn tennis shoes on the tour instead of my fancy thong sandals. So much for fashion.

Ten minutes after climbing back on the bus, we reached

the cemetery. "This way, everyone," Aunt Vera said as she led us inside.

Silky, decorative ghosts hung from tree branches; black wreaths adorned headstones. Small candles lined each pathway. The entire scene, especially with the influx of cool fog, felt spooky.

All of the tour attendees, each of whom carried battery-lit candles, were dressed as witches, including Rhett and me. Thankfully, although he possessed a wicked sense of humor, he didn't go with the wizard-in-the-goofy-hat look. He wore a black shirt, black jeans, and boots. Vampire-like makeup finished the costume. With his shirt unbuttoned halfway and his manly chest partially exposed, he looked like a guy you'd see on the front of a romance novel—downright sexy.

"This is the first graveyard ever established in the area," Aunt Vera said.

Crystal Cove was a lovely California seaside town, rich with history. Rolling hills bordered the town to the east; the ocean lay to the west. Settlers moved into the area in the 1850s, but the town was officially founded in 1883.

"Rumor has it"—my aunt lowered her voice—"that every year Old Man Carlton, the first settler in Crystal Cove and a moral soul, rises from his grave and flies over the town to make sure no evil lurks within."

A teenaged girl at the front of the pack uttered an unnerving, albeit sarcastic, wail.

"Don't disparage rumors, young lady." My aunt shook a finger as she neared a crypt. "Nor superstitions, for that matter. Some may consider them irrational or false conceptions, but I happen to know"—she raised her arms overhead—"that we believe what we will because of surprising occurrences."

Suddenly, a skeleton leaped from behind the crypt. It swooped toward the teenager, who shrieked. As fast as it appeared, the skeleton ducked out of sight. People erupted into giggles. The girl, who was accompanied by another teen, punched her friend. I wondered which Winsome Witch had dragged them along.

"Scared?" Rhett said.

"Not with you nearby," I murmured. Following Bailey's instruction, I snuggled into him. Delicious desire coursed from my head to my toes. "By the way, thank you for the flowers."

"What flowers?"

"The gerbera daisies. In the black cat vase."

"I don't know what you're talking about."

"You left them on the shop's doorstep. The card said they were from"—I gestured with quotation marks—"'the one who adores you.'"

"Sorry. I didn't send them." His mouth quirked up on the right. "Should I be jealous?"

"No, of course not," I sputtered. If Rhett hadn't left the gift, then who had?

"Just to be safe . . ." He brushed his lips against my forehead.

As he did, I caught a couple of women in the group eyeing me with envy. *Let them*, I thought, though heat warmed my cheeks. My deceased husband hadn't been one for public displays of affection. It appeared Rhett was, and I liked it.

"Say, is that Dr. Thornton?" Rhett whispered.

Ahead of us, Pearl walked with Bingo. They were deep in conversation.

"I barely recognized her," he said.

As High Priestess of the Winsome Witches, Pearl had dressed accordingly. Her floor-length black gown and pointed hat were covered with sequins. She nearly glimmered in the moonlight.

A few weeks ago, Rhett had confided that he'd met with Dr. Thornton to deal with his fear of fire. He left his job as chef of The Grotto when the restaurant burned down, due to arson. His takeaway from his sessions—*takeaway* was a term Dr. Thornton used—was that Rhett had to deconstruct the lies so he could get to the truth. "See the sunrise, not the sunset," he whispered.

That was another of Pearl's, um, *pearls* of wisdom.

"You know"—I bumped him with my hip—"in this

quiet-as-a-tomb environment, we can invoke the cone of silence. Care to tell me more about you?" I wasn't one for keeping secrets. I'd learned way too late that my husband had kept loads of them. He stole clients' funds and he hid gold coins in a statue, to name a couple. In the few months since I'd met Rhett, I had gleaned a bit of data about him. He lived in a cabin, he owned his own business, and he had attended culinary school years ago. He loved to fish and whittle, and he liked to read many of the same books I did. But I wanted to know more. Heck, I wanted to know everything. Did that mean I was ready for a deeper relationship after all?

"For instance?" he asked.

"Parents?"

"What about them?"

"Do you have them? Are they—" I paused awkwardly.

"Yes, they're still alive."

"Where do they live?"

He hesitated. "Napa Valley."

"What do they do?"

"Dine on fine French food."

I poked his rib cage. "Don't be cryptic."

"They're in the business. They own a restaurant."

"Really, which one?"

"Intime."

I gasped. "You're not fooling?"

"Nope."

Intime—in French it meant "intimate"—was a renowned restaurant in the wine country, second to the French Laundry; both were located in Yontville, north of Napa. I had eaten there twice. I remembered a lovely woman, the owner, who had reminded me of my mother, tall and slender with dark curls feathering her face. She had beautiful blue eyes. Now looking at Rhett, I could see the resemblance. Honestly, I would melt into his eyes if he'd let me.

"Why didn't you tell me that before?" I said.

"My father . . ." He worked his tongue inside his cheek. "Strapping guy. Very tan." He looked like the kind of man who could have run a huge vineyard or ranch. "Sort of stern."

"That's him. He disinherited me."

"Why?"

"Because I eloped with the daughter of his best friend. Within the year, we were divorced. Her choice. Heartbroken, I entered culinary school, but when I didn't pursue the art of French cooking, which further incensed my father, I became the black sheep."

"How did your mother feel about your father cutting you off?"

Rhett had risked his life to run back through the fire in The Grotto to save his mother's prized recipe box. Now I understood why he had taken the risk. Those recipes were not merely family keepsakes; they were the essence of a successful business.

"She wasn't pleased, but she wouldn't buck him. We communicate via my sisters."

"You have sisters?" I had no idea I would get such a rich account. Maybe having a secret admirer was the impetus. Yay for me. "Do they have names?"

"Scarlett and Ashley."

I grinned. "Your mother loved *Gone with the Wind*."

"She adored it. Doesn't every young girl?" Rhett toed the ground. "My father wanted a partner in the family business. He didn't expect my sisters to comply. I sorely disappointed him."

"Does he know what happened to you? Your career? The fire?"

"He does."

"Hasn't he tried to mend fences?"

Rhett shook his head, then pressed a finger to my lips. "No more talk of him."

"My aunt intimated that you had some run-ins with the law." She hadn't revealed more. She believed all people should tell their stories in their own time.

A moment passed before Rhett said, "About a year ago, when your aunt insisted on giving me a palm reading, I let slip that I'd stolen a car. That wasn't entirely true. When I eloped with Alicia, I borrowed my father's car. He reported it stolen. In the dead of night, I returned the car, and Alicia and I hitchhiked for a month. To look for America."

"Like the Simon and Garfunkel song."

"Pretty much. I don't have a police record."

"Back to the buses, everyone," Aunt Vera said. "Jenna, Rhett, don't lag."

I squeezed Rhett's arm and said, "At some point, you're going to tell me about Alicia and any other ladies in your past." My aunt had also warned me that Rhett was a *bit of a rogue*. What did that mean? Was I falling in love with a man who would one day break my heart?

As we neared the bus, Rhett said, "Who's that?" He pointed at a freckle-faced woman climbing out of a Corvette.

Emma Wright jammed a witch hat on her short-cropped hair and blew a kiss to the driver, her husband, Edward. Whenever I saw the man, I winced. He was fairly attractive with his lean Nordic look, chiseled jaw, and rock-hard eyes. His blond hair was a little slicker than I liked on a man, but that had nothing to do with my reaction to him. No, I winced because he was a dentist. The sound of the drill. The masks. The smells. The phantom pain. Yes, I went to a dentist—not Edward—but only because I wanted good teeth and not dentures when I entered my golden years.

Edward gunned the sports car and sped away. Emma watched him leave, her expression pinched, but she quickly put on a smile and joined Bingo and Pearl.

"Don't you know Emma?" I said. "She'll be the newest inductee to the Winsome Witches. She owns Pet Taxi, the service that shuttles animals to the vet or the groomers." Emma, like my pal Bailey, was blessed with boundless energy and enthusiasm. "She can talk a blue streak." Maybe that was why she spent most of her daylight hours with non-human-talking pets. I wondered how her husband dealt with that. Dentists did all the talking in their profession. I'd heard Edward was a cave explorer in his spare time; maybe he communed with bats. "You've never used her service?" I went on.

"I take Rook to all his appointments myself." Rhett owned a Labrador retriever. He liked big dogs. "He won't get into a car with a stranger. I'm not sure what happened to him before I found him at the pound, but I'm pretty sure it was something awful that involved cars."

"Poor pup. Do you happen to know Emma's husband?"

"Edward. Sure. He's a weekend spelunker. He comes into Bait and Switch a lot. Long neck."

"Really? That's all you remember? Edward has a long neck?"

"I'm a guy. What more do you want?"

Our next stop on the tour was The Enchanted Garden nursery, one of my favorite places to visit in Crystal Cove. I could spend hours browsing the plants and glazed pots. Recently I'd purchased herbs for my front porch: basil, parsley, mint, and thyme. Some weren't doing so well, although the parsley was thriving. I supposed even I, who didn't have a green thumb, couldn't kill parsley.

On the other hand, the owner of the shop, Maya Adaire, was skillful with a garden. Her shop, which was the first established in town, teemed with plants and beautiful ironwork sculpture. She offered many of her homegrown vegetables for sale: heirloom tomatoes, exotic mushrooms, zucchini, and pumpkins. A daily dose of mushrooms, she advised, could cure cancer. As if the rest of her accomplishments weren't enough, Maya had also penned a cookbook of healthful vegetarian recipes.

As we entered The Enchanted Garden's main shop, I inhaled. The scent of fall flowers filled the air. The interior was aglow with tiny white lights. Strands of orange pumpkin cutouts hung from the coarse wooden beams overhead. A blessing broom, which was hand-wrapped with ribbon, leaned against the checkout counter. A sign posting the way to Salem and Sleepy Hollow stood in the center of the garden near a birdbath waterfall. Maya had cleverly placed decorative art and bird feeders throughout the shop. Bowls of wrapped Halloween candies sat on wrought-iron tables and potting étagères.

Maya, a slender, almost ropy woman, her lean look the result of a vegetarian diet, greeted us as we entered. She wore a witch hat decorated with black satin and white bell-shaped flowers. She had woven the flowers into her curly tresses, as well. As we entered, she handed each of us a business card. I already had one, but I didn't decline. I loved the lily of the valley logo. I remembered doing an advertising campaign for an online florist. Unlike my typical humorous ads, the LOV ad—that's what we had called it—featured what I believed was every schoolgirl's dream wedding: exquisite bouquets of lily of the valley with their pretty white bell-shaped flowers and streamers of white chiffon blowing in a gentle breeze. On a previous visit to The Enchanted Garden, I had asked Maya about the logo. I learned her mother had named her Maya Lily: *Maya* for May, and *Lily* for her mother's favorite flower, which bloomed in May. How sweet was that?

"This way, y'all," Maya said with a subtle Southern accent. She was born in South Carolina but had migrated to California after college. As she led the way, she rubbed her hands like a witch beckoning Hansel and Gretel into her cottage, which made me giggle. All part of the act, I assumed. "On your right, you'll see a number of unique plants that might benefit you, should you be so inclined. Jacob's Ladder, otherwise known as Ladder to Heaven, can increase your mental abilities as well as your joie de vivre. Lavender, I'm sure you all know, attracts affection. It is especially good when used in love-type potions."

A few of the visitors giggled.

"Think about adding some dried lavender whenever you're writing a love note. Y'all still do that, don't you? Write?"

More laughter.

"In addition, the aroma of lavender encourages long life. Some people carry lavender in order to see ghosts. Have any of you seen a ghost?"

No hands shot up.

Maya grinned. "Me, either, but I hope to someday. Now, sage"—she fingered a grayish-green plant—"is wonderful when added to a bath. It can purify you of all past evils and negative deeds. If you burn sagebrush, sort of like burning incense, you can drive away malevolent forces." She moved on to a section of trailing plants. "Rosemary, when burned, is powerful, as well. Pay attention: if you place a sprig of rosemary beneath your pillow, you'll get a good sleep. It also"—she beckoned us near, then whispered—"attracts elves."

"Jenna has seen elves," Rhett joked. "The Keebler kind."

I knuckled his arm.

Emma, who had been hanging back with Pearl and Bingo, sidled up to Maya. "Tell them about the history of this place."

"Didn't you tell them, Vera?"

My aunt shook her head.

Maya offered a mock scowl. "Fine. Leave the heavy lifting to me. The main building of The Enchanted Garden was erected in 1901. The garden shop was passed down from generation to generation, until the last of the family died, with no survivors. Some believed the original owners were witches."

"No," someone from the back of the pack said.

Maya raised a finger. "Aha, I hear disbelievers among you. It's true. Witches dwelled in Crystal Cove. The bay has mystical properties."

My aunt clucked her tongue and winked at me.

"Really?" a teenage girl asked, not the same one who had yowled in the cemetery.

Maya nodded and waved a hand dramatically. "I purchased the garden site specifically to draw on these properties. I have dedicated my life to finding just the right herbal potion for everyone who asks." Maya was the herbalist I had scheduled to teach our customers how to make potions. "Now, follow me for more of the tour." She crooked a finger. We trailed her until she came to an abrupt halt. "Can y'all hear me?" She motioned to a lush pot of herbs. "In this pot you will spy sweet basil. Sometimes it's known as St. John's wort. It's often used in protection spells. In addition to basil, you might notice hyssop, peppermint, and sassafras."

Emma said, "Sassafras is used in root beer."

"That's right," Maya responded. "By the way, witches often decorate their herb pots with unrefined gemstones like bloodstone and tiger's eye." She held a finger to her mouth and said, "Shh. That's insider information. As a side note—"

My aunt cleared her throat and twirled her finger. "Wrap it up, Maya. You're losing them."

Maya laughed. "Yes, I'm afraid that's a bad habit of mine. Too much information."

"Eek," a woman in the crowd shrieked.

A large, ebony-colored cat bounded through the tour members and lurched at Maya. It stopped at her feet, and then, as if reconsidering, it leaped upward. At Emma. She caught the cat just in time and wedged her thumbs beneath its forearms.

"There, there, Boots," Emma said, while scratching his ears. "What spooked you?"

"He probably saw a ghost," Maya retorted.

I recognized the cat. I'd seen him around The Enchanted Garden on previous occasions. I couldn't tell if he was a Bombay or Burmese, but he had no markings on him. Certainly no white *boots*, as his name inferred. I glanced at Maya, who was twirling a curl of her hair, a gamine smile tugging at her lips. Had she enticed Boots to dash in and scare everyone?

"Poor little guy," Emma cooed.

Rhett leaned into me. "He's not so little. Looks to be about twenty pounds."

I giggled, then turned to Emma. "He sure seems to like you."

"Only because I've been carting him back and forth to the vet for the past few weeks for treatment. He's got hot spots on his rear legs, and he keeps licking them."

"Where was I?" Maya said. "Oh, right. For the farewell—"

She paused, distracted by something to her right. "Oh no you don't."

While we'd been chatting, the rowdy teenage girl and her girlfriend started tiptoeing toward an exit door at the rear of the garden shop.

Maya sprinted toward them and blocked their exit. She raised her arms overhead. "Do not touch that handle. Pooh-pooh." She blew out bad air. "Whatever were you thinking? You always exit through the door you came in. It's a Southern tradition."

Emma said, "I thought that was an Irish superstition."

"Whatever it is, you simply don't do it. It has something to do with entering and leaving this life as a good person, and y'all want that." Maya steered the group toward the front, offering a few more words about herbs as we moved. When we neared the exit, she said, "Thank you for coming. As you exit, take the small pots of rosemary I planted for you. Set them to the right of your front door if you want to keep witches away. Unless you don't believe. It is, after all"—she chuckled—"just a superstition."

Outside the shop, a whistling wind kicked up. The teens, who were now wound up to a frenzy, howled along with the wind and hurled their teeny pots of rosemary on the ground. I wasn't one to believe in superstitions, but as the clay shattered, the evening's light mood and good vibes vanished, and I shivered with fear.

On the bus ride to Traveler's Tavern, Rhett couldn't stop laughing about the crowd's reaction to the black cat at The Enchanted Garden. As we climbed off the bus, he said, "Working down at The Pier, you won't believe the superstitions I've heard."

"Like?"

"Don't whistle on board a ship. Don't leave port on Friday. Don't bring a banana on board."

"A banana?"

"Don't even wear yellow on a ship."

I giggled. "Darn. Yellow's one of my favorite colors."

"You two, get a move on," Aunt Vera said. "No dilly-dallying." She pushed me toward the front of the old restaurant.

Traveler's Tavern, which was undergoing a shoring-up renovation, was established over 160 years ago. Walking in, I could sense the history. How many explorers had passed through the heavy oak doors? The walls and ceilings held signatures of all who had visited before us.

"Whoa." Rhett stopped me from walking beneath the wooden scaffolding that stood in the center of the room. "You may not believe in superstitions, but that's just flaunting skepticism."

"Thanks." Gazing at the signatures, I had completely lost sight of where I was.

Built entirely of stone, mortar, and wood, the tavern was chilly. The bar was set up for a ghoulish party. Eerie green candles set the mood. I could imagine bawdy nights back in the Gold Rush days when people, hungry for chunks of the precious metal that might change their futures forever, downed tankards of beer or whiskey. While the tavern's colorful owner told us the history of the place, we dined on Halloween spiced popcorn, mini ghost cupcakes decorated with white icing and black licorice eyes, and Black Cat brew, which was a lusty mix of root beer laced with cinnamon.

As we were leaving, yet more black cats crossed our path. A few in the crowd shrieked; others laughed. Had the cagey tavern owner, like Maya, set the cats loose on purpose to scare us, or were they stray cats on the prowl? Whatever the reason, I was sufficiently shaken *and* stirred.

Chapter 4

FOR THE LAST stop on the tour, we headed to Pearl Thornton's place, an elegant two-story showplace that had been featured in many magazines. As we approached the house, which was set high on the mountain, the damp, foggy weather lifted. A full moon, like a beacon of hope, cut through the clouds and lit a path to the front door.

The interior of the home was exquisite, with high ceilings and expansive rooms, although the extensive use of the color ecru was a little bland for my taste. The view through the plate-glass windows of the living room matched my father's view—the twinkling lights of Crystal Cove below and eons of miles of ocean. Beautifully carved jack-o'-lanterns flickered on various antique tables. Glossy black bats hung on clear thread that had been slung between the rafters. Actors dressed as vampires or ghouls moved among us. A red goblin rounded the corner and screeched at a pair of women. The women tittered and fanned themselves.

Similarly to our other stops on the journey, we were invited to take a tour of the house. Pearl acted as guide.

"Let's start with the kitchen," she said. "That's where I've set up the bar. We're serving a Witchy Woman cocktail. Demon rum is the secret ingredient."

The kitchen was fitted with state-of-the-art appliances, hand-painted tiles, and top-of-the-line granite counters.

Rhett handed me a sugar-rimmed martini glass filled with a frothy, bloodred beverage. "Happy early Halloween."

"Cheers." We clinked glasses.

As I took my first sip—the drink was deliciously sweet— the kitchen door leading to the garage opened. A woman in her early twenties stormed through the doorway, her umbrella still open.

Pearl yelled, "Trisha, close that umbrella now! It's bad luck."

"Bad luck, Mother?" Unlike her plump mother, Trisha was angular and rangy and had possibly the worst skin I'd ever seen. I couldn't tell if it was a dietary issue or a nerves thing. Her loose clothing did nothing to enhance her figure. She hoisted her crocheted purse and raggedy backpack higher on her shoulder and pushed her hank of black hair that reminded me of furry yarn away from her face. "I've already had twenty-three years of bad luck being your daughter."

Ouch! The ten or so people in the kitchen gasped.

"What's up with my cell phone?" Trisha shook the umbrella free of moisture and snapped it closed. "I can't get the darned thing to turn on. Did you cancel the contract?"

"That's it, young lady. Into the pantry." Pearl muscled her daughter into a small room at the far end of the kitchen. Sadly, the room wasn't far enough away. We could still hear every word the two said.

"You did, didn't you?" Trisha shouted. "You canceled the contract. How dare you."

"Your expenses are mounting up," Pearl responded, her voice raspy with anger.

"I've got to live."

"Within a budget."

Aunt Vera whispered to me, "Trisha is taking a year off between college and grad school. She goes to UCSC, her father's alma mater." UC Santa Cruz, a branch of the University of California, was situated in Santa Cruz, a short hop north of Crystal Cove.

"Is Pearl paying all her expenses?"

"It would seem so."

"That's pretty gracious."

"You and your budgets," Trisha continued, her voice shrill and unkind. "Why don't you admit what's really irking you? It's my boyfriend. You don't approve of him. I heard you talking to Bingo when she was over the other day. You called him a lab rat."

Pearl said, "I never said that."

My aunt and I peeked at Bingo, who flushed red, confirming that Pearl had, indeed, said that. Oops.

"Daddy liked him, Mother," Trisha countered.

"Your father is no longer alive."

"Because you drove him to his grave." Pearl's husband, a respected geologist, met an early demise. Thanks to foggy conditions, he accidentally drove off a cliff. "You and your witches and your crazy people, and your—"

"That's enough. Hush."

"Or what, you'll cut me off completely? You've been threatening to do that ever since I moved home. I want my phone turned on, Mother. Do you hear me? Sean has to be able to get hold of me."

Bingo cleared her throat and waved a hand at the gawking crowd in the kitchen. "Ahem, everyone. Let's not eavesdrop any longer. Let's convene in the den."

Aunt Vera latched onto Rhett's and my elbows. "What a shame," she said as she accompanied us from the room. "Privacy is so hard to preserve."

The crowd followed us into what turned out to be not just a den but also a grandiose display room. I'd heard of the

Thornton Collection, but I had no idea of the collection's vastness. Glass cabinets lined the walls. Each was internally lit, the lights illuminating large irregularly shaped masses of rocks and minerals. A small placard identified each: *azurite from Arizona*, *topaz from Russia*, *hematite from Switzerland*. Among the mix were a number of large gray rocks called *Thorntonite*, named after Pearl's husband, Thomas Thornton, who discovered the rock a mere week before he died. Where the specimen had come from was anyone's guess. His last trek had taken him from Yosemite all the way to Mt. McKinley.

The pièce de résistance of the Thornton Collection, a large blob about the size of a tennis ball of grayish indigo stone, stood inside a glass box mounted on a pedestal at the center of the room. Its placard read: *rough sapphire, Kashmir.* What quality of gem lay hidden inside the blob had to be worth millions. A half-carat cut sapphire ran in the neighborhood of eight hundred dollars. My husband had wanted to buy me a sapphire for my thirtieth birthday. We'd laughed out loud when we heard of the sale of a twenty-two-carat sapphire going at auction at Christie's for over three million dollars. Of such dreams are memories made.

"Wow," I uttered under my breath and moved closer for a better look.

"Copy that," Rhett said.

"Ditto." Maya, who had closed The Enchanted Garden and joined the rest of the Winsome Witches for the party, drew near. "Can you imagine how many hours it would take to polish that stone?"

Emma said, "The veterinarian I assist would give an arm and a leg to get her hands on some of the shavings."

"Shavings?" I said.

"When a stone is polished, it leaves shavings," Emma explained. "Sapphire, if worn or ingested, has been credited with the ability to cure all sorts of mental and physical conditions."

I said, "But the shavings wouldn't help, would they? Doesn't it have to be the stone itself?"

"Maya, do you know?" Emma said. "Aren't all aspects of minerals used in New Age concoctions?"

"I don't know for certain, sugar. I work mostly with herbs."

Emma nodded. "Yes, all aspects. I'm positive. My husband told me so. I've seen something like that mentioned in articles, too. At the library and online. Have you heard of *Paradigm Solutions* and *Aquarius Awareness*? Wonderful e-zines. I like to stay current, don't you?" Like I said, Emma could talk up a storm. "Some pundits say stones are magical, right, Maya?"

Maya raised an eyebrow. "People believe what they want to believe."

I grinned. "Which means we will never know whether they work or whether it's a person's mind doing the healing."

Rhett elbowed me and whispered, "Don't be a cynic."

Pearl joined the group. She looked teary-eyed. Her cheeks were flushed. I gazed past her for signs of her daughter, but Trisha was not to be seen. Everyone welcomed Pearl, and then she joined the conversation, acting as if nothing untoward had happened. "I see you're admiring the sapphire. Thomas was so proud of that find. He discovered it on a trek through the northernmost part of India."

"It's certainly not for every woman's budget," I joked.

"I have an amethyst necklace," Emma said. "My husband gave it to me. Amethyst is supposed to stimulate psychic intuition."

"I've heard that, too," Aunt Vera said.

Pearl frowned. "Hogwash."

"It's true. Amethyst has healing properties," Emma went on. "In Greek folklore, the story goes that the god of wine—"

"Bacchus," Maya chimed in.

Emma nodded. "Bacchus was mad at humans. But the

goddess Diana intervened and turned a young woman into amethyst to protect her. Bacchus, realizing his evil, cried, and the stone turned purple from his tears. Isn't that romantic?"

"My, my," Pearl said. "Aren't you being emotive?"

"Don't be dismissive, Pearl," Maya said. "Many of our superstitions come from folklore. I noticed you have all the chairs on your patio facing the ocean. Why is that? Feng shui?"

Pearl said, "Uh, because the sun sets in the west, Maya."

A cat yowled. A woman swore. Then a calico darted into the room and raced around in a circle, gazing upward as if searching for its owner. Trisha stomped in after the cat, a tall glass of something amber-colored in her hand. "Darned nuisance. I've told you to bell the cat, Mother."

Emma clicked her tongue as a cue. The calico darted to her and leaped into her arms.

"Are you telling your guests how much everything costs, Mother?" Trisha continued. "Are you lording it over them like you lord it over me?"

"Trisha, please."

"Hey, everyone." Trisha tapped her glass with her stubby fingernails to get the crowd's attention. "Did my mother tell you she has been approached by at least a dozen museums asking her to donate the Thornton Collection? No? She hasn't? Surprise, surprise. Did she tell you that she won't give it up? Not even a sliver. She claims my father wouldn't have wanted her to. But he did."

"He did not," Pearl snapped.

"Yes, he did, Mother. He told me the night before he died that the rocks he hoarded were evil."

"You're lying."

Trisha whirled around, her backpack swinging to and fro with the quick move, and glared at Maya. "You think they're evil, too."

Maya recoiled. "No."

"Yes. I saw you at the history museum. Two months ago. You were with a little boy. Sandy hair, freckled cheeks. He was tugging you toward the rock room. That's what he called it. But you wouldn't let him enter."

Maya glanced from Pearl to the rest of us. She looked helpless. "My nephew," she conceded.

"Why didn't you want to go in?" Trisha sneered. "I'll tell you why. Because rocks are evil, that's why. You know it. I know it."

Maya shook her head. "He was being a brat. I don't think they're evil. I—"

"In the end," Trisha interrupted, "my father believed the old saying, *Ashes to ashes*. What belonged to the earth should return to the earth. He wanted to get rid of the whole thing."

Pearl sniffed. "He never said that."

"Yes, he did. I told you, Mother, he confided in me. Why is that so hard to believe?"

"Because you and he were not close. This is a fairy tale you've made up in your mind. You miss your father and want to believe that he held the same beliefs you did. He didn't."

Tears sprang to Trisha's eyes. She pointed an accusatory finger at Pearl. "Why do you keep them, Mother?"

"Because it's all I have left of him."

"Wrong. You have *me*, but I guess that's not enough." Trisha jutted her chin. "If you sold these collections and that ugly hunk of rock"—she pointed to the rough sapphire—"you could donate the money to charity or research. Heck, you could probably add an entire geology wing at UCSC. You'd even have enough to fund libraries across the country," Trisha persisted. "But you won't because you're selfish."

"Enough." Pearl clapped her hands. "I know your endgame, young lady. You want the money for yourself. Well, you can't have it. You are no longer welcome in this house. Leave."

Trisha slammed her beverage glass on the display case. "Over my dead body."

"Whatever it takes."

"Witch," Trisha muttered—or something very close to that—as she stomped out of the room.

Bingo hurried to Pearl and offered her arm. Pearl clutched it like a lifeline. Bingo said, "Why don't we head outside? The moon is full, the weather temperate. It's time for the Welcoming."

The crowd murmured its relief. One of the guests lit the fire that was preset in the fire pit centered in the all-brick patio. Flames curled toward the sky in a plume.

Pearl, as the High Priestess of the Winsome Witches, took up a position on the opposite side of the fire. With the darkening ocean as her backdrop, she said, "Good evening to all. It is time to induct Emma into the fold. Put on your hats if you have removed them."

Everyone obeyed.

Rhett leaned into me. "I didn't think I was allowed to stay for this moment."

"Remember, they're not real witches. My aunt told me the ceremony is as harmless as bridging from a Girl Scout Brownie to a Junior. You have sisters. You must know what I mean."

He held up three fingers and started to recite the Girl Scout promise: "On my honor—"

I laid a finger across his mouth to quiet him. He kissed it and a zing of passion ran straight to my toes.

"Emma, come forward," Pearl said.

Emma, with her scarlet witch hat slightly atilt and her eyes glowing with excitement, hurried to Pearl. After righting Emma's hat, Pearl patted Emma's cheek.

"What makes a woman a Winsome Witch?" Pearl asked the throng. She didn't wait for a response. "We seek balance and harmony. We seek to help others. We use our kinship to brighten this world. We are fire, we are energy, and we are all things positive. We welcome you, Emma Wright, as the newest member of the Winsome Witches. Do you accept this honor?"

"Aye," Emma gushed.

"You will be my handmaiden for the next year." A handmaiden, Aunt Vera had told me, helped the High Priestess in all ritual purposes. Each year's new inductee—and there was only one—assumed the responsibility. "Are you prepared to take on such a task?"

"Aye."

"Then welcome, Emma Wright, into our family."

The crowd applauded, and Pearl handed Emma a gold box wrapped with a gold bow. The pair exchanged a few quiet words, and then Emma moved toward me.

I stopped her and said, "Is your husband here to celebrate?"

Emma blanched. "Um, no, he . . . he . . ." She seemed panicked and unable to form a sentence.

I felt the urge to steady her but held back. Maybe she was overstimulated from the ceremony. "What happened? Couldn't he break free from work?" I asked.

"Not exactly. He—" She shuddered. "He said he wouldn't be caught dead in the presence of witches."

WHEN I ARRIVED home, I was wound tighter than a top. The evening's affairs that had included the spooked Boots, the trio of black cats, the anxious calico, and me almost walking beneath a ladder—well, scaffolding—not to mention the raw emotions pouring out of Trisha, and finally, the dread that Emma displayed following her induction, had set me off. Sleep was out of the question for at least an hour.

I cuddled Tigger, freshened his water bowl, and ogled the empty antique bookcase I had purchased last week. Way back when I was eight years old and had needed to stay home sick with the flu, I became an avid reader. I read the entire set of Nancy Drew novels that week, and even though I couldn't cook, I devoured *The Nancy Drew Cookbook: Clues to Good Cooking*, too. How could I resist? I graduated to *The Chronicles of Narnia*, and then, thanks to Bailey's mother who was a devout reader herself, I discovered books like *The Secret Garden*, *The Yearling*, *Black Beauty*, and more. Over the years, I bought and saved my favorite titles, but when David and I married, because he liked to live in a sparse environment that didn't attract dust, I packed up my books and stored them. It was time to put them on display.

The cottage I lived in was like a bachelor apartment with a tiny kitchen at one end, a living space complete with fireplace in the middle, and a bedroom setup at the other end, lovingly decorated by my aunt with the addition of a Chinese cabinet I'd brought with me . . . and now the bookcase. I fetched the boxes filled with books that I had stowed on the far side of the brass bed.

"No time like the present." Tigger scampered to me as if he were going to help. "Back up, little buddy," I said. "I don't want you getting bonked with a hardback." I arranged the books in alphabetical order by title, not author: *The Giver*, *Gone with the Wind*, *The Grapes of Wrath*, *To Kill a Mockingbird*, *Old Yeller*, *White Fang*. I managed about thirty books on each shelf. At the bottom of the case, I set up the array of adult cookbooks I was amassing, including titles by celebrity chefs like Flay, Garten, and Bourdain.

As I was placing the last grouping of cookbooks on the shelf, I paused. The *Betty Crocker Halloween Cookbook*, which had an adorable purple cover adorned with pumpkins, black cats, and foodie pictures, made me think of the Halloween party I'd offered to throw. Now, as the hour neared midnight, I wondered what had possessed me to suggest such a ridiculous thing. Me? Hostess a party? Gack. Sure, I had been practicing in the kitchen, but I wasn't a cook. Would my friends and family mind if I changed the menu to potluck?

My pulse began to race. *Get a grip, Jenna. You can do this.*

I opened the cookbook and reviewed the table of contents. Each section sounded so fun: *Bewitching Bites and Drinks* and *Mystifying Main Dishes*. Some of the recipes, most accompanied by photographs, made me laugh out loud: Wart-Topped Quesadilla Wedges, a Brie jack-o'-lantern, and Bugs in a Blanket. There was even a section for planning the party, complete with hints on how to decorate the table. After a few minutes, my heart rate settled back to normal; I could do this.

Divining a menu might be a good idea; beverages first. A memory from college came back to me, and I started to giggle. I remembered attending a frat party. As a few of my dorm mates and I entered, a guy dressed in a toga handed us oranges and Sharpie pens. We were supposed to draw a face on our oranges, like you would a pumpkin, and then, using a flavor injector that looked like a syringe, we were told to insert a shot's worth of vodka into the fruit. While we obeyed, Toga Guy gave us a lecture about hypodermics. He explained that the first hypodermic involved animal bladders and goose quills. One of my pals heaved. Though I would forgo the history lesson at my party, I decided that something whimsical like funny-faced, liquor-infused oranges would be fun.

I switched on my computer and did a search for food injectors. I found one that was quite stylish with a green handle. I purchased a few so we would be able to offer them for sale in the store. Next, I considered the main course. I tracked down a recipe for turkey basted with maple syrup. Yum, I thought, until I read through the ingredients. Over fifteen. Yipes. And the steps were complicated. I started to perspire, but rather than go berserk, I did the rational thing. Just as I would when preparing for a new ad campaign, I wrote a list, or in this case, an industrious menu. It consisted of seven courses. I paused, crossed off two items, and settled on five. Next, I made a shopping list, which by the end—*heart be still*—seemed to be as long as my arm.

More deep breaths.

I folded the list and stowed it in my purse and suddenly felt better. Stronger. Nearly confident. I could pull off this party. I could.

When I went to sleep, the spooky events of the night were all but erased from my memory.

However, at 6:04 A.M. Wednesday morning, when the telephone jangled, I bolted to a sitting position in my bed. Tigger awoke, too, and bounded from my feet to my chin in two seconds flat. He kneaded my arm.

"Stop. Off, kitty." With my heart hammering my rib cage, I switched on a light and snatched up the phone. "Hello?"

"Jenna, darling. It's so . . . oh, dear—" Aunt Vera's voice cut out. The line crackled with static. "She's—" Aunt Vera gasped. She sounded freaked out. "Bingo—" More static. "She's dead."

Chapter 5

ᏣᎬᎪᏯᏩ

I SHOOK THE cobwebs from my brain and glanced a second time at my clock. I was an early riser, but after a late-night party with only me, my cat, and my bookcase, waking up at this hour was proving difficult, to say the least. "Slow down, Aunt Vera. Where are you?"

"Pearl's house. Come quickly. It's so—" More fizzling static. I hated cell phone reception sometimes, but what would we do without the darned contraptions?

The connection ended. I scrambled out of bed, dressed in seconds, fed Tigger, and promised I would return for him before going to the shop.

A few minutes later, I arrived at Pearl's house. At rush hour, a person could drive across town in less than ten minutes. At the crack of dawn and speeding, less than that.

Four cars stood in the driveway. The front door hung open. I parked my VW bug behind the last car and raced inside. Voices rang out in the backyard. I hurried in that direction.

Bingo, wearing all white and looking as determined as an avenging angel, tore past me, nearly knocking me down.

"You're not dead!" I shouted with glee. My aunt had been wrong. Or I'd heard her wrong. She must have been talking to Bingo when she'd called me on the telephone. Did it matter? Bingo was alive. I chased after her. "Where's my aunt?"

Bingo charged onto the patio while waggling her cell phone. "Girls, girls. I finally got through to 911. Reception up here is horrible. EMTs are on their way."

"911?" I said, a new bout of panic surging through me. "EMTs?"

My aunt, who stood with Maya on the patio near the fire pit, rushed to me. She embraced me as she sniffed back tears.

"What's wrong?" I asked.

"It's Pearl. She died during the night."

"Pearl?"

Maya stepped to the side and I saw Pearl, sprawled face-down across the cold fire pit.

My hand flew to my mouth. "What happened?"

"That's the thing," Aunt Vera said. "We don't know. We arrived for our early-morning coffee."

Way too early, I mused.

"We had to discuss the program for the luncheon," my aunt went on. "We have an agenda, but sometimes we run too long. Pearl wanted to cut a few items. I brought muffins." She pointed to a pastry bag sitting on the ground beside her tote bag.

"I brought coffee," Maya said. She held up a tray of four coffees. Her fingers were gripping the edges so hard her knuckles were pasty. "Pearl liked half caf. One sugar." Her hands started to shake.

I dashed to her, removed the tray of coffees, and set them on the wrought-iron dining table. Afterward, I returned to the trio of women. "Go on."

"We think she suffered a heart attack," Bingo said.

My aunt nodded. "Remember how Pearl said she was being treated for type 2 diabetes? Maybe . . . maybe . . ." She pressed her lips together.

I remembered Pearl's *fake* death at the outdoor faire and how she had laughed at tricking her friends. Not so funny now.

"Maybe she went into cardiac arrest due to complications," Bingo said. "It appears she was drinking. Diabetics shouldn't drink."

I said, "Not all diabetics follow that rule." An assistant at Taylor & Squibb drank and fell into a coma. She never woke up. "Besides, Pearl was just recently diagnosed. Maybe she didn't know to stop drinking."

Bingo hitched her head toward a pair of wicker chaise lounges. Beyond the chairs were banks of white roses and drifts of lavender-colored aster. On the table set between the chairs stood a martini glass with a tad left of what was most likely the bloodred Witchy Woman concoction. I spied Pearl's witch hat resting on one of the chaises. Why had she moved to the fire pit? If she was having a heart attack or lapsing into a coma, why not head indoors toward a telephone?

"She looks like she was reaching for something," Aunt Vera said.

My aunt was right. Pearl's right arm was outstretched and twisted, palm upward. The sleeve of her elegant dress was bunched up around her bicep. The crook of her arm was slightly red.

The sound of pounding footsteps drew my attention toward the house. A pair of young men in emergency medical technician uniforms hustled onto the patio. "Back away, ladies," the tallest said.

"She's dead," Bingo offered. "There's no pulse. I fear she's been dead for hours."

"Let us do our job," the lead EMT said.

"Listen to the man," a woman ordered. I recognized the voice. Cinnamon Pritchett, our chief of police, strode onto the patio. She wasn't dressed in her usual brown uniform. She wore a coral-colored sweater and jeans and looked downright casual. She didn't have on any makeup, not that she ever donned much. She was a natural, sun-splashed, girl-next-door type. She tucked her bobbed dark hair behind her ears. "Good morning, everyone."

"Why are you here?" I blurted. Dumb question. My aunt had contacted 911.

"I could ask you the same thing, but I won't, although"— she added under her breath—"this is becoming a far too regular occurrence."

You're telling me. Until that moment, I hadn't realized that I was shaking. All over. Another dead body. Three in three months. Each was someone I'd known. Death was a natural occurrence—ashes to ashes and all that rot—but, honestly, what in the heck was going on? Was I—was my presence—in some otherworldly way, responsible for attracting this evil to Crystal Cove?

Cinnamon toured the fire pit while the EMTs checked Pearl's vitals. "To answer your question, I'm here because the police are called in all instances of death when 911 is involved."

"I know that."

"I'm first because I was close by."

Close by *where*? I wanted to ask, but didn't. Not my business.

Cinnamon said, "What do you think happened, Jenna?"

Why did she nominate me to be spokesman? Fine. I quickly explained about Pearl's recent diagnosis. "She must have lost consciousness."

"Shame," Cinnamon said and meant it. She pursed her lips as she eyed the side table holding the martini glass. "Was she drinking alcohol?"

Bingo said, "Possibly. At last night's party, she was serving Witchy Woman cocktails."

"A sweet concoction made with rum," my aunt added.

"Was Dr. Thornton a heavy drinker?" Cinnamon asked.

Bingo shook her head. "No. She is . . . *was* . . . a lightweight in that department."

"It could have been someone else's cocktail," I said. "There were a lot of us here." I filled her in on the haunted tour that ended at Pearl's house.

A shriek rattled the quiet. A stout, gray-haired woman in black uniform and white apron raced onto the patio. "Heavens. It's—" She had the uncomely face of a female Alfred Hitchcock, with a hooked nose, pointed chin, and flabby neck, and she had an accent right out of *Downton Abbey*. She peeked past Cinnamon, then wailed again. "Is that the missus? Is she dead?"

One of Cinnamon's subordinates, a moose-faced man, hurried in after the woman. "Got your text, boss. I'm here. What's up?"

"In a sec." Cinnamon addressed the frantic woman. "Ma'am, who are you?"

"Mrs. Davies." She slurped back a sob. "The house-keeper. I wondered why there were so many cars outside. I didn't think much about it. Maybe the party ran long, I says to myself, so I started with my chores. When I noticed it was gone, I came looking for the missus."

"When you noticed what was gone?" Cinnamon asked.

"Heavens, that means—" Mrs. Davies glanced again at her employer. "She didn't know. The missus didn't have a clue that it's missing."

"What's missing?" Cinnamon said, her tone steady. She must have run into all sorts of frenzied characters as a police chief.

"The sapphire."

"The sapphire's gone?" I blurted. "As in someone stole it?"

Mrs. Davies nodded like an out-of-whack bobble-headed doll.

"What sapphire?" Cinnamon asked.

"Thomas Thornton was a collector," I explained, even though I was sure she knew. She hadn't left Crystal Cove like I had. Had she investigated his death by car accident, too? "He has a display room filled with minerals, and one of his great treasures was a rough sapphire probably worth millions. He found it in Kashmir."

Mrs. Davies intertwined her gnarled hands, which looked like they were permanently afflicted with writer's cramp.

Did she spend her weekends diarizing the lives of her wealthy employers?

Stop it, Jenna. Not nice.

"Miss Pearl was such a wonderful woman," Mrs. Davies said. "Everyone loved her. Who would do this ghastly thing to her?"

"What ghastly thing?" Cinnamon said.

"Why, murder her, of course. She's been stabbed, hasn't she?"

"No, she hasn't been stabbed," Cinnamon said.

"Why else would she be lying that way?"

Everyone turned and took note of Pearl. Had she been murdered? How? There wasn't any blood.

Aunt Vera gasped. "Are you saying someone killed her to get the sapphire?"

"Trisha must have done it!" Bingo shouted. "She and her mother had a horrible fight last night. She stormed out of the house."

Maya stepped forward. "Trisha wanted to sell the Thornton Collection. Remember, y'all? She said the stones were evil."

Bingo nodded and looked at the others for confirmation. "Pearl refused. She claimed her husband wouldn't have wanted her to sell them. Maybe Trisha came back and pushed her mother into the pit."

"Maybe Pearl bumped her head on the stone," Aunt Vera theorized, "and died instantly."

"And Trisha ran off with the sapphire," Maya said.

"Pearl isn't burned," I said, "which means she must have been killed after the fire cooled."

"Hold it!" Cinnamon barked. "We don't know that she was murdered."

"But she's not lying in a natural way," I countered. "If she'd passed out, wouldn't she have slumped to the ground, not pitched forward?"

Cinnamon clapped her hands. "All right. That's enough speculation."

"You have to admit the two crimes must be connected," I said. "The sapphire's missing, and—"

"Jenna. All of you. Stop. Please." Cinnamon herded everyone into the living room, warned us to stay put, and then returned to the EMTs, who were still examining Pearl's body.

The Moose—his real name was Marlon Appleby—approached her. I heard Cinnamon ask about the cause of death. The lead EMT pointed to the redness I'd noticed on Pearl's arm. I heard Cinnamon say, "A toxicology test will have to be run."

Had someone injected Pearl with poison or something she had an allergic reaction to?

Cinnamon directed the Moose—Marlon—to bag the cocktail glass and take pictures of what was evidently shaping up to be a crime scene.

My aunt started to cry. "Pearl was the inspiration for the Winsome Witches. What will happen to the group and all the fund-raising we do?"

I encircled her with my arm. "The group will continue. You have each other to carry out Pearl's wishes." Better question: what would all of Pearl's patients and her daughter do without her?

As if thinking of Trisha conjured her up, she barged into the living room. Her hair was frizzed out around her face like a fright wig. She inched her crocheted purse higher on her shoulder. "What's going on here?"

"Your mother," Aunt Vera said. "She's . . . dead."

"No way."

Mrs. Davies pointed.

Trisha raced past us toward the patio. "Mother? Mom?"

Cinnamon sprinted to the French doors and blocked Trisha from progressing while introducing herself.

Trisha tried to dodge around her. "My mother. I have to go to her."

"There's nothing you can do," Cinnamon said.

"No-o-o!" Trisha keened.

Cinnamon's voice turned supremely gentle. "I need you to stay in here. Can you do that?"

Trisha sniffed back tears but nodded. When Cinnamon

released her, Trisha's purse slid from her shoulder as she folded in on herself. "She's really dead?" She looked up, her eyes pinpoints of worry. "How did she die?"

"We're not sure. We'll be running tests."

"How can you not know?"

"It's complicated. She was sick. There's no obvious evidence of foul play."

Trisha gasped. "Do you think she was murdered?"

I said, "Chief, is it possible someone injected her with something?"

Cinnamon scowled at me. "Trisha, when did you last see your mother?"

"At the party." Trisha's eyes widened as realization hit her: she was being interrogated. "I didn't kill her, if that's what you think. Yes, we fought. They all saw me. But I stormed out. I left the house."

"Hold on," Maya said. "You ran off with a backpack on your shoulder. Where is it now?"

"Why do you care?" Trisha hissed.

"A very expensive sapphire seems to be missing," Cinnamon said.

"The sapphire is gone? We were burgled?" Trisha blew out an angry breath. "I warned Mother to install an alarm system, but do you think she listened to me?"

Mrs. Davies sidled up to Cinnamon. "The display case isn't busted. Someone opened it with a key. Whoever did it must have known that if the glass broke, it would set off an alarm. Trisha knows where the key is kept."

Trisha's face grew hateful. "You think I took the stupid rock, you wicked shrew? Don't be ridiculous."

Cinnamon didn't say a word. That kind of patience was a rare commodity.

"Fine," Trisha said, the silence spurring her to talk. "Here's the truth. I didn't leave right away. I went up to my bedroom to drop off my backpack and change my clothes. My backpack is still there. Search it. You'll see. The sapphire is not in it."

Cinnamon set her subordinate on the task.

Minutes later, Deputy Appleby returned carrying the raggedy backpack. "Is the sapphire a big blue-gray rock?"

"About the size of a baseball," I offered.

"It's in here." He handed the backpack to Cinnamon and then returned to the patio.

"Uh-uh, no way," Trisha shouted. "I did not take that stone. Emma. She must have planted it in my bag. She's trying to frame me."

"Emma Wright, the Pet Taxi girl?" Cinnamon said. "Why would she do that?"

"She doesn't like me."

"Nobody does," Mrs. Davies muttered under her breath but loud enough for all to hear.

Trisha shot her a cruel look. "Emma was here. Last night. It was her induction into the Winsome Witches coven."

"Coven?" Cinnamon looked from one woman to the next. Maya, Bingo, and my aunt stood taller.

"It's not a real coven," I explained. "It's a charity group that gets together every Halloween to raise money for literacy." How could Cinnamon not have heard about them? She must be asking rote questions.

Trisha said, "After I changed clothes, I . . . I went for a walk. I was steaming mad. When I returned"—she jammed her foot against the carpet—"I saw Emma. She was with my mother. Emma was crying. Mother looked like she'd been crying, too. I didn't want to intrude. That's when I left. For real."

"Why didn't you interrupt?" Bingo said, acid in her tone. "You didn't seem to have any compunctions earlier about barging in on the party and dressing down your mother in front of everyone."

"Bingo, don't." My aunt petted her arm.

Bingo shook her off.

Trisha continued. "I . . . I went to my boyfriend's place. Emma must have stuck around and killed my mother, and then she stole the gem and planted it in my stuff."

"Why would Emma do that?" Bingo said. "She doesn't have a mean bone in her body."

"How do you know?" Trisha responded. "Why do you think I did it? You don't know me."

"As a matter of fact, I do, young lady. I was one of your mother's best friends. She confided in me."

Cinnamon cleared her throat. "What time did you arrive at your boyfriend's place, Miss Thornton?"

Trisha crossed her arms. "Ten."

"Can he corroborate that?"

"No, he . . . he wasn't there, but you can tell I was. I left dishes in the sink. Someone must have seen the lights go on and heard me pacing."

"Because you were mad at your mother," Maya pointed out.

"Stop it. All of you." Trisha spun in an arc to address us. "I did not poison her."

Cinnamon said, "I didn't say she was poisoned."

Trisha's face turned dark. "Yes, you did. You said she was injected with something."

"No, I didn't." Cinnamon cut a quick look at me, warning me to keep my mouth shut. Had I guessed correctly? Had Pearl been poisoned?

"You said you'd be running tests," Trisha said. "That suggests poison. No, wait!" She held up a finger. "Mother was recently diagnosed as a diabetic. Did she mess up her insulin?"

Deputy Appleby reappeared at the French doors. "Boss, the EMTs have everything they need. We're waiting for the coroner. I took copious pictures."

Cinnamon said, "Rope off the area and track down Emma Wright."

Bingo cleared her throat. "Excuse me, Chief Pritchett, I don't mean to sound crude, but will we be allowed to hold the luncheon despite our friend's death?" By default, Bingo was now the leader of the Winsome Witches. She looked to the others for support. Maya and my aunt grabbed her hands. "Big donors are coming. We can't afford to cancel."

"Yes, of course." Cinnamon gave a quick nod. "I'm sorry

for your loss. Now, if you'll excuse me." She joined her colleagues on the patio.

My aunt hurried to me and gave me a huge hug. "Thank you for coming. The three of us were so distraught. Bingo was grinding her teeth to chalk. Maya was running in circles with that idiot tray of coffee. We needed someone reasonable. It's so tragic."

"Poor Pearl," I said, feeling an acute loss. Pearl—Dr. Thornton—was the person who had helped me recover from the shock of finding my husband's suicide note two years after his death. The revelation had rattled me to the core. Pearl had convinced me that I couldn't have done anything to prevent his death. Suicide victims rarely revealed their plans ahead of time.

Aunt Vera said, "Do you really think Trisha could have killed her mother?"

"I don't know what to think. The police will find the truth. Look at Cinnamon, still gathering evidence."

Cinnamon had donned gloves and was crouched down inspecting everything from leaves to dust. She signaled for Deputy Appleby to take another photograph.

"What about a memorial?" my aunt asked.

"I'm sure you'll have to wait for the coroner's report," I said. "It'll be a while until the department is willing to release the body." I paused, nearly gagging at what I sounded like. I wasn't a professional. I shouldn't know—or think I know—as much as a policeman when it came to murder. Three murders in three months. My stomach turned sour.

"Trisha says she saw Emma with Pearl," Aunt Vera whispered. "But what if somebody else showed up after Emma? In that case, I suppose anyone could have killed her, including all of us."

Her comment caught me off guard. Was she right? I surveyed the others in the room. Trisha stood in the far corner, talking to someone via a cell phone. Hadn't she said last night that she couldn't get the darned thing to turn on? Had she stolen not only the sapphire but also some cash to reinstate her account? The housekeeper had moved into the foyer and was dusting. Her mouth was turned up in a pained smile. Maya, who was coughing through tears, stood near the large plate-glass window peering at the yard. Bingo lingered at the French doors. She seemed to be assessing everyone, too, one by one, and I swear, she looked victorious.

Chapter 6

WHEN I ARRIVED at the shop later, I found another gift on the doorstep—a miniature pumpkin with an intricate black cat drawing painted on it. The attached note read: *You will soon know of my love for you.* What the heck? This was a joke, right? I set the pumpkin on the counter and continued about my business.

For the remainder of the morning, all the gossip in The Cookbook Nook teemed around Pearl's murder. Had her daughter killed her? Was one of her clients a murderer? Had a Winsome Witch done her in? I knew the often-asked questions when it came to murder investigations, but one unrelated question continued to plague me: had I, by my return to Crystal Cove, cursed the town? Guilt gnawed at me. I felt I needed to do something to fix the problem, but what could I do? Leave? Return to San Francisco? Move to Antarctica? I liked penguins.

Picking up on my anxiety, Tigger, my sweet kitty, sought me out. I cuddled him for a while, and then to keep my mind and hands occupied, I set about carving a pumpkin. Not the pumpkin left by the secret admirer. A big pumpkin about fifteen inches in diameter. Bailey joined me.

After a half hour of silent carving, Bailey held up a smaller pumpkin she had been working on. "What do you think?"

I choked back a snort. "Really? One tooth?"

She jutted her chin, obviously peeved. "I think he's cute. What have you carved?"

I twisted my pumpkin—like hers, he was grinning, but mine had a little more bang for the buck. I'd given him bright eyes, bushy eyebrows, hair, ears, and a bow tie.

She gawked. "Guess I missed Pumpkin Carving 101 in college."

"Blame my mother." She had loved carving intricate designs in pumpkins like castles or leafless trees or the word *boo* in a jeering mouth. "You do know there's a citywide pumpkin contest in addition to the Spookiest Window Display contest, don't you?"

She moaned. "How can I compete with yours?"

"You don't have to. We're a team. Did you see the array of pumpkins in front of Aunt Teek's? I think one is a cutout of the Bates Motel from *Psycho*. I'll bet Bingo used a pattern."

"Cheater."

A while later, as I was arranging pumpkins outside the entry, Tito, the reporter for the *Crystal Cove Crier*, pulled to a stop on his mountain bicycle. He looked quite fit in snug biker pants and shirt. I knew he worked out. Had he doubled up on his regimen? A lock of dark hair spilled from beneath his helmet. He tucked it back in and grinned. Bailey believed he might have had some dental work done. She was probably right. His incisors didn't look nearly as fanglike.

"*Hola, chica*," he said, then quickly revised, "Hi, Jenna." I'd made it very clear that I hated when he called me *chica*. "Beautiful day, no?"

"Yes."

"It is a shame about Dr. Thornton."

"Yes, it is."

"She will be missed. Is there a story there?"

"What kind of story?" I asked, deliberately being evasive.

He offered a wry look. "Care to comment?"

"No." I held up my hands. "Ask the police."

As he rode off, a pack of ladies all dressed in gingham and looking like Dorothy in *The Wizard of Oz*, right down to their pigtails and freckles, hurried past me, each chattering with excitement. "Hello," they trilled in unison.

I trailed them into the shop. No one in the store blinked an eye at the women's outfits. It was almost Halloween, after all. Each lady carried a cloth tote emblazoned with a movie image of Dorothy, the Tin Man, the Lion, and the Scarecrow skipping along the yellow brick road.

"Ooh," one of the women said as she browsed the display tables. "Look, girls. An Oz cookbook." She plucked a book from a specialty shelf. I had ordered cookbooks that featured movies and television. "*Cookin' in Oz*. How darling." She turned to me. "Miss, are you the owner? We're a Wizard of Oz book club. Can you help us?"

I had heard of dedicated groups like theirs. Most had read the entire set of Baum books. I remembered my grandmother reading original copies of *The Wonderful Wizard of Oz, The Marvelous Land of Oz, Dorothy and the Wizard*, and more to me. I'd blissfully reread them in my teens during an especially rainy week. Sometimes there was nothing better than a dreary day when all I could do was read. With the trauma of Pearl's death still cycling through my brain, I wished for one of those rainy days right now. I would close the shop and cuddle beneath a comforter and cry. But that, as my father would say, would not be productive, and I needed to feel productive.

To take my mind off the murder, I joined the women by the display. They clustered around me and gazed expectantly, as if I were the Wizard himself.

"We eat, drink, and sleep Dorothy if we can," the woman who seemed to be the organizer continued. "Is that what this book is about?"

"Peek inside," I said. "The authors have put together recipes and little anecdotes, not just about the movie but about the Broadway production and its collaborators, as well. Each shares his or her own story and possibly a recipe. It's fun."

She browsed the pages. "Hey, I didn't know Art Carney was the scarecrow on Broadway. You know who Art Carney is, don't you?"

I had a vague idea. Old actor on the Jackie Gleason television show.

"Ooh, I love learning something new." She closed the book. "Do you have a dozen on hand?"

I gulped. "Only the one."

"But you can order more and ship, yes?"

"Of course."

As the ladies purchased other books and gift items, I learned they were from nearby San Jose. They had specifically come to town for the Winsome Witches luncheon. I also learned about a Wizard of Oz collector in the Stanford area. A retired orthodontist, he had immersed himself in all things Oz. He owned nearly two thousand Oz-related books; he had even built a yellow brick road in his collectibles room. Amazing.

When the ladies departed, Bailey joined me at the register. "Weren't they enthusiastic?" she said. "Do you remember your favorite scary book?"

"Why scary?"

"Weren't you totally freaked out reading *The Wizard of Oz*? The scene about the monkeys and the wicked witch. Ewww." She shimmied with mock fright.

"Now that you mention it." I vividly remembered shivering as my grandmother read the part about Dorothy being swept into the cyclone. "The second in the series wasn't much tamer. If I recall, a little boy named Tip escapes from a witch with the help of Jack Pumpkinhead."

"Perfect for Halloween."

"However, nothing scared me more than *Dracula*."

Bailey's mouth dropped open. "You read *Dracula*?"

"And *Frankenstein*. Do you know the idea for

Frankenstein came to Mary Shelley in a dream? She and some buddies were competing about who could come up with the best horror story."

Bailey said, "Did you read *The Strange Case of Dr. Jekyll and Mr. Hyde*?"

"Yes. I loved the way Stevenson laid out the secrets, morsel by morsel. Brilliant."

On and on the two of us went, sharing book titles we had read over the years. By the time we reached the popular Goosebumps series by R. L. Stine, Katie appeared carrying a huge tray of popcorn balls.

"*Curse of the Mummy's Tomb*," Bailey cried.

"*Monster Blood*," I responded. We had come up with about fifty titles so far. Stine was so prolific.

"Treats," Katie said.

Bailey frowned. "That's not a Goosebumps title."

"No." Katie wiggled the tray. "It's snack time. I'm putting them in the hall. You two get first dibs."

"They're so teensy," I said. Most popcorn balls I had sampled were the size of tennis balls. These were little golf ball–sized tidbits. I nibbled on one. "Yum. Butter and caramel and something else."

"Marshmallows," Katie said. "It makes them taste like corny Rice Krispies treats, don't you think? Hoo-boy, that's not what I meant. Not corny. Corn-filled . . . whatever." She ambled into the breezeway between the shop and the café and set the tray on the table where we offered goodies for our customers. Half a minute later, she returned. "By the way, where is your aunt? I wanted to review the café menus for the week. I've conjured up all sorts of fun items using Halloween recipes."

I glanced at the clock above the checkout counter. Two P.M. Where was my aunt? She had gone directly from Pearl's house to the precinct. Surely the police were done questioning her by now. I was dying—bad choice of words—to find out whether Trisha or Emma had killed Pearl. I kept imagining the crime scene in my mind in little snippets, like a storyboard for one of my ad campaigns: the windblown patio, the scattered leaves, the empty martini glass, Pearl's hat abandoned on the chaise lounge, Pearl's body out-stretched across the fire pit. Someone mentioned that she looked like she was reaching for something. What could it have been?

Katie said, "Do you think the Winsome Witches will cancel the luncheon?"

I shook my head. "Cinnamon said they didn't have to."

As much as I was saddened by Pearl's death, I truly hoped that life in Crystal Cove would get back to normal soon. Our economy thrived on having groups like the Winsome Witches throwing gala parties. I was looking forward to the events we had planned at the shop. In addition to the magician and herbalist, we had considered having a special fortune-telling session—communing with imaginary ghosts would be involved—which made me think again about my aunt. Where was she? Should I be worried? I hoped Cinnamon hadn't figured out some way to implicate Aunt Vera in the crime and locked her behind bars. I rang my aunt but reached her voice mail. I left a message for her to call me back.

For the next few hours, I focused on the upcoming special events day. We were planning on having a drawing. Every-one who bought a book would get a chance to win a Cook-book Nook gift basket. I'd had so much fun assembling the basket, which was filled with Halloween goodies like a goblin's hand, a *Witch Parking* sign, rubber snakes, a glow stick for trick-or-treating, a black cat mug, and of course, a couple of dandy children's fiction books including *Angeli-na's Halloween* and *Scary, Scary Halloween*. The cost had run about a hundred dollars, but I figured it was worth the investment because the basket would attract tons of eager-to-win shoppers.

At 6:00 P.M., after closing The Cookbook Nook, I moved to the display window area to set the gift basket among the books.

Aunt Vera rushed past the window with her turban tucked beneath her arm. Her hair looked ironed to her head. The folds of her caftan fluted out. Even through the glass, I could hear the copious strands of beads around her neck rattling like old bones. What was up?

She raced into the shop and let the door slam behind her. "Oh my," she cried. "I've lost them."

I'd never seen my aunt so flustered. I dashed to her. "Lost what?"

"My powers. I can't see the future. Not a whit."

Honestly, I believed she made up everything. Was I mistaken?

"My eyes are fuzzy. My head is swimming with confusion."

"Sit." I forced her into a chair beside the vintage kitchen table. I pushed aside the unfinished jigsaw puzzle of wine bottle corks—we always had a foodie-themed puzzle in progress—and I gripped her hands. "Where have you been? I thought you were at the precinct."

"I was, but I left there and went with Bingo to her shop. She needed my support."

I didn't ask why she hadn't called me. It was obvious she was distraught.

"How could I say *no*?" my aunt continued. "Bingo is the new Head Priestess. There's so much to do. She needed calming and asked me to predict her future, but Jenna, I couldn't read her aura." Her face turned into a mask of pain. "My power is gone. My channels are blocked."

"Aunt Vera."

"Stop. I know you're not a believer, but I am. Truly. Next, I tried reading her palm. Nothing. I couldn't make sense of even one line. I had a deck of tarot cards with me and asked Bingo to withdraw a card. She did, and I got nothing. Nothing. I—" She pulled a pack of tarot cards from the pocket of her caftan. "Draw one."

"No."

"Do it. Please. Don't doubt me. Try."

I obeyed. I drew the Devil card. It was upside down. I gasped.

"Inverted," Aunt Vera said. "Not so bad. The Devil card is not as frightening as you think. When reversed or inverted, the card reminds you that a situation that may seem to be trapping you is an illusion. It's not real. You have options, and help from family and friends is always available."

I gestured with my pinky. "There. You see? You have nothing to worry about. You can tell the future."

"That's not the future. Tarot cards provide data. Simple facts. I get nothing else. No vibes." She wiggled fingers beside her head. "I don't know what situation you'll be facing. It was the same with Bingo. I was blank. It's because of my anger. Anger at this whole affair. Anger that Pearl is dead. Anger that I can't do anything about it. I'm not the angry type, Jenna."

Maybe my aunt's blockage was being caused by something else. Was Bingo guilty of murder? Was her aura so black that my aunt didn't dare break through?

Stop it, Jenna, you don't believe this stuff. Yet . . .

I said, "What card did Bingo draw?"

"The Nine of Swords."

I knew the card. A man sat in bed with nine swords lined up on the wall behind him. He was draped with a checkerboard quilt. In the course of my relationship with my aunt, I had learned the meaning of many of the cards. The Nine of Swords signified that the person had reached a realization of just how bad a situation was, essentially waking up from a nightmare. The quilt signified that he had been playing a game with himself. He had to take responsibility. "What did you say?"

"Not a word. I couldn't interpret. But I felt fear. Right here." She tapped her solar plexus with three fingertips.

"That means you're getting something."

"No, I'm not. I'm getting nothing. Nada. Zip."

"C'mon, breathe." I rested a hand on her shoulder. "At least it wasn't the Ten of Swords." A month ago, after I learned the real reason for my husband's death, Aunt Vera insisted she tell my future. She knew how upset I was. I would have done anything to find my center. I'd pulled the Ten of Swords, a card with a man impaled by ten swords. Yipes. Even I knew that card was universally known as the get-out-of-Dodge card. But Aunt Vera had tweaked the reading. She had pointed out the light in the card to me. She told me that each beginning must come from an end. "In Bingo's case, you're picking up on her anxiety. One of her best friends has been murdered. She's going to be the new High Priestess. That's a lot of responsibility. In addition, she's getting married."

Aunt Vera sighed. I moved to a spot behind her and massaged her shoulders, trying to rub life and spunk into her.

When I released her, she said, "That's it," and leaped to her feet. Literally. She spun to face me and grabbed my face in both hands. "I may be a psychic mess, but I know my course. I have to solve the crime. Pearl was my dear friend. So is Bingo. To ease both of their souls, I must get involved. Maybe, if the fates are with me, Pearl will help."

"Pearl? From the other side of who-knows-where?" Uh-oh. "Aunt Vera, slow down. The police—"

"Darling, the police can either abide my help or not. It won't matter to me." Without another word, she dashed from the store.

"Wait," I called after her. "Katie wanted to discuss—"

But Aunt Vera didn't stop. She popped into her classic Mustang, a car she'd had since she was a teenager—she always understood the value of a good investment—and sped off.

I raced to the sales counter and called my father for advice, but he wasn't answering his phone. He hated the contraptions. If he could have life his way, people would still write letters and drop in for a cup of coffee. Even when he worked at the FBI, he was against anything being recorded. E-mails? Digital transmissions? Forget about it.

I dialed Bailey next, but her message went to voice mail, too. If she was hanging out with her paddleboarding pal, Jorge, she wouldn't answer until morning. Shoot. I couldn't talk to Katie; she was swamped with customers at the café. I considered calling Rhett but worried that if I did, he might think I was making a booty call. I wasn't quite prepared to take the next step in our relationship.

"Tigger, it's you and me, pal." I scooped him into my arms. "Ready to listen?"

I BENT MY kitten's ear for the entire ride home. As I drove past my aunt's house, I scanned the windows for activity. The place was dark. The moment I entered my cottage, I felt lonely and edgy. Quickly, I lit a dozen vanilla-scented candles and turned on a Judy Garland CD—listening to Judy was also a throwback to my mother; she adored the way Judy crooned—and then I pulled out the fixings for fudge. Katie repeatedly reminded me that cooking was all about the preparation. Having drilled that tidbit into my brain, I now, at all times, kept my cupboards and refrigerator filled with items I needed to make candy or cookies. I adored sweets. And salty things. And fruit. What didn't I like to eat?

Using a recipe I found in a *Betty Crocker Cookbook*, I whipped up a batch of fudge. Luckily, my aunt had the foresight to add a candy thermometer to my set of kitchen tools. After the fudge cooled to 120 degrees, I stirred in the vanilla and spread the fudge in the pan to set. Then I ate a quick dinner of cheese, crackers, and avocado slices paired with a crisp sauvignon blanc. I know, the meal wasn't great on the healthy list, but I was fidgety. Salt and crunch helped.

When I finished, I opened a potion cookbook I'd brought home. The book was filled with healing potions. Thanks to Maya, I knew there were herbs and spices that made me feel better, like the scent of lavender or rosemary and the taste of cinnamon and nutmeg.

After reviewing the steps in a calming potion recipe, I snipped off some pieces of the herb garden I had planted on the front porch, and I returned to the kitchen. I dumped the sprigs into a bowl. Using the back of an ice cream scoop—I didn't have what cooks called a muddler—I pressed the oil out of the herbs. I wrapped the potpourri into the toe of an old stocking, old because I hadn't worn stockings since I'd moved back to Crystal Cove. Lucky me. I pondered why I had kept them. On the chance that I might return to the world of advertising? Never.

I tucked the mock sachet beneath the pillow of my bed and instantly felt calmer.

While snacking on fudge, I took a long, luxurious bath doused with lavender-scented salt. A half hour later, I climbed on top of my bed and fell asleep wrapped in a towel. Tigger snuggled into my stomach.

During the night, I had one fitful dream after another. I was swept up in a cyclone. I wasn't Dorothy. I was Glinda the Good Witch of the North. In my bubbly childhood costume. The cyclone suddenly vanished, and I was seized by killer monkeys. With their talons clenched, they flew me across fields of poppies, right to the Witch of the East's castle. Where my aunt was being held captive. In a gigantic bucket of water. The tune "Ding-Dong! The Witch Is Dead" started blaring in my brain.

I bolted upright on my bed, drenched in perspiration. I smacked the coverlet. "That's it, you dope. Fudge is out of your diet after nine P.M." I swung my legs over the side of the bed and padded to the bathroom for a long drink of water.

As I stared at my raggedy image in the mirror, I wondered if the dream had significance. Was my aunt in danger? Did a fellow witch intend to melt her? Did I have to act as fairy godmother to save her?

Chapter 7

ON THURSDAY MORNING, my jog/walk along the beach was about as crazy as my nightmare. For the entire span of time, I dodged a seagull that thought I was its breakfast. Did the silly bird know about my chaotic Oz monkeys dream?

After a quick shower, I rang my father. This time I reached him. I told him I was worried about Aunt Vera. He tried to calm me and asked me if I had eaten. When I said I hadn't, he suggested I meet him at Nuts and Bolts, the hardware store he had invested in after leaving the FBI—to keep busy, not to make money; we would go from there for a quick bite.

"Jenna," he said with a hint of formality as I entered.

"Cary."

"Don't sass."

"Morning, Dad."

"You look good, sweetheart." He looped his arm through mine and walked me out of his spic-and-span shop.

"Really?" I had dabbed on a touch of lipstick and put on a pink mini halter dress, hoping the sun's reflection would bounce off the fabric and add color to my wan face. Apparently, my stabs at normalcy had worked. "I didn't sleep all that well."

"You can't tell, and you know I never lie." My father wasn't one to pay compliments, but he had become extra sensitive toward my feelings ever since I found my husband's suicide note.

We walked along Buena Vista Boulevard toward Latte Luck Café. Thanks to the temperate weather, folks were out in droves: moms, dads, nannies, grannies with strollers, people on bicycles, and Rollerbladers. Some heads turned, probably because my father and I were an eyeful. Kid you not, he looked like Cary Grant in his sixties—silver hair, strong jaw, tall and slim. I, dressed in my mini halter that was more suitable for summer, looked downright leggy.

We, along with the rest of the folks, ogled the Halloween window displays. The Pelican Brief Diner had added strings of glistening pumpkins to its windows, which were regularly adorned with nets and fish. The beauty salon had filled its round, portal-style window with a variety of decorative pumpkins and scarecrows.

"Wow." I pointed at the Play Room Toy Store. "That's a good display."

A carousel filled with ghosts and goblins as cute as Casper the Friendly Ghost twirled with delight. A sound system piped out a children's song telling monsters to *go away*. Kiddie-sized costumes and books like *Boo!* and *The Teeny Tiny Ghost* decorated the background.

"That's my favorite, too," my father said. He steered me into Latte Luck Café, which had hung sparkling vampire faces and bats in its windows.

Two feet inside the café, I spotted Rhett chatting up the person who stood in line in front of him. A shiver of lust ran through me. He was wearing the same thing he had worn the first day I met him: fisherman's knit sweater and tight jeans that fit just right. A smile lit up his face. Sheesh, but I liked the guy. Were we meant to be a couple? Would we be able to think each other's thoughts in forty or fifty years?

Rhett turned and winked at me. I felt myself blush and quickly convinced myself that he hadn't turned because he'd sensed my presence. He simply must have caught sight of me in the mirror that ran the length of the wall behind the counter. He waved for my father and me to join him in line.

I shook my head. I hated when people cut in. We waited our turn, ordered two café lattes as well as a banana-walnut muffin and a Greek yogurt to split, and then joined Rhett at one of the modest tables.

"Rhett, my boy." My father clapped him on the back. "How are you?"

"Good, Cary. You?"

"Excellent." Now that my father was retired, he was a die-hard fisherman and often went to Bait and Switch Fishing and Sport Supply Store for fishing supplies and a fish tale or two. Over the course of the last year, he had bonded with Rhett because he had done a few repairs at Rhett's cabin. Although Rhett was fully capable of doing his own fix-it jobs, he didn't want to waste the time. Besides, my father enjoyed his new role as handyman extraordinaire. "Except," my father continued, giving Rhett a wry look, "we're about to embark on a discussion concerning Jenna's aunt."

Rhett grinned. "I'll leave."

I clutched his arm. "No, stay." I shot my father a peeved look. "Dad."

"Sweetheart, you know how I hate to poke my nose into anyone's affairs, unlike some people I know. Namely, y-o-u. But if we must, we must." Up until a few months ago, my father and I had struggled with our relationship. I hadn't been very sensitive to his needs at the time my mother died because, well, my husband and my mom died within weeks of each other. My return to Crystal Cove and my occasional request for my father's advice had helped us mend fences. The fact that my sister and brother didn't live near enough for Dad to pester daily also made a difference. My sister lived in Los Angeles. She was rearing three children and running a home business. My brother was a successful, in-demand architect in Napa. When he wasn't working, he took vacations at monk-style retreats. No phone calls. No conversation. Adorable but boring.

My father continued, "Other than your nightmare, what's on your mind? I assume you're worried about your aunt's relationship with that man."

The way he said *that man* made my curiosity feelers prickle with alarm. "Who? Which man? She's dating someone and hasn't told me?"

"I'm not sure they're dating. It doesn't matter." Dad waved a hand. "What did you want to discuss?"

Rhett snickered.

I said, "You, hush."

He pressed his lips together to keep from laughing.

I pushed concern about my aunt's dating life aside and said, "Dad, you heard about Pearl Thornton, didn't you?"

My father shook his head.

"Where have you been?" I covered my mouth. Did I shriek? I hadn't meant to. Sotto voce, I added, "She's dead. She died yesterday. Well, not yesterday. Tuesday night, but she was found yesterday morning."

"I'm sorry to hear that. I've been working day and night on a mansion. New tile floors, at the cost of one-eighty a square foot, throughout. I—" He leaned forward and set his elbows on the table. "Never mind about me. Tell me about Pearl. Was she ill?"

"I think she was murdered."

"Really?"

"And Aunt Vera thinks she should investigate."

My father groaned. "That's what this is about? No, sir. No way. My sister is not going to stick her nose into anything. You goaded her into this, didn't you?"

"I did no such thing." Anger rose up my throat. I tamped it down. I did not—*not*—want to argue. "Aunt Vera is a grown woman. She makes her own decisions. Right now, she intends to investigate. She says her channels are blocked—"

"Her what?"

"Her psychic channels. They're blocked because of all

the anger she's feeling. She has to solve the crime if she wants to get her powers back."

"Her *powers*." My father huffed.

Rhett said, "Cary, why not let Jenna tell us everything."

"Sure. Fine. Keep talking."

I ignored his dismissive tone and quickly summarized yesterday's events: Aunt Vera and her friends finding Pearl dead, Cinnamon's investigation, and my aunt's meltdown after closing the shop. "Between you and me, I get the feeling Aunt Vera thinks Pearl might contact her from the beyond."

My father pushed his coffee and the muffin aside. I could see the muscle that held his jaw in place ticking. If only I could crawl inside his mind and see what he really wanted to say. What came out of his mouth was, "Jenna, I want you to put this worry from your mind. Your aunt will realize how inane this plan of attack is in a few hours, and she'll cease and desist."

"Dad, I've never seen her so flummoxed." I described the state of my aunt's hair and the strained timbre of her voice. "It doesn't help that I had that nightmare."

"About?" Rhett said.

I felt my cheeks warm a second time. Not from anger, from embarrassment. I didn't want him to think I was nuts. Even so, I recapped the dream as speedily as I could. Glinda, the monkeys, the castle, the gigantic bucket of hot water. When I was done, I mentally vowed for a second time: *No more fudge at night. Ever.*

"Hot water spells trouble," Rhett said.

"Precisely." I wanted to hug him for being so supportive. "Don't you see, Dad? I have to help Aunt Vera get clear."

"Jenna, no." My father spanked the table.

Sound in the café stopped. Dead. People stared at us.

More heat shot up my neck and into my cheeks. For all I knew, I had red blotches all over me. That was what happened when I couldn't contain my emotions. Not pretty. I diverted my gaze from the onlookers to my cuticles. If only I had eyes in the sides of my head so I could see if they had stopped staring.

My father, ignorant of the onlookers' rapt attention, continued his tirade. "I tolerated when you got involved after Desiree died." Desiree, my college roommate and popular celebrity chef, had been strangled and buried beneath the sand. "I kept quiet when you investigated after that Mumford woman died." The owner of Mum's the Word Diner, a competitor in the Grill Fest a month ago, was murdered in the alley right outside our café. "But this has got to end. You are not a crusader."

"I'm not the one investigating. Aunt Vera is."

"You just said you needed to help her get clear, did you not?"

I hated that he had such a keen memory.

"You'll get involved," he went on. "You can't help yourself. You're so . . . so—"

"I'm her niece," I snapped, then bit my lip. *Don't blow your top. Don't, don't, don't* cycled like a mantra through my mind. After a long moment, I said, "Family means everything to me."

"Your aunt should not get involved. I'll tell her so."

I guffawed. Truly. A big walloping laugh erupted from my belly. "Yeah, Dad, like you can tell her anything. She's as bullheaded as you are."

"I am not—" My father chuffed like a tiger. He glowered at Rhett. "Care to chime in?"

Rhett's mouth quirked up on one side. "And miss the fun?" He wagged his head. "Not on a bet." He leaned back in his chair and folded his arms. "Don't mind me. I'd pay handsomely for a ringside seat to this debate."

Silence fell between my father and me. Well, actually, throughout the café. I could hear the old clock behind the counter ticking. Swell.

After a minute, my father mirrored Rhett's folded-arm pose, and he smiled. I thought I'd melt in my chair. Was his beef with me defused? I glanced at Rhett and had to curb the urge to throw my arms around him and plant a full-blown kiss of thanks on his lips. Not here. Not now. Later, maybe.

Then, out of nowhere, the worry I had suffered earlier

resurfaced. I put words to my concern. "About Pearl's death . . . What if . . ." I placed both hands, palms down, on the table. "What if by moving back to Crystal Cove, I have opened the floodgates to bad karma?"

"Huh?" my father muttered.

"Dad, what if it's my fault?"

His eyes widened. He knew I was serious. "Sweetheart, evil exists everywhere. Our small town is not exempt." Working for the FBI, he knew better than most about evil. I didn't know the entirety of what role he had played during his stint there, but I was sure he had seen horrible things.

"But murder with this kind of frequency?" I argued. "I came back, and wham, someone died followed by someone else and, now, Dr. Thornton."

Rhett leaned forward and ran a finger along my forearm. "Jenna, maybe it's your fate to have returned so you could help the families."

"What do you mean?"

"Maybe, because of your own trauma, you have a gift to help them deal with theirs."

"I'm not a counselor."

"I'm not saying you are. But perhaps you know or suspect the truth before the police do."

"Are you saying I have some kind of magical power?"

He nodded. "Crystal Cove, like much of the coast of California, bears mystical properties. Perhaps you pick up on the supernatural, like your aunt."

"Don't encourage her," my father muttered and pulled the plate holding the muffin toward him. He peeled off the muffin's wrapper, cut the muffin in half, and picked up one section. He pushed the remainder toward me. "Eat."

I took a bite. The flavor was rich with bits of banana. I followed with a sip of coffee.

"But it's true, Cary," Rhett said. "Crystal Cove is special, and you know it."

"So what if it is?" my father replied.

I nearly choked on the coffee. "Dad, did you just imply that it's true?"

"No, I said—"

"You do not believe in ESP," I cut in. "You think tarot cards are bunk. In fact, you think everything Aunt Vera says about the future is baloney."

He shot a finger at me. "I would never admit this to my sister, and you'd better keep your pretty mouth shut"—a faint smile graced his lips; a twinkle sparkled in his eyes—"but there are times I've had a sense of something metaphysical going on here."

"No way."

"I have, too," Rhett said.

I gazed between the two men in my life, not shocked that they were agreeing, but stunned that they would admit this . . . *belief* . . . to me.

"Mind you, I'm rational," my father said.

"Understatement of the century," I quipped.

"I always look for the reasonable explanation."

"As do I," Rhett said.

"Me, too," I added. "I'm extremely levelheaded." I might be an artist, but I also see things in black and white. It's the curse of a Gemini. Right brain, left brain, yada yada. "But there are times—"

A hand gripped me from behind. I spun in my chair, expecting to see someone I knew. I shrieked when I found myself staring into the eyes of a giant Casper the Friendly Ghost. I recoiled and slid my chair backward. Into Rhett. He steadied me by placing his hands on my hips. I felt another flush of heat course through me, not due to contact with him, although that was a given, but because he was laughing louder than anybody else in the café.

Yes, they were all laughing. Let's hear it for Jenna the Spectacle.

"Can it," I muttered.

"So much for being levelheaded," he gibed.

I wrenched from his grip and glowered at the ghost. "You have a lot of nerve scaring me like that. Who are you?"

"Mine to know," the ghost said, but I recognized the

voice. It was the toy shop owner, a semi-infantile thirty-something with cherub cheeks.

I shook a finger. "You could have given me a—" I sucked in air as I flashed on Pearl, fooling around at the faire the day before, pretending to have a heart attack. Had her performance given the murderer the idea to poison her?

Chapter 8

MY MIDMORNING BREAK with my father and Rhett did nothing to quell my worry. I returned to the shop, still wondering what to do about my aunt. As I arrived at Fisherman's Village, I spotted Pepper Pritchett riding up on her bicycle. Wearing a long black sweater and black scarf that caught the wind, she looked for all intents and purposes like the nasty woman who hated Toto in *The Wizard of Oz*. She parked her bicycle, an old relic like the one I had inherited from my mother, complete with the basket and bell, in the stand outside Beaders of Paradise. Her shop would have been a darling place to browse, if not for its acerbic owner. Pepper was a wizard at beading and teaching beading; she lacked something in the personality department. She swooped off the bicycle, cinched the belt of her sweater, and gazed over her shoulder at me. If looks could kill. What had I done this time? Pepper didn't like my family for a variety of age-old reasons. I was doing my best to win her over, but it was hard being nice to someone so downright nasty.

I waved and smiled while flashing on last night's nightmare. In the dream, I was Glinda. Did I, as Rhett intimated at breakfast, have powers that I hadn't yet realized? Could I utter a chant, albeit a fake chant, that would change Pepper's demeanor? It was worth a shot.

Be nice, be nice, be nice, I whispered while clicking my heels—okay, I was trying to double-channel Glinda and Dorothy, and okay, flip-flops were definitely not as effective as ruby slippers—but I swear Pepper smiled at me. Next on my to-do list was making that amulet that Bailey had suggested with the Be Nice potion. Maybe I could conjure up some homemade candy to sweeten the deal. What was Pepper's favorite? Did she even eat candy, or did her diet consist solely of lemons and limes?

I snickered under my breath and headed toward The Cookbook Nook. Before entering the shop, I caught sight of another bicyclist. Cinnamon Pritchett, dressed in her brown uniform with her broad-brimmed hat hanging by a chin strap over her shoulders, hopped off her state-of-the-art mountain bike, removed her helmet, looped it over the handlebars, and slotted her bike next to her mother's. However, instead of entering her mother's shop, she marched toward the Nook Café.

Desperate for an update, I rushed toward her. "Cinnamon, wait up." If she had solved the mystery of Pearl's murder, my aunt could give up her quest and move forward with her life. I caught up to Cinnamon near the entrance to the café. The aroma of freshly baked biscuits wafted out the door. How I adored Katie's biscuits. Lots of butter. Maybe a drizzle of honey. My stomach grumbled. Half of a banana muffin was not going to suffice until lunch.

Cinnamon and I exchanged pleasantries. Yes, the day was gorgeous and the weather crisp. But then I got right to the point. I knew how much Cinnamon appreciated directness.

"How's the investigation going?" I asked.

"It's moving along."

"Did you arrest Trisha Thornton?"

"I've released her."

"She's not guilty? I could have sworn she was lying. Does she have an alibi?"

Cinnamon cocked her head.

"C'mon," I said. "Dr. Thornton—Pearl—was my therapist."

"Why do you go to a therapist?"

"I'll give you a dozen reasons, starting with my husband's suicide and financial duplicity."

"I'm sorry. That was thoughtless of me."

"Lots of people see therapists. It's almost chic to go. Why, I'll bet some cops, er, policemen, see shrinks." I winked. "But back to Trisha. Her alibi seemed weak."

"It turns out it was stronger than imagined. She went to her boyfriend's place, and then she went to UC Santa Cruz. She was at school, from ten P.M. until one A.M., conducting a laboratory experiment on rats looking for the effects of diabetes."

"She can do that?"

"She's a chemist."

"Why wouldn't she have told you where she was at the start?"

"She was alone at the lab. No witnesses." Cinnamon drew in a breath and exhaled. "To make things worse, she's on probation. Revealing her indiscretion—"

"You mean trespassing."

"Revealing her *whereabouts* could get her expelled for good."

I shifted feet. "I heard she was taking a year off between college and grad school."

"Nope. She started graduate school, but she's on probation for cheating on a test."

"So she's a cheater."

Cinnamon gave me a wry look.

I ignored it. "Can you tell me what the time of death was?"

"The coroner figures between ten and midnight."

At the exact time Trisha claimed to be at the lab. How convenient.

"Does Trisha inherit her mother's estate?" I asked.

"She does."

"Including her father's rock collection?"

"Yes."

"Wow! That has to be worth millions upon millions. Isn't that a huge motive for murder?"

"It would be, except the lawyer for the estate assures me Trisha will have to rely on a modest allowance until she's thirty-five. She won't be able to touch the bulk of the estate because of a stipulation in the trust. That's years away."

"If you rule her out, who else is there?" I asked. "Emma Wright? According to Trisha, Emma was the last to see Pearl alive. Did you track her down?"

"That's why I'm here. I went looking for her but couldn't find her."

"She's missing?"

"Not exactly. I got in touch with her husband, Edward. He was frantic. He hadn't seen or heard from her since Tuesday night."

"Not since the murder?"

"Right. He called everyone he knew. No one had seen her. But then I got a tip. Emma is here dining in the café."

"Here? Who told you?"

Cinnamon raised an eyebrow. *As if*, her gaze said. I wasn't dense. I could figure it out. Her mother, Pepper, must have caught sight of Emma and contacted Cinnamon, hence the two riding into Fisherman's Village on bicycles at the same time. Cinnamon pressed past me.

"Wait," I said. "You don't want to question her in public, do you? I mean, wouldn't someplace like my office be a better choice?" Okay, it wasn't much of an office. It shared space with the stockroom. A desk, chair, file cabinet, and computer. What more did we need? "It's cramped, but it serves its purpose."

"Good idea."

I'm not typically an eavesdropper, but after showing Cinnamon and Emma to the stockroom—Emma came willingly, though she looked nervous—I hovered halfway between the sales counter and the archway leading to the stockroom.

Bailey sneaked up and said, "What're you doing?"

I hushed her and motioned for her to tend to customers. Three were perusing the Halloween section.

"Bossy," she muttered.

"Curious." I waved her away and craned an ear toward the stockroom. Luckily, Cinnamon wasn't whispering. Neither was Emma. She sobbed when she heard that Pearl was dead. She sobbed harder when she was informed that someone had seen her having a private conversation with the doctor.

After calming Emma down, Cinnamon said, "Where have you been since you left the doctor's house?"

"At ten P.M., I returned to work and discovered a pet missing from its confine. Mrs. Hammerstead's Havanese. The dog's a sneaky little thing. He can open any cage. I didn't want to tell my boss. I might lose my job. I spent two hours looking for him. When I found him, around midnight, I took him back to the clinic."

"And then you went home?"

"No. My husband hates when I disturb his sleep, so"— Emma hesitated—"I walked."

"Why?"

"I needed time to—" She slurped back something that sounded like tears.

"Time to what?"

"Think."

"About?"

"Something." Emma's voice dropped to a whisper.

I inched closer. Why was she being so evasive?

"Where did you walk?"

"Anywhere. Everywhere. The beach. The road. I browsed shop windows."

"All night?"

"Yes."

We had a few homeless people in Crystal Cove. The weather was moderate, which made it an ideal place to tuck in for the night. But Emma had a house. And a husband. What had stirred her so much that she walked all night? Had she killed Pearl? Was she trying to fashion an alibi?

"You didn't go home in the morning," Cinnamon said.

"No."

"Why not?"

"I . . ." Emma clicked her tongue. "I drove up to see my mother in Santa Cruz."

"Your husband said he called her. She hadn't seen you."

"She was lying. She knew I . . . I needed time." More slurping.

"Here's a tissue." I heard Cinnamon pull a Kleenex from a box. Emma blew her nose. "Let's go back to your last minutes at Dr. Thornton's home. Did you and the doctor argue?"

"What? No." Emma sniffed. "Look, she was alive when I left."

"I have something to show you. Do you recognize this?"

Emma gasped. I ached to peek through the break in the drapes and see what Cinnamon was holding, but I held back.

"Is this your wedding ring?" Cinnamon asked.

"I don't know."

"There's an inscription and the date of your wedding inside. Care to revise your statement?"

Emma started crying again. "Yes, it's mine. Where did you find it?"

"I think you know," Cinnamon said, revealing nothing, leaving me hanging. "We wondered why Dr. Thornton was sprawled across the fire pit. That prompted me to do a search of the ashes. My people found your ring."

Why would Emma's ring have been in the ashes?

"I was"—Emma hiccupped—"asking Pearl for advice."

"About your marriage."

"I wanted to leave my husband."

"Is that all?" Cinnamon said.

Emma didn't respond.

I imagined the scenario on the patio. Pearl probably told Emma to keep a clear head and wait until morning to

address her problem. But Emma wouldn't listen. She was
upset with her husband for whatever reason. She tossed her
ring into the fire pit. Pearl tried to catch it. I paused. No,
that wasn't right. Pearl wasn't burned on any part of her
body. She had fallen or lain across the fire pit after the ashes
cooled. I was missing something.

"Talk to me, Mrs. Wright," Cinnamon said. "You're not
telling me everything. You wanted to leave your husband
for what reason? Did he cheat on you?"

Emma remained silent.

"Did he abuse you?"

"No."

"Did he threaten you in any way?"

"No. Edward is kind. He adores me. It's . . . I . . . I was
in love with Pearl. I needed to know if she felt the same."

I gasped. *Knock me over with a feather.* Realizing Cinnamon could have heard my outburst, I quickly covered by
saying, "Ow, Tigger, don't scratch me." Poor little guy was
halfway across the shop dallying with an elderly customer
who came in every day to give Tigger an ear scratch. My
outburst must have put Cinnamon on alert. Her voice
dropped to a whisper. So did Emma's. I glanced around the
shop. Bailey was tending to customers. No one was looking
in my direction. Curiosity getting the better of me, I dared
to creep closer to the curtain.

"I've loved Pearl since the day I met her," Emma
continued.

"Were you her patient?"

"No. She and I met while working on the Winsome
Witches luncheon. I was so inspired by her. She was such a
giving person. I've never had feelings like that before. Ever.
My husband . . . He doesn't understand me like Pearl did. I
didn't want to hurt him, but what could I do? Deny what was
turning me inside out? I wanted to be with Pearl for the rest
of my life."

"What happened next?" Cinnamon said. "After you
told her."

"She said in very clear terms that she was not in love

with me, nor would she ever be. I told her I could make her love me. She said I was transferring or something like that."

Doctor-patient transference. A common incident.

"I said she was wrong, and I'd prove it to her. I took off my ring and hurled it into the fire. She tried to catch it but missed. We stood there for a moment, staring at each other. Then she said I shouldn't have done that. She said she didn't feel the same about me. She never would. She was in love with a man. She wouldn't tell me who."

"And that made you mad."

"No, not mad. I was embarrassed. My heart was pounding so hard. I ran out." Emma wept loudly. "After that, I couldn't go home. You understand. I couldn't face my husband. I still love him, too. I couldn't hurt him like that. So I went to work. And then, in the light of day, I realized I had to talk to somebody—not my husband—so I went to see my mother."

Had Edward found out about Emma's yearning anyhow and gone to Pearl to confront her? Was he the one who killed her?

"Pearl said I had to come to grips with reality. Around nine A.M. this morning, I came back to Crystal Cove, but I had to eat before confronting my husband."

"Why didn't you call him?"

"I know it was bad of me. He must have been worried. But I didn't want to say anything wrong on the telephone."

Inexplicably, I felt as if someone were giving me the evil eye. I turned just in time to spy Pepper marching toward me. How did Bailey miss seeing her enter? How did I miss hearing her thundering footsteps?

Pepper gripped my arm. "What do you think you're doing, Miss Snoop?" I tried to wrench free. Man, she was stronger than I assumed. She propelled me forward, through the stockroom curtain. "Cinn," she said to her daughter. "Look who I found listening in on your conversation."

Cinnamon's gaze blazed into me. My cheeks stung with guilt. "What did you hear, Jenna?"

My mother often warned my siblings and me that spying

on people would get us in trouble. I was never certain whether she was equating being a childhood sneak to whatever it was my father did for the FBI. My siblings and I were pretty sure uncovering secrets were part of his job description. Finally, I admitted, "Everything."

Emma moaned.

"Do you have any questions of your own?" Cinnamon said with a bite.

I knew she was being sarcastic, but come to think of it, yes, I did have some questions. "Emma, you said you went searching for Mrs. Hammerstead's Havanese after you left Dr. Thornton's house. Did anyone see you?"

"I wasn't paying attention," Emma said. "Ho-Ho responds to a dog whistle. I was blowing it."

Pepper said, "Was that you near Azure Park around eleven P.M.?"

All of us turned to face her.

Pepper shrugged. "What are you staring at? You know I take late-night walks."

A few months ago, on one of her infamous walks, she claimed to have seen me herding my friend—the celebrity chef who was killed—to the beach. Her statement, until she rescinded it, nearly implicated me in that murder.

"I heard someone yelling," Pepper went on. "The person was all crouched over. I couldn't make out the face. Was that you? You were wearing a yellow shirt."

"Sweater." She gestured to her top. "Yes, that was me. Thank you for noticing." Emma hurried to Pepper and clutched her hands. "Ho-Ho likes to crawl under bushes." Tears flowed from Emma's eyes. "Thank you, Mrs. Pritchett. Thank you. I don't know how to repay you."

"I like chocolate," Pepper said. "The bitterer the better."

I stifled a snort. Why hadn't I figured that out on my own? Pepper was as bitter as horehound.

"If that's everything." Emma looked expectantly at Cinnamon.

"Hold it," I said, as a new angle that could make Emma

very culpable flitted into my head. Cinnamon cut me a questioning look. "I'm sorry," I hastened to add. "I know it's not my place, but Cinna—" I reverted to her official title. "Chief Pritchett, are you convinced, because Emma's alibi is confirmed based on your mother's statement, that Emma couldn't be the killer? Is the time of death that fixed?"

"I didn't do it," Emma cried.

Cinnamon, visibly unmoved, said to me, "Go on."

"You work with a veterinarian, Emma."

"So?"

I liked Emma—everyone who used her services swore by her tenderness with animals; I even entrusted Tigger to her—but I wasn't completely convinced she didn't kill Pearl. Emma had fallen in love with Pearl. By her own admission, Pearl had rejected her. Emma could've lashed out. Having observed actors during my advertising career, I knew how easy tears were to manufacture. I said, "Chief, you believe the killer injected Pearl with something. I'm assuming a type of poison."

She nodded, confirming my suspicion.

I addressed Emma. "You have access to hypodermic needles."

"I have a phobia of needles," Emma said. "I faint at the sight of them. That's why I'm not a veterinarian. That's why I shuttle pets around. I"—she gazed at us, her eyes wide—"remember something. I heard movement in the house, like there was someone else at home. It must have been Trisha. She and her mother fought. Trisha must have come back and killed her mother after I left. It wasn't me. I swear."

Chapter 9

CINNAMON ASKED EMMA to come to the precinct to provide an official statement. Pepper left, too. She was less than cheery. In fact, she was mumbling under her breath about her disappointment. In *me*. "Why do you always feel the need to offer your two cents?" was one of her complaints. Of course, I wondered why she wasn't asking herself the same question.

I joined Bailey at the sales register where she was ringing up the last of the customers. A stack of assorted cookbooks, for everything from candy to vegetables, stood on the counter. She whispered, "We have a novice cook in the mix. These are the first cookbooks she's ever bought. She can't wait for Katie's next cooking class."

"Did you recommend the Fannie Farmer book?"

"Of course, and *The Joy of Cooking*." When Bailey finished setting the books into bags, she tied ribbon around each. As the customers headed out with their purchases, she said, "So, spill. What was Pepper spluttering about as she left? Sometimes I wonder if she might be cuckoo."

"She's not." I filled her in. "How can I win Pepper over and make her accept me? I don't like having enemies."

"None of us do."

I peered through the bay window toward Beaders of Paradise and saw something glisten in the shop's window—a green stained-glass frog—and an idea came to me. "Pepper likes frogs." I hurried to the cookware section of the store.

Bailey followed, no doubt wondering if I was the one who was cuckoo.

"She has lots of frog-themed things in her store," I said. "I've peeked in after hours."

"You haven't."

"Heaven forbid I draw near during the day. She might think I was spying on her." I scoured the hanging items on the wall and on the endcaps of the bookshelves.

"What are you searching for?"

"We have frog-shaped chocolate molds, don't we?"

Bailey went right to them. I swear the girl had the entire place memorized. She would have made a great librarian; I'm sure she could nail the Dewey decimal system. One drawback: she didn't like quiet.

"Go ask Katie if she can teach me how to make dark chocolate," I said. "The bitterer the better."

"Bitter?"

"I'm not making them bitter out of spite. Pepper likes bitter. Go."

"Aye-aye, Captain." Bailey saluted and trotted off.

I would wrap the goodies in green plastic with a bow and write a lovely note to Pepper. Maybe then—

The door opened and Aunt Vera entered in normal attire, no caftan, no turban. She was wearing a pair of slacks, a light sweater, and sandals. Her hair was swept off her face. She wore no makeup.

My heart snagged in my chest. She never wore normal attire. Never. At least not out in public. I rushed to her. "Where have you been? You didn't come home last night. I didn't see your car in the driveway."

"I . . ." She flushed pink, then frittered her hand. "Have you been spying on me?"

Gosh, I was going to get a horrible reputation if people always assumed I was snooping. It wasn't in my nature. Not really. However, during these past three months . . .

I said, "I was worried."

"I'm not a teenager."

"I didn't say you were." I released the breath I was holding. "I'm just glad you're safe."

"Did I see Pepper leaving the store as I was parking?"

I nodded. I told her about Cinnamon's findings and her chat with Emma Wright. *Poor dear*, my aunt repeated more than once. I added, "Emma claimed she heard someone in Pearl's house at the time that she was revealing her true feelings. It was probably Trisha. She admitted she saw Emma there."

"But you said both of them left prior to ten P.M. What if there was a third person?"

"The housekeeper?"

"Somebody."

"Are you getting a feeling?" I wiggled my hands beside my head.

Aunt Vera didn't respond. She sidled past me and stowed her purse in the stockroom. When she reemerged, she finger-combed her hair, then moved to the vintage kitchen table and slumped into a chair.

I joined her and grasped her hands. Her face looked damp, as though she had splashed it with water while in back. Her eyes looked glossy with moisture. I allowed the silence to enfold us.

After a long moment, she shook her head. "I can't get over that Pearl is dead. Gone. She was so good to me. To everyone."

"To her patients, too," I said. "She had a way about her, in therapy, that put me at ease. I was growing more trusting. She was encouraging me to see more of Rhett."

"He was a client, too, wasn't he?" my aunt said. "I wonder how many clients Pearl had."

"Good question. People confided in her. Do you think

it's possible that one of her clients, someone who wasn't even at the party, killed her to protect a secret?"

"That certainly widens the list of suspects." Aunt Vera released my hands and picked up a piece of the wine cork jigsaw puzzle. She twisted it right, then left. After she found a spot for it and pushed it into place, she tapped it with her fingertip. "I keep trying to visualize the crime scene."

"What do you remember?"

"That's just it. I don't."

"Then you're not really visualiz—" I pressed my lips together. I wasn't going to nitpick.

"Something seemed out of place."

"Close your eyes," I said. "Try to picture it." I remembered Pearl asking me to do the same. I didn't lie on a couch at her office; I sat in a chair. Shutting my eyes, she advised, would take me out of the present and put me at the scene. How did David's note feel in my hand? How did I feel as people at my mother's funeral stared at me? "Come on, Aunt Vera, humor me."

Her eyes fluttered, then closed.

"See Pearl," I ordered. "Lying across the fire pit. See the rest of us standing there. Maya held the coffee tray. Bingo was making a telephone call. See—"

Aunt Vera's eyes snapped open. "That's not working."

"You're not trying hard enough."

She rose from the chair. "I must go."

"Where?"

"To Pearl's house." She fetched her purse and darted out of the shop.

I nabbed Bailey, who was strolling down the hallway with a plate of cookies in her hand, and said, "Watch the shop," and then I bolted after my aunt.

"LET ME DRIVE," I shouted, but Aunt Vera wouldn't listen. She whipped her car keys from her purse and dashed to her Mustang.

Resigned, I climbed in on the passenger side. I noticed

an overnight bag on the floor and detected a hint of what I considered a man's cologne, Clive Christian in fact, heavy with lime and mandarin oranges, with a hint of cedarwood and spice. The essences of lily of the valley and rose were its base. I remembered the scent because it had been my husband's favorite; David had expensive tastes.

"Are you seeing someone?" I said as I latched my seat belt. "Do you have a new beau?"

"Yes . . . No . . ."

"Which is it, yes or no?"

"It's nothing," Aunt Vera replied and ground the car into reverse.

"C'mon. Tell me. Is it that sweet mustachioed manager of the bed-and-breakfast?"

She didn't answer. I didn't press. I wanted her focused on the road. Aunt Vera wasn't the best driver. She was easily distracted.

As we arrived at Pearl's house and were walking up the path, the front door opened.

"Is that Bingo?" I said.

Bingo nearly flew past us, head down, her wide jaw set. She was clutching her purse tightly to her chest.

"Bingo, dear," Aunt Vera said. "Slow down. What's the hurry?"

Bingo looked up. Wisps of hair hung loosely around her face. She batted them away and adjusted her wire-rimmed glasses. "I'm late. Sorry. Forgive me." She briskly hugged my aunt.

"Why are you here?" Aunt Vera asked,

Bingo tapped the arm of her glasses. "I left these the night of the party. So silly. I meant to search for them the morning . . . the morning—" She jammed her lips together. The morning Pearl died. She inhaled and continued. "I can't see anything up close without them. I don't know how I managed. Mrs. Davies let me in." She glanced at the house and back at us. "Must run. I'm meeting my fiancé and the wedding planner, and then the banquet manager for the luncheon, and afterward an antique collector. So much to do.

If only Pearl—" She covered her mouth, shook her head woefully, and hurried to her car.

Before we pressed the doorbell, the front door opened. Mrs. Davies, the housekeeper who reminded me of a female Alfred Hitchcock, greeted us and beckoned us inside with the tips of her feather duster. How had she known we were there? Maybe she had been peeking through the sidelight windows, watching Bingo depart.

"Such a tragedy," she said as we strolled into the tiled entryway. "Did Ms. Bedelia tell you?"

"Did she tell us what?" I said.

"It's horrible. Ghastly. The missus would be so upset."

"About what?"

"She was such a gracious lady and so in love with her husband." Mrs. Davies worried the handle of the duster. "I came to work this morning. I don't know what else I'm to do. No one's given me direction."

I wondered whether the new buyers would still employ Mrs. Davies, once Pearl's estate was settled and the house sold—I assumed Trisha would want to sell the house and the trustee would allow her to do so, returning the proceeds to the trust. In an apartment near the college, Trisha would have no need of a housekeeper, and from what I sensed the other morning, there was no love lost between the two of them.

"Do you like it here?" I asked.

"I'm glad I moved to the States, if that's what you mean. I've been thankful for the work. I'm good at what I do." Mrs. Davies shook her head. "Who else but I would have noticed another theft? It's simply ghastly."

"What are you saying?" I asked. "Something else was stolen? When? The night Pearl died?"

"Must have been."

"Was it the doctor's Tiffany filigree heart-and-key pendant?" Pearl often wore the diamond-studded necklace. I remembered her toying with it at a few of our sessions. Her late husband had given it to her on their tenth anniversary. It had to be worth a pretty penny.

"No, not jewelry." Mrs. Davies clicked her tongue. "It was the rock."

"The sapphire was found."

"Not that rock. The other. The Thorntonite."

"Are you saying the Thorntonite was stolen the night of the murder?"

"Not all, mind you, only a portion, which is why I didn't notice until this morning." She pointed toward the room that held the Thornton Collection.

"Could it have been stolen at an earlier time?"

"Not likely. I dust every day. I simply stopped yesterday after finding the sapphire missing."

"Why would someone steal Thorntonite?"

"The rock is rare. To date, geologists haven't discovered any more of it."

"Could a small piece of it go for a hefty price?"

"I haven't a clue. It is an ugly thing, indeed. Packed with sele-something, the missus told me, as if that would matter to me." Pearl's calico cat scampered into the entryway and yowled. Mrs. Davies shooed it with the duster. The calico hissed. The woman knelt down and scratched the cat under the chin. "Poor dear. I know. We are all upset. Now scat. To the kitchen with you." The cat darted from the room. Mrs. Davies rose and returned her attention to us. "I believe it was Miss Thornton that stole the rock. She's bloody cheeky, that one."

Why would Trisha steal a portion? With her mother dead, she owned the entire collection. And hadn't she been adamant about selling the collection? She said it was *evil*.

"Why do you suspect Trisha?" I asked.

"Trisha is the only one who knows where the missus kept the keys to the cabinets."

Aunt Vera said, "Don't you know the location, as well?"

Mrs. Davies cut her an anxious look, then flushed pink. "Of course I do, but I would never steal from the missus. Not in a million years. She was too good to me."

"Where did Dr. Thornton stow the key?" I asked.

Mrs. Davies pointed. "In her study. In the drawer of the desk that holds the will and other important documents."

"Is the study locked?"

"No, miss."

"Is the desk?"

"No, miss."

"So, really, anyone could have stolen it."

Mrs. Davies mulled that over and offered a curt nod. "I've rung the police. They're on their way. Why have you come?"

I glanced at my aunt. We had a small window of opportunity to snoop around.

"Because"—Aunt Vera licked her lips—"I, like Ms. Bedelia, left a pair of glasses here."

Not a polished lie, I mused, but quick.

"I believe I left them outside," my aunt added.

Mrs. Davies eyed us warily. "Wouldn't the police have collected them, seeing as it was a crime scene?"

"Possibly," my aunt conceded. "But Bingo found hers."

Had Bingo really come to look for glasses, or had she, like us, used the excuse to snoop? She could have pulled a pair from her purse.

I said, "Could we have a look around?"

"Feel free, but don't go in the display room, please. The police will need to dust for fingerprints."

Mrs. Davies led the way to the kitchen. As we passed the den, I peeked in. Nothing seemed out of place. All the cabinets were closed. The collection of Thorntonite looked like I remembered. Numerous gray rocks, all about the size of a child's fist, sat stacked on a mirror plate within the clear glass case. I wondered how the housekeeper had noticed a portion was missing, until I realized that was what she did. She tended to the house. She probably knew the count of the silver, the stemware, and the china, too.

Or she was lying to throw suspicion on Trisha.

We strode through the kitchen and out to the backyard. The temperature had warmed since we left the shop. I shaded my eyes and surveyed the area. Aunt Vera drew near.

"Do you remember what you might have seen?" I whispered.

"No, but I feel something deep in my soul."

"Didn't you tell me you lost your powers?" I teased.

"Don't, Jenna dear. Please."

"Sorry."

She paced the patio, scouring beneath and behind the chaise lounges. A tingling sensation slithered up my spine. I started searching as hard as she did. Was I sensing something on her behalf? No, I didn't have her powers. I didn't believe in her powers.

The French doors leading to the den burst open. Trisha Thornton shrieked, "You!"

Aha. I must have picked up on Trisha's presence. So much for not intruding on the second crime scene, I thought, though her fingerprints had to be everywhere in that room. Or did they? Believing the rocks to be evil, perhaps she went out of her way to avoid touching the cases. A solitary fingerprint would implicate her, wouldn't it?

"How dare you invade my home!" She charged toward my aunt.

"We're not invading," Aunt Vera said. "We came to look for a pair of glasses."

"That's a lie. You're creeping around. I saw you." Trisha shot her hands forward as if she intended to strangle my aunt.

Without hesitating, I inserted myself between her and Aunt Vera. I wasn't tough, but I occasionally kickboxed along with an instructor on television, and I'd become quite good at Dr. Oz's seven-minute workout. I could defend my aunt if necessary, especially from someone as lean as the storm cloud facing her. "Look, Trisha, we're sorry for your loss," I said, "but we cared for your mother, and we want to help."

"Stop butting into our affairs. The police are doing their job. Do you hear me? Now, leave." She pointed to the door.

What could we do? She was, after all, the new owner. I nabbed my aunt's elbow and steered her toward the exit.

As we departed through the kitchen, I recalled the fight between Trisha and her mother on the night of the party. It involved money. What if Trisha had lied to Cinnamon about being in the lab at school? What if Trisha had stuck around after Emma ran off and argued with her mother again? What if Trisha had revealed to Pearl that she was not taking time off from school; she was on probation? How would Pearl have reacted? Would she have been mortified? Enraged? If she had threatened to cut Trisha off for good, Trisha might have lashed out and killed her mother to ensure that she didn't change her will. Granted, Trisha wouldn't inherit everything right away, but she was guaranteed an allowance—one she didn't have to beg for—and she could look forward to receiving a substantial sum in less than twelve years.

Chapter 10

AS AUNT VERA and I drove back to the shop, we chatted about the crime scene and what she remembered after seeing it for a second time.

"The angle of the chaise lounges seemed off," she said.

"The police could have moved them."

"Pearl's witch hat was no longer there. The martini glass was gone, as well."

"The police could have taken any of those for evidence." Though why they would've wanted the hat was beyond me. Maybe Mrs. Davies put it back in Pearl's closet. The notion caught me off guard. Tears pressed at the corners of my eyes.

"The leaves on the ground looked messy." Aunt Vera paused. "A breeze or the police trampling them could have caused that, I guess." She pulled into a parking spot at Fisherman's Village, but she didn't turn off the engine. "Jenna dear, I've got a headache. I have to rest. Will you be okay without me for the afternoon?"

I nodded. "Take as long as you need."

Around 3:00 P.M., I called her to check in, but she didn't answer her telephone. I tried again at 4:00 P.M., with the same result. By close of business, I was wrung out with worry. She was my pillar. I couldn't stand for her to be hurting.

Rather than call her again and possibly irritate her—she was, after all, a grown-up and able to deal with tragedy—I wrangled Bailey and Katie, and we went to Vines, the wine bar on the second floor of Fisherman's Village. Tigger was a little miffed at not being included and turned up his tail at treats that I offered, but an enormous amount of cuddling—which I think I needed more than he did—settled him down. I nestled him into his kitty bed in the stockroom, along with the cookbook *Purr-fect Recipes for a Healthy Cat: 101 Natural Cat Food & Treat Recipes to Make Your Cat Happy*. The book was a great source for teaching me not only about what to feed my cat but about which nutrients he needed. Tigger couldn't care less what was written on the pages or how dutiful a human I was becoming. He fell in love with the six beautiful cats that graced the cover and, now, liked to sleep with his head on the book. He dozed instantly. Lucky him.

Vines Wine Bistro was always an inviting place for anyone who wanted a quiet conversation. All the handcrafted tables were small, set to seat four patrons or less. The ten-foot-long curving bar allowed for limited chatter. Classical music played through a speaker system. Strings of lights in the shapes of vines added a twinkle to the room.

However, tonight, as Katie opened the heavy oak door, noise spilled out. She thrust out her hands to block us. "What's going on here?"

I peeked around her. The bar was hopping with people, many in Halloween costumes. "Wow."

"A little early for dress-up, isn't it?" Bailey said.

I grinned. "Halloween is only a few days away. Some people live for it. Didn't you see those women who came into the shop dressed in Dorothy costumes? Have you ever heard of Comic-Con? Talk about costume lovers." Comic-Con is a convention for fans of comics, graphic novels, movies, and more.

"Will we be able to hear ourselves think?" Katie said.

"Yes. Move inside," Bailey ordered.

A lithe waitress in an understated black sheath led us to one of the tables at the back. Just beyond our table was a glass-enclosed room. Within, a party of ten was having a private wine tasting.

"What's going on over there?" I asked. A throng, three people thick, crowded a wall.

"That?" The waitress laughed. "It's the boss's way of pitching in to the Winsome Witches event. We're having a Pin the Bat on the Pumpkin contest. Didn't you get a flyer?"

"I did," Bailey said. "I forgot to show you, Jenna."

No wonder she had looked so sneaky walking up the stairs to the bar. Bailey loved a party.

"Can anyone play?" I asked.

"Sure. Donate a buck to the pumpkin." The waitress hitched a thumb at one of the largest pumpkins I had ever seen. Not one that would win a biggest-in-the-world contest, but *big*. It perched on the end of the bar. "The money goes to the literacy fund."

"Me first," Bailey said after we ordered a bottle of an Oregon pinot noir and a cheese plate appetizer. In addition to partying, she was always eager to play a game. She hurried from the table, plopped a buck into the pumpkin, and then jostled her way to the front of the throng. A man in a cowboy costume handed her a rubbery bat, blindfolded her, and twirled her around three times.

While Bailey navigated her way to a grinning paper pumpkin that had been stuck to the wall, the crowd doing its best to distract and disorient her, Katie said, "By the way, I'm glad to help you make the bittersweet chocolate to sweeten up Pepper. They'll be the best ever. We'll add a little cayenne."

"To chocolate?"

She nodded. Her curls bounced. "Delish, promise. By

the way, did I tell you how happy I am with our new chef hire?" In addition to the assistant chef position, Katie had been looking for another chef. She couldn't work twenty-four hours every day; she needed a respite. She had hired him yesterday. "He's got the most fabulous stuffed chicken recipe. Basil, goat cheese, and peppers in a tomato–sour cream sauce."

"Sounds yummy."

"He's fabulous with the rest of the staff. They're respect-ful. And he's on time."

"So far."

"Don't jinx it," she said. The chef she had hired a month ago didn't work out. He was often late and tipsy. "I need to have a personal life again."

"Speaking of which, how is your new boyfriend?"

"Super sweet, but"—she scrunched up her nose—"I'm so afraid I'll blow it."

"Why?"

"I've never had a boyfriend before. Ever. I mean, I went on a few dates, but while working for Old Man Powers"—Katie's former boss, a widower who lived well into his nineties—"life sped by. I didn't have time to get to know someone and have him get to know me."

Her boyfriend was the amiable ice cream guy who bicy-cled around town serving up homemade ice cream, which he kept cold by using the power of his pedaling. He often stopped into the Nook Café to see if Katie needed a delivery of ice cream, which she rarely did since she made fabulous ice cream all by herself.

Our waitress delivered the wine and cheese platter—an American trio that included a round of Cowgirl Creamery's triple cream called Mt. Tam, named for Mt. Tamalpais; a small sliver of Humboldt Fog; and a wedge of Wisconsin cheddar. After decanting the wine, she left.

I poured the wine into three glasses, then took a sip from mine and swooshed its velvety smoothness around my mouth. Divine. Oregon's climate was favorable for lush red wine.

Katie swirled the wine in her glass. "Enough about me. Tell me what's going on with your aunt."

I summarized our trip to Pearl's house, including learning about the missing minerals and our run-in with Trisha. "Aunt Vera is distraught. She feels she should be getting all sorts of extrasensory input about the murder since she was close to Pearl, but she's mentally stymied. The fact that Trisha lit into us didn't help."

"Bad aura?"

"That girl—" I stopped myself. I sounded way older than my nearly thirty years; Trisha was only six or seven years younger than I was. "Trisha said we should trust the police to investigate. Does that make her innocent?"

"What's her alibi?"

"She claims she was at school doing a research project about her mother's illness. No witnesses."

"Did Cinnamon buy that?"

"She seems to have." I took another sip of wine. "I doubt Trisha will search for any witnesses because she's on probation for cheating on a test. She doesn't want anyone to know she sneaked onto the premises."

"Hmm," Katie said. "I could have sworn your aunt told me Trisha was taking a year off." Katie was a gossip hound. She knew a bit about everyone in town.

"I heard the same thing. I guess Trisha lied from the get-go."

"Or her mother fibbed to your aunt because she was embarrassed."

When leaving Pearl's house earlier, I had considered the same thing. If that was the case, Pearl had known about her daughter being on probation. The question was, when did Pearl learn the news? The night she died?

"C'mon, help me out, people," Bailey cried.

I watched as she forged blindly through the crowd and approached the paper pumpkin with a wiggly rubber bat. She neared the left side, but the crowd moaned, which threw her off. She pivoted and headed toward the crowd again.

More moans and a few gasps. Watching her grope made me think of something.

I said, "How do you think Trisha got into the lab?"

"A key."

Bailey swung around again. She neared the nose of the pumpkin. The crowd cheered. She must have thought they were fooling her because she made a right turn.

"Not if she had been booted out of school," I said.

"Someone must have let her into the lab."

"Which means she wasn't working alone; she had help. She's lying about there being no witness in order to protect someone."

"Or she's lying about being there at all."

"To give herself an alibi." I drummed the bowl of my wineglass with my fingertips. "I'm sure, now that a piece of the Thorntonite has gone missing, Cinnamon will do a little more digging."

"Ha-ha, that's funny." Katie chortled. "Digging. Rocks. Geology."

"Unintended pun."

Katie sipped her wine and hummed. "You sure pick a nice wine."

I had to thank my long-lost husband for that. Before I met him, David had considered going into the wine business. He didn't, but he had an educated palate and taught me to have one, as well.

"Back to Trisha," Katie said, not losing track of our conversation. "Couldn't you—"

"I hate games." Bailey, wearing a witch hat decked out with funereal-looking black roses and ivy, plopped into a chair. "I never win."

"Where'd you get the hat?" I asked.

"Some cute warlock wearing a Zorro-style mask gave it to me." Bailey pointed. "See him? The next victim. When he gave it to me, he crossed his fingers and blew me a kiss. Like I would bring him luck. Sweet."

The crowd roared. People parted. I could see someone

slinging a blindfold over the masked warlock. He had rugged bone structure and tan skin.

"He's here to attend the Winsome Witches luncheon." Bailey picked up her wine and took a sip. "He had the most gorgeous, undistinguishable accent. Maybe European? Yum."

I wasn't sure whether she was referring to the wine or the guy.

"Would you throw over Jorge for a stranger?" I said.

"*Jorge*. Bah." Bailey huffed. "We broke up. His mother hates me."

I wondered if the guy in the Zorro-style mask was, indeed, Jorge, toying with her. "His mother has never met you," I said. "She lives in Mexico."

"I know. But she doesn't want him dating an *Americano*. If a man listens to his mother, is he the man of my dreams?"

"Some men, yes."

"What century are you living in? *Not*. All daughters-in-law should be menaces to their mothers-in-law." She snickered, then took another sip of wine. "Okay, you're right. I want my future mother-in-law to like me."

I petted her hand. "I'm sorry."

She shrugged. "If it's not meant to be, it's not meant to be. Jorge is just one more name on the men-from-my-past list." She sipped more wine. "So . . . what're you guys gossiping about?"

"Trisha Thornton," Katie said. "I was just about to tell Jenna that she knows lots of people, and she should call someone at UC Santa Cruz and ask about Trisha's status at school." She summed up Trisha's claim to be on probation.

"I'm sure Cinnamon has called the school," I argued. "Besides, the registrar won't reveal anything to me."

Katie said, "You donate to the alumni association, don't you?"

"To Cal Poly"—where I attended college—"not UC Santa Cruz."

"Forget the school status angle for a second." Bailey righted her slightly tipsy witch hat. "Let's focus on why

Trisha was really there. Jenna, you said some of the Thorntonite was missing. What if the housekeeper is right and Trisha stole it? What if she took it that night to the lab?"

"To do what?" I asked.

"Your aunt mentioned she's a chemist of some sort. Let's say Trisha lied about looking for a cure for diabetes. Maybe she was experimenting with the rock. You know, doing an alchemy project."

"Witches do alchemy," Katie said.

"True. My warlock"—Bailey gestured toward the Pin the Bat on the Pumpkin area—"and I were talking about potions. He said he could make the perfect love potion."

I'll bet he could. "Did Warlock Zorro ask for your number?"

"No, the skunk."

Katie rapped the table. "Stay on topic. Trisha. With the Thorntonite. In the laboratory. Why?"

Bailey nodded. "She was angry with her mother for being a witch—"

I held up a hand. "Pearl wasn't a witch."

"But she was the leader of the Winsome Witches," Bailey argued. "Trisha, being conservative—"

"Conservative?" I wasn't following her logic.

"She thought the rocks her father collected were evil." Bailey raised a skeptical eyebrow. "C'mon. Really? Evil? They're rocks, for Pete's sake."

"Maybe," Katie said, "Trisha stole the Thorntonite to see if she could turn evil into good."

"Or maybe she decided to experiment in black magic," Bailey countered.

I shook my head. "Not very conservative."

Bailey glowered. "Just listen, both of you. Perhaps Trisha wanted to see if she could make her mother come around to her way of thinking. She took the Thorntonite, ground it into a potion, and *poof*"—Bailey clapped her hands like a magician—"she magically coerced someone to murder her mother."

"Whoa." Katie held up a hand. "That's not the direction I was heading at all."

"Hold it." I mirrored the raised hand. "Let's try a whole new angle. What if someone else with a grudge against Pearl believes herself to be a *real* witch and stole the Thorntonite to do what Bailey said?" I replayed my aunt's and my morning visit to Pearl's house. "Aunt Vera couldn't see what it was about the setting that had bothered her. What if she wasn't remembering something she had viewed but something she intuited? Like pervasive evil." I thumped the table. "Come to think of it, I felt something was off, too, right before Trisha Thornton caught us snooping."

Katie tapped her head. "Oho! You're getting the gift."

"I am not. No way. But don't you ever get a feeling? A tingling sensation?"

"That's it! That's the gift," Katie said. "My mother has . . . *had* . . . the gift." Her mother was suffering from early-onset Alzheimer's. Katie's father, a harsh man on the best of days, couldn't handle the disease. He only visited Katie's mother at the assisted-living center once a year, on her birthday. Katie wiggled her fingers. "There's all this spiritual energy flowing around Crystal Cove. You're picking up on it."

"Uh-uh," I said. "I don't believe it."

"For heaven's sake, Jenna." Katie hugged herself and wriggled in place. "Stop fighting whatever is going on inside you. It's a gift. Embrace it."

Bailey mimicked Katie. "Yes. Embrace it."

"It's not a curse," Katie said.

"Spirit of the wine bar." Bailey threw her hands overhead like a traveling-show healer. "Fill Jenna with the sight."

"Cut it out." I batted her hands.

"It's not a curse," Katie repeated.

"I don't think of it as a curse." I didn't. I thought it was insane, idiotic, and totally outside the realm of possibility. But not a curse. "We're done with this discussion."

My pals tried to bring up the subject two more times before we said good night for the evening.

When I arrived home with Tigger, I was wired. Silly made-up ditties coursed through my head: *Curses and witches and pumpkins, oh my!* Why? I don't know. Maybe it was the fact that Katie, Bailey, and I had talked about potions; maybe it was the fact that I was hungry. I hadn't eaten anything other than tidbits from the cheese platter while Katie and Bailey chowed down on Italian salads loaded with salami, garbanzo beans, and olives. Why hadn't I eaten more? At least some protein? A chicken breast or steak would've been a good choice. I hadn't because my appetite had flown the coop when we started talking about curses and the spiritual energy floating around Crystal Cove.

Well, it didn't matter. I would eat now.

I tore into the kitchen, fetched Tigger a snack, and then, intent on practicing my skills at making food for the Halloween party, I opened one of the cookbooks I'd toted home: *Ghoulish Goodies: Creature Feature Cupcakes, Monster Eyeballs, Bat Wings, Funny Bones, Witches' Knuckles, and Much More!* How hard could it be to make a bag of dirt or a cup of worms? I stumbled onto a page that was filled with tips, one of which caught my eye: *Don't drive yourself nuts*. The author suggested, when throwing a party, to have fun and to be willing to ask for help. I couldn't do the second right now. "You're not quite a sous chef," I said to Tigger. "Are you?" He meowed.

However, taking the *fun* suggestion to heart, I flipped to a section in the cookbook highlighting candy.

In the mood for something salty but sweet—so much for protein—I found *Boo-rific Seed Brittle*. I felt a moment of panic as I gathered the ingredients. I didn't have pumpkin seeds, but I had sunflower seeds; they would make a good substitute, right?

With kitchen mitts protecting my forearms and hands, I boiled the sugar, water, and corn syrup. As I stirred the bubbling concoction with a wooden spoon, I thought of the Shakespeare play I'd acted in during my senior year of high school. I had wanted the part of Lady Macbeth, but I ended up cast as one of the three witches. Lady M went to Sloan

What's-her-name, as all the starring roles had. No one could compete with full-of-herself Sloan, who left Crystal Cove to make it on Broadway. The last I heard, she was in a touring company. Not everyone wound up a star. In the opening scene, we witches stood around a huge black pot chanting, "Double, double, toil and trouble. Fire burn and cauldron bubble."

The memory zinged me back to my conversation with Katie and Bailey at Vines. Was there a real witch among the Winsome Witches, one who was practicing some kind of dark magic? Did I believe real witches existed? Perhaps one of the witches murdered Pearl to gain control over the other Winsome Witches. Except what kind of control could she wield, more fund-raising?

Get real, Jenna. I moved the boiling brew off the burner and stirred in the butter and sunflower seeds. The recipe asked me to cook the mixture for another five minutes. As I did, I inhaled. The smell was sweet yet salty. Heavenly. Precisely what I was in the mood for. Tigger roamed the kitchen floor, weaving in and out of my ankles begging for another tidbit. I was pretty sure he was hoping to score human food. Not a chance.

I tossed him another kitty treat, then added the requisite baking soda to the pot. Next, I poured in the vanilla, remembering to stand back because the author warned that the vanilla would make the concoction *spit*. It did. Thanks to the kitchen mitts I'd donned, none of the hot liquid scalded me. Yay! I stirred the pot one more time before pouring the candy onto a baking sheet greased with butter.

While it cooled, I decided to take a walk on the beach. Tigger begged to come along. How could I refuse?

The cool air hit me with a punch, the good kind. I kicked off my shoes and raced to the ocean's edge. A full moon peeked from behind a cluster of clouds. Soon, it emerged fully and cast a path of golden light across the ocean, right to my bare feet.

"Isn't it pretty?" I whispered to Tigger. He nuzzled my chin with the top of his head.

A flash of light caught my eye. South of me, a bonfire came to life. Crystal Cove allowed campfires, but the town didn't create fire pits. Beachgoers had to dig their own pits and provide their own wood.

The group surrounding the fire whooped with glee, and then they grasped hands and started to dance in a circle.

I drew nearer. The dancers were girls, all dressed as fairies. Their wispy skirts blew in the breeze; their wiry wings flounced behind them. One raised her voice above the rest and chanted words that sounded like an incantation in another language. Her fellow fairies cackled. They raised their arms, still connected by the hand, overhead.

The one doing the reciting broke free. She brandished a wand. At the top of her lungs, she yelled, "Bibbidi-bobbidi-boo!"

Like a group of kindergartners playing Ring around the Rosie, the group of women all fell down and burst into hysterics.

Oddly enough, seeing them making light of something so grave made me shiver. I tucked Tigger close to my chest and thought of Pearl and her fellow witches again. Yes, they came together once a year for a good cause. Yes, it was all in fun.

Except this year it wasn't.

What if one witch considered herself or himself a real witch? What if she . . . or he . . . had admitted as much to Pearl in a therapy session? Had the killer murdered Pearl to protect the secret?

Chapter 11

I AWOKE FRIDAY, cranky and edgy. My aunt didn't show up at work. I called; she didn't answer. She did leave a message with Bailey that she was fine and safe and I shouldn't worry. Yeah, like that would help. I went through the day worried about her and her psychic blockage while still wondering who could have killed Pearl. Eating only greens and protein and downing glass after glass of water didn't seem to help my mood. Bailey suggested caffeine. I refused to indulge. I hoped a good night's rest would do the trick.

But it didn't. I woke up Saturday feeling much the same.

Giving in, I fixed one of the strongest cups of coffee I had imbibed since college days. No sugar. No cream. No half-caf concoction. Pure, unadulterated caffeine. Bailey would have been proud. I downed the entire contents of my cup and whispered, "Ahh."

Tigger, who was nibbling his tuna, gave me a curious look.

"Just on the mend, bud." In ten seconds flat, my body felt energized—okay, sure, it was fake energy, but I was enlivened—and the cobwebs in my mind started to dissolve. Requiring even further stimulation, I turned on the local news. I never did that in the morning. I liked to start fresh, with no input from the outside world, but today was different.

Instead of the top story covering an event in Santa Cruz or Watsonville, the reporter focused on Crystal Cove. Our mayor was concerned about the increase in bonfires on the beach. She insisted the cooler weather had something to do with the surge, but because the area was drier than usual . . .

I switched off the television, my buoyant mood gone in a flash. My thoughts flew to what I had seen the night before last on the beach. Were those dancing, giddy girls merely having fun, or were they taking witchcraft to a whole new level? I reflected on what Bailey had suggested at Vines that night. Was one of the Winsome Witches a real witch? Was Trisha Thornton practicing alchemy? Was Pearl dead because of some incantation Trisha had cast?

Before taking my morning run/walk, I did what Katie had advised the night we went to Vines and I called UC Santa Cruz because, in the wee hours of the morning, I'd remembered that an old college friend worked in the administration office. Yes, it was a weekend day and offices were closed, but I had her cell phone number, and I knew she was an early riser. The phone rang a few times. On the fourth ring, I reached her voice mail. After her message, I said hello and asked how she was doing. I added that we needed to catch up. Then I launched into my query. I wanted to find out all I could about Trisha Thornton and whether it was possible for Trisha to get into a lab on the campus premises by herself. Without a key. While on probation. I asked whether, if Trisha had stolen in, there was any way to corroborate her presence, like perhaps security camera footage? I ended by begging my friend to call me as soon as she could.

After a brisk run and a brisker shower—seriously cold showers could be incredibly beneficial and healing; they improved circulation, boosted white cell activity, and balanced hormones, all of which I needed—I dressed in a peach-colored shift, had a quickie power breakfast of scrambled eggs topped with Parmesan cheese and a side of fruit, and then gathered up my sweet kitty and hurried to The Cookbook Nook.

I switched on our music loop, which was food-related. The first in line was "Bread and Butter" by the Newbeats. That got me singing and made me forget the edginess I had felt for the past two days. I settled at the table in the children's section of the store and began flipping through kiddie cookbooks, trying to decide which covers to turn outward to lure customers. The spine of a book didn't always do the job. Not all of the books in stock were Halloween-themed, but I didn't care. What mother could resist a title like *Fairy Tale Feasts: A Literary Cookbook for Young Readers and Eaters*? The book was more than a collection of stories and recipes. In it, the author and her daughter encouraged young readers to be creative storytellers themselves.

Bailey entered and gave me a wry look. "Planning on auditioning for *You've Got the Beat* anytime soon?"

"Not a chance." Although I loved to croon, my voice wouldn't get past round two hundred in a competition on the popular television reality show. I had breath issues, a music teacher once told me. I didn't care. I continued to sing.

Bailey plopped into a chair opposite me and eyed *Fairy Tale Feasts*. "*Booklist* gave that cookbook thumbs-up for its easy language and whimsical illustrations."

"Rightly so." I opened to a page. "How can you pass up a recipe for stone soup made with a real stone?"

The telephone at the sales counter rang. I handed the book to Bailey and said, "Make this area shine today, would you? It's a weekend day. Families will be flocking in." I dashed to the phone and answered. "The Cookbook Nook."

"Jenna?" It was Rhett. How I loved the sound of his voice. He, I imagined, could carry a tune. "I was wondering if you were free Tuesday."

Would I sound too eager if I screamed *Yes!* at the top of

my lungs? "Perfect." I didn't yell. I had learned a modicum of composure in my previous career. "Where will we go?"

"On a hike with a group of day trekkers, and we'll finish at my place. I'll cook."

I gulped. *His* place. I hadn't visited his cabin yet. It was located at the top of the mountain, near a lake. Rhett said it was peace personified. "Sounds lovely."

"Super. I'll pick you up at ten in the morning. Do you have good walking shoes?"

"Flip-flops are out?" I joked.

"Definitely."

"I'll dust off my best tennis shoes."

When I hung up, I was giddy with excitement. What was it about Rhett that turned me on so much? His eyes—*yes*. His slightly crooked but sexy smile—*uh-huh*. The confident way he walked, arms hanging easily by his sides, chin held high—*definitely*.

Bailey leaned on the counter with her elbows. "Was that lover boy? You're looking all goggle-eyed and dreamy."

"I am not."

"Yes, you are." She batted her eyelashes with fervor. "What's up?"

"He asked me on a date."

"You've been on a few already. What's the big deal?"

"It's for the entire day. Hiking and ending with dinner at his house."

"Ooh la la. His house? Good for you. You're taking the plunge."

"No, I'm not."

She bobbed her head. "Next thing you know, he'll invite you to meet his mother."

Not likely. Not until he and his family had mended fences. I had to admit I wanted to meet them. A girl could learn so much from a guy's family, and let's face it, I wanted to dine at Intime again, this time knowing the owners. Imagine what specialties I might score from the kitchen.

A silver-haired older woman with glistening eyes and a

vibrant smile entered the store with four middle schoolers. "Ooh, look at this place. It's a cookbook shop. Hey, my little loves, did you know Gran collects cookbooks?"

"No, Gran," the tallest of the children said.

"Well, I do. Tons of them." Gran removed her fuchsia-colored shawl and draped it over her arm. "We're going to become regulars here. Why hasn't your mommy told me about this shop? Bad mommy." She ushered the children into the rear of the store. "Wait until you see all the cookbooks I have in the boxes that were delivered to the house. From church bazaars and all sorts of charitable organizations." She waved at Bailey and me. "Do you have cooking classes?"

"We do," I said.

"Goody. For children, too?"

"Indeed. The next children's class is in three weeks, right before Thanksgiving." We didn't want kids to come to the candy-making class. Too dangerous.

"Perfect. I just moved to town, hence the boxes."

"At least fifty," one of the children said.

Gran laughed. "It took a bit of arm wrestling to get me to move, but now that I'm here, I love Crystal Cove, and your store is going to become my new home." She told each of the children to pick something, then went to browse for herself.

"Ka-ching," Bailey whispered.

I swatted her arm.

"No kidding. Did you see that shawl? That's a *shahtoosh*, made from the wool of a chiru."

"A what?"

"A type of antelope from the snowy white mountains of Tibet. A *shahtoosh* is the softest, warmest shawl ever and the most expensive, sort of like Manolo Blahnik shoes for the shoulders." Bailey tapped my hand and whispered, "You know, Gran, or whatever her name is, reminds me of your aunt. Too bad Vera didn't have children. She would have had a gaggle of them with her at all times. Speaking of which, where is your aunt?"

"Hasn't she checked in today?"

"She did at eight A.M., but it's nearly ten."

My worry sensors went on high alert.

"Yoo-hoo." Katie rounded the corner with a plate of mini muffins. "Look what I've got. Apple spice with mascarpone frosting. Quite delicious, with an extra spritz of nutmeg." She joined us at the sales counter. "Jenna, you haven't eaten, I can tell."

"Yes, I did."

"Not enough. Another protein breakfast?" She clucked her tongue. "C'mon, you're salivating. Take one."

I peeled off the muffin wrapper and popped the morsel into my mouth. "Love it. The texture is fabulous, but now I need a glass of milk."

"Coming right up."

As Katie started toward the breezeway, Maya, the owner of The Enchanted Garden, raced into the store and straight to the counter. Her slim body looked even leaner in skintight leggings and rib-clutching T-shirt. Her curly tresses flew wildly about her face. "Help!"

"What's wrong?" I said.

"My cat. Boots." The black cat with no white markings. Maya outlined him like she was participating in a game of charades. "He's gone." With her Southern drawl, the word *gone* stretched into three syllables. "Missing. Disappeared."

"Maybe he's helping take care of a litter."

"Boots is a *he*, not a *she*," Maya snapped, then quickly covered her mouth. "I apologize, y'all. I didn't mean to holler. I hollered, didn't I? It's just that he's never left before."

Katie said, "Are you feeling all right, Maya?"

"You mean other than scared out of my mind?"

"Sometimes cats leave their owners when they aren't feeling well, even over something as silly as a cold, and well, you're hoarse."

"You would be, too, from screaming after him. I need help. Is Vera here? Maybe she'll be able to sense where he is."

Honestly, some of my aunt's clients relied too heavily on

her powers that weren't really powers. She gave them confidence; she calmed them down. Then, in time, whatever it was that irked them seemed to dissolve. It was what she liked to call *emotional* magic.

Without waiting for an answer, Maya tore to the stockroom. Bailey leaped out from behind the sales counter to block her. Only employees were allowed in the stockroom. And cops with suspects.

Maya yelled past her, "Vera?"

"She's not here," I said.

"Where is she?"

"Running late, I assume." I tried to put the unease that had surfaced moments ago from my mind, except I couldn't. Where was Aunt Vera? She was never this, well, unpredictable.

"Please, can you call her?" Maya begged. "I need to find Boots. The Black Cat Parade is this afternoon. He's got to win. He's so . . ." She threw her arms open wide. "So beautiful. So special."

I glanced at Tigger, who had found his way to the group. He meowed. "Yes, you're beautiful and special, too," I cooed.

"But not as singular as Boots," Maya said.

I don't know. I thought Tigger was singular with the white tuft of hair down his chest, and the tawny color of his stripes was like none I had ever seen on a ginger cat.

"Boots is going to win this year," Maya went on. "He didn't win last year, but he's destined to snare the prize this time. He's bigger and so much more handsome than he was. From the point of his ears to the tip of his tail. I've been feeding him all organic food. Raw tuna. Homemade treats."

Not everyone ascribed to the raw diet for cats. First, it was hard to maintain—I, with my limited kitchen skills, would fail miserably—and second, I had heard that too many germs could pass through cats' systems and, thereby, infect little kids who might touch them and put their fingers into their mouths after an affectionate cuddle. But I wasn't the vet. I wouldn't dare attempt to educate another cat owner.

"Hello-o-o," Emma called from the doorway. "Where's

my adorable Tigger?" She shuffled inside in a sort of crouch, arms outstretched. "Are you ready for your s-h-o-t-s?"

Tigger couldn't spell, but he could read body language, and he was having none of it. Could he remember Emma taking him for his DRCC/FVRCP vaccination? In addition, he needed a rabies vaccine and possibly a FeLV/FIV vaccination. But that would be the end of them for a long time. He dashed to the rear corner, ducked under a chair, and poked his nose out.

"C'mon, Tig-Tig," Emma said and clucked her tongue.

The children who had come in with the vivacious Gran thought Tigger was begging to play with them. One dropped to all fours and attempted *catch the paw*.

"Stop, Emma," Maya ordered.

Emma gaped. "But Tigger needs his shots."

"No, I mean stop. Right. There. You did it, didn't you?" Maya advanced on Emma.

Emma froze. Her face flushed. "No . . . I didn't." Did she think Maya was accusing her of killing Pearl? Her eyes filmed over. Was she going to burst into tears?

"You stole my Boots."

"What? No." Emma looked to me for help.

"Boots is missing," I explained. "He ran off."

"Another pet ran off? What is going on, bad karma?" Emma hurried to Maya and grabbed her hands.

Maya wrenched free. "What did y'all do with him? Drown him?"

"No. I wouldn't. Why would you even think—"

"Maya," I cut in. "You know Emma is wonderful with animals. She would never harm one." I said it with such authority that I wondered if I truly believed Emma could have hurt Dr. Thornton, the woman she claimed to love. Thanks to Pepper Pritchett, she had a verifiable alibi.

Tigger, as if trying to back up my allegation, darted from beneath the chair and dashed to Emma. When he allowed her to pick him up and caress him, I had to assume the poor little guy didn't have a clue what was in store for him. Nobody liked shots.

Maya pointed at Emma. "She wants her own cat to win."

"Yes, of course," Emma sputtered. "Everyone wants her cat to win."

"But yours isn't as special as Boots."

Feeling the urgent need to do what my aunt would in order to stabilize the escalating situation, I rested a hand on Maya's elbow. "Maya." I focused on sending imaginary rays of white light through her to calm her. "You're scared about Boots. Don't blame Emma."

"It's his turn to win."

"There will be hundreds of cats there, Maya," I said. "Lots of competition. It's anybody's guess who will win." I was entering Tigger. He wouldn't walk on a leash like some of the other cats, but owners were allowed—and encouraged—to carry their pets in the parade. The prize was a dozen Halloween cupcakes from the Seaside Bakery.

Maya broke free of my less-than-spiritual hold over her and whirled on Emma. "You knew Boots would win. That's why you stole him."

"This is ridiculous," Emma said. "I am not a thief, and I am not a—" The floodgates burst. She couldn't curb them any longer. "I'll prove it. I'll find Boots for you." She handed Tigger to me. "The vet will do his shots next week, okay, Jenna? A few days won't make a difference." She aimed a finger at Maya. "I promise you, I'll bring Boots to The Enchanted Garden inside of an hour, or I'm not a cat whisperer."

Maya looked less than convinced. Her jaw was clenched; she was breathing high in her chest. She pivoted and tore out of the store, leaving me to wonder about the animosity brewing between the Winsome Witches. What was going on? Was someone in town casting spells upon these poor women, or was it simply getting too near the bewitching hour?

Where in the heck was my aunt?

Chapter 12

A S NOON APPROACHED, Aunt Vera still hadn't shown up at the shop. I finally gave in and called her at home.

She answered on the second ring. "Hello, Jenna."

"How did you know it was me?"

"Caller ID."

Of course. Silly me. "Are you all right? Why didn't you ring me back?"

Aunt Vera sneezed. "I'm sorry, I spoke to Bailey. Didn't she tell you?"

"Yes, but I thought—"

She blew her nose. "Were you worried sick?"

Worried to distraction was more like it. She was obviously the one who was under the weather. "How are you feeling? Have you come down with something?"

"I've been in bed since I dropped you at the shop on Thursday. It's just a cold."

"Would you like me to bring you some chicken soup? I'll have Katie whip up a batch. Heavy on the noodles." I would even bring her a copy of *Chicken Soup for the Soul: 101 Stories to Open the Heart and Rekindle the Spirit.* I kept copies of it in the general fiction section of the store. We invariably had to reorder it. The book was a cult success, with heartwarming stories and poetry.

"No, sweetheart, I'm fine. I've been drinking plenty of liquids. I'm just run-down."

"And emotionally strung out."

"Yes, it's been a hard week. Losing Pearl. My powers floundering . . ." Her voice trembled.

"Aunt Vera," I started, but stopped. I wasn't going to refute her powers, not when I was feeling so many mixed emotions about my own spiritual awakenings.

"I promise I'll be in tomorrow."

"No, that's not why I called. I mean, yes, I love when you're at the shop, but we don't need—" I stopped blathering. "Rest up. I'll check in with you later."

She blew me a kiss and hung up before I could ask her what else she might need. Cough syrup, antihistamines, tea?

Rather than call her back, I dialed my father and put him on the case. He was pragmatic. He wouldn't take no for an answer. He would see her in person, or else. *Tag, Dad. You're it.*

LATER THAT AFTERNOON, when it was time for the Black Cat Parade to begin, I left Bailey in charge of the shop, dressed Tigger in his cute witch hat, and headed out. The mayor and her committee had done a bang-up job of decorating Buena Vista Boulevard. Black wire outlines of cats were attached to every lamppost. Black parade banners with fringe hung across the streets. Prior to 6:00 A.M., all automobiles had been diverted through neighborhoods. Only foot traffic was allowed.

Hundreds of participants with cats showed up. There were tabbies, black cats, Burmese, Siamese, and ragdolls. An American shorthair with a white tufted neck had the sourest face; he clearly didn't like the devil's ears his owner had put on him. A smug Persian wore a crown and was draped with jewels. I even saw a Maine Coon, like the cat in the Cat in the Stacks Mysteries that I had just finished reading. The cat was huge and wore only suit-type cuffs around his ankles. When I asked the owner what his cat was dressed as, he grinned and said a stripper. I laughed out loud.

Dogs were not allowed at this parade. The mayor had made a decree. Cats and dogs didn't mix. Owners didn't seem to be put out. At the upcoming Winter Holiday Carnival, adorable canines would rule.

Like people do in New Orleans at Mardi Gras, many were trolling the streets handing out strands of black and orange beads to put people in a festive mood. Others were singing along with the music being piped through speakers: an instrumental of "Black Magic Woman," followed by "The Lion Sleeps Tonight" and "What's New, Pussycat?"

I was surprised—but not very—to see Cinnamon Pritchett among the mix. She was cuddling two cats, one under each arm. Both wore teensy red hats. At first, I thought they were devil-style witch hats, but then I realized the horns were deer racks. Cinnamon had named her cats Donner and Blitzen because she found them last Christmas. I approached her and allowed Tigger to sniff the strangers. "Cute costumes," I said, delighted to have a conversation with her about something other than murder. "Are they Santa's magical helpers?"

"Yep. In December they'll be flying around, but in October, they're grounded." She smiled. "Aren't all the kids in costumes cute?"

A group of Winsome Witches stood beside a booth handing out treats to any child in a costume. Some of the witches looked frighteningly scary; others looked as docile as the fairies in *Cinderella*.

"I was wondering," I began.

Cinnamon shook her head. "No shop talk. Not at a parade. Think *fun*, Jenna. Life is supposed to be fun. Besides, I'm late meeting up with my handsome fireman."

"Are you two getting serious?"

"As serious as a cop and a firefighter can be. The chemistry is good. We'll have to see if the flame fizzles." She moved south.

Tigger and I headed north. As we neared the Purr-fect Pet Adoption booth, where dozens of kittens and grown cats were housed in an air-conditioned vehicle nearby and ready for someone's love, Tigger snuggled into me and started to quiver. Had he picked up a scent? Did fear work like a dog whistle, so high-pitched that only animals could sense it?

"It's okay, Tig," I cooed. "You aren't going anywhere. No way am I giving you back." I still wondered why he had been abandoned; if only he could tell me.

I heard laughter and turned. Tito Martinez stood at the head of the adoption line. He must have asked the curly-haired woman handling the adoptions a funny question. He held a mini tape recorder in front of her mouth.

As I passed by, Tito said, "*Hola*, Jenna. Hold up." He bid good-bye to the woman and raced to walk with me. "You look pretty."

My hair was pulled into a knot, and I hadn't put on a speck of makeup. *Pretty* was stretching it.

"I'm doing an article for the *Crier* about the parade," he said. "So, how did you hear about it?" He thrust the tape recorder in my direction.

I raised an eyebrow. "Really?"

"Okay, dumb question. Everybody in town got a flyer." He grinned. "How do you think all the *turistas* found out?"

"Because our savvy mayor put the word out via the Internet and elsewise. Ads. Radio. She's fearless."

"Care to comment about Dr. Thornton's murder?" Talk about a guy with no grace when segueing.

I said, "The answer is still no."

"I was talking to her housekeeper the other day at the coffee shop. She said the doc was having trouble with her daughter. Now do you care to comment?"

"Tito." I didn't mean to sound exasperated, but I couldn't

help myself sometimes around him. He seemed to have no nuance. From zero to sixty in less than three seconds. A roller-coaster designer would do well to study Tito.

"It relates to my article about pet adoption," he went on. "The daughter asked Dr. Thornton to get rid of their cat. Doesn't that speak to the young woman's character?" He waited. I didn't respond. "No? Nothing?"

"Chief Pritchett is right over there." I pointed.

"Yeah, like she'll talk to me." He hurried off in the opposite direction. Was he in hot water with Cinnamon?

At the booth for Cat Food Consortium for Organic Cat Food—a name as long as a cookbook title—the folks were offering homemade pet treats. I purchased mini-sized tuna oil and oatmeal treats. When Tigger finished the first, I worried that he might leap out of my arms for more samples. I held on to him with all my might.

"Hi, Jenna." The local veterinarian, an Asian woman with the most gorgeous blue-black hair, approached and scratched Tigger's ears. "How are you doing, little guy?" She didn't take her eyes off him. Emma had told me that Tigger was so scared the first time he went in for shots, he was shivering down to his teeth. Now? He didn't shy away from the veterinarian. I chalked it up to the doctor's incredibly warm demeanor. "He looks real good, Jenna."

Her words were like gold to me. I was being a good kitty parent.

"Doctor, I was wondering if I could ask you a question about Emma. She said she fainted at the sight of—"

The vet cleared her throat and pointed to something over my shoulder. "Ahem. I think we'll have to talk later. A handsome man wants speak to you."

I spun around. Rhett was approaching while waving his arm.

"What a surprise to see you here," I said as he drew near.

"Yeah, I considered boycotting. No dogs. What was the mayor thinking?" He grinned. "I'm actually taking a midday stroll, then heading back to Bait and Switch. How is your aunt holding up?"

"She's under the weather. Stress can cause the nastiest colds."

"Tell her to try a mixture of lemon juice, hot water, and garlic."

I scrunched my nose. "Ick."

"Works like a charm every time. Gotta go." He took my hand and pulled me in for a quick kiss.

Then he loped off, leaving me breathless. Let's hear it for public displays of affection.

Maya caught up with me, also breathless but not for the same reason. She was perspiring. "Jenna, have you seen Emma?"

"Not yet. Still no Boots?"

Maya shook her head. "I went back to The Enchanted Garden. Emma didn't show up." Her eyes were red-rimmed, her thin shoulders hunched.

Tigger mewled. I scruffed his neck. "Yes, I know. It's so sad." I eyed Maya. "Look, I'm sure your cat will reappear. How could any feline resist coming to the parade?"

"Emma stole him. I'm sure of it."

"Why would you say that? Is there a history of bad blood between you two that I don't know about?"

"Bad blood? No!" Maya's voice rocketed upward. "It's just . . . well, ever since Pearl died, Emma's been so different. You know, closed. Like she's got a secret."

She does, I thought, but it was not mine to tell. "Do you think she's an international cat smuggler?" I teased.

"You're making fun."

"A wee bit."

"Maya," Dingo shouted as she rushed toward us, her red hair swept off her face in a tight bun, her face devoid of makeup. Clad in a black dress accompanied by striped knee socks, she looked even more witchlike than ever. I bit back a smile. Add a broom and some might think she was the Wicked Witch of the East. "Maya," she repeated. "Did Emma find you?"

"No."

"She's got your cat. She has Boots. She's at the registration table." Bingo pointed. "All is good, by the way. The cat sneezed right in front of me. That's a wonderful omen. A sign of future wealth. Or maybe it's future health." She chortled. "Pure superstition, but sometimes we have to be believers."

Maya broke into a smile, which did worlds for her beleaguered face. "Thank you, thank you." She raced away.

"Well, my, my," Bingo pointed. "Take a gander over there. Trisha has come with her mother's calico."

Trisha wore a yellow sundress and had tamed her fuzzy black hair into a knot at the nape of her neck. The cat, which was dressed in a black cape decorated with purple stars, squirmed in her arms. Didn't Tito just tell me that Trisha had wanted to get rid of the cat? *Please tell me she didn't bring him to the parade to abandon him.*

I said, "I thought she hated that cat."

"Don't let her fool you. She loathed how her mother doted on the cat. Animals and children can be quite competitive. But look at her. She seems to be in seventh heaven. How sweet."

Sweet or sinister? Dressed in that costume, the cat could woo a new master in a matter of seconds.

"Bingo, what do you know about Trisha?" I said. My friend from college hadn't called me back yet. I wondered if she would. Revealing private information to me might hamper her career. "I heard Trisha was taking a year off from school, but then I learned she was out on probation."

Bingo pursed her lips, which looked dry and chapped. Why did some women eschew makeup? It seemed to be a recent trend for her. Had her religious fiancé requested she go au naturel? "I don't want to talk out of turn," she began. "On the other hand, you might as well hear the truth. Trisha upset Pearl beyond belief. They always argued."

"So I noticed."

"They fought because Trisha was dabbling . . . in drugs." She glanced around.

So did I. No one was listening in on us. "Go on."

"Amphetamines and cocaine. Pearl believed Trisha had

cleaned up her act, but then Trisha went back to her old habits. Pearl found the stash. She put her foot down. She wouldn't pay for another day of college until Trisha went into rehab. She threatened to cut her off entirely."

"Wow." I ogled Trisha, paying particular attention to her abused skin. I had known an accountant at Taylor & Squibb who was so revved up by drugs she had picked her skin raw. Ultimately, when my associate became drug-free, she had needed extensive dermabrasion to smooth out the mess she had made with her fingernails. I said, "But according to Trisha, she's not on probation for using drugs. She got booted out because she cheated on a test."

"Cheated? No, never. That's not possible." Bingo crossed her arms. "Despite her apparent proclivities, Trisha is a straight-A student. She would have no reason to cheat. She aces everything. She's as brilliant as her father was."

"Get your treats!" A vendor carrying cotton candy and drinks passed by. "Treats for the sweets!"

The aroma of warm sugar made my mouth water. I was hungry. I had skipped lunch. But straight sugar wasn't the answer. Not after the deliciously rich apple spice muffin I'd downed midmorning. I needed protein. A fish burger or something.

Tigger started to squirm. "Yes, yes," I said to him. "We're going to register."

Bingo said, "I'd better hurry off. I promised to join my fiancé. He's parading his little munchkin." I had recently learned that a munchkin wasn't just an endearing name for a small cat. It was a new breed of cat with supershort legs.

Before Bingo could leave, however, Emma and her husband, Edward, approached.

Emma said, "Hello, Bingo. Jenna."

Edward was carrying a ginger cat larger than Tigger in his arms. He nuzzled the cat's chin, then handed the cat to Emma and said, "I'm going to get a pumpkin cupcake. Want one?"

Emma shook her head and brushed her fingertips along his bicep. I wondered if she had told him her secret yet. He didn't seem cool to her, but he didn't seem warm, either. He strolled away, his gait long and catlike. While tucking his hair behind his ears, he gazed at the surrounding crowd, as if hunting. Did he know his wife had fallen in love with her doctor? Was he searching for a replacement spouse?

Bingo gave Emma a hug. "I see you're black cat–less, which means you must have met up with Maya."

"I did." Emma looked so relieved. "She's over the moon."

"At least one good thing happened. We must start racking up the positive." Bingo hurried off.

Emma watched her with fixed concentration. When Bingo disappeared into the crowd, Emma pivoted and held her cat beneath the armpits to let him sniff Tigger, nose to nose. "Make nice," she cautioned. Emma's cat pawed at Tigger, who, in turn, sniffed with curiosity. Neither hissed. "Good boy." Emma tucked her cat into her arms. "Do you need to enter Tigger into the parade?"

"Yes."

"I'll go with you."

As we headed in the direction of the registration desk, we passed another vendor selling freshly made pretzels. Better than sugar, I mused. The vendor assured me he had made the pretzels with almond flour, so I would get some protein. I bought one and tore off a tiny nibble for Tigger. He lapped it up. I downed the rest, savoring the salty warmth while wondering how hard it was to make pretzels. They were one of my favorite snack foods. Back when David and I lived in San Francisco and were clawing our way to success, we had eaten lots of pretzels-and-soda dinners. Memories. I nudged them into the past and, instead, imagined the upcoming dinner at Rhett's house. What would he prepare? Should I take clothes to change into after the hike, maybe that backless little number I had purchased at a local boutique? It was near perfect with a plunging neckline and a flirty skirt. A shiver of delightful anticipation ran through me.

Emma cut into my dreamy thoughts. "Jenna, ever since I learned Pearl was murdered, I've been thinking about who might have wanted her dead. I hate that anyone could imagine I did it. I really did love her."

"Have you told your husband, you know . . ."

Emma shook her head vehemently. "No, and I never will. I'm turning over a new leaf. I'm dedicating myself to him. We have a good marriage. It was my mistake. I was weak. I'm not going to look at another man or woman that way ever again." She fingered the hair at the nape of her neck. "Anyway, as I was saying, I've been thinking. When we talked to Chief Pritchett"—respectfully, she didn't add that I had inserted myself into the conversation—"you mentioned that a hypodermic needle might have been used to kill Pearl. I'm not kidding; I faint at the sight of them, but Bingo wouldn't. She was a nurse."

I gaped at her. Why would she point a finger at the new leader of the Winsome Witches? "Don't you like Bingo?"

"Of course I do, and I respect her, too. She's the High Priestess, and I'm her handmaiden. But I was trying to think of other suspects. Bingo would know all about needles and what kinds of poisons to use, wouldn't she? Nurses learn about that kind of stuff. Just between you and me, she's always wanted to be High Priestess. Pearl told me so. Bingo could have had an agenda, and get this . . ." Emma looked right and left and back at me. She lowered her voice. "I saw Bingo in her antique shop the night Pearl died, when I was out looking for Mrs. H's dog."

"That gives her an alibi."

"Does it?" She mulled that over. "Well, anyway, she was practicing spells."

"Spells?"

"A book in one hand, a wand in the other." Emma balanced her cat on one hip and used her other hand to demonstrate. "She had all sorts of bottles and mixing jars on a table in front of her. I wouldn't be surprised if she was working on a potion to snare that fiancé of hers."

"She didn't need to snare him." In truth, I didn't like the turn of this conversation. I didn't think my aunt would appreciate it, either. Bingo was a friend. A good woman.

Just because she looked like a caricature of a witch didn't make her one. Yet I flashed on a moment at Pearl's house right after we found her, while the police were investigating. Bingo was eyeing the others with a look bordering on triumph.

"I'm certain there's something Bingo isn't telling us." Emma pressed through a knot of people blocking the end of the registration line. "Excuse us. Thanks." She lined up behind three others. I stood beside her. "Bingo's been acting cagey for the past few weeks."

"Cagey, how?"

"Have you noticed that anytime her fiancé goes near one of her friends, Bingo spirits him away?"

I hadn't, but then I barely knew the Reverend. I had only met him once, at a diner while he was picking up a to-go meal. He was the pastor of a small congregation, a studious type with longish hair and a beak nose.

"Did you notice that he didn't go on the haunted tour? He didn't come to the party at Pearl's house, either."

Neither did Emma's husband, but I wasn't going to quibble. I said, "Perhaps he was working on his sermon."

"He rarely goes anywhere other than church. It's like Bingo doesn't want us to get to know him. What if she's put a spell on him?"

I snorted. "C'mon, Emma, you don't really believe that, do you?"

"Bingo acted like Pearl's friend, but she wasn't. I heard her on the haunted tour. She was arguing with Pearl. She said Pearl couldn't be trusted to keep her mouth shut."

"About?"

"That's just it. I asked Pearl. She wouldn't tell me. Why not? Because she *could* keep her mouth shut."

Sadly, I thought, that would be forever.

Chapter 13

᯾ᯕᯕ᯽

THE PARADE WENT off without a hitch. Tigger didn't win the competition. Neither did Maya's cat, Boots, which Maya surprisingly took in stride. I think just having Boots back in her arms made her realize how silly competitions were. The Persian wearing the tiara won the parade. How could the judges resist all the glitz and glamour? Only another Persian beribboned like a Miss America beauty pageant entrant would've stood an equal chance.

After I arrived home that night and set Tigger in the cottage, I strolled to my aunt's house. I saw a light on in her bedroom. I rang the doorbell. She didn't respond. "Aunt Vera?" I yelled.

No answer.

I wasn't usually one to out-and-out panic, but something didn't feel right. I fumbled with my keys and inserted my copy of Aunt Vera's key into the lock. I opened the door and hurried inside. "Aunt Vera?" I rushed to her bedroom. She wasn't in her bed. A pile of clothing lay on the bedspread.

The door to the bathroom was ajar. I checked inside. Maybe she had fallen on the tile. She wasn't there, either.

I raced to the patio. The moon was still full. I didn't see any walkers. There were no bonfires. Unease turned to dread. I hurried back inside and dialed my father. He answered after one ring.

"What's up, Tootsie Pop?" he said, using the nickname he had given me way back when. No matter how old I got or what career path I chose, I would always be his *little* girl.

"Aunt Vera. Did you check in on her?"

"I couldn't reach her."

"Couldn't—" I drew in a sharp breath. "Why didn't you call me back?"

"Sweetheart, your aunt is very protective of her privacy."

So much for *Tag, you're it*. That just cemented the fact that if I wanted a job done well, I had to do it myself. Sheesh.

"Dad, she's sick."

"So she'll sleep it off."

"That's just the thing. She's not in her house."

"She's not?"

"No. She's gone. Her car is here, but she's nowhere to be found. I'm afraid she may have done something stupid."

Dad scoffed. "Your aunt? She's never done a stupid thing in her life. Well, except that time . . ." He chuckled.

"Dad. Focus! What if she went for a late-night swim, thinking the chill would kick out her cold?"

"Then she'll be back. She's a strong swimmer. She won all sorts of awards in her day."

"She did?"

"She had her eye set on the Olympics, but Mother wasn't supportive."

For some reason, I had assumed my aunt's career dreams had included dancing, perhaps becoming a prima ballerina. She would often swirl and swish around the shop. She had such grace. I said, "Grams dashed her dreams?"

"*Dashed* is a little strong. Mother said Vera wasn't ready to commit to the work an Olympic hopeful had to do."

"Grams called Aunt Vera lazy? She is anything but lazy."

"Nowadays. But back then——" He hummed. "She had boys on her mind. All the time. And rock and roll. And roaming the world. She wasn't much of a student, either."

"But she's so smart."

"By Vera's sophomore year in high school, Mother was able to coax her to focus. Mother also insisted that we choose service-oriented futures. I wound up in the FBI. Your aunt spent a year in the Peace Corps."

"The Peace Corps?" What else didn't I know about my aunt?

"She ultimately found her calling by working with charities. In the long run, it was a win-win."

"I guess I was lucky Mom supported my dreams."

"Your mother was a pushover for all you kids." He chortled. "I'll call Cinnamon and put her on the case." My father and Cinnamon Pritchett had a relationship that was different than any I could have imagined. Cinnamon's father had walked out on her and her mother. During high school, she hung out with a rough crowd. My father became her mentor. With his guidance, Cinnamon turned her life around and chose law enforcement. "She'll send a deputy out looking for your aunt. Go home and wait for my call."

My father was a big believer in *Let the police handle it*. Except the police didn't always handle things, at least not in a timely manner. I needed things done *now. ASAP*.

"Dad, I don't like your tone."

"You don't?"

Up until I moved back to Crystal Cove, I had never been good at telling my father how I felt. "You sound like you're FBI-ing me."

"Ha! A new verb. I like it." He laughed. "Yes, that's what I'm doing. I'm FBI-ing you. Go. Get some rest. I'm on the case. Promise."

I trudged to the cottage and slogged inside. Tigger, unhappy with being cooped up in my purse for the foray into my aunt's house, tore across the cottage floor. He skittered beneath the kitchen table, lost traction, and wound up sliding into the wall. He yowled his discontent.

"Careful, buddy. *Look before you leap* is an age-old warning for a reason."

He meowed, not understanding.

I scooped him off the floor. "Too much unbridled energy can send you into a tailspin." I gave him a hug and set him down. "Eat and settle in for the night."

But he wouldn't quit. He darted after me as I strolled to the kitchen to make myself a cup of green tea and a chicken breast. I had heard the tea was a good remedy to stave off dementia. With all the stress cycling through my brain, dementia couldn't be far away. The chicken was going to be nothing fancy, purely for fuel.

After putting the water on to boil, I removed the chicken from the refrigerator. While opening the package, I thought again of my friend who worked at UC Santa Cruz. Was she being a chicken about calling me? She was a strong, vibrant career woman. Surely, she had the courage to buck the system.

I fetched my cell phone and dialed. My message rolled into voice mail for a second time. Shoot. My friend and I had been pretty tight back in college. I had introduced her to her husband—cute guy, now a prestigious Central Coast winery owner. She owed me, didn't she?

"Phooey." I stabbed End on the phone and dropped it on the kitchen table with a *thunk*.

Cooking ought to calm my nerves. But not cooking chicken. For some reason a chicken breast even doused with my favorite spices and paired with a glass of wine didn't tempt my taste buds. Truth? Nothing did. But I needed to get my hands busy and occupy my brain cells.

Yesterday, I had taken two minutes to drop into the grocery store and purchase oranges and inexpensive vodka to do a trial run for the Halloween party. I'd also bought a flavor injector, which was clear and not nearly as stylish as the green-handled ones I had ordered online.

Though my knees still knocked, figuratively, about throwing a party by myself, there was no time like the present to practice. I fetched a black Sharpie from a drawer and bumped the drawer closed with my hip. It didn't go in all the way. I bumped it again. I had a bad habit of leaving drawers slightly ajar and dozens of bruises to show for it. Next, I drew huge pumpkin-style grins on both oranges. I set them on a cutting board, then filled the injector with vodka. If I recalled correctly, I needed to thrust the injector straight through the navel where the orange was pulpy. I tried once, but the needle didn't push through. I jabbed again. The tip missed its target and skidded off the peel. The fruit went flying off the cutting board. I lurched to catch it and hit my forearm on the counter's edge in the process.

"Ow!"

Tigger leaped onto the chair beside the kitchen table and ogled me.

"Don't worry. You're not in trouble."

I twirled a finger so he would nestle down on the chair seat, a trick we had been working on for over a month. He followed my finger and turned in the circle, but he wouldn't rest. I fetched a pea-sized kitty treat, patted his rump, and said, "Lie down." I know. He wasn't a dog, but he got the idea. When he settled, I handed him the treat. Afterward I washed my hands and started over.

I fetched the wayward orange and rinsed it off. With my left hand, I steadied the fruit on the cutting board, then carefully slid the needle into the navel. Success. I pushed in the plunger. Juice squirted into the orange. I removed the flavor injector, set it on the counter, and shouted, "Ta-da!"

Tigger meowed.

I explained. "I did it. I infused an—"

I stopped as two scenarios flashed in my mind: my ineptness with a flavor injector, and Pearl lying dead. She had been injected with poison. Who among her friends and enemies knew how to use a syringe? Emma claimed that she fainted from the sight of needles. Was she lying? She worked with a veterinarian; she had to know *how* to use a hypodermic. She had good reason to kill Pearl—to keep her husband from finding out about her love for Pearl. And I couldn't rule out Emma's husband, Edward, could I? He was not the warmest of souls. Would he have killed Pearl to save his marriage? He was a dentist; he used a syringe to inject lidocaine or whatever the current drug was for numbing the mouth. Emma claimed that Bingo, a former nurse, would be quite adept at using a syringe. Did Bingo want Pearl dead so she could become the High Priestess? What had Bingo and Pearl argued about on the night of the haunted tour? Had anybody heard the conversation?

Next, I considered Trisha Thornton. She was a chemist. She might have used a syringe in her lab studies at some point in her education. Did she kill her mother for the basic reason that any child would kill a parent, to eliminate the one person who controlled her in order to get her hot little hands on her inheritance whether or not she had to wait a dozen years to access it?

I peered out the window at my aunt's house. She was determined to solve Pearl's murder. Was she deliberating along the same lines as I was? Did she figure out who had murdered Pearl? Was she frazzled enough to have approached the killer by herself? Was that why I couldn't reach her? Was she hurt . . . or worse . . . dead?

The notion made me tense up so fiercely I thought I might be sick. I dialed my father again on the cell phone. My call went to voice mail. Dang. Trying to keep my composure, I asked him to telephone me as soon as he could to give me an update. Then I dialed my aunt's cell phone.

No answer. No rollover to voice mail.

"Shoot!"

Someone rapped on my door. "Aunt Vera?" I nearly skipped to the foyer. I peeked through the peephole and drew up short. It wasn't Aunt Vera or my father. It was Rhett. He held a largish square brown box in his hand. I glanced at my watch. Eight P.M. On Saturday. Nowhere near our date night of Tuesday. Did he have ESP? Sensing how fraught I was, had he come over to comfort me?

"Jenna," he called.

No way did I want him to think I was a helpless wreck. I checked myself in the tiny mirror to the right of the door. Not bad. My mascara and lipstick were intact. No orange pulp adorned my cheeks. I shook out the tension in my shoulders and opened the door as I forced a big, happy smile onto my face. "What brings you to my neck of the woods?"

He held up the box. "I bought you a present."

No bow. No wrapping. "Um, what is it?"

"A hibachi. I want to teach you how to grill."

I tilted my head. "Did my father put you up to this?"

"Your father?"

"Lately, you two are as thick as thieves. Did he call you? Did he tell you I was fretting about my aunt? Truth."

Silence.

I said, "I value the truth."

Rhett nodded. "Yes. He called me."

"Which means Cinnamon and her deputies haven't tracked down my aunt. Ugh. I knew it. Something's happened to her. She's in trouble. I'm sensing it right here." I tapped my solar plexus. "I've tried to push the feeling aside, but I can't."

A new wave of bad vibes, or whatever you would call them, zinged through me. I wrapped my arms around myself.

Rhett moved toward me and drew me into a one-armed hug. "Shh. Don't go there. She's fine. I'm sure of it."

Tears pressed at the corners of my eyes. When they retreated and I felt assured I wouldn't cry, I inched out of Rhett's embrace. "Thank you."

"You're welcome."

"I appreciate the gift, but let there be no misunderstanding, I'm nowhere near ready to learn how to barbecue on a teensy grill that requires charcoal." I hitched a thumb at the mess in the kitchen. "I'm barely learning how to inject a . . . no!"

Tigger, the scamp, had figured out how to leap onto the

counter. A kitchen chair seemed to be his launching point. He was licking the unwrapped chicken. "Off," I squawked.

He bounded to the floor and scurried to safety beneath the couch. He peeped from beneath, his eyes as wide as saucers.

"You'd better hide, cat," I warned. That would teach me to leave food unattended on the counter. I hoped Tigger wouldn't get sick. He wouldn't, would he? Cats were natural predators. They could eat mice and all sorts of delectable *ick* fare. I eyed Rhett, who was stifling a smile. "Come in," I said. "A good rinsing will remove his germs, won't it? Cooking will probably kill them, too."

"You bet." Rhett set the box holding the hibachi on the table beside the couch. "I'm assuming, by the uncooked nature of that chicken, you haven't eaten dinner. Do you want to go to The Pelican Brief and grab a bite?"

"No."

He looked hurt. "No?"

"I mean, yes, I'm hungry, but I'm truly concerned about Aunt Vera." I fluttered my fingers. "I know I'm acting like a worrywart, but call it a sixth sense. Pearl's murder has undone me, and my aunt's disappearance is downright disconcerting." I frowned. "Would you mind a to-go helping of cheese and crackers and a vodka-infused orange so we can search the town for her?"

Chapter 14

RHETT OPTED FOR no snack, but he was more than willing to help me locate my aunt. For some reason, as I
closed the door of my cottage, I got another vibe. A *positive*
vibe. I needed those by the dozens. What was so good about
it? Yes, my aunt was sick, and yes, she was heartsick over
the loss of a friend, but I got the distinct feeling that she
wasn't injured, and she sure as shooting wasn't dead.
Granted, acknowledging the vibe was crazy and worthy of
a finger twirl beside my head, but I let myself hold on to the
hope.

We started at the south end of town and walked along
the east side of Buena Vista Boulevard, checking out a few
of my aunt's favorite places to shop.

At the beautiful old brick grouping of stores called
Artiste Arcade, we stopped beside Adorn Yourself, a darling
accessory shop. Aunt Vera enjoyed browsing jewelry and
antique stores. The display window held a boxful of man-
nequin arms and hands, each hand featuring ghoulish

jewelry or holding a glittery spider handbag. Peering beyond the display, I didn't glimpse my aunt inside the store.

At the shopping complex I liked to call our mini San Francisco, an octet of bayside structures, we entered Home Sweet Home, a potpourri, candle, and home accessory store. I asked the chatty owner if she had seen my aunt. She hadn't. She said there was a Four C's meeting going on at the Aquarium. Perhaps I should check in there.

I nearly did a head smack. The Four Cs, otherwise known as the Crystal Cove Coastal Concern, was a pet project of my aunt's. The group took it upon itself to keep our residents and interested tourists informed about how precious our environment was. The aquarium was a mile up the road, at the Y where the main egress out of town met Buena Vista. Usually the group convened on Wednesdays. Why was there a special Saturday meeting? Did it matter? Sick or not, Aunt Vera would find a way to attend.

As we were passing Nuts and Bolts, I gripped Rhett's arm and pulled him to a stop.

"What's wrong?" he said.

"Nothing. Look." I laughed and pointed.

In the time since I had met my father at the hardware shop, he had put up a window display. It consisted of a piece of plaster and a dummy witch—you know the kind, only the rear half of the witch, her legs wrapped around a broom, her feet in the air. The witch had soared into the plaster, head first. Beneath, Dad had added a sign that read *Don't Text and Fly*.

"Who knew my father had such a good sense of humor?" I said.

"I did. He's a great guy, Jenna. You're too close to the situation to see, but he's extremely bright as well as introspective."

"Introspective. Big word."

"He sees the world in global terms. If he'd taken another career path, he probably could have become president."

"High praise." I nudged him. "Let's keep moving."

The lighting store's windows were usually filled with

sconces and elaborate chandeliers. For the Halloween display competition, however, the owner had set out a collection of pirate-style hands, each holding a lantern. Beneath was a sign: *In the Days of Old.* It was a perfect tribute to the beginning of Crystal Cove.

"Whoa," Rhett said as we neared Aunt Teek's, which was Bingo's antiques and collectibles store. "This display is above and beyond."

He was right. In addition to her intricate set of carved pumpkins, Bingo had created a display window that could have been featured in a home decorating magazine. The presentation focused on a Gothic haunted house, complete with tall columns on the front porch. The house was dark inside, although the attic was lit. Lightning bolts attacked the house from all angles. On the porch stood dollhouse-sized miniature patio furniture. The swings on a battery-operated miniature swing set swung to and fro in the yard in front of the porch. Tiny toys were scattered around the swing set. Shards of crystal carpeted the ground. A light above the display shone down and made the crystals gleam. As I looked closer, I noticed a graveyard beyond the hotel, almost tucked out of sight. Two women were approaching the graveyard, one dressed in black, the other in white. In the graveyard stood a tombstone. On top of it sat a small black cat figurine.

"Jenna?" a woman called.

I whipped around, hands raised defensively. I instantly dropped my arms to my sides when I spied my aunt walking toward us, her hand slung around the elbow of a man. Not just any man. Nature Guy, the ruggedly handsome one who was the leader of the Four C's. I felt a cosmic jolt to my psyche. Was this her new beau? The one she didn't want to talk about when I rode in her car and detected the scent of Clive Christian cologne? My aunt, clad in a white ankle-length cotton dress and strappy sandals—no caftan, no turban—looked slim and healthy. Her face was flushed, her smile broad.

"I thought you were sick," I said. Did I sound petulant?

I hadn't intended to. I hurried to add, "I mean, you were sneezing and coughing earlier. Are you better? Are your powers restored?"

"My pow—" Aunt Vera hesitated. She flitted a hand. "Pfft." She glanced at Nature Guy like she didn't want him to know she was a fortune-teller. How could he not know? Everyone in town knew. Why would she keep that a secret from him? My aunt continued, "I *was* sick, but I took a good elixir, something Maya whipped up for me. She hated that I was downing that store-bought stuff. She's a whiz with potions."

I felt confused, like I was suffering verbal whiplash. Talking about potions in front of her new beau was okay, but mentioning her powers wasn't?

"Maya says herbs are magical," Aunt Vera went on. "We shouldn't play around with them, of course. Whoever uses them needs to know what she's doing, but Maya has the best remedy suggestions. Dill to cure hiccups. Eucalyptus under the pillow to guard against colds. I wish I'd known that a day or two ago. Here's a silly one she told me, not that I'd ever do this." She squeezed Nature Guy—Greg's—arm. "If you suffer from dizziness . . . mind you, this is somewhat drastic . . . you're supposed to run naked after dark through a field of flax. Can you believe it? Run naked and you'll be cured."

Greg chuckled.

Rhett said, "Although you'll probably catch a cold."

"Too-ra-loo." Aunt Vera giggled like a schoolgirl. "It's not like we have any flax fields in Crystal Cove. Anyway, Maya made me something packed with vitamin C, geranium, ginseng, and henna, and within no time, I was feeling great." She winked at Greg. "I'm being bad. Jenna, Rhett, this is Greg Giuliani."

I shook his hand and said, "We've met before."

He nodded. "At a Coastal Concern meeting, if I'm not mistaken, and at the memorial last month." As minister for the Internet-based Collective Life Church, Greg had presided over the service of the diner owner who was murdered.

His eulogy had been inspired, his concern for all humankind genuine. "Care to join us? Vee and I are going to dinner at Paolo's."

I drew up short. *Vee?* Not *Vera?* Exactly how far along was this relationship? Greg was a good twenty years younger than she was, which was okay, of course. I wasn't judging, or at least I was trying not to. My aunt deserved every happiness in the world. But *Vee?* Really?

Rhett must have picked up on my distress. He said, "We'll pass on dinner. We're window browsing."

"See you in the morning, then." Aunt Vera prodded Greg to move on. A few steps later, she stopped and turned back. "By the way, Jenna, you can tell your father to stop calling me. I'm a big girl. I'm fine." She didn't tell me to back off, too, but I knew her warning was implied.

"Will do."

As she and Greg strolled away, I noticed her white dress again, and a feeling of dread swelled within me. I spun around and gazed at the display in the window at Aunt Teek's. The woman in white was walking toward the graveyard. The woman in black was following her. Was the woman in white representative of my aunt? Was the one in black Bingo? Had Bingo fashioned the window to be a warning of some kind? Aunt Vera hadn't spent two seconds looking at the display. Was she at all concerned?

Stop it, Jenna. Bingo had no way of knowing Aunt Vera would wear white tonight. My aunt never wore white; she adored colorful attire. So why had she worn white, and why did she look ultra fit? Had she been working out to impress Nature Guy Greg while hiding her new figure under her daily choice of caftan? I wondered again how long she had been seeing—*dating*—him and whether I should be worried.

Then a crazy notion ran through my mind. Had Greg Giuliani hired Maya to make a love potion so he could entrap my aunt? She was a wealthy woman. Was he after her money, whether for himself or to finance the Four C's?

Aunt Vera, as my father mentioned earlier, had found her calling in helping needy organizations.

"Hello." Rhett tapped my elbow. "Where did you go?"

"My aunt was nervous that her powers to see the future were hampered by Pearl's death. What if she's right?"

"I thought you didn't believe in that stuff."

"I didn't. I don't. But what if she's incapable of seeing her own future? What if she's in danger?"

"From Greg?"

"From Dr. Thornton's killer. We don't know the motive for the killing yet. What if someone is out to get the Winsome Witches? Aunt Vera has been quite vocal about investigating."

"Breathe." Rhett slung an arm around my shoulders. "Your aunt may have told you her plans, but I certainly had no clue. Breathe."

I sank into him, savoring his calm demeanor. David, my husband, would have fanned the emotional fire and stirred me to do something rash. *Ah, David.* His death had left me feeling like a kite without a string. Now, with his final letter to me tucked away in the lockbox in my closet and the mystery of his death solved, I was becoming grounded again. Would I be able to find new love? Was Rhett the man for me?

"Hey, Rhett," a man called.

Rhett released me and spun around. "Bucky," he said warmly, then added, "Cinnamon." He said it neutrally with no bite.

Cinnamon was walking hand in hand with the hunkiest fireman this side of the Rockies. Bucky had a chiseled chin and warm brown eyes, a thick set of dark curls, and a quick smile. Cinnamon nodded to both of us. "Jenna. Rhett." Also no bite.

My tense shoulders eased up. Were Cinnamon and Rhett finally going to overcome their dislike of each other? At one time, they had dated, but the arson at The Grotto restaurant had put a glitch in their relationship. Cinnamon considered Rhett a suspect because he was found inside, pinned under a beam. Rhett told her his theory—that the former owner, now living in New Orleans, swapped out the artwork in the restaurant before torching the place—but Cinnamon didn't buy it. Her doubt had ended their budding romance. Maybe her newly found ease around Rhett had something to do with her dating the poster boy for the fire department, who was also a good friend of Rhett's. I thought of the morning of Pearl's death when Cinnamon arrived in civilian clothing—soft sweater, tousled hair. Had she spent the night at Bucky's? Was love in the air for everyone?

I grinned.

"What's so funny?" Cinnamon said.

"Nothing." I stifled a giggle.

She glowered at me, and I knew *she* knew what I was thinking. She ignored me and peered at the Aunt Teek's window display. "Hmm. Bingo Bedelia has quite a vivid imagination."

Bucky said, "You should see the display at the fire department."

"You don't have a sales window," Cinnamon said.

"True, but we have a front lawn. Tombstones, severed heads, blood, guts, and gore. It's right up there with gross."

We all laughed.

"We're going to dinner at The Pelican Brief," Rhett said, revising his earlier statement to my aunt and Greg that we were passing on a meal. "Want to join us?"

"We'd better not," Cinnamon said. "It might be considered a conflict of interest if I'm seen dining with Jenna."

A frisson of fear shot through me. "Conflict how? You can't possibly suspect me of—"

"Not you. Your aunt."

"What?" My voice skated up an octave. "You're kidding."

Cinnamon's face grew grim. "I'm telling you straight. Do you happen to know her alibi for that night?"

I didn't. I hadn't thought to ask.

Cinnamon said, "A witness saw her in the vicinity of Dr. Thornton's house around eleven P.M."

"No way. Which witness?"

"I've called Vera to ask her in for questioning," Cinnamon went on, ignoring my question, "but she's not returning my calls."

Had Aunt Vera been dodging Cinnamon? Was the white dress sans turban actually a disguise? I didn't dare glance in the direction my aunt and Greg had headed. I wasn't about to turn her over to the police. Not until she was good and ready. Cinnamon Pritchett and her deputies could darned well do the jobs they were paid to do without my help. However, I could still argue on my aunt's behalf. "Cinnamon, you can't believe Aunt Vera is a killer. She is the kindest, gentlest human being on the planet."

"Everyone is capable of murder if driven to the brink."

I drew in a quick spurt of air and blew it out. "I repeat, which witness?"

Cinnamon screwed up her mouth. "I'm not at liberty to say."

Man, she could be so exasperating. "I can't believe you. First, you don't believe Rhett is innocent." I motioned to him. "Then me." For the murder of my friend Desiree. "And now my aunt?" Rhett brushed my arm. I ignored him. "Tell me, why are you so cynical?"

Cinnamon gawked. "I'm what?"

"Cynical. Distrustful. Suspicious." I knew why; it was a low blow on my part, and yet I couldn't stop the words from spewing out of my mouth. Up until a few moments ago, I had wanted to be Cinnamon's friend. Now, I wasn't so sure.

"Jenna," Rhett cautioned.

"No. I'm right and she knows it. This has got to stop. Bullies—"

"I am not a bully," Cinnamon said, matching my intensity.

"Yes, you are."

"I'm doing my job. In a professional manner. If you hinder my investigation—"

"Hinder? I would never *hinder*. I would only help."

"I repeat, if you interfere with me or my team in any way, shape, or form, I will arrest you for obstruction so fast your head will spin. Do you hear me?" Her gaze grew dark and foreboding. "Do. You. Hear. Me?"

Yeah, I did. Loud and clear.

Chapter 15

ALL NIGHT LONG, I fretted about my aunt and whether she would return Cinnamon's calls. Most of Sunday morning, I wondered whether she would be thrown in the clink for insubordination. I hoped not. It was the *big day*. The Winsome Witches luncheon was scheduled to start at 11:30 A.M. Between 10:00 and 11:00 A.M., I called Aunt Vera several times but got no response. At a quarter past eleven, I put Bailey in charge of The Cookbook Nook, changed clothes, and hurried to Nature's Retreat.

The hotel, built in the hills above Crystal Cove and surrounded by gorgeous oaks and other indigenous trees, was the only hotel in town that had a ballroom grand enough to hold over three hundred attendees.

I entered the ballroom and stared with wonder at the splendor. The room was typically elegant with its natural wood panels and lavish crystal chandeliers, but the Winsome Witches decorating committee had done a number, too. Each of the fifty-plus tables was draped with black cloth and

adorned with a dramatically tiered centerpiece. At the base
were silver pumpkins and shiny red leaves. Bramble dripped
off the tiers. On top of each perched a silver witch hat encircled with more red leaves. A string quartet situated at the
far side of the ballroom was playing "Bewitched, Bothered,
and Bewildered."

I noted a number of men in attendance. Tito stood beside
the head table with a plump-faced man. Both wore suits;
neither wore a witch hat. Tito seemed to be regaling the
plump-faced man with a story.

As I passed near their table, Tito reached out to me. "You
look pretty, Jenna."

"Thank you." I had donned a Chanel-style black sheath,
gold beads, gold strappy sandals, and the same gold witch
hat that I had fashioned for the faire.

Tito said, "Are you flying solo? No Bailey?"

"She's managing the store."

"Of course. How is she doing with that boyfriend of
hers?"

I had forgotten that Tito and Bailey had talked at Latte
Luck Café a few days ago.

He added, "Jorge does not appreciate her enough."

"How true. They broke up."

"Some love is not meant to be. Tell her to wish upon a
star." Tito twirled a finger in the air. "It is good luck and
will bring new love into her life."

Was everybody in town superstitious? I wondered, then
chided myself. Wishing upon a star wasn't superstition; it
was an act of hope.

"Thanks, I will. Um, forgive me for asking, but why are
you here, Tito?"

"Here? At this table? We"—he gestured to his
tablemate—"are guests of Dr. Thornton's, may she rest in
peace."

"Were you a patient?"

Tito guffawed. "Me? Go to a shrink? Never."

The plump-faced man grinned. "Tito donates a ton of
money to support literacy. The doc loved him."

Tito blushed and shrugged. "Kids have to read, no?"

I looked at Tito curiously. When had he become a nice guy and not the obnoxious braggart I'd taken him for?

"Jenna, dear, over here." My aunt, who was dressed in a fitted black gown and a grandiose witch hat brimming with black lace and black ribbon, waved to me.

The sight of her made my heart light. She was free, not incarcerated. Had she spoken to Cinnamon yet? I bid good-bye to Tito and his friend and hurried to where she stood beside a table with Maya and Emma, also dressed in witch outfits.

Aunt Vera extended both arms. "Sweet girl." She pulled me in for a kiss on both cheeks. "Welcome."

I whispered, "Did you contact Cinnamon Pritchett?"

"Whatever for?" she said, matching my hushed tone.

"She's been calling you. She thinks you're a suspect in Pearl's murder."

"Nonsense. She couldn't possibly."

"She does. Someone saw you that night. In the area near Pearl's house. Does Greg live up there?"

"Dear, I won't discuss my personal matters."

"But Cinnamon—"

"Ah, Cinnamon. That girl." Aunt Vera whistled softly. "Don't you worry another second. I'll contact her, okay?" Raising her voice, she added, "Don't you look lovely?"

"So do all of you," I said, following her lead.

Emma picked at her flouncy frock. "I think this makes me look poofy at the waist, don't you?"

Maya said, "Sugar, you look adorable."

Emma blushed with the praise. "No, you're the one who looks good. You're so thin. Have you lost weight?"

"A little."

"And you put on blush," Emma said. "I don't think I've ever seen you wear makeup. It looks good. It gives you a nice glow."

"Didn't you know? I'm hoping to be the next *cougar* in town." Maya primped her hair. Emma giggled. Apparently they had made up, the concern about Maya's lost cat a thing of the past. Maya gestured at the ballroom. "Look at all the handsome warlocks. I must have a shot with at least one of them, don't y'all think?" She dragged out the last few words in sassy, Southern belle style.

In addition to Tito and his friend, there were quite a few men in the audience, many of whom were single. A number of them were dressed in warlock costumes complete with purple or black capes; others, like Rhett, wore suits. Rhett was talking to a powerfully built blond man whose hair was secured with a rubber band at the nape of his neck.

"Emma, isn't that your husband talking to Rhett?" Maya wiggled a finger to indicate the muscular man.

"No, that's not Edward."

"Sure it is, sugar. I'd recognize your Nordic god anywhere."

Why was Maya being so persistent?

"It's not Edward," I said. "His neck isn't long enough," I added, remembering how Rhett had described Edward.

"Edward wouldn't step foot in here," Emma said between clenched teeth. "He won't have anything to do with this whole witch business."

"Why ever not?" Maya asked.

"Dentists are very practical."

Maya snorted. "You call a guy who goes hunting for stalagmites on the weekends practical?"

"He doesn't hunt for . . ." Emma blew out an exasperated breath. "He's an amateur photographer."

"I heard he collects rock samples, too. Y'all support his hobby. Why won't he support yours? Don't you two have anything in common?"

Emma's shoulders sagged.

Maya must have noticed Emma's discomfort because she hastened to say, "I'm sorry, sugar. I shouldn't put you on the spot." She petted Emma's arm in condolence. "By the way, Jenna, that Rhett is yummy. I hope you are jumping into the kitchen with him."

I gawked. "Jumping into the kitchen?"

"You know, mixing it up. Cooking up something saucy."

Rhett glanced in our direction and winked at me. I felt a rush of desire but squelched it. Not the time, not the place. "Um, we're taking it slowly." Last night's dinner at The Pelican Brief had been easy and unstructured. We didn't talk about my aunt, or Nature Guy Greg, or the murder. We discussed movies that we liked. I was partial to old-style romance and mysteries; he liked adventures on the high seas. When he dropped me off at the cottage, we kissed on the porch. I could still feel the warmth of his hand cupping my neck.

"Don't take it too slowly," Maya advised. "Keep the heat in the kitchen, if you know what I mean. If you don't, I might have a mind to steal him away." She toyed with her hair again. "On the other hand, who is the blond guy he's talking to? Maybe I should mosey over there." Maya had been married once; her husband left her ten years ago to pursue his dream, whatever that was. She had dated others in town, but I remembered her telling me that it was hard to make a connection with men who didn't understand her passion for gardening. "He's tan. Maybe he likes the outdoors. Wait, he's turning around. Well, shoot, it's that nature geek. Greg Something." Maya snapped her fingers. "What's his last name, Vera?"

I got the distinct impression Maya was toying with my aunt.

"Giuliani," Aunt Vera said, then deftly switched subjects. "Did any of you see the silent auction baskets? Maya put up a gorgeous offering."

Dozens of tables circled the room, each holding a number of items that were up for auction. I had peeked at a few: tours of the town, dinners at restaurants, a sailing outing, and an evening on a murder mystery dinner cruise.

"Tell them what's in your basket, Maya," Aunt Vera prompted.

"It's nothing, really." Maya frittered a hand. "A year of personal service, provided by me, to make sure the garden is growing at its best. Not everyone understands soil and mineral conditions around here. Coastal climes can be tricky."

"I've made a bid on it," Aunt Vera said.

"Why on earth?" Maya raised an eyebrow. "Your garden is lovely, Vera. The azaleas are some of the best specimens in the area."

"One can always learn something new." Aunt Vera gestured toward the far end of the room. "There's also going to be a live auction. Two levels. First, see those items over there? Home Sweet Home is giving away a basket filled with candles and handblown Christmas ornaments—they're stunning—and Play Room Toy Store has offered up a Christmas stocking filled with heirloom toys. There are even a number of book offerings; the theme for the auction, after all, is Reading Can Be Magical. For the final segment of the auction, we have two stunning donations: four nights at the Bellagio in Las Vegas, including airfare, and tickets to a celebrity car race with an opportunity to meet some stars. Isn't this fun? Oh, look, there's Bingo." Aunt Vera waved and beckoned. "Bingo dear, over here."

I gulped when I saw Bingo Bedelia, the Winsome Witches' new High Priestess, waltzing toward us in what had to be her take on Glinda the Good Witch. Her white silk dress nearly glistened in the glow of light from the chandeliers. The chiffon overskirt floated an inch above the ground. She carried a glittery wand that matched her white witch hat. She seemed to be granting wishes to guests as she moved. I flashed on the display window at Aunt Teek's. Had Bingo fashioned the white witch in the display to represent herself? Was she afraid of a black witch?

Jenna, get real. Why was I conjuring up such peculiar theories? It was a window display. End of story.

"Wow, Bingo," my aunt said. "You put the rest of us to shame."

"No one said we had to wear funereal black." Bingo flinched the moment the words left her mouth. So did everyone else. Talk about awkward.

Aunt Vera petted Bingo's shoulder. "A little gallows humor. Too-ra-loo. Pearl would have howled, wouldn't she, ladies? C'mon, Bingo, show off your dress."

Bingo pinched her skirt on either side and did a twirl.

"You look like Glinda," Emma said.

Bingo raised an eyebrow. "Glinda?"

"From *The Wizard of Oz*," Emma responded.

Bingo shook her head. "I've never seen it."

"What?" all of us nearly shouted.

Aunt Vera said, "You've never seen the movie *The Wizard of Oz*? Haven't you read the book?"

"I led a sheltered childhood," Bingo said, then swatted my aunt's arm. "Of course I've read it, you gooses. I'm putting you on. I've seen the movie at least a dozen times. Pearl would say—" Her eyes grew moist. She started again. "Pearl might not be here, but she is in spirit, and she would say—" She couldn't finish. She waved the wand as if to orchestrate a new conversation. "Pearl would have loved the whole thing. The hats, the décor, the energy." She raised her wand as if proposing a toast. "To Pearl."

We each mimed hoisting a glass. "To Pearl."

Maya said, "Poor thing. What do y'all think happened? Are the police doing everything they can to find the killer?"

Suddenly, I realized this was first time the group had convened since they had found Pearl's body. "Yes," I said. "Chief Pritchett knows the means. Now, she has to figure out the motive."

"What was the means?" Aunt Vera asked.

"Poison," Emma chimed in. "Someone used a hypodermic needle."

Maya moaned. So did Bingo.

"Emma, let's keep that to ourselves," I cautioned. "I'm sure the police don't want that getting around."

"She died between ten and midnight," Emma added, not heeding my warning. "The police are establishing alibis. I've given them mine, and it's been corroborated."

It was iffy, I mused, but I didn't say so out loud. Pepper

Pritchett, who was also at the banquet and looking surprisingly sporty in a cocktail dress and cloche-style witch hat, stood nearby. Without a doubt, she would take me on if she heard me refute her as a witness. Who needed the aggravation?

"What's your alibi, Bingo?" Maya asked.

Bingo blanched and put her hand to her chest. "You couldn't think that I—"

"No, silly," Maya said, "but the police are bound to ask. They asked me. I was home in bed reading a lovely culinary mystery set in the White House. Jenna turned me on to the series. You know the one I mean, with the chef."

Bingo set her wand on the table. "I was doing bookkeeping at the shop."

Aunt Vera threw her a skeptical look. "You were? I don't remember seeing lights on when I drove past."

"What were you doing out and about?" Maya asked.

"We were—" My aunt paled, as if she hadn't meant to offer that much information. "I had to make a grocery run."

Maya raised an eyebrow. "You said *we*, sugar."

"I meant *I* had to make a grocery run." Aunt Vera twisted a strand of hair at the nape of her neck. "*I*"—she stressed the singularity of the word a second time—"was out of milk. I can't stand dry cereal in the morning."

"No, no, no, Vera Hart." Maya waggled a finger. "You can't slip out of this one. You said *we*."

"This discussion is over." My aunt straightened her spine.

"Hmpf." Maya's mouth twisted with frustration. She got the message; Aunt Vera was not going to answer.

Maya returned to the subject of gardening. The others joined in, arguing the wonders of herbs.

I nudged my aunt to the side and whispered into her ear. "Were you with Greg that night?"

"I already told you, I won't discuss personal matters."

"What about Bingo? Do you think she's lying about her whereabouts?"

"What? No. Of course not."

"You seemed dubious of her alibi. Emma told me she saw Bingo in her shop that night."

"Maybe so. I didn't see the light on, but Bingo wouldn't lie."

I mentioned Emma's concern that Bingo was a nurse in her prior career. She would know how to wield a syringe.

"Bingo wouldn't have killed Pearl. She's a kind soul. But this discussion has piqued my interest. I'm going to get to the bottom of things, no matter what. Pearl deserves my devotion."

"Not to mention, you deserve to be proven innocent."

She waved her hand dismissively. "I am innocent. Cinnamon knows that."

For a woman in her sixties, she was very naïve.

"By the way," Aunt Vera went on, "if I didn't mention it before, I have my own theories."

"Like what?"

"Listen up." My aunt rejoined the conversation at the table, cutting off yet another round of basil-trumps-rosemary as far as hardy herbs were concerned. "Ladies, do you think the murder weapon could have been something other than a hypodermic needle?"

"Like what?" Maya asked. "How else could you transmit poison?"

"Via an open wound," Bingo said.

"Like a scratch?" Maya said. "Made with, let's say, a nail?"

"How about an old record needle?" Emma suggested.

"Or a sewing needle," Bingo offered.

Aunt Vera nodded. "Something that could make a pinprick similar to the prick of a hypodermic needle." My aunt addressed me. "Do you happen to know what kind of poison was used?"

"Why would I—"

"You listened in at the crime scene, dear."

I squeezed my lips together and felt my cheeks warm. If Aunt Vera had seen me, had the others observed me, too? "I don't know, and I wouldn't venture a guess. That's private police information." I scanned the room for Pepper. She was glowering at me. Did she know what we were debating? Would

she call her daughter and claim I was overstepping boundaries?
Would Cinnamon arrest me for obstruction? I could not do jail
time. Not only didn't I look good in orange—peach was fine—
but on a daily basis I need blue skies and open spaces.

"C'mon." My aunt squeezed my arm. "We're in this
together. We want this crime solved as much as the police do."

"Aunt Vera, please. Cinnamon Pritchett is very good at
her job."

"Pearl's death should be avenged."

Bingo said, "You're right, Vera. We should help solve the
case."

"Ladies, ladies," Maya cut in. "Listen to Jenna. She's a
voice of reason. The police are doing their job. Let's stick to
what we're good at. We're entrepreneurs, not investigators."

"But we're Winsome Witches," Emma chimed.

"Enough of this chatter," Maya said. "It's giving me—all
of us—the heebie-jeebies." She slipped a hand inside Bingo's
arm and pulled her aside. "By the by, Miss High Priestess,
I've been meaning to ask you a question about today's
schedule."

As they moved to the far side of the table, Aunt Vera
cozied up to me. "What do you think that's about?"

"I'd say Maya was just trying to defuse the situation."

Maya lifted a program from the table and displayed it to
Bingo, who pulled a pair of glasses from her clutch purse
to read. I flashed on Bingo exiting Pearl's house when Aunt
Vera and I had arrived to snoop around the backyard. Had
she really left her glasses at the house, or was she the murderer, and had she gone there to gather what evidence she
might have dropped? If only I could visualize the crime
scene inch by inch.

Bingo peeked at her watch and said loudly enough for all
to hear, "I had no idea of the time. We've got to get a move
on." She handed the program back to Maya and hurried
toward the dais.

Seconds later, Bingo welcomed the crowd and everyone
took their seats.

At the same time, Emma's cell phone buzzed inside her purse. She answered and her mouth turned down in a frown. A couple of times she said, "Yes, of course." She ended the call and gazed at each of us. "Emergency. A vomiting cat of a shut-in client. I've got to go. I . . ." She glanced at the dais where Bingo stood. "What am I supposed to do?"

"Go, dear," Aunt Vera said. "The handmaiden doesn't need to lift a finger at this function."

"Thank you so much." Emma dashed out of the ballroom.

Using a microphone, Bingo began to tell a happy tale about Pearl and how she'd founded the Winsome Witches, while waiters started delivering glorious-looking appetizer salads of mixed greens topped with cold grilled vegetables, fresh herbs, and toasted pumpkin seeds.

Despite the noise, I leaned toward my aunt and said, "I forgot to tell you. The other day at the Black Cat Parade, Emma told me she heard Pearl and Bingo arguing on the haunted tour. Bingo warned Pearl to keep quiet about her secret."

"Secret?"

"How much do you know about Bingo's past?"

"Enough."

"The other day, when she drew a tarot card, the Nine of Swords, you didn't see anything."

"I was blocked."

"What if you didn't see anything because you didn't *want* to? On that card, a person wakes up in bed from a bad dream. What if the card was trying to reveal Bingo's nightmarish past to you?"

My aunt petted my hand. "Jenna, sweetheart, you don't believe in all this hoodoo voodoo."

"Whether I do or don't, this whole affair has me spooked. Tell me the truth. Bingo lost someone close to her, didn't she? She moved here soon after. Was it a man? A fiancé? Do you know anything about him?"

My aunt grew quiet. "Bingo is my friend."

Maya drummed the table with her fingertips. "C'mon, sugar, spill."

"You're listening in?" Aunt Vera said, somewhat miffed.

"Honey, I have eagle's ears. C'mon. Tell Jenna what she wants to know. What was it Agatha Christie said? Every murderer is someone's friend, isn't that right?"

Aunt Vera shook her head. "I promise you, Bingo's secret is not worth killing over."

Maya winked. "Let us be the judge of that."

Chapter 16

M Y AUNT WAITED while a waiter delivered a cheddar-filled popover to each bread plate, then said, "Bingo was set to be married years ago. It didn't work out. Her fiancé left for college and never called her again. He's the one who gave her the nickname."

"After a dog?" Maya said.

"After the interjection *Bingo!*, meaning you've got it." My aunt touched her nose and pointed at Maya. "He said he knew the moment he met her that she was the woman for him. She was ecstatic."

"She doesn't know why he never contacted her?" I asked. "Did he die like—"

"Don't." Aunt Vera's expression turned inward. She fiddled with her napkin. Over thirty years ago, a man left her at the altar. He married someone else the next month. He and his wife didn't have any children, so he hadn't married the woman because she was pregnant. My aunt never found out the reason why he abandoned her because he died within the year. His death was the reason she sought ways to communicate with otherworldly spirits.

Maya looked from my aunt to me and back to my aunt. "That's it? That's Bingo's secret? A guy dumped her? Why would Bingo care if Pearl revealed that?"

"Did something dire happen to him?" I asked.

"Truly, I don't know," Aunt Vera said. "Jenna, are you sure Emma isn't lying about Pearl and Bingo arguing?"

"She seemed adamant."

Maya clucked her tongue. "There's a lot going on with Emma. Are y'all picking up that there is trouble in marital paradise? Has the chemistry disappeared between her and her man? Speaking of chemistry, you won't believe what I heard earlier today about Pearl's daughter."

"Trisha is on probation at college," I said. "Supposedly for cheating, though I hear she is a straight-A student, and she might be on probation because she uses drugs."

"My heavens. I had no idea," Maya said. "But, no, that's not my story. A client came into The Enchanted Garden, and we were talking about the Thorntonite that was stolen from Pearl's house."

I gasped. "You know about that?"

"Honey, that housekeeper has a big mouth. Don't they all? Anyway, my client said she believes Trisha stole it."

"Why?"

"She has a daughter who used to be friends with Trisha. She knows Trisha pretty well. She said Trisha is wound tighter than a sofa spring. We talked about Trisha's plans. Who knows whether she'll have any if she goes to jail?"

"I'm not sure she will go to jail," I said. "Chief Pritchett seems to be buying Trisha's alibi."

Maya clucked her tongue. "She might change her mind when she hears this. I'm sure you know that one of the main focuses at UC Santa Cruz is sustainable agriculture. Why, there are so many vintners and environmentalists that come out of that school, it's mind-boggling. Trisha double-majored. In food science and environmental science."

"I thought she was a chemist," I said.

"They go hand in hand." Maya nodded in rhythm as she spoke. "Y'all know where I'm going with this. Trisha knows how to use a hypodermic needle, and, well"—she took a sip from her water glass—"it turns out, Trisha, according to my client, is also fascinated with rocks. *Fas-ci-nated*. Many times the woman has seen her daughter and Trisha doing experiments on rocks, dousing them with vinegar or baking soda and the like. One time she caught Trisha teaching her daughter how to grind and polish stones. So, tell me, why did Trisha cry foul and call those rocks of her father's evil?" Maya spanked the table. "To divert suspicion from herself, of course."

We chatted about Trisha for another few minutes, each of us theorizing about her guilt, but when the live auction started, we tabled the discussion and paid attention.

Bingo and the literacy chair, a dark-haired Bulgarian beauty, worked the room into a frenzy. By the end of the first segment, every attendee was chanting: *Going, going, gone!* I bid on an assortment of children's books that included some of my favorite titles—*The Indian in the Cupboard*, *Matilda*, and *Stuart Little*—and I won. Rhett and Tito vied for an autographed copy of a Bobby Flay cookbook that I had worked hard to acquire for the event; Tito snagged it. Maya was the victor in a bid for an autographed set of Harry Potter books.

Moments after I collected my stack, I realized if I didn't go to the restroom, there was no way I was going to be able to take a bite of the French silk fudge cake dessert. It looked rich and creamy and was topped with a dollop of whipped cream—one of my all-time favorite things. I even liked whipped cream straight from a spray can into the mouth. Who didn't?

A line had formed outside the ladies' room. I stood at the end and checked my cell phone for messages. One was from Bailey asking when I would return to the store. She'd had a run on Halloween aprons. We had purchased a dozen orange ones with cartoon-style witches riding brooms. The artwork reminded me of the opening segments for the TV show

Bewitched. Each was inscribed with the words *Whisk me away.* Adorable. The other message was from my father, who wrote that he'd spoken to my aunt, and she was fine—as if I didn't know. He then asked if I needed help for my upcoming Halloween party. He happened to be a good cook. I was able to answer both texts before the line moved. Minutes later and thoroughly relieved, I strolled to the mirrors to reapply lipstick. I was standing by my lonesome when the door to the lounge opened and Maya hurried in, sneezing.

"Are you all right?" I said.

"I think I'm catching a cold. It's your aunt's fault." She shuffled past me to a pretty floral Kleenex box and plucked a tissue from it. "If only she hadn't insisted on taking all that syrup made with artificial dyes." She blew her nose.

"Aunt Vera said you gave her a potion to cure her. Can't you take that?"

"Sugar, once the damage is done, it's done. Potions can soften the impact, but they can't eliminate what has started to fester." Maya blew her nose a second time, then sidled next to me.

My nose twitched at the odor emanating from her. I knew the smell from my college days and open-air concerts. Lots of students smoked marijuana. I opted not to. I wasn't a Goody Two-shoes, I just didn't like smoke of any kind, and the oily, herbal scent of weed made my stomach turn.

"What?" Maya said, catching my reaction via the mirror.

"Did you just take a toke outside?"

Maya's eyes widened as if she wanted to deny it, but she didn't. A Cheshire cat grin spread across her face. "Just one hit. I thought it might help with whatever this cold thing is."

"You do look a little jaundiced."

"Makeup helps." She giggled while unlatching her purse and accidentally bobbled it. The contents toppled onto the counter. "Oops." Out fell a couple of tubes of lipstick, a face powder compact, a bottle of pills, a lighter, and plastic-wrapped toothpicks—the kind you get at restaurants. "What a klutz." She scooped the items back into the purse, retaining the compact. "You won't tell a soul, will you? Just between girlfriends, I grow the weed. For medicinal purposes. The night Pearl died, I lied about being home. I was really tending to my crop. If only I'd stayed around and helped Pearl clean up after the party." She blew her nose again, then tossed the tissue into a wastebasket. "I haven't told the police, of course. How could I?"

"Some people get licenses to grow marijuana if it's for medicinal purposes. You do potions. I would imagine you could do the same."

"Don't get me started." She waved her hand. "Talk about the Dark Ages when it comes to that. I've applied for a license. Who knows when the state will bless me with its approval? A cousin who lives in Hawaii got his license lickety-split. But don't worry, if I need to corroborate my whereabouts, I will tell the police that a client stopped in to make a purchase. Of course, they'll expect a name, which will cause a snag, because I won't ask my client to vouch for me."

"Because it's illegal," I finished.

"You got it." Maya sighed. "Everyone has secrets." She applied powder around her nose where the tissue had rubbed off her makeup and plopped the compact into her purse. "Why, even your aunt has secrets. She thinks we don't know, but some of us do."

"Know what?"

"That she's dating that hunky Greg Giuliani. He's a whole bunch younger, but she doesn't give a hoot. Thank heavens Pearl didn't find out. She would not have been happy to learn that little tidbit."

"Why?"

"Because Pearl had the hots for Greg, too. Didn't you see him sit down at the head table?"

I hadn't noticed.

"Pearl invited him to attend the luncheon with her. She was so excited about the prospect. I remember the first time your aunt dragged Pearl to attend a Coastal Concern meeting. She went kicking and screaming, but she told me later that it changed her life. She had found the man of her dreams. Who knew two good friends would be interested in the same man?"

Who, indeed? Worry fluttered like bats inside my stomach. If Cinnamon Pritchett found out about this bit of gossip, would she think my aunt killed Pearl to get rid of her competition? Would Cinnamon arrest my aunt and never let her out of jail?

BREATHING HIGH IN my chest, I returned to the ballroom in search of Aunt Vera. I needed to nab her and fill her in, but I was too late. She was on the dais receiving a gavel from Bingo.

"All right, everyone, now the fun begins," my aunt said. She pounded the lectern. A witch in a lavender hat decked out with cascades of lavender flowers approached the podium. She handed a glittery envelope to my aunt. "Four nights for two at the Bellagio in Las Vegas, plus airfare," Aunt Vera said, reading from the envelope. "And, this just in, the donor has added two tickets to the latest Cirque du Soleil show. The opening bid will start at one thousand dollars. Do I hear one thousand?"

Someone in the back of the room shouted, "One thousand."

"Two," another attendee yelled.

Aunt Vera said, "Two. Do I hear three? Three thousand?"

At that point, the bidding proceeded with lively enthusiasm, rising by two hundred dollars every few seconds. The winner paid five thousand dollars for the trip. Pockets were running deep.

At the end of the final round of the auction, a crowd of winners swelled toward the dais. I couldn't get within fifty feet of my aunt. At least Cinnamon Pritchett had not arrived with a posse to arrest her. Yet. So I waited. And waited.

When I finally reached her, I seized her by the elbow and escorted her to a private corner.

"What's wrong, Jenna?" Her face was etched with worry.

I explained.

"That settles it," Aunt Vera said.

"Settles what?"

"I told you I'm going to investigate, and investigate I shall."

"All I want you to do is talk to Cinnamon. Be open. Tell her everything. Did Pearl know you were dating Greg? Was she angry?"

"Of course not. She had no interest in him."

"Maya says she did."

"How could she possibly? Pearl and Greg didn't have a thing in common. No, Maya's wrong." Aunt Vera spun me around and propelled me toward the exit. "Go back to the shop, dear. Don't worry about a thing. I'll put an end to this nonsense."

As I headed out, I saw Greg Giuliani striding toward my aunt with a big smile on his face.

She gripped his hands and said something. His expression grew grim. After a moment, he nodded.

Without warning, I felt like I had sunk chin-deep into quicksand. I could barely breathe.

Chapter 17

A T 7:00 A.M. Monday morning, as I was heading out to the beach for a run/walk, I looked for Aunt Vera's car. It wasn't parked in the driveway. Had she contacted Cinnamon Pritchett and convinced her she was innocent, or was she playing footsie with her new boy toy?

Stop it, Jenna. That's beneath you. But I was worried. About her health and her freedom, and, honestly, I didn't want her heart to be broken again. I wanted her to find a man who treasured her, in all aspects. Was Nature Guy Greg the right guy? He was a man of great spiritual depth, and he'd dedicated his life to helping the environment. But what else did he have that he could offer my aunt? Was a good soul enough?

An hour later I arrived at work. To distract myself, I dove into the boxes of new cookbooks that had come in late Saturday. Not every one of them focused on Halloween. Already, we were stocking books for Thanksgiving and Christmas. Gift items were arriving, too. I had found the most charming three-by-three-inch rustic boxes with hand-painted sayings on them like *The best things in life aren't things* and *You are the shake to my bake*. They made me smile. I was pretty certain my customers would love them, too. They would make great stocking stuffers. I was contemplating a holiday display of culinary mysteries, too, with a sign that said *Stalking Stuffers*. Would people get the play on words?

Around 10:00 A.M., Katie rolled a cooking cart into the shop. On it were bags of dark chocolate chips, sugar, butter, a salt shaker, and utensils. "Ready?" she said.

"For?"

"The candy-making class. Did you forget?"

"On Monday? With everything else we have to do?"

She nodded. "We have ten adults coming."

"What are you conjuring up?"

"It was a tough decision. I had to choose between chocolate fudge, peanut butter pretzel bonbons, and chocolate brittle."

"No candy corn?"

"Those are primarily kid treats."

Huh, who knew? They were one of my favorite indulgences at this time of year. Did that mean I was a kid at heart?

Katie said, "I went with chocolate brittle. Sweets taste great with a dash of salt. Have you ever paired bacon and chocolate?"

"Can't say that I have."

"Delish." Katie anchored the cart using a foot brake, then helped me set up the chairs in a semicircle.

"Do I get to be your assistant?" I asked.

"If you aren't scared of spitting sugar."

"*Moi?* I'll have you know I made sunflower seed brittle the other night at home. It spit and I didn't get burned." I polished my fingernails on the front of my shirt. "To quote Mark Twain: 'Courage is resistance to fear, mastery of fear—not absence of fear.'"

Katie applauded. "I'm proud of you." She withdrew a marble cutting board from the cabinet beneath the cooktop.

"What's that for?" I asked.

"Spreading the candy out. We could do it on a metal baking sheet—"

"That's what I used at home."

"But marble cools candy much more quickly. It has thermodynamic properties that draw heat out of the sugar."

"Ha. I learn something new every day."

Minutes later, the class members started to arrive. One woman carried a glazed pot planted with herbs. She shoved it at me. "For you."

"That was nice. You didn't have to."

"I didn't. There's a note attached."

The message read: *May a window close and a door open.* Odd. Did whoever was sending the gifts hope that I would end my newfound relationship with Rhett and open my arms to *him*? Who was this anonymous wooer?

Tigger bumped my legs. *Oof.* I set the herbs on the sales counter and scooped up my kitten. "Fie, fie, knave. Do not frighten me so." It was a feeble attempt at Shakespeare, but with all that was going on, including Aunt Vera's whimsy, Pearl's murder, and Katie's possibly aggressive candy, how was I supposed to respond to some gift giver making secret advances on me? Needless to say, I was feeling emotional and vulnerable. I didn't like secrets and rarely liked surprises.

I gave Tigger a quick kiss and nudged him back toward the stockroom. "That's where you stay until after the class. Go on." He obeyed. I squirted my hands with sanitizer lotion.

"Jenna, dear." Helen Hammerstead, a pear-shaped woman with a doughy face, scuttled toward me. She held her pampered Havanese in her arms. "Do you mind if Ho-Ho attends the class?" She nodded to the dog. "I just couldn't leave the house without my baby." She rubbed noses with the dog. "No, I couldn't. You know I couldn't." The dog licked her nose. She eyed me pleadingly.

I sighed. There was one drawback to offering cooking classes in the shop. Although we had gotten the okay from health regulators, we had to ensure that animals didn't come anywhere near the food or preparations, ergo, the reason why I had banned Tigger from the proceedings.

"I'll tuck Ho-Ho into my purse. He's a nonallergenic, nonshedding breed," Mrs. Hammerstead said. "Please, pretty please?"

I smiled. "I get it. You can't bear to part with him now that's he back."

"Back from where?"

"The other night."

Her face pinched into a frown. "Whatever are you talking about?"

"When he went missing from the veterinarian's office."

She gasped. "He went missing?"

"Yes, Emma tracked him down." Was the woman daft?

Mrs. Hammerstead arched an eyebrow. "I never heard about this." She lifted her dog, thumbs wedged beneath his forearms, and planted his face against hers. "Did you run off, you bad boy? Did you? Why didn't you tell me?"

Yeah, like he can talk, I thought, but Mrs. H's concern set my mind into gear. Had Emma kept the truth from her client to protect her reputation, or had she lied about looking for the Havanese to give herself an alibi? Pepper swore she saw Emma roaming Azure Park. She even knew Emma was wearing yellow. On the other hand, Pepper had been known to fabricate—all right, out-and-out *lie*—about events. The woman had a deep-seated need to be in the thick of things. But why lie this time? How would she have known what color sweater Emma had been wearing? Also, Emma claimed she saw Bingo practicing spells in her antique shop, which meant she had definitely been out and about, but was she roaming Crystal Cove at the precise time the murder occurred? I intended to find out.

I said, "Ho-Ho has to stay in your purse and no escaping, deal?"

Mrs. Hammerstead giggled in a hissy way, like hot foam oozing out of a coffee machine. "Of course, dear. Ho-Ho is a good doggie." She lifted the pup again. "Yes, you are. Yes, you are." She tucked the dog away, placed a tiny blanket over his back, and then cleaned her hands with a sanitizer wipe.

Before the class started, I slipped away to the stockroom and discreetly dialed the precinct.

"Crystal Cove Police Department, Deputy Appleby speaking."

"Deputy, it's Jenna Hart."

He cleared his throat. "What's up, Miss Hart?" I heard a chair squeak and a bit of a groan. Was Deputy Appleby sitting taller to talk to me? A curious notion swept through me. Weeks ago, he had suggested we go for coffee; at the time, I'd thought he was teasing me. Baiting me, even. Was it possible that the deputy was my secret admirer? I was pretty sure he would be better suited to someone a little more passive than I was.

I decided to skirt the prickly subject. "Is Chief Pritchett there?"

"She's out."

"May I leave a message? It might pertain to Pearl Thornton's murder."

"I can address your concerns."

"I'm sure you could, but—"

"Jenna, speak."

I recoiled. "No need to talk to me like a dog."

"I wasn't . . . I didn't mean . . . Sorry, Jenna . . . Miss Hart. What's on your mind?" His bumbling reinforced my concern that he might be my mysterious gift giver. Uh-oh. Talk about awkward.

"I'm skeptical about Emma Wright's alibi." As much as I liked Emma, I wanted Cinnamon to have someone other than my aunt on her radar. I explained about Emma's client not knowing her dog had been at large.

Deputy Appleby snickered. "Not every babysitter blabs about the antics of a bratty child for fear of not being hired again."

"True. Just call it intuition."

"You? Intuitive?" He chuckled. "If you were intuitive—" He paused. Was he debating whether to ask me if I'd guessed who was sending me the tokens of affection?

I refused to give him the satisfaction. "You'll make sure the chief gets that message?"

"You betcha."

Talk about *not* making friends and influencing people. I didn't care. If he was my secret admirer, he would have to work harder than leaving a few gifts outside the shop door—not to suggest that I would ever consider him a prospect. I imagined my last kiss with Rhett and the memory warmed me through and through. I could barely wait until tomorrow's date.

Bailey hurried in with a cup of coffee from Latte Luck Café. Her hair looked windblown. Her eyes, which were the same color as her turquoise outfit and beads, glistened with fiery energy. "Let's hear it for caffeine." She took a sip of her coffee as she sidled behind the sales counter and settled onto a stool. "Nice crowd. Do you think they noticed the candy cookbook displays I set on the front table? They're not all for Halloween. For example, *The Sweet Book of Candymaking from the Simple to the Spectacular* has all these fabulous tips on how to get started. There's a whole chapter dedicated to caramels."

The full title was *The Sweet Book of Candymaking from the Simple to the Spectacular—How to Make Caramels, Fudge, Hard Candy, Fondant, Toffee, and More*. A mouthful in any language.

"The other one I adore," Bailey continued, "is *Handcrafted Candy Bars: From-Scratch, All-Natural, Gloriously Grown-Up Confections*. Get this chapter title: 'Dream Bars: Healthier, Spicier, Sexier.' Yum-yum. The book has been highly recommended by the owner of a culinary bookshop on the East Coast. It's filled with recipes for all-time favorite candies. The dark chocolate–dipped almond-coconut bars look downright sinful." She cocked her head. "So did the crowd browse?"

"Most went straight to their chairs, but I'll make sure they view your wizardry afterward."

"Oh, I almost forgot"—Bailey set her coffee aside—"I

saw Trisha Thornton at Latte Luck. She was with her boy-friend. Boy, did they canoodle. They have no compunctions about kissing in public. Me? I had a boyfriend in college who nipped that practice in the bud. 'No public displays of affection,' he warned me repeatedly, and it has stuck with me."

"What did he look like?"

"Raggedy. Gaunt face, big teeth. He was a genius. Also not my type. I'm so glad we ended that doomed affair."

"Not your college boyfriend, you goon. Trisha's guy."

"Holey jeans, faded T-shirt, shaggy tired hair. Like a bear that had been awakened from a long winter's nap. Any-way, I overheard them talking."

"About?"

"Your aunt."

"Vera?"

"Do you have another?"

I sneered. She knew I didn't. My father had one sister. My mother had been an only child.

"He said, 'Vera Hart has to be stopped,' and Trisha said, 'What's she doing now?' and he said, 'Poking around at school. If she finds out—' That's when Trisha cut him off. I think she spotted me listening in. She said, 'Don't worry, she won't.' "

"Won't find out what?" I asked.

"Do I look like I know?"

"What if Trisha lied about being in the lab on the night her mother was murdered? What if someone can corroborate that the lab was empty? I've got to find out."

"How—"

"Jenna!" Pepper dashed into the store and screeched to a halt short of the semicircle of chairs. Her face was flushed. She held her cell phone overhead and pressed a hand to her chest to catch her breath. "Jenna, come quick. It's"—she gulped in air—"your aunt. She's been in a car accident. She was rushed to the hospital."

Chapter 18

TO MY SURPRISE, Pepper couldn't have been more supportive and concerned. She pushed me toward the exit. She offered her car, which I didn't need, and her cell phone, which I also didn't need; I'd had sense enough to grab my purse. As I dashed from the shop, Bailey promised that everything at The Cookbook Nook would go off without a hitch.

I scooted into my VW and jammed the car into gear. Pepper was still within range. I yelled out the window, asking who had alerted her.

"Maya."

"Why didn't she call me?" I shouted.

"She did. You didn't answer."

I glanced at my cell phone's readout. Indeed, there was a missed call from a telephone number I didn't recognize.

"Maya's at the hospital with your aunt," Pepper added. "She'll explain . . . Just go. Mercy Urgent Care."

There was a big hospital near Santa Cruz, but there were

two decent-sized emergency clinics in Crystal Cove. Boating, surfing, and swimming accidents occurred often in a beach community. Mercy Urgent Care was on the road heading up into the hills.

I raced to Admitting. A kind nurse directed me to the second floor. When I arrived at Aunt Vera's room, I paused in the doorway. My stomach clenched at the sight of my stalwart aunt looking so feeble. She lay in bed, the back of the bed raised to a forty-five-degree angle. Her skin was pale; her face was stained black and blue. Tubes weaved out of her like spiderwebs to machines that pulsed with light and vibrated with tones. A young female doctor, who appeared no older than I, was in attendance checking my aunt's pulse.

Maya stood by the window with her arms wrapped around her body, hands shoved under her armpits. Her curly hair looked bedraggled. Her slender frame was overwhelmed by the loose-fitting, green hemp dress and knitted shawl she wore. When she saw me, she hurried to me and clutched my hands. "I watched the whole thing." Her voice sounded hoarse. "She was driving erratically. I was in the car behind yelling for her to stop."

"I'm sorry, you were where?"

"Here's how it started—"

"Thank you, Doctor," Aunt Vera said. Her voice was gravelly and tired.

The doctor wrote something on the chart and, without a word to Maya or me, left the room.

I broke free of Maya and rushed to my aunt's side. "What happened?"

"I don't know." Her eyes were glassy. The blue-and-white gown the hospital had provided washed out her usually ruddy skin.

Why couldn't hospitals come up with gowns in bright pink or red? Something cheery and hopeful. If I were to take on the campaign to promote this hospital, that would be one of the first things I would address. *Mercy Urgent Care. Not wishy-washy. Not bland. Full of hope. Because we urgently*

care that you face life with energy and enthusiasm . . . or
something like that. Years ago, I would have spent months
perfecting the slogan for a campaign. Now, they flitted
through my mind in an instant, quickly replaced by what I
needed to do at The Cookbook Nook.

"One minute I was driving along the road," Aunt Vera
continued, "and the next, bam."

"Bam?" I cried.

Maya nodded. "She plowed into a tree."

"A tree?" I moaned. "Did Trisha Thornton or her boyfriend try to run you off the road?"

"What?" Aunt Vera looked perplexed. "Why would they
do such a thing?"

"Bailey overheard them talking at Latte Luck Café. Bailey said they were worried because you were snooping
around UC Santa Cruz. By yourself."

"I went to the school to talk to a counselor about Trisha.
I thought I might intercede on her behalf with this probation
thing. However, I couldn't find anyone to help me. Not a
soul."

I sighed. "Really? You would do that for her? Even while
everyone thinks she killed her mother? You are positively
the kindest person in the world." I lifted her hand and
squeezed gently.

Aunt Vera said, "Let me backtrack. Nobody ran me off
the road. It was my own doing. It all started at yesterday's
lunch when you got me thinking about Bingo."

"This is my fault?"

"Of course it is, dear. Everything's your fault." She
winked—an effort that made her wince—and then she
waggled a teasing finger, her energy slightly more vibrant
than her skin tone. "Jenna Starrett Hart, don't even go there.
I did not crash because of you or anything you did. You
know how I drift off when I drive. If I were Chief Pritchett,
I'd take away my driver's license ASAP. Don't tell her I said
that." She snickered. "Something like this . . . running into
a tree? It's never happened before." She flinched again. The
tubes weren't making talking easy. The tape holding them

in place was puckering. "Anyway, after our chat at the luncheon, I thought back to times when I'd asked Bingo about her former fiancé or her past. I remembered how she would snap off conversations with a wave of her hand—a misdirection, a magician might call it. All she had ever told me about her high school sweetheart was what I told you already: he left for college and dumped her. End of story. Well, I wanted to know the truth, so I telephoned her, but she didn't answer. That's why I went to Aunt Teek's. To look for her. She wasn't there. A sign read, *Back in 10 minutes*. But the door was unlocked. She often forgets to lock the door. She says it's a Midwesterner's habit. They're so trusting, they never lock their houses. Can you imagine?"

I couldn't. In California, that just wasn't done. There were areas that were safer than others, but locked doors were a must. If only the world's inhabitants could be more trusting . . . and trustworthy. Open doors. Open books. No violence. No death.

I tucked a loose hair behind my ear and said, "Go on."

Aunt Vera drew in a sharp breath. She grimaced, as if something in her rib cage hurt. She exhaled slowly. "I went inside to wait. While I was there, I glanced around and saw a pile of books on Bingo's desk. I wondered if any might be a diary or a photo album, anything that might give me the slightest peek into her past. I'm not typically a snoop, but I owed it to Pearl, didn't I? At least I convinced myself I did. If I could learn something more about the man who broke Bingo's heart, maybe I would understand why she was so evasive about him. I wondered if there was some deep, dark secret that Bingo needed to hide—would kill to hide. I don't know if she was Pearl's client—we've never talked about that, either—but what if something horrible happened to the man, and Bingo mentioned it to Pearl? Who better to talk to about that kind of upset than a therapist?"

"Are you wondering whether Bingo killed the boy?"

"No. Heavens, no. I don't . . . No." Aunt Vera picked up a glass that had a lid and a straw and slurped down a long drink of water. "What I found next . . . forgive me, but when

I didn't discover a diary or personal calendar on the desktop, I decided to rummage through the drawers. What can I say? A niggling notion just took over. It was like I was possessed. Not truly possessed, mind you. No exorcists needed today." She tittered as she set the glass back on the bedside tray. "Anyway, in the second drawer on the right, I found a bottle of arsenic."

Maya gasped.

Aunt Vera nodded. "I know. Arsenic, the king of poisons. Then I found an antique hatpin about six inches long that looked stained at the tip. Remember how Bingo suggested a sewing needle as a weapon when you were theorizing at the luncheon? Well, I got to pondering how else poison might have been administered to Pearl in a way other than a hypodermic. What if Bingo dipped a hatpin in arsenic and poked Pearl?"

I said, "Do you think Bingo was taunting us? Giving us a clue?"

"No, it can't be." Maya waved a hand. "Bingo is not a killer. She is so . . . good."

"She is, and I would hope it's not her," my aunt said, "but why did she stash those items out of sight? Right about that time, Bingo, Emma, and Maya entered the shop."

I looked at Maya. She concurred.

"Needless to say, I was caught off guard," Aunt Vera went on. "I dumped my findings back in the drawer and stood, bumping my knee on the underside of the desk. It'll be black and blue tomorrow."

I didn't have the heart to tell her what her face looked like. It would probably turn a horrific greenish-yellow in a few days.

Aunt Vera continued. "It seems the trio had met, without me, that morning to plan a celebration tea."

Maya said, "You were invited, but for some reason we couldn't track you down. Your cell phone must have been switched off."

I glanced at my aunt. She tinged pink. Earlier, I hadn't seen her car in her driveway. She must have spent the night at Nature Guy Greg's place. *No judgment, Jenna, no judgment.*

"We went to Latte Luck Café to chat," Maya went on. "We thought it would be nice to hostess a high tea at Nature's Retreat for all those who put their heart and soul into the luncheon. You know how these events are. They take a year to plan—the faire, the haunted tour, the luncheon—and then *whoosh*, it's all over in a nanosecond. Everyone is exhausted and wondering what tornado hit her. That's why Vera got a cold. Me, too. Emma came up with the idea for the high tea. She said Pearl would have approved. Bingo embraced the idea with open arms."

"How did you wind up at Aunt Teek's?" I asked.

"Silly Bingo needed her datebook. The woman doesn't do anything in the digital age. She doesn't have an iPhone or Blackberry. It's amazing, don't you think?"

My boss at Taylor & Squibb was very old school. No social media. No hashtag communications written in 140 characters or less. He said the New Age was ruining our ability to communicate face to face. He and my father met one time and talked like they were lifelong buddies.

"When we arrived at the shop," Maya continued, "we must have startled Vera. Now that I know why she was there, it makes all the sense in the world, but she seemed flustered. You did, Vera." Maya eyed my aunt. "You stuttered, and your face was as flushed as a rutabaga. Not a pretty color, by the way. Sort of mottled. Now, you look . . ." Her mouth turned down.

Aunt Vera said, "What? What do I look like? Give me a mirror."

"No!" I yelled.

"That bad?"

"You'll need a little makeup for a few days, that's all," I lied.

"More than a little makeup," Maya said.

I glowered at her. "Go on. Tell the rest of the story. You, Bingo, and Emma walked in on my aunt."

Maya coughed as she knotted the ends of her shawl. "Bingo asked what Vera was doing there."

"Her voice had an edge to it," Aunt Vera cut in. "Of course, I could have been reading something into her tone because I was nervous. I fibbed and told her I needed some lace for something we were decorating at the shop. A pumpkin, I think. I'm sure she knew I was fibbing."

Maya said, "But Bingo laughed and said, 'What's mine is yours,' and then she proceeded to make tea for all of us. I started to help, but I was so hypercaffeinated by that time—I'd had three cups of tea trying to rid myself of this nagging cold—I excused myself to the ladies' room. When I returned, we kept the conversation light. No mention of Pearl or the tragedy. Halfway through our chitchat, Vera started acting funny."

"How so?" I asked.

"She was pulling on her hair and fidgety. Suddenly, she bolted to her feet and hightailed it out of there."

Aunt Vera's eyes widened. "Did I look that edgy? Truth be told, I was thoroughly embarrassed that I had questioned whether my friend of many years could be a cold-blooded killer, but what in heavens might she need arsenic for?"

I said, "Maybe arsenic just happened to be included in the items she'd purchased along with the antique shop. You know, arsenic was an old-time remedy. Back in college, I took a human biology class, one of those classes that was totally useless to a journalism and art major. The project required us to research medicines and how they were used to treat ailments. It turned out doctors used arsenic, and sometimes mercury, to treat syphilis before penicillin was discovered, and they used opium to help with coughing and other digestion ailments."

"Who knew?" Maya hiccupped out a laugh. "Did you know marijuana, because it stimulates hunger, is good for people with eating disorders?"

Aunt Vera gave her a curious look.

"Sorry." Maya waved a hand. "I get off track sometimes."

Was she trying to tell my aunt she had a thriving medical, albeit unlicensed, marijuana business? Not mine to reveal.

Aunt Vera said, "So, Jenna, you think finding arsenic in Bingo's things could be harmless?"

"She could have found the arsenic and decided that it was safer to stow it in her desk."

"Rather than throw it away?"

I nodded. "I can't tell you how many things I put someplace thinking I'll get rid of them and find them years later. Back to you. What happened next?"

"I drove toward home, contemplating my next step."

"Your next step?" Maya said. "Vera, you've got to stop investigating. It's not wise. We have a good police force."

"I know, but it's my duty. I can't sit idly by and watch them bungle Pearl's case."

"They're not bungling it." Maya heaved her narrow shoulders. "All I can say is it's lucky I came onto the scene. You see, Jenna, because I thought your aunt was acting erratically, even for her—"

"Too-ra-loo," my aunt warbled.

"Call me crazy, but you made me so anxious. I worried you'd gone back to taking that over-the-counter cough medicine junk. All those unhealthy red dyes. The stuff can make you not only itchy but sleepy, and worse. So I followed you. You missed your exit. I didn't know where you were off to, but then you started to weave. You were getting too close to the cliff."

"What cliff?" I nearly shrieked, trying to imagine the terrain.

"South of the pier," Maya said.

There were lots of hills in and around Crystal Cove, but not many cliffs. However, along Highway 1, southward toward San Simeon, there were sheer walls of rock. I remembered when my father was teaching me to drive along the route. Every second, I worried that I would plunge into the ocean.

"Aunt Vera, why were you all the way down there?"

"I can't remember."

"I thought maybe you'd fallen asleep," Maya said. "That's why I was honking."

"I remember wondering who was dogging me from behind. It was hazy. I couldn't make out a car or face in the rearview mirror. At one point, I turned my head to see who was being so rude. I guess that's when I lost control of the steering wheel. I swerved. I hit the tree and banged forward."

My heart started to pound so hard I could feel it drumming my ribs. "Didn't the airbag inflate?" I said.

"What airbag? In my ancient Mustang? I hit my forehead and my cheek." She started to reach for her face.

I said, "Don't."

"Give me a mirror, now."

"No."

"Don't baby me."

"Don't be a baby."

She pulled up the covers of her bed and tucked them tightly under her arms. "Well, I'm alive and that's all that matters. Now, I'm getting sleepy."

"We'll go," I said, "but I want you to promise to do everything the doctor orders." I took hold of my aunt's hands. They were shaking. She was anxious. So was I. Replaying the events in my mind, I couldn't help wondering if Bingo had slipped something into my aunt's tea to make her so drowsy she would drive herself to an untimely death.

Chapter 19

AROUND 11:00 A.M., as Maya and I were leaving Mercy Urgent Care, my father rushed into the foyer. Pepper had tracked him down, too. Would wonders never cease? I quickly updated him. He promised he wouldn't leave my aunt's side, just in case someone wanted to do her in. He wouldn't need a gun to protect her. At one point early in his FBI career, before he became a clandestine spy, he had served as a defensive tactics or, as the bureau called it, DT trainer. He knew everything from jujitsu to krav maga. Although he hadn't taught me or my siblings hand to hand fighting, he did teach us how to run. Running, he often advised us, was the best response; standing one's ground was asking for trouble.

Though the sun blazed overhead when Maya and I exited the facility, the air was chilly. A shiver ran down my spine and my stomach grumbled. I hadn't eaten anything since dawn. I wondered what Katie had put on the lunch menu at the café. I was hoping for one of her rich soups, like creamed broccoli topped with grated cheddar cheese.

Maya threw herself at me and clutched me in a desperate embrace. "Jenna."

My fingers felt her lean frame beneath the drapes of clothing. She could probably do with a little of Katie's home cooking, too, I mused.

"I was so worried," she said.

"I know," I cooed. "I was worried, as well."

"Your aunt is wrong. Bingo can't be the killer. She just can't be."

"I hope she isn't, but I intend to find out."

"You know I'd help, but I have to get back to work. I've got two employees out sick. Forgive me?"

"You've done enough."

Maya bussed my cheek and hurried to her Prius.

Before I satisfied my hunger, I needed to talk to Cinnamon Pritchett. I climbed into my VW bug and dialed the precinct. I quickly learned that Cinnamon was dealing with a fistfight at The Pier. Before heading there, I called Bailey, who assured me everything was hunky-dory at the shop.

The Pier, which was about two hundred yards of weathered wood located at the south end of town, was a destination spot. People from all over came to rent boats, fish, take a sunset cruise, ride the carousel, play a carny game, or shop and dine.

One of the restaurants, Mum's the Word diner, had been the center of attention last month; its owner was murdered during the Grill Fest. However, once again, The Word, as the locals called it, was thriving. A line of customers snaked out the door. Just beyond The Word stood the Seaside Bakery. I am particularly fond of its spun sugar. I know; no advice warranted. Pure sugar is not good for the body, but I can't help myself sometimes. I blame my mother. She used to treat me to a wand of Pink Froth after our art-on-the-beach outings. Ah, memories.

I saw a group of people convening beyond the bakery. I also spotted Rhett sitting with Bucky on the bench opposite the diner. Both held fishing poles. Bucky was laughing at some story Rhett was telling. I didn't disturb them and wended my way through the crowd.

Cinnamon stood in front of a ring toss carny game. She faced off two men, one I dubbed Mutt, the other Jeff. Mutt was huge and furry; Jeff was skin and bones and much shorter than his adversary. His jeans hung down around his hips and only managed to stay up because of a belt. His nose was bleeding and his cheek was bruised. Cinnamon looked forceful, standing with her right hand gripping the butt of the pistol in her holster. She pointed the index finger of her left hand at Mutt. "Your turn to speak."

From what I could glean from individuals in the crowd, Mutt and Jeff worked together at the ring toss carny game. Mutt claimed Jeff was having an affair with his wife. Jeff had retaliated, saying he would never set hand on Mutt's wife because she was uglier than a monkey's armpit. Mutt, fueled by a couple of early-morning beers, had slugged Jeff. Cinnamon happened to be at The Word having a bite to eat when the set-to started.

I waited while she defused the situation. The men ended up shaking hands and walking off together, Mutt's arm slung over Jeff's shoulders. I didn't envy Mutt's wife when he arrived home. According to the woman next to me, Mutt was certain she was having an affair with *someone*. I hoped Cinnamon would send one of her crew to monitor the reunion.

I caught up to Cinnamon as she headed back toward The Word. "Chief."

"Jenna." Her gaze was filled with concern. "I heard about your aunt. Mother texted me."

"Your mother—"

Cinnamon held up a hand. "Don't say a word. I know she can be confrontational."

"No, she was great," I said. "She was sincerely worried about my aunt. I'd like to thank her for coming straight to me."

Cinnamon offered a wry smile. "Thank her? Really?"

"At some point, she and I have to make amends. Do you think I could win her over by giving her a batch of bitter-sweet chocolate?"

"Only if Katie makes it." She laughed.

"Ha-ha." Apparently my secret about not being an expert in the kitchen was out. "I'm a work in progress."

"Me, too."

"Listen, about my aunt's accident—"

"She's not a very good driver, is she?"

"Let's just say her mind drifts on occasion, but this wasn't because of her inability to focus. I think someone might have dosed her tea to make her woozy." I gave Cinnamon an account of the morning's events.

She blew out a long stream of frustrated air. "Vera was investigating?"

"She's not guilty. She wants to know the truth as much as you and I do."

"That's not the point. I could haul her into jail for breaking and entering Aunt Teek's."

"The door was unlocked."

"Really?" Cinnamon's tone dripped with sarcasm. "Do you think that defense would hold up in court?"

"I don't know, would it? I didn't go to law school." I matched her tone.

She glowered at me. "What did Vera hope to find?"

"She thinks Bingo Bedelia might be hiding something from her past."

"Your aunt and Bingo are good friends. Don't they talk about these things?"

"Are you telling me you don't have secrets that you keep from your best friend?"

Cinnamon hesitated. "I don't have a best friend."

That rocked me to the core. As a cop, had she cut herself off from the rest of the world?

"My aunt is trying to be unbiased," I said, pressing onward. I didn't add that I hoped Cinnamon would be impartial, as well. About my aunt. Had she discovered yet that Aunt Vera and Pearl had vied for the same guy? I sure wasn't going to tell her.

"What does she need to be unbiased about?"

"A piece of gossip she gleaned. Emma claimed to have overheard Bingo arguing with Pearl a few nights ago, warning her to keep a secret." I held up a hand. "No, I don't know what secret."

"Sounds cryptic."

"My aunt wondered if the secret involved the man who broke Bingo's heart. She went to see if she could find evidence, like a diary or something."

"Do women still write in diaries?"

"Tons do. We have some beautiful spiral recipe diaries at the shop for people who like to keep track of menus and family recipes."

Cinnamon wagged her head. "Not I."

"Me, either. But I hear it's an art, a way to pass along tradition. Anyway," I continued, "my aunt was on the hunt, but then Bingo and the others showed up."

"Which others?"

"Emma and Maya." I explained about the morning tea to discuss a thank-you event for Winsome Witches volunteers. "Can you send someone to Aunt Teek's to see if Bingo put something in my aunt's tea that might have made her drowsy and unsteady behind the wheel?"

"I would imagine if Bingo did, the cup has been rinsed by now."

Her comment ricocheted me back to the morning we found Pearl dead. "Wow," I said. "I hadn't thought of that."

"Of what?"

"Pearl's cocktail glass."

"What are you talking about?"

"Pearl's killer couldn't have simply jammed her with a hypodermic needle. She would have needed to subdue Pearl first."

"Or he."

"How could she or *he* have injected Pearl without leaving a bruise? When I have to have blood drawn, I pray for a good technician who can find a vein and not leave my arm a mass of purple. Pearl didn't have a bruise, only the rash in the crook of her arm. I heard one of your people mention you'd be doing a toxicology report."

She frowned. "You heard *me* mention it."

"Fine. But I wasn't eavesdropping on purpose. You weren't whispering. You're a singer." My aunt said Cinnamon had a voice like an angel. "You project."

"Swell."

I shifted feet. "Pearl wouldn't have let someone inject her willingly. I suppose someone could have switched out the insulin in her hypodermic. Trisha suggested that. And, yes, Pearl could have dosed herself, but I didn't see a hypodermic lying around. Did you? Think about it. Pearl drank a cocktail." I ticked off points on my fingertips. "The glass was still on the table beside the chaise lounge when we found her. What if the killer put something in that drink?"

"Have you been spending a lot of time theorizing about this?"

"The notion just came to me. Do you know if Pearl was sedated?"

"Yes."

"Yes, as in *yes*, she was?"

Cinnamon flicked a fly off her neck.

"With . . . ?" I said, leading her.

"An imidazopyridine class of drugs."

"An *immy* what? What the heck is that?"

"The lab thinks it was zolpidem, the generic name for Ambien. Maybe three to five milligrams. When mixed with alcohol, it's enough to make a person sleepy but cooperative."

"How hard is that to get?"

"Not very. It's about fifty cents a pill, street value."

I reflected on Emma's husband, the dentist. I'd bet he could write a prescription for those pills. What if he knew about Emma's feelings for Pearl? He didn't attend the party. According to Emma, he wouldn't come within a mile of witches. What if he waited until the party disbanded and Emma left, and then he stole into Pearl's house? I paused. Why would Pearl have let Edward near enough to dose her drink?

Then I thought of another angle. "Could Pearl's murder have been a mercy killing? Is it possible she was sicker than she let on? Maybe she didn't have type 2 diabetes, she had . . ." I couldn't say the word. My mother died of lung cancer. Not due to any fault of her own. She hadn't smoked a day in her life. "Maybe Pearl let, or even encouraged, someone to give her the shot."

"We checked her doctor's records. She definitely had type 2 diabetes." Cinnamon shifted feet. "Is this sudden passion for theorizing the reason why you left a message with my deputy for me to call you?"

I had forgotten about that conversation. "No." I told her about Mrs. Hammerstead's visit to the store for the candy-making class. I described our conversation about the night her dog Ho-Ho went missing. "If I were you, I'd check with the vet. If Ho-Ho wasn't missing, Emma Wright might have lied about her alibi."

Cinnamon sighed, clearly frustrated with me. "I'll follow up."

"Also, you should know that Bailey overheard Trisha Thornton talking to her boyfriend at the coffee shop. They were worried about Aunt Vera nosing around UC Santa Cruz. I had no idea she went there. If only she'd told me. I've called a friend—"

"You called what friend?" Cinnamon blurted out. "Where? At UCSC?"

Open mouth; insert a fistful of *uh-oh*s. "A friend who works in the administration office."

"Jenna."

"I just wanted to find out about Trisha's finances." I didn't add, *And her alibi and her ability to use a hypodermic, yada yada*. "I learned her mother was about to cut her off financially."

"Who told you that? This *friend*?"

"No. Bingo Bedelia. What if, when Trisha realized she wouldn't get her inheritance right away, she came up with the idea to steal the Thorntonite? It's very rare. A single piece could rake in some big bucks."

Cinnamon raised a hand to silence me. "I can't believe you. You have no right to ask around."

"Sure, I do. Everyone has a right to question what

happened. I haven't done anything in an official capacity. I have not misrepresented myself."

"Didn't you just tell me you did not study the law?"

"My father taught me to be curious. I want to solve Pearl Thornton's murder. She was my advisor and one of my aunt's best friends. Not to mention, I want my aunt to be off your suspect list. Is she?"

Cinnamon remained mute. Not a *yes*, not a *no*. Dang.

"What if Trisha drugged her mother?" I continued. "Trisha is a user. Did you know that? Cocaine and amphetamines."

"Did Ms. Bedelia tell you that, as well?"

I nodded.

Cinnamon pursed her mouth. "In a murder investigation, ninety-nine percent of the suspects lie or subvert the truth. If one points a finger at another, then usually that person is hiding something of her own."

"Do you think Bingo is lying?"

"I didn't say that."

Was everybody in the Winsome Witches coven good at *misdirection*, as my aunt termed it? "If Trisha has a drug source," I continued, "she could get her hands on something like Ambien or zolpidem."

"Did you forget that she wasn't at the house when her mother died?"

"Doesn't that kind of drug require time to take effect?" I waited while Cinnamon digested that tidbit. "Trisha could have gone to the lab—if she really went to the lab—and returned to do the deed once her mother fell asleep. By the way, Trisha is also into alchemy."

"According to Ms. Bedelia?"

I shook my head. "Maya Adaire told me that."

"Okay, that's enough." Cinnamon shot her finger at me. "Right now I feel like we're playing a bad game of telephone. Who said what to whom and when? I know gossip is the lifeblood of a small town, but I've listened to enough chatter. Go back to work and let me do what I do best. I promise I'll take everything under consideration."

"And deem my aunt innocent?"

A woman yelled, "Chief Pritchett."

Cinnamon's eyes widened.

I pivoted and gaped, surprised to see Trisha Thornton exiting Mum's the Word Diner.

"Chief Pritchett," she said. "There you are."

Trisha hurried toward Cinnamon, her arm outstretched. She was carrying a blue leather-bound book. "I found something I think you'll want to see." She drew up short when she caught sight of me. She glanced at Cinnamon, who shrugged as if she were getting used to me being privy to information.

"What do you have?" Cinnamon held out her hand.

Trisha forked over the book, which was about five by seven inches. On the front cover, gold lettering spelled out *Datebook*. "I was sitting on the couch last night, watching television, and I spilled popcorn. I went fishing for the kernels between the cushions and . . . and this was there. It's my mother's." She helped Cinnamon flip open the book, and she pointed to the entries. "See these?"

Appointments were written in pairs of block letters, every day Monday through Friday, at each hour between the hours of nine and five. I could make out: *RJ*, *EW*, *MA*, *BB*, and so many more.

"We'd been wondering where this might have gotten to," Cinnamon said. "The calendar on her computer was blank."

I felt relieved to know that Cinnamon and her people had searched Pearl's office for clues.

"I don't know why my mother entered an appointment with Ma," Trisha said, pointing to the *MA* entry. "That's my grandmother. She lives in Santa Cruz in a nursing home."

I said, "Are you sure those letters signify your grandmother? The other appointments are all initials." I recognized my own, *JH*, scrawled in at 3:00 P.M. a week ago Friday. It had been our final session. Pearl had declared me ready to *move on*. "*MA* could be someone else. Maya Adaire, perhaps."

"Or Marlon Appleby," Cinnamon said, referring to her deputy. "Or a horde of other locals."

"Do you think one of them killed her?" Trisha said.

"They must all have terrible problems. Why else would my mother be so secretive about their names?"

"I don't think she was being secretive, Miss Thornton, only discreet."

Trisha nodded, looking younger and more uncertain than on previous occasions. She clutched the strap of her crocheted tote with both hands. "Well, I thought you should have the book. In case." She hurried away.

Cinnamon held up the book. "What do you think, Jenna? She brought this to me of her own accord. Doesn't that make her seem pretty darned innocent?"

I huffed. "Didn't you just tell me that whoever points the finger at someone else could be guilty herself?"

Cinnamon frowned, apparently not appreciating my steel-trap memory. An awkward silence fell between us.

I broke it. "How are things with you and Bucky?"

She tilted her head. "That's it? We're resorting to chitchat?"

"He's quite charming," I said. "And he's friends with Rhett, which means he has good taste."

"Rhett," Cinnamon muttered.

Shoot. Why had I been naïve the other night to think she had moved on and forgotten the past? "Talk to Bucky. He's obviously good friends with Rhett. Or don't you trust his judgment?" I hitched my thumb at Rhett and Bucky, who were still sitting beside each other. Bucky was talking this time and Rhett was laughing. "Is that the laugh of a guilty man? No, it's not. Here's a suggestion. When you're done solving Pearl Thornton's murder, why don't you revisit the arson at The Grotto and check out the former restaurant owner in New Orleans? Maybe Rhett's right. Maybe she still has the art that supposedly burned in the fire."

Cinnamon ground her teeth together. Was she wondering whether her bias, based upon suspicion developed years ago, clashed with her current reality, or was she upset that Bucky and Rhett were friends? Either way, she didn't want to say something to me that she might regret.

As for me? I didn't care. I had given her food for thought.

Chapter 20

I RETURNED TO The Cookbook Nook about the same time the candy-making class was wrapping up. A few hours had produced a wealth of chocolate brittle as well as a bevy of satisfied customers.

Katie said, "Terrific, you're back." She handed me a wedge of candy. "Taste."

The morsel crunched and melted in my mouth. The combination of sugar and salt was heavenly. "Delicious."

"Hand these out." Katie had fashioned adorable checkered boxes in which each of the attendees could pack their goodies. She also provided labels: *Homemade by* with a blank for the attendee's name. "Wait, before you do, tell me who *that* is from." She gestured to a tiny box on the counter. "The note says, 'From your secret admirer.' Care to share who that might be?"

I opened the box. Out sprang a Slinky toy. So did another notecard. "What the—" I gasped. I picked up the notecard.

"What's it say?"

" 'I know how much you like retro. Enjoy.' " I snorted. "I do not like retro. I mean, yes, I like a yo-yo and a hula hoop, but a coil of wire? Who is this guy?"

"Are you sure Rhett isn't joking around with you?" Katie asked.

"These gifts are not from him." I jammed the toy back in the box and shoved the gift under the counter. I had to figure out who this admirer was and put an end to it. If Deputy Appleby was the culprit, I would give him a piece of my mind in the bargain. "Moving on." I passed out the candy boxes to the students.

As they packed their sweets, the chatter among them was electric. The class had been fun, insightful, and most definitely tasty. All agreed that Katie was an excellent and enthusiastic teacher, and they looked forward to another class. I couldn't have been more thrilled. Positive buzz always helped a business thrive.

Meanwhile, Katie and I started folding chairs and resetting the movable bookshelves.

Katie said, "How's your aunt? You look relieved, so she must be okay."

I gave her a brief recap.

"Do you really think she was drugged?" Katie asked.

"Maya said Aunt Vera was acting edgy and different. That's not a good sign."

When we were done rearranging, I sent Katie in search of a bowl of soup—she hadn't made broccoli with cheddar, but she did have lobster bisque on hand, my second favorite—and I went to the counter to help Bailey, who was manning the register. Each attendee, thanks to the ten percent off coupon we had provided, had gone in search of something, whether a cookbook, a work of fiction, or giftware.

As they approached the checkout counter, I set the purchases into our tangerine-striped gift bags, specially ordered for the fall season, and tied them with bows.

When the last student left the shop, Bailey said, "I heard you telling Katie about your aunt. What did I miss?"

I filled her in. I added that Trisha showed up at the end of my chat with Cinnamon.

"Which reminds me." Bailey twisted and untwisted her turquoise beads. "Did you ever hear back from your friend at UCSC?"

"No."

"Meaning we still don't know about Trisha's school records or her school debt, and we don't know whether she was really at the lab when she says she was."

"No, but she brought that book to Cinnamon."

"Which proves nothing." Bailey whipped a ledger from the drawer beneath the cash register and shoved it at me. "Here. Take this to Cinnamon. It's our cash receipts book. It shows we earned money today."

"Huh?" I said. "I'm not following."

"Does this book prove anything? No, it does not. A date-book with initials in it is worthless. It doesn't verify that anybody killed anybody. All it proves is that people with initials were Pearl Thornton's patients, but it doesn't do more than that. My initials, Bailey Bird, are the same as Bingo's. So, was I one of Pearl's patients?"

"I don't know. Were you?"

Bailey smirked. "Like I'd ever go to a shrink. I would never be able to leave the couch with all the junk going on in this noggin." She tapped her temple, then laughed. "Only sane people should go to a shrink, in my humble opinion. The others should do their best to pretend they're sane. In other words, fake it. Speaking of Bingo Bedelia . . . let's face it, she is not all that sane. Did you see the display window at Aunt Teek's? It's out there." Bailey twirled her finger next to her head. "What do you know about her?"

"She grew up in Ohio, became a nurse, and moved here about twenty years ago. She was engaged at one time, but she never married."

"So why does she own an antique shop? Why isn't she still a nurse?"

"She would need to get a California license."

"Why not do that? Is there something in her past that might prevent her from continuing that career?"

"Like?"

"Like did she kill someone in Ohio and flee?"

I shuddered; I had wondered the same thing. Where was that boyfriend who supposedly up and left her?

"C'mon," Bailey said. "Once a caretaker, always a caretaker. Being a nurse is a calling, isn't it?" Bailey hurried to the computer and swung the screen to face me. "Let's twink her."

"I don't want to twink her." Twinking was a new social networking program. You twinked someone; they twinked you back. You could see their pictures; they could see yours. The idea was to write little stories to accompany each photo, not just share photos. I had gotten into it because of all the pictures I had of Tigger. I also twinked photographs of the store. I found twinking was a great marketing tool. People loved twinking books and kitchenware. Katie twinked the photos of her food. We shared a few links to recipes on our website.

"Bingo isn't her real name," Bailey said, her hands hovering over the keyboard. "What is it?"

"Barbara."

Bailey typed Barbara > Bingo > Bedelia into the Twink search space. Up popped a ton of pictures for a site run by someone named Mr. Mysterious. All of the pictures were older ones, circa thirty years ago. Bingo looked to be about sixteen. I was sure they were photos of her; the lantern jaw and nose were unmistakable. All of the photographs of other teens had funny names attributed to them: Musketeer, Mouse, Babykins.

As if she knew we were snooping into her life, Bingo hurried into the shop. Talk about bad timing.

"Quick, Bailey," I whispered. "Turn it off. Now."

"Jenna." Over a Pilgrim-style black dress, Bingo wore a black cape that flapped like bat wings behind her. She rushed toward us.

"Turn it off, Bailey," I rasped. "Off. Off."

She obeyed with a grumble.

"Is Vera here?" Bingo used her hands to talk, each movement jerky and tense.

"Aunt Vera? No, she's at the hospital."

"Still?" Bingo started for the door. "Why did Maya wait this long to tell me about the accident?"

"Bingo, hold up." I darted from behind the counter and blocked her short of the exit. I didn't touch her. She looked positively spooked. "I've got to ask you something."

She tried to dodge me. "I must go. Your aunt needs me."

"She's resting. She'll be in the hospital overnight."

"Maya said Vera crashed into a tree." Bingo sniffed. "When will she learn to focus as she drives?"

"Maya said my aunt seemed woozy after drinking tea at your shop."

"Tea doesn't make a person woozy. No, this is all about Vera and her driving skills. A car is a two-ton piece of machinery. She can't be idle behind the wheel. Doesn't she realize driving requires total concentration? She—"

"Bingo. Stop. Aunt Vera is going to be fine." If Bingo was this worried, maybe she didn't have anything to do with my aunt's accident. If Aunt Vera wasn't unsteady, maybe she had zoned out, yet again, while driving. I decided to speak to my father about the problem. He would insist my aunt get a full medical examination. She would argue but ultimately obey. "May I ask you a question?"

"About?"

"Pearl."

"What about her?"

"Were you one of Pearl's patients?"

Bingo stiffened. "That's . . . privileged information."

"I was a patient. I don't mind saying so. I had to deal with the grief of losing my husband. Why did you see her?"

"Why is it important to you?"

"My aunt . . ." I paused. No, I wouldn't involve Aunt Vera. This was my line of inquiry, not hers. But how could I find out the secret Bingo wanted Pearl to keep? She had a secret. Emma heard her say so, and Bingo's gaze . . . well, if her eyes were laser beams, she could cut me in half. "Your Halloween display."

"What about it?"

"There are two women running toward a cemetery. Is one of them you? Is there someone you're frightened of? Perhaps a past that you're running from?"

Bingo looked me straight in the eye. "Jenna, I believed you of all people would discern the significance."

"I'm sorry? Why me?"

"You love books. Your aunt tells me you are an avid reader. The display is my depiction, my interpretation if you will, of *Rebecca*."

"By Daphne du Maurier?" How had I not figured that out? *Rebecca*, a sinister psychological tale about jealousy, was one of my all-time favorite books. *Last night I dreamt I went to Manderley again* . . . "You're telling me your display involves the *new* Mrs. de Winter being chased by—" I hesitated. "Who does the woman in black represent, Mrs. Danvers or the first Mrs. de Winter?"

"Both. Don't you get it?" she huffed. "It doesn't matter. I really must go to your aunt."

"Wait." This time I touched her. "One more question. You and Pearl were overheard arguing on the night of the haunted tour."

"Who heard us?"

"That's not important. You wanted Pearl to keep a secret. Whatever it was, she took to her grave."

"You couldn't think—" Bingo's eyes misted over. "You do. You think I killed Pearl." She pinched her lips together. "Mercy. I would never kill to keep the secret, and it's bound to come out."

"What is it? Please tell me."

"He . . ." She chewed her lip.

"He, who?"

Bingo gripped my elbow and drew me outside. A cool breeze curled around my ankles and legs. I fought off a shiver.

"I was engaged as a girl," Bingo said sotto voce. "In high school. My fiancé left for college, and in a blink of an eye, it was over. I was heartbroken, but after a long while, I moved on."

"You settled in Crystal Cove. You started a new life."

She nodded.

"You gave up nursing. Why?"

"I only became a nurse because my mother had been one. It was not my passion. I always loved antiques."

"Go on."

"A few months ago, out of the blue, my former fiancé began calling me." Bingo worried her hands together. "Somehow the Reverend's and my nuptial date made it onto social networking. I didn't post it; neither did the Reverend. I only revealed the official date to Pearl. He . . . this man . . . learned I was getting married, and he . . ." More worrying. She looked like she would rather be anywhere else than outside our shop. "I was sure Pearl was the one who had posted something. I accused her. She swore she didn't do it."

"Maybe her daughter, Trisha, leaked it."

Bingo sucked in air, then exhaled. "I hadn't considered that. Trisha doesn't like me. Not a whit."

"Go on. So this guy is calling you. It's throwing you into a tailspin. Why?"

"Because he's . . . blackmailing me."

"Why on earth?"

Bingo chewed on her lip. "Because I posed nude for him."

Now I understood the tarot card she had drawn. I said, "He kept the negatives."

Bingo's eyes misted over. "I have done everything I could to lead a good life. A charitable life. I've been anxious all these years that the negatives would surface. Now that I'm marrying the Reverend, well, you can understand why. I offered to pay the jerk for the photos, but he wouldn't go for it."

I was confused. "Didn't you just tell me he was black-mailing you?"

"Not for money. He wants to *see* me. He claims he still loves me."

"If he did, he wouldn't threaten you."

"I asked Pearl's advice. She said many youths make mistakes they regret in their later years and not to blame myself. She told me not to make contact. I was afraid he would post the photos on the Internet. The worry hung like the sword of Damocles over my head." The sword of Damocles came from a Greek tale between Dionysus and Damocles, ending with the moral that with great power comes great peril. "Pearl advised me to confess fully to the Reverend, but I couldn't. I didn't dare. And lose him? No, no, no." Bingo shook her head. "Then a few days ago, Pearl started acting strangely. She became critical of my work ethic for the Winsome Witches. She often grew snippy as we neared the big luncheon, but this time she was worse. That night, during the tour, she banned me from participating with the Winsome Witches ever again if I didn't come clean to the Reverend. She valued honesty above all else. We exchanged words. In a fit of peeve, I called her selfish and domineering." Bingo clasped my hands. "By the end of the haunted tour, Pearl apologized, as did I, and I was certain my secret was safe."

"Bingo, I'm afraid to tell you that my aunt found a stained hatpin and a bottle of arsenic in the drawers at Aunt Teek's."

Bingo smirked. "Hmph. I knew she'd been poking around in my stuff. I wasn't sure for what."

"Is the hatpin stained with arsenic?"

"Heavens, no. That arsenic has never been opened and never will be. I should probably take it to a chemical disposal site." She nodded as if making a mental note.

"The hatpin?" I prompted.

"The tip of my old fountain pen was bent out of shape, so I got creative and I dipped the hatpin in ink and used it as a quill. Didn't you see the lettering on my display? It's so fine, it's eerie."

It was such a reasonable explanation, I didn't question it.

"On the night Pearl died, Emma claims you were in your shop, but my aunt didn't see you there."

"Emma. She tries so hard." Bingo sighed. "By giving us all an alibi, the girl was trying to do the right thing. But she lied. I wasn't in my shop. I was at the cemetery."

"Why?"

Bingo hesitated. She lowered her chin and looked at me from beneath her lashes. "I was practicing incantations."

Emma claimed that Bingo was taking the witch thing way too seriously. She even said she had seen Bingo practicing magic at the store. Had she seen her do so on other occasions?

I said, "Are you a real, practicing witch?"

"No, and I'm not a Wiccan, either, although did you know Wicca is now a religion recognized by the United States military?"

"Really?" A client of Taylor & Squibb was a Wiccan. A few years ago, she had invited me to a coven circle in the city. Hoping I might come up with a great ad campaign, I attended. On the way to the event, my friend explained that Wicca was a pagan religion, which was typically duotheistic, worshipping both the netherworld and a horned god that associated with forest animals, and a mother goddess that associated with the moon, stars, and fate. The Wicca religion involved the ritual practice of witchcraft, but none of the members were considered witches. I had a good time at the circle. We sang and bonded. It had all been harmless yet satisfying in a mystical way.

Bingo said, "I was only practicing so I could be the best leader of the Winsome Witches."

"Why would you feel the need to do that? Pearl was the leader."

"Her health . . ." Bingo ran her thumb and finger along the seam of her cape, then stopped abruptly. "She asked me to be prepared in case she stepped down."

I was right. Pearl was sicker than she had led us to believe. "Does your future husband mind that you are the High Priestess?"

"The Reverend is a wonderful man. He values me as a person. He knows that we aren't real witches, and we do this all in fun. 'Anything for a good cause,' he would say. He's a very open-minded minister and a voracious reader. He reads across genre. Not just biblical text. He devours mysteries and fiction. He wouldn't go so far as to read something *racy*, but he likes a good whodunit. By the way, you must tell Katie, he loves to cook Italian food. His pasta pomodoro is to die for. How fabulously lucky am I?"

"Yet you still haven't told him about the photos?"

"I'm warming to the idea."

Her alibi didn't ring true. Why spend two hours in a cemetery? How much practice did she need? "Bingo, did anyone see you that night in the cemetery?"

"I saw a man wearing a fedora. I don't know if he saw me. I told the police."

"You did?"

"I'm very forthright. I went straight to them after the luncheon realizing that everyone, as Maya said, should be aboveboard. It's the only way the police can get to the truth. As I said, I'm not sure if the man in the fedora saw me. He was walking with a cane and carrying a bouquet of flowers. They were white and caught the moonlight. Daisies, I think. He went to a grave to the east of me, up the hill. When he arrived at a gravestone, he did the oddest thing. He twirled once before setting down the flowers."

Tears sprang to my eyes as I realized she was describing my father. He and my mother used to twirl around the living room, laughing until their sides hurt. My mother had adored daisies. Dad must have been visiting her grave. I blinked to hold the tears at bay and whispered, "How long was he there?"

"As long as I. Two hours."

Chapter 21

I DRANK MY lobster bisque from a to-go cup as I sped to Mercy Urgent Care. I was eager to talk to my father and get the scoop. To my surprise, he wasn't there. Neither was my aunt. She had been released.

"Released?" I barked at a nurse who didn't deserve my wrath. "She was on tubes and bruised and—"

The nurse ran away and fetched the doctor, who returned quickly. Probably to tame the crazy woman, namely *me*. "Your aunt was fully alert; she denied pain medication," the doctor said. "Her vitals were strong, and she had no head injury. She asked to be released. We didn't have the right to hold her."

She's in danger, I wanted to say, but didn't. Instead, I called my father. "What happened?" I cried when he answered. "Where are you? Where's Aunt Vera? You promised you wouldn't let her out of your sight."

"Calm down, Tootsie Pop. She's fine. She wanted to go

home. I had a client to see, but I found a trustworthy policeman to watch your aunt at her place."

"Who?"

"Marlon Appleby."

"What?" My voice crescendoed.

"You don't like my choice? Why not? Don't you trust him?"

"Sure, I trust him. Why wouldn't I?" I growled. Deputy Appleby. Was the guy insinuating himself into my life?

"Marlon is off duty," my father went on. "He's thrilled to make the extra income. Turns out he has a couple of kids to support."

"He's not married."

"That doesn't mean he doesn't have kids." My dad chuckled. "He's going to stay with your aunt for twenty-four hours." He laughed again. "Needless to say, she's not happy with the arrangement, but she has accepted her fate."

I told him I needed to see him in person and hurried to Nuts and Bolts.

As I entered the narrow shop, a cuckoo popped from its hiding hole in a clock that my father had retooled. The wooden bird sang out a single "Cuckoo," signifying half past noon.

Beside the checkout counter stood Old Jake, a wealthy widower with a gnarled body and face—he reminded me of one of those old trees that lived in the Forest of No Return in the Disney classic *Babes in Toyland*. Jake eyed the clock and scanned his wristwatch. "Got that thing down to a second, don't you, Cary?"

My father, who was rummaging through an assortment of nails, nodded. He loved fixing things. As usual, the place was super tidy. With his heightened need for order, my father should have been a Navy man instead of FBI.

"Good day, Jenna," Jake said. "I hope you have wonderful things planned for yourself."

It was Jake's standard line. "I do, sir, and you?"

"Haven't gone but one day without doing something that

pleased me." That *one* day was the day he buried his wife. "Have at it, Cary," he yelled to my father.

"Have at it," my father echoed.

The old guy left with a Nuts and Bolt bag in hand.

"Make yourself comfortable, Jenna," my father said, continuing to search through the nails.

I moved to the checkout counter and glanced at the Seneca plaque hanging on the wall. Its quote was seared in my memory: *The primary sign of a well-ordered mind is a man's ability to remain in one place and linger in his own company.* The quote epitomized my father; he was his own best friend. I was on a path to becoming my own.

After a long moment—I never rushed my father—he said, "Found it." He held up a single nail as if it were a prized trophy. "This is the reason I don't let people handle the wares themselves. Things get out of place." He set the nail on the counter and strolled to me. "Old Jake had an emergency. You know I never deny him."

Only recently, I'd found out that Old Jake had saved my father's life. When my father was twelve, he went surfing. Alone. A wave tumbled him and his board struck his head. Jake, not much older than my father, happened to be on the beach that day. He was a drifter. He saw the accident and rescued my dad. My grandfather saw promise in Jake. As payback for his Good Samaritan act, my grandfather tutored Jake and taught him how to invest. Ten years later, Jake, like my aunt, made a killing in the stock market. He and my father had remained fast friends. Day or night, whenever Jake felt a weird whimsy to repair his multimillion-dollar home, Dad accommodated him.

Dad said, "What's up?"

I didn't answer. I didn't know where to begin. He had visited Mom's grave. How often did he do that?

"Jenna?"

"You were seen . . ."

"Seen?"

"Doing . . ." The words wouldn't form.

"Doing?" Dad's mouth quirked up on one side. "Two can play this game."

When had my father developed this wry sense of humor? After my mother died, he turned dour. So did I. But I was on the mend. Maybe falling in love with Bailey's mother was transforming my father. Lola, who owned The Pelican Brief Diner, was a bundle of good energy and good vibes. On the other hand, if my father was in love with her, why did he go to the cemetery?

"Jenna," my father prodded.

"You were seen. At the cemetery. At night."

"Who saw me?"

"Bingo Bedelia."

"Aha. I should have known it was her." Dad gestured to his chin. "She has such a distinctive silhouette with that long nose and square jaw. What do they call that kind of jaw?"

"Lantern jaw."

"That's it. Like Popeye."

"Dad, you were walking with your cane."

"I often use a walking stick in unsteady territory. What's your question?"

"You were putting flowers on Mom's grave."

"Yes."

"Do you—" I sank against the counter, the hard edge pressing against the underside of my rib cage. "Do you miss her?"

"Of course I miss her. I lay flowers twice a year. On the day of her death, as an honor to the life she led, and on the day we met, as a reminder that we will see each other again."

"See each other?" I shook my head, not understanding. "Are you saying you believe in the beyond?"

"I know everything in the physical world leads me to believe there is no beyond, but I continue to hope. I have faith, as the pundits call it. I will see your mother again."

"But, Dad—"

"Don't you hope you'll see David again?"

I wasn't sure. After all I had learned, what would I say

when I saw my husband? *How could you leave me? How could you take your own life? Did it hurt to die? Wasn't I worth changing your bad habits for?*

"Of course you would," my father answered for me. "If you've loved someone, you continue to love them even after they are gone."

My chest grew tight with sorrow. "What about Lola?"

He smiled. "Lola was your mother's best friend. She would like to see your mother, as well." He grinned. "Don't look at me like that. There won't be room for jealousy in the future. Only healthy reunions."

My dad had been volunteering with all sorts of do-gooder projects like Habitat for Humanity and more. Had his belief in peace and harmony come from those sessions?

Tears pressed at the corners of my eyes. Man, was I ever becoming a waterworks factory. "I want the faith you have."

"Sweetheart." My father hurried around the counter and put his arms around me. "We all come to our beliefs differently and at a different pace. Heartache like yours can rip someone's faith to shreds. Faith has to be rebuilt. Your aunt . . . it's one of the reasons she does all that card reading and such. She doesn't want to be superstitious, but she does want to believe. She continues to try to contact Stuart."

The man who left her at the altar and died less than a year later.

I said, "Hey, did you know she's dating Greg Giuliani?"

My father's eyes widened. "Dating? Don't be silly."

"I saw them together. She was all dolled up. Isn't he the one you were referring to the other day? I think—" I bit my tongue. I did not need to tell my father about Aunt Vera staying the night at Greg's. It was not my business; it was certainly not my father's.

"Greg isn't for her," my father said.

"You tell her," I joked.

"Not in her condition. She's mad enough that she crashed her car."

"Wait until she sees her face in the mirror."

"I made Marlon swear she can't go near one."

"But you know Aunt Vera."

In unison we said, "Stubborn," then laughed.

My father brushed my shoulders, as if sweeping away specks of dust; it was his way of balancing me. "All this talk about faith and your aunt's dating life aren't why you showed up here. You came to ask me about my trek to the cemetery. Why?"

"I wanted to corroborate Bingo's alibi."

"Aha," my father said again. "I won't even ask why you are investigating. It seems I have no say in keeping you within twenty yards of the law."

"I told you. I feel like my presence has drawn this bad karma to Crystal Cove. I've got to fix it. In addition, Cinnamon Pritchett has her eye on Aunt Vera as her main suspect."

My father said, "Don't worry. I'll have a word with her."

I huffed. Did everyone in town think they could change Cinnamon's mind? I sure couldn't.

"In the meantime," my father went on, "tell me why Bingo Bedelia is a suspect in Dr. Thornton's death."

I explained.

"All solid reasoning. Protecting a secret from one's past is definitely a good motive for murder, but I'm afraid Bingo should be eliminated from your list. She was indeed in the cemetery from approximately ten until well after midnight."

"How do you know she was there that long?"

My father smiled, but there was a sadness in his eyes. "Sometimes I read to your mother. She loved poetry by Dickinson. What a lonely soul the poetess must have been, living almost entirely in seclusion as an adult. Your mother's favorite was one of Dickinson's poems about lovers being kept apart, with only the door ajar."

I kid you not, nothing my father ever did in his life again would shock me as much as right now. He knew about Dickinson's life? He could paraphrase her poetry?

"But back to Bingo," my father continued. "She was doing what looked like calisthenics. Arms raised. Arms lowered. Up, down." He demonstrated. "Quite comical."

"She was practicing incantations."

"As in witch chants?"

I gave Bingo's reasoning.

"You don't believe Bingo could have had anything to do with harming your aunt, do you?"

"I don't know what to think. Someone did."

"Your aunt—" He mimed steering a car.

"Is a bad driver, I know. But this was different. Maya said she couldn't get Aunt Vera to pull over. She was honking and everything. I think Aunt Vera was drugged. Right before, she was drinking tea at Aunt Teek's with Maya, Bingo, and Emma." I halted.

"What?"

"Maya said she went to the restroom. What if Emma slipped something into Aunt Vera's tea? She has access to drugs, both at the veterinarian's office and possibly"—I paused for effect—"from her husband, the dentist."

The cuckoo burst from its hiding hole in the clock and sang out, "Cuckoo."

But I didn't think my theory was so crazy. How could I prove it?

Chapter 22

BEFORE RETURNING TO The Cookbook Nook, since I was on a mission to find out the truth about everything—including my own secret admirer mystery—I swung by the Play Room Toy Store. Where else would my secret admirer have purchased a Slinky? Online at eBay, possibly, but the owner of the toy store sold retro toys. He often put them in his window displays. He wasn't at the store. The ancient clerk couldn't remember anyone in the past few months having purchased a Slinky, other than the new jumbo rainbow version.

Frustrated but not beaten, I proceeded to The Enchanted Garden. The salesperson, a thick woman nearly twice Maya's size in height and stature, reweaved her waist-length braid as I explained my dilemma. My secret admirer must have purchased the green-glazed pot filled with herbs here. No other shop in town sold such beautiful garden items.

"No, ma'am," the clerk said. "I don't remember anyone purchasing a gift like that."

"Is Maya here?"

"Yes, ma'am, but she doesn't want to be disturbed when she's"—she waved the tip of her braid like a wand—"doing her magic."

"Her what?"

The clerk beamed; her smile was infectious. "You know, doing that voodoo that she *do* so well." She wiggled a finger. "She's out in the hothouse working on the potions demonstration that she's giving at your store on Wednesday."

I thought of the prized mushrooms Maya grew in the hothouse and hoped she didn't plan to use any of *those* in her presentation.

"Say," the clerk went on. "I just remembered, we used to sell those glazed pots you were asking about. They were sort of passé. We haven't carried them in years." She leaned forward in confidence. "You know, maybe Lover Boy bought the pot way back when and planted it with herbs from his own secret garden."

Swell. I had established that the admirer was a hoarder. He had a Slinky and an out-of-date glazed pot to give out as love tokens. What else did he have? Trolls and pet rocks? Who was this guy? He certainly wasn't going to win my heart with his loony advances.

Putting the affair from my mind, I returned to the shop. The rest of the afternoon sped by. Because it was already Monday again, we had to do cash tallies and book orders, and restock the shelves, and then, of course, there was taste testing for the café. I loved taste testing. Katie had made an assortment of candies from the *Handcrafted Candy Bars* cookbook Bailey had raved about. Man, was she ever right. The dark chocolate–dipped almond-coconut bar was downright sinful.

A half hour after closing, Bailey, Katie, and I, with Tigger tucked into my big tote, headed to Azure Park. The park was the largest in town, about two square city blocks of grass, oak trees, and boxwoods, and it was within walking distance of Fisherman's Village. Monthly, the park featured live music. Nearly the whole town showed up. People camped out on blankets or brought picnic sets. Because the nights grew cooler in October, people also came loaded with coats, scarves, and gloves.

"Isn't it beautiful?" I said as we arrived. The sun had set; the moon hadn't yet risen. Stars were beginning to sparkle in the twilight. Event planners had strung lights around the park and had set up a bandstand-style stage at the north end. I shrugged into my denim jacket and buttoned the buttons.

"Who do you think will win?" Bailey said. At tonight's event, the mayor would hand out the awards for the best window displays as well as decorated pumpkins.

"The owner of Play Room Toy Store," I said. "He always wins."

"Look," Katie pointed. "There's your aunt."

Aunt Vera was sitting at a portable picnic table with none other than Deputy Appleby. So much for my aunt staying home and resting. Where was Nature Guy Greg? Was I wrong about him and *Vee*? Aunt Vera and the deputy seemed to be playing mahjong, a game I would never learn in even one of its varieties: Chinese, American, and more. A college friend had tried to teach me. I could distinguish between bams, craks, and dragons, but I couldn't get the hang of passing around tiles to get a complete hand. Nor did I have the patience. I wouldn't learn to play bridge, either. To relax, I preferred a good book or a walk on the beach and, now, cooking.

Beyond my aunt and her escort, I saw Cinnamon walking beside Bucky. No public display of affection, I noted. They weren't even holding hands. I also caught sight of Bingo and the Reverend. They seemed almost entwined and looked completely in love. With my father's testimony, I truly believed Bingo was innocent; she had no reason to kill Pearl and I doubted she had drugged my aunt. She had come clean to me about her past. Had she told her fiancé the story? Had he helped her contact the former fiancé? I hoped she would be able to keep the guy from posting the nude photos on the Internet. She didn't deserve to be punished for silly choices she had made as a teen.

Bailey and I laid out our blanket. I set Tigger on a corner and warned him to stay. He wasn't a roamer. He turned in three circles, clawed, stretched, then plopped down and went to sleep. Katie unpacked the picnic basket she had brought. Included in the feast were wine, cheese, salami, freshly baked sourdough bread, and an assortment of vegetables paired with her delectable dill sour cream dip.

"Simple fare," she said humbly. "For dessert . . ." She set out an assortment of bonbons. "The pumpkin pecan chocolates are mouthwatering."

I went for a backward dinner—dessert first. I downed a bonbon, agreed with her assessment, and said, "What's on tonight's musical slate?"

"The stylings of The Quartet." Katie was wearing a shiny orange tee and matching jacket over black trousers. She had even donned makeup and added a sparkly bow to her hair. "Boy, I can't wait."

"Who, pray tell, make up The Quartet?" I asked, as if I didn't know. Rumors abounded that Katie's boyfriend had started a band.

"Keller and five of his pals."

"That makes six." I held up fingers, showing I could do the math.

Katie grinned. "They didn't think The Sextet had the same ring."

"What do they sing?"

"Old standards. Four-part harmony. The extra two guys offer vocal percussion. No instruments. Prepare to be blown away."

Bailey rolled her eyes and mouthed: *Geek*. I slugged her.

"Whoa," Bailey said, slugging me back. "Get a load of those."

Four people dressed up in colorful goblin costumes traipsed alongside the crowd toward the bandstand.

Katie said, "I think the one leading the pack, the really

short one with the purple cowl and big green ears, is the mayor."

I grinned. "The creature does have a familiar jaunty gait."

The mayor took the stage and tapped a live microphone. "Testing, one, two, three."

Out of nowhere, a spotted owl swooped low across the stage. The mayor, clumsy in her garish costume, spun around so hard she stumbled off the stage.

The audience let out a collective gasp.

Bailey shuddered and moaned.

I gripped her arm. "Are you okay?"

"If you see an owl during the day, there will be a death close to you," she intoned as if under a spell.

"Stop that," I ordered. "It's nighttime. Shake it off. Where do you get all these silly superstitions?"

"My mother. My friends."

"Not me."

"I'm fine," the mayor announced, scrambling to her feet. "Please welcome The Quartet!"

Bailey poured each of us a glass of wine as The Quartet took the stage, all six of them. The audience hushed. We never knew what to expect at these musical outings. One time a talented maestro led a high school band, and they sounded as glorious as the Boston Pops. Another time, we had three legendary rock stars who could barely hold a tune.

Keller picked up the microphone and, solo, cackled like a ghoul. When the crowd hushed, he sang the opening words to "The Monster Mash."

People roared their approval.

During the chorus, the entire sixsome sang. Then Keller pointed the microphone at the audience, which responded in kind. It was a rousing success.

The set consisted of more Halloween favorites, including "Superstition" and "Ghostbusters." The group finished with a speedy version of "Thriller." People who knew the "Thriller" dance leaped to their feet and strutted along, Bailey, Katie, and I among them.

When the music ended, the mayor hurried to the stage. "Now, the moment you've all been waiting for." She waggled a gold statuette. "The winner of the Crystal Cove Halloween pumpkin-carving contest is . . ." Someone offstage beat a tabletop like a drum. "It's a tie between Play Room Toy Store and Home Sweet Home, and the winner of the best window display is . . . "

I knew the pumpkin I had carved wasn't the best. Bushy eyebrows and a spastic grin. Big deal. I would take more time next year when I got into the groove of being a shop owner. But our window display was top-notch. I crossed my fingers.

"Aunt Teek's," the mayor announced.

Cheers from the crowd. It was the first year Play Room Toy Store didn't make a clean sweep.

As the winners approached the stage, Bailey leaned in to me. "Speaking of Aunt Teek's, if Bingo Bedelia didn't kill Dr. Thornton, who did?"

I told Bailey and Katie about my aunt's foray into Bingo's store and how Maya, Emma, and Bingo walked in on her.

"It couldn't have been Emma who drugged the tea," Bailey said. "I mean, I know she had a deep, dark secret, but it's out, so what reason would she have to harm your aunt? And I've seen her with animals. She's so loving."

"It doesn't look like Emma's husband would agree with you." Katie hitched her head.

Edward was sitting by himself on a blanket, one bottle of water, one sandwich, obviously alone.

"That doesn't prove anything. Emma could be working," I said, although I had to admit, Edward looked pretty forlorn. A memory flashed in my mind. I had seen the initials *EW* in Pearl's datebook. Emma mentioned that Pearl had warned her about doctor-patient transference, which indicated she had been a patient, but did that rule out Edward? Had he seen Pearl professionally, as well? If he had, that might explain why the doctor would have allowed him into her home the night she was killed. He could have found out earlier from Emma about her love for Pearl and, incensed, gone to Pearl's house to eliminate her from the equation.

Bailey flicked my arm with a fingernail. "Where did you go? What are you thinking?"

I told them.

Katie said, "No, it can't be true. I go to Dr. Wright. He's a good dentist."

"That doesn't mean he isn't a killer," Bailey said.

"Ew. Ick." Katie waved a hand. "Jenna, what about Maya? Maybe she has a secret she's hiding. Are you sure she didn't put the poison in your aunt's tea to keep her from finding out?"

"Maya didn't have opportunity. She went to the restroom. She was also the one who followed my aunt and honked, trying to get her to pay attention to the road."

"I still think Trisha is the best bet to have hurt your aunt," Bailey said. "I know she wasn't at Aunt Teek's, so she couldn't have drugged Vera, but you intimated that it's possible Vera wasn't drugged. Did they do a tox screen on her? Do they know for sure?"

I wasn't certain.

"Look, your aunt is nervous. She's lost her powers. She has every right to feel anxious, maybe even woozy." Bailey stabbed the blanket to make her point. "Trisha Thornton has need of cash. She has loans to pay. Maybe she killed her mother because she believed her mother's estate would be settled quickly. Don't forget, she and her boyfriend were upset that your aunt was snooping around UC Santa Cruz. What about the rock that's missing?" Bailey sipped her wine. "What if Trisha stole it and pawned it so she could have enough money to bribe someone at college to clean up her record and readmit her?"

Katie didn't agree. "Why not steal the entire set then?"

"Because Trisha banked on the housekeeper, Mrs. Davies, not noticing one portion missing."

"Oho!" Bailey laughed. "What about Mrs. Davies? You know, the butler did it, except in this case the housekeeper did it."

I glowered at her.

"Okay, just making light." Bailey grinned. "Back to Trisha. Call your buddy at UCSC again and see if she'll give you at least a financial update."

Knowing Bailey wouldn't let up until I obeyed, I fetched my cell phone and dialed my friend.

She surprised me by picking up after one ring. We chit-chatted for a second, about her husband, her dog, and The Cookbook Nook. She promised to stop into the store soon.

Then I said, "You must have gotten my messages. Can you answer any of my questions?"

She didn't respond.

"Does Trisha owe money to the school?" I begged.

Finally she said, "Jenna, look, I've talked to the police. If it helps, I was able to convince them that they should chat again with the girl. You were right to ask about the security camera." She hung up.

I looked at my pals and grinned. A security camera meant either someone did see or didn't see Trisha on campus. Either way, her alibi was in question.

Chapter 23

S LEEP DIDN'T COME easily for me. When I drifted off, I
dreamed a nightmare that shook me to the core. I often
experienced vivid dreams. Over the years, I'd learned that
creative people remembered their dreams better than most.
But this one was ridiculous. It could have been written by
Shakespeare or, better yet, Stephen King. On an autumn
night, people in ghoulish costumes chased each other
through a pumpkin patch. I ran after Trisha Thornton
demanding *the truth and nothing but the truth*. Someone—a
masked man, my secret admirer—hounded me. As he
sprinted after me, he flung herbs. I knew, deep in my soul,
that if any hit me, I would be drugged by a love potion and
swept under his spell.

I woke heavy-headed and vowed, yet again, to foreswear
eating chocolate at night, this time moving the timetable up
to after dusk. I would have to see if I could keep my promise
in the weeks to come. I owed it to my sanity to be vigilant.

Eager to start my day on a cheery note, in less than a half

hour, I exercised, dressed, and dropped Tigger at Aunt Vera's. She had been more than amenable to taking him. Though I knew she wouldn't admit it, after booting out Deputy Appleby—she needed her space—she felt slightly vulnerable; worry flickered in her eyes.

A half hour later, Rhett picked me up for our date.

"Tough night?" he said as he maneuvered his Ford truck around a tight curve of the road.

"I only had one glass of wine. Too many sweets were the culprit. I tossed and turned."

"Did you eat breakfast?"

I shook my head. "I forgot to."

"I've got an antidote. Reach in the backpack. Grab the string cheese. It's a good balance for a sugar high. Or you can eat a protein bar."

I sorted through the pack that sat at my feet and pulled out two tubes of string cheese and a bottle of water. Minutes later, after downing the snack, I felt steadier.

When we reached the trailhead, Rhett drove into a parking area. We were meeting up with a group of people. Some would trek to what was known as the Hell Hole, a claustrophobic cave site near the Moore Creek Preserve. Others, like us, would divert and hit the two-mile hike that provided incredible vistas of the ocean. I told Rhett there was no way I was going into the spooky cave with the daredevils. I had seen pictures. The passage was so narrow that chests and noses hit walls.

"The hike today should do you good," Rhett said.

"Just being with you will do me good." I grinned, then eyed the rest of the group that had formed. About a dozen people. "Hey, isn't that Edward Wright?" I pointed. A tiny shudder shimmied down my spine.

Rhett nodded. "He's the leader of the group."

"Is Emma joining us?"

"I don't see her." Rhett placed a hand at the arch of my back and guided me forward.

"How well do you know Edward?" I asked. Was it the fact that he was a dentist that gave me the willies? Or was it something about his lanky Nordic look? He reminded me of any number of killers in James Bond movies. Katie liked him, and Emma said that he adored her.

"He's a nice enough guy. A die-hard caver."

"So I've heard."

"He takes amazing photographs of stalagmites and stalactites."

"Because they remind him of teeth?" I joked.

Rhett chuckled.

"All right, everyone, let's move out," Edward commanded. He wasn't wearing a hat or visor. His shoulder-length blond hair gleamed in the sun.

The coast of California offered some of the most scenic hiking in the world. The terrain was lush and emerald green. The bays and oaks provided plenty of shade.

Along the way, we stopped to rest. Some of the hikers scoured the area for raw gemstones. Edward picked up a rock and buffed it with the sleeve of his shirt. He handed it to another trekker, a twenty-something woman in a big floppy hat. She smiled flirtatiously. He smiled, too, though the smile was tight—no exposed teeth—and his gaze was downright flinty.

Another chill ran through me. I itched to know more about Edward, specifically whether he had been Pearl's client. I revealed my need to Rhett.

He rubbed my shoulder. "Please don't. I'm not comfortable with you grilling him."

"I'm not going to *grill* him, but admit it, there's something different about him."

"There's something atypical about all cavers."

Exactly.

I drew near to Edward and the young female trekker. Her mouth was moving. Rhett, doing his best to hide what I had to imagine was exasperation with me, held back.

"Really?" she said, midconversation. "You like rocks, and yet you don't believe in alchemy?"

"I like caving," Edward said. "There's a distinction."

"Alchemy is all the rage around here," the young woman

said as she admired the facets of the buffed stone. "It's the ability to transform base metals into noble metals."

Edward shifted feet. "I don't believe in hoodoo stuff."

"It's not hoodoo, silly." She batted his arm. "Alchemy isn't a religion."

"It's about magic and myth, isn't it?"

"You're stubborn, you know that?"

Edward offered a cruel grin.

Silence fell between them giving me the opportunity to cut in. "Edward, I'm Jenna."

"She's with me, Edward," Rhett said, shoring up the space behind me. I appreciated the protective warmth of his body, not to mention the mental support of his presence, even if he didn't totally agree with my intent to ask Edward a couple of questions.

"Hey, Rhett, good to see you." Edward jutted out a hand. They shook amiably.

I said, "Your wife drives my cat around."

"You have a wife?" his female companion said.

"No," Edward sputtered. "I mean, yes."

The woman rushed to another group of female rock collectors. She started talking animatedly, probably saying Edward had led her on. Hadn't she noticed the wedding ring on his left hand? He hadn't removed it.

Edward picked up another rock and cleaned it with his sleeve. "I saw you at the Black Cat parade, Jenna. You own the cookbook shop and the ginger kitten."

"That's me." The guy took enough care to note what kind of cat I owned. How bad could he be? On the other hand, his jaw was ticking with tension. I said, "I see you're into rocks. Rhett tells me you photograph them."

Rhett added, "Edward has put on a couple of exhibitions."

"Really?" I tried my best to act like a fan. "There are some special rock collections in the area. Have you ever viewed the Thornton Collection?"

Edward didn't respond.

I said, "That's a nice rock you're holding."

"This isn't for me," Edward said. "It's for Emma. She likes to collect raw garnet. It's her mother's birthstone. January."

I recalled Bailey coming up with the theory that Trisha Thornton had ground stones and turned them into a potion to coerce someone to kill her mother. Was it as absurd a notion as it sounded? What if it was Emma, not Trisha, doing the grinding?

"I overheard part of your conversation with the young woman." I jutted a finger; the woman was still eyeing him with hostility. "Do either you or Emma practice alchemy?"

Edward dropped the rock as if it were hot and brushed off his hands. "I don't know much about minerals. Only stalactites and stalagmites."

"Explain the lure of caving to me," I said.

He stretched his back and rolled kinks out of his neck. "It's all about negotiating the pitches and squeezes. Drinking in the way caves formed. Discovering their age. It can give a guy quite a rush."

"Or a girl."

A faint smile graced his hard mouth.

"I hear caving is an extreme sport nowadays," I said. "Are you a risk taker?"

"I don't throw caution to the wind, if that's what you're asking. Caves can be dangerous places. Cavers have to be aware of flooding, loose rocks, and physical exhaustion."

Rhett retrieved the stone Edward had discarded. He popped it up and down on his palm. Had he sensed the same thing I had? Edward was growing increasingly tense. He was holding something back. Rhett said, "Have you explored a lot of caves?"

"I've hit nearly all the ones in the western states. Black Chasm, Lake Shasta Caverns, Boyden Cave. I hope to explore all the caves in the U.S. After attacking America, I'll go international, starting with Europe and then Africa."

"Does Emma explore with you?" I asked.

"Emma and I . . ." He hesitated. "Look, you're prying. I get it. You're my wife's friend. Are you a witch, too?"

"Emma's not—" I paused. "Were you seeing Dr. Thornton as a patient?"

He cocked his head. "That's a non sequitur that ranks right up there with *nosy*. Why do you want to know?"

"The initials *EW* are in the doctor's datebook."

"How did you—" He paused. "No, I wasn't a patient, but Emma was. She—" His eyelid started to twitch. His nostrils flared. A guy I worked with at Taylor & Squibb suffered the same ailments whenever he asked for a sick day . . . and he wasn't sick. "You know, don't you?"

I nodded. "I do."

Rhett said, "Know what?"

I whispered Emma's secret in his ear. His eyes widened.

Edward said, "Emma filed for divorce."

I gawped. Emma had told me she intended to stay married to her husband.

"I don't want her to leave," Edward went on. "I want to work on the marriage. I love her."

"Enough to kill your rival?"

"I didn't—" Edward sputtered. "Emma told me Pearl—Dr. Thornton—rebuffed her. I've asked her to reconsider."

"You'd stay married knowing her true feelings?"

"For better or worse. That was the vow we took." He shifted feet. "Look, just to set the record straight, I've told Chief Pritchett everything. She asked me for my alibi. It's rock solid."

I bit my lip. *Rock* solid? Did he really say that?

"I was at a meeting with a bunch of other cavers."

"People saw you?"

"They couldn't miss me. It was my slide show. My photographs. I was the presenter. Eight P.M. to midnight. I guess that's why Emma thought she had time to talk to Pearl. She didn't kill her, either."

"How can you know for sure? You were busy."

"True. But I know her. She's not capable." He glanced at his watch. "Time to go." He scudded his boots, one at a time, across a boulder to rid the soles of pebbles and debris and then raised a hand overhead. "Okay, everyone, let's get going."

As he moved on, I glimpsed the debris left behind. The raggedy leaves made me think of the crime scene. Leaves had clustered around the legs of the chaise lounge where Pearl was found. Where had they come from—Pearl's garden, or had someone like Edward tracked them in?

RHETT AND I spent the next few hours of the hike drinking in the views of the ocean. He asked how I knew about Emma's love for Pearl. I told him I was a curious soul and I had good ears, honed from hours of listening in at my boss's door whenever he was making a new hire. I wanted to know ahead of time with whom I might be working. Rhett warned me not to anger Cinnamon. He had experienced her wrath from a front-row seat. I assured him that she and I were friends; she knew how passionate I felt about justice for Dr. Thornton as well as for my aunt.

After a while, Rhett and I tabled the discussion and turned our conversation to safer topics like how much we both liked to travel and where we hoped to go. I had yet to visit the British Isles. Rhett wanted to visit Ireland. I was eager to go to Paris for a second time. I loved the artwork and statuary there. Rhett wanted to see Egypt, if it was safe, so he could explore the pyramids. I wanted to travel to exotic islands where I could sip mai tais and read, read, read. Rhett wanted to tour Italy and taste the flavors of every province.

At dusk, we wound up at his cabin. We entered through the garden in the back. He wanted me to view the rows of fresh vegetables he had planted before the sun disappeared completely and the light grew dim. The garden was luscious and wild, like him. His tomatoes were on their last legs. He had thriving autumn plants like Jerusalem artichokes, scallions, beets, and spinach. For herbs, he had planted oregano, lemongrass, rosemary, and more. Barrels of annual flowers stood among the perennials.

He let me help him gather items for supper, but he

wouldn't let me assist with the cooking. Smart man. I was invited to sit at the granite counter dividing the kitchen from the living room and sip wine while watching his handiwork. As I savored appetizers of pears wrapped with prosciutto paired with a glass of pinot noir, I took in my surroundings. His home was very male with a leather couch, an overstuffed reading chair, and Shaker-style furniture. A floor lamp stood beside the chair as well as a stack of at least thirty books. The décor included a television, but it wasn't one of those huge HDTVs. The kitchen was the room to which Rhett had devoted most of his attention. Copper pots hung from a rack. Utensils and oven mitts were plentiful. A floor-to-ceiling bookcase beside the Wolfe double oven was jam-packed with cookbooks that even I, a cookbook store owner, coveted. Many were autographed first editions.

For dinner, we sat side by side at the dining table, looking out the plate-glass window at the sunset. Over a delicious meal of maple-glazed salmon served on a bed of grilled spinach and scallions, Rhett told me more about his family. His mother's name was Melanie, which was another reason why she loved *Gone with the Wind*. His father's name was Hugo. They met at cooking school at age eighteen, Rhett said at first, then revised that. They had actually met as line chefs at a well-known restaurant in New Orleans, which taught them everything they knew. They had never been with anyone else and, to this day, were still in love. That was one of the reasons why Rhett didn't understand his father putting up a fuss when he had eloped with Alicia.

"But he objected, and I hate to say it, he was right. We weren't meant to be together. We were too young, too raw." Rhett wrapped an arm around the back of my shoulders. "Face it, if I had stayed with Alicia, I wouldn't have met you. You look beautiful, by the way."

I fingered the stem of my wineglass. "Uh-huh, right. In a T-shirt covered with dust from the trail mixed with the scent of warm perspiration." So much for changing into the little sexy number I had brought with me. The garden tour had nixed that idea.

Rhett nuzzled my neck. "All I smell is the perfume of your skin." He worked his way up my neck to my ear.

Passion coursed through me. Through us. I set aside the wineglass, turned my face to meet his, and our lips met. We kissed for a long time.

When we came up for air, my heart was pounding so hard I could feel it in my throat. I whispered, "I can't."

"Can't what?"

"I want to but I can't. Not yet."

He ran a finger along my jawline. "I understand."

"You do?"

"You've got a cat at home," he teased. "Obligations."

If only he knew how scared I was to give myself over to a man. I couldn't yet. But soon, I vowed. Very soon.

Rhett twirled a lock of my hair and gently tugged my head backward. The move exposed my throat. He grazed my skin with his mouth, then released me. "C'mon, I'll take you home."

"I can drive."

"Not without a car."

Right. His caresses had thrown me for a loop. I wasn't sure I knew which way was north. After collecting myself and my purse, I headed for the front door. "Thank you for a lovely day and evening."

"No, you don't." He gripped me by the wrist. "You're not leaving that way."

"Which way? We ate. We kissed. I properly thanked you."

"You only leave through the door you came in. Please." He was talking about the door leading to the backyard. "It's an old Irish tradition."

A wave of laughter—and tension—pealed out of me. "You and superstitions. Don't tell me one of your buddies down at The Pier gave you this one, too."

"Nope. Blame my mother."

Chapter 24

WHEN RHETT DROPPED me off at my cottage, we kissed again, better than before if that were possible, and then like a true gentleman, he opened my door, pushed me inside, and said good night.

The hour wasn't late, but it was cool. I threw on a sweater to walk the few yards to my aunt's house to fetch Tigger. As I exited the cottage, I turned to catch the door before it slammed shut. Too late. Swell. I had forgotten to take a key. I would get that from Aunt Vera, too. I hadn't thought ahead and hidden one in a garden pot or under a mat.

A branch or something snapped. I spun around and froze. Did I hear footsteps? I peered into the dark.

All right, *yes*, I'd also forgotten to turn on the porch light. At least there was moonlight.

Another sound. Heavy breathing.

"Who's there?" I asked. "Don't come any closer," I added, as if the meager threat would scare off someone. Maybe it was Old Jake, who liked to walk through the neighborhood at night. His mansion was located at the northernmost end of the beach homes. "Jake, is that you?"

When no one answered, fear knotted in the pit of my stomach.

Suddenly something yeti-sized ran at me. Was it Edward Wright? Had he come to set the record straight? I threw up my arms in defense. Every muscle started quivering. I was tall but no match for a yeti.

In the dim light, I made out Trisha Thornton—not a yeti. Shadows could play havoc with my imagination. Trisha's fuzzy hair stuck out around her head like coiled snakes. "You!" She didn't lash out. She didn't stick a gun in my face. In fact, her hands were jammed into the pockets of her peacoat. "What did I ever do to you? Why did you call UCSC?" Trisha shifted from foot to foot as if hopped up on something. Drugs? Booze? "Why did you sic that administrator on me? She called the cops. She talked to Pritchett. She told her everything."

"What's everything?"

"Why did you do it?"

Because I think you're guilty of murder, I wanted to say.

"Now my boyfriend's in a heap of trouble."

"Your boyfriend?" Did he kill Pearl? I returned to Bailey's assumption that Trisha, not Emma, had created some kind of potion using the Thorntonite to coerce someone to commit murder. Had Trisha lured her boyfriend into the plot?

"He's getting kicked out of school, all because of me." She huffed. "No, not because of *me*. Because of *you*. Sticking your big fat nose into my affairs." For the record, my nose was of the small, ski-jump variety. "You! Always squirreling around looking for clues."

"I don't do that."

"Yes, you do."

"I sell cookbooks," I countered, not to be sassy but because I was petrified and didn't know what else to say. Or do. Normally, I would have taken my father's advice and *run*. But Trisha had me hemmed in and my feet felt like lead. Where was the fight-or-flight adrenaline that I had read about in stories?

She wriggled one hand out of her pocket. I flinched. Did she have a weapon? She wagged a tissue at me. I breathed a tad easier, but only a tad.

"You're not making friends at the police precinct, by the way." She dabbed her nose with the tissue. "There are a couple of people down there who are not happy about your sleuthing."

Like who? I wanted to say, but I didn't have to. I knew. Maybe I should write a book titled *How to Make Enemies and Not Influence People*. Dale Carnegie, watch out.

Trisha slurped back a tear. "I wasn't supposed to be on campus that night. My boyfriend let me in."

"You really were there?"

"Aren't you listening?" she shrieked. "Yes, I was there. It was all caught on security footage. Time-stamped."

"You said there were no witnesses."

"I didn't want to get Sean in trouble, but now he is. Big-time. Because of you."

"I'm sorry. Truly." I held out my hands, palms up. "Did you really go there to work on a cure for diabetes?"

"Yes," she said with such vehemence.

I wasn't sure I believed her, but the fact that she hadn't punched me or mauled me yet was giving her some credence. "Your mother told my aunt you were taking a year off. Did she know you were on probation?"

"Yeah, she knew all right."

"For cheating?"

"I didn't cheat. I . . . I was caught with some illegal substances. I'm clean, now. I'm in a program."

"Did your mother find out the night she died?"

"Oh no. Way before that night. That's why she put me on an allowance. That's why we fought. If I messed up, which I did a lot, she made it very clear that I had let her down. Straight As? Forget it. Graduating college with honors? Ha!"

"The drugs?"

"Look, no matter what I did, it was never good enough."

"You don't sound like you liked her very much."

"I didn't, but that doesn't mean I killed her. Didn't you hear me? I have an alibi. A solid alibi. On camera. With time-stamped footage. Just so you know," Trisha went on, "if I'd wanted to kill my mother, I wouldn't have used poison. I would have strangled her." She shook clenched hands in front of my face. "I'd have twisted the life out of her just to shut her up. Her and all her advice. She couldn't seem to help herself. She always told me what I *should* do. Like she knew. Like she had the perfect recipe for how to live life. Get off drugs. Clean up your act. Take responsibility." Tears welled in Trisha's eyes. Spent, she dropped her arms to her sides, and then as if she didn't know what to do with her arms, she wrapped them around her body.

I let a long moment pass before I said, "I don't think you hated your mother, Trisha."

"I did."

"Yet you wanted to find a cure for her."

She gazed at me.

"Trisha, was your boyfriend with you the whole time?"

"What? No. He let me in and . . ." She made a fist with one hand and smacked it into the palm of the other. "Uh-uh. No way." The fire returned to her eyes. "He did not kill my mother. You will not pin this on him."

"The rock that is missing from your father's collection. You're the only person who could have taken it."

"That's not true. Mrs. Davies could have. That woman has sticky fingers. Did you know she swiped an expensive brooch of my mother's? I'm sure of it. I scoped out her stuff, looking for it. I thought it might be buried beneath all those newspaper articles Davies keeps. *Dear Abby*–type crap. It seems Davies wrote the stuff in London. Her photo is on every one."

I remembered thinking Mrs. Davies's hands looked afflicted with writer's cramp.

"She's a hoarder," Trisha continued. "I'll bet she has the rock, too. Some place. She's just waiting to pawn it so she can send more money back to her mother in England. I think the woman is hard up." Trisha sniffed. "I remember how mad Mom was when I told her about the brooch."

I didn't know if Trisha was to be believed. She could have stolen the brooch herself and blamed the housekeeper. "Do you practice alchemy?"

"Are you nuts? I would never do experiments with rocks."

"Someone saw you."

"Someone's lying."

"You were pouring something over rocks, making them bubble."

"Are you kidding me? Do you think I'm a witch like in *Macbeth*?" Give the girl two points; she was well read. "I'm nowhere near a witch. I wanted nothing to do with that whole phony-baloney stuff my mother did. I did not work with rocks. I only work with plants. I'm planning on being a plant physiologist. I'm studying the morphology of plants, their structure, and the phytochemistry as it pertains to ecology and medicine."

Whoa. The multisyllabic words spilled out of her with such confidence. But I wasn't going to let that stop my interrogation. "The woman who saw you said you were practicing alchemy at her house. With her daughter."

Trisha swore under her breath. "That's Mrs. Paxton for you. Who did she tell, Maya Adaire? They're thick as thieves. Mrs. Paxton is always overreacting. Her daughter and I were not doing alchemy. We were doing a high school science project about the reaction between vinegar and baking soda. It creates chemical volcanoes."

The door to my aunt's house opened. Aunt Vera stepped onto the porch. "Jenna, is that you?" She held a hand over her eyes to block the glare of the porch light.

Trisha didn't stick around. She bolted off. Seconds later, I heard a car sputter to life.

Breathing high in my chest, I raced to my aunt's house. She ushered me inside. Tigger leaped into my arms. His chugging calmed me.

Aunt Vera closed the door and twisted the lock. "What happened out there? Who was yelling?" My aunt was once again dressed in a caftan, this one covered in blue sequins. She had clipped her hair in pin-curl fashion around her face. Though she looked agitated for me, she seemed more at peace than she had in days.

I told her about Trisha. "Despite her weird behavior and her hatred for her mother, I don't think she killed Pearl."

My aunt laid a hand over her heart. "Thank heavens. I didn't want it to be her."

"You didn't?"

"Pearl adored Trisha."

"Trisha doesn't think so."

"But she did. Pearl talked glowingly of her. If she was hard on Trisha, it was only because she saw such potential in the girl."

"Enough about Trisha. How are you?" I grabbed her hand. Steady as a rock. "You look amazing. Was someone here?" I detected the faint hint of a man's cologne. "Greg?"

"Greg?" She raised an eyebrow. "Why on earth would he have come here?"

"The two of you. You're dating."

My aunt shook her head. "We *were* dating for a nanosecond."

"It's over?"

"We didn't have enough in common."

"What about the Coastal Concern?"

"A shared interest, nothing more. He likes hiking and fishing and spending hours on the sand. He's not into food. I don't believe he's ever looked inside a cookbook." She tinged crimson. "The sex was good, don't get me wrong, but I quickly realized I didn't want to go into my golden years wishing I were younger so I could hold on to him."

"Then who was here?"

"Deputy Appleby. He came to check on me." She chuckled. "Actually, I think he was trying to see if you were home."

"Me?"

"I think he's interested in you."

"No way."

"*Way.*" She buffed my shoulder. "He's not half bad. In fact, he's quite charming. He plays a mean game of mahjong. Did you know he's a widower?"

"I'm sorry to hear that, but can we not discuss him?"

"Whatever you say, dear. Tea?"

"Sure."

Aunt Vera moved into the kitchen. As she put up a pot of water to boil, she motioned at the deck of tarot cards on the table. Three were turned over. The Three of Swords, the Two of Cups—reversed or upside down—and the Hermit. What a trio. Now, as much as I didn't believe in any of this stuff, I knew my aunt did, and from what I remembered, the Three of Swords—with swords piercing a giant heart, rain cascading from the clouds, and a hint of sunshine behind the clouds—represented the end of a relationship that might be pretty new. The Hermit card was self-explanatory; it represented a time of isolation and perhaps reflection. The reversed Two of Cups, which depicted two lovers flipped on their heads, signified a mutual parting of ways.

I placed Tigger on the floor, then gripped my aunt's shoulders and gave a squeeze. "You can do readings again."

"I suppose I can. That's my life in a nutshell." Aunt Vera gathered up the cards. She closed her eyes as she solemnly shuffled the cards, not in the typical bridge fashion, more shimmying them together so the cards never bent.

"Can you do another reading and get a feeling about who killed Pearl?"

"Sadly, I can't. And my crystal ball is out of order."

"You're mocking me."

She winked. "Who do you suspect?"

I told her about Bingo's alibi, corroborated by Dad, and my concerns about Edward and Emma. "I can't figure out for the life of me why Maya would want Pearl dead." Though saying her name out loud made me wonder if her initials, not Marlon Appleby's, were the *MA* in Pearl's datebook. Had she been a patient? Did she, like so many others, have a secret to hide? "Also, Trisha tried to implicate Mrs. Davies."

"The housekeeper? There might be something there. Pearl hinted at having helped the woman out of a scrape."

"Trisha said the woman has sticky fingers. She stole a brooch from Pearl."

"Maybe that was the final straw for Pearl, and they argued."

"Would Davies know how to wield a hypodermic?"

"Darling, don't you think anyone could do it? There are how-to instructional videos everywhere on the Internet nowadays."

Chapter 25

WHEN I ARRIVED at The Cookbook Nook the next morning, I found another gift. This one was a paperweight in the shape of two infinite hearts with the words *Infinite Love* tooled into the metal. A big orange balloon looped with black ribbon was tied to the paperweight. At the knot of the balloon was a note: *To my love. SA*.

Secret Admirer. Even I could decipher that cryptic message.

I marched into the shop and jiggled the gift. "Does anyone know who is leaving these?"

Bailey and my aunt had beaten me to work and were busy relocating bookshelves to make space for the magic and potion demonstrations. Over fifty people had responded to our flyers and Internet newsletter saying they wanted to attend. The store was going to be packed, but I wouldn't turn anyone away.

"Got me," Bailey said. "Just so you know, that wasn't outside when I came in."

"Then how could you not have seen who left it?" I didn't mean to sound snarky, but the phantom gift giver was starting to get on my nerves. I had one mystery to solve. I didn't need two.

"Are you suggesting I wouldn't tell you? Puh-leese." She swatted the balloon. "How very Halloween. It's sweet."

"It's got to stop."

Bailey pinched me. "Forget about it and help us rearrange the furniture."

Tito knocked on the door frame. *"Buenos dias, señoritas."* He strutted into the shop. "I hope I am not too early."

I whirled around. "The presentation doesn't start until ten, Tito."

"Aha, then I have plenty of time to set up."

"Set up what?"

"I am your magician." He hoisted a black leather bag. "Your man had to cancel, so he asked me to replace him."

"You? Do magic?" I didn't mean to falter, but truth be told, Tito didn't strike me as the suave and magical type.

"I have hidden talents." Tito flapped his hand and a bouquet of silk flowers materialized. He offered them to me, head bowed, not making eye contact. "For you. A most beautiful lady."

Something triggered inside me. I glanced from the flowers to the infinity loop I was holding. Hadn't it appeared magically, too? *No way.* Tito was not the secret admirer.

He moved past me to Bailey. "For you, *presto.*" He shook his hand and a card popped into it. "Hmmm. No, that is not right." He chuckled—amusing himself—then flicked the card onto the vintage kitchen table and repeated the move. Up popped a single fake rose. *"Perfecto."* He pressed it into Bailey's hand. "A rose by any other name."

She thrust it back at him. "Thanks, but no thanks."

"Ah, but you must. It is bad luck to refuse a gift."

Bailey snarled. "Fine. Sure." She took the rose and flung it on the sales counter. "Bad luck comes in threes."

Tito, whose ego was so strong that he could probably endure having his feelings hurt by ten girls at the same time, set his bag of tricks down and rubbed his hands together. "I am here to help."

Bailey pointed toward the stockroom. "Get the six-foot foldable table." When Tito disappeared from view, she rolled her eyes at me. "Really? Tito, a magician? Do you think we can make him vanish into thin air?"

I giggled. "Let's give him a chance. We've both agreed that we like his reporting style. Maybe he'll grow on us. Besides, we made a promise to our customers. Lots of children are coming. They're expecting a magician. Even a bungling one will do the trick. By the way, you don't think—" I held up the infinity loop and inclined my head toward the stockroom.

"Tito? Ha! Not likely. If he is, why wouldn't he just say so?"

"Yeah, you're right. He's a bit of a—"

"Braggart."

"Not to mention he doesn't have that much romance in his little pinky." I tossed the infinity loop with the attached balloon onto the sales counter to be dealt with at another time.

"On the other hand," Bailey went on, "maybe he is the secret admirer, but he's scared if he admits it, you'll bite his head off."

"Yeah, I'm so scary." I wiggled my fingers in her face and said, "Boo!" followed by, "Get real."

An hour later, the shop was ready for the crowd. We had stocked a number of magic-titled books on a table, including *The Disney Magic Kitchen Cookbook* and *Magic Foods: Simple Changes You Can Make to Supercharge Your Energy, Lose Weight, and Live*. In addition, we had included kid-related fiction. One that tickled me was a Magic School Bus story called *Food Chain Frenzy*. Kids could learn facts about the ecosystem as well as eating habits. Cool, right? For fans of Maya's potion lesson, I'd included *The Spice and Herb Bible*, a practical reference guide from a revered spice merchant. For our book club fans—numbers of them had responded to the invitation—I had stocked copies of *The*

Book Club Cookbook, which included recipes and food for thought from a variety of books, like hot cocoa and chocolate fondue from the whimsical *Chocolat*. Tasty!

In the breezeway, Katie had set out caramel popcorn balls using the same recipe she had made a few days ago. Each was wrapped in pretty orange cellophane to be given out as gifts to all that attended. She had also baked miniature *magic* cupcakes. Half were double dark chocolate with gold-foil icing adorned with magician hats or canes. The other half were blueberry cupcakes topped with whipped vanilla frosting and decorated with tiny bunnies in tuxes. For a snack, I had feasted on one of the dark chocolate cupcakes. Besides Tootsie Rolls, I adored dark chocolate. Not being proud, I begged Katie for the recipe. I wanted to serve them at my Halloween party. She suggested I use a simple buttercream frosting instead of making the more difficult gold foil. Who was I to argue?

"Tito," I said. "We're nearly ready."

Tito, who stood in the breezeway dining on the sweets, said, "Coming." He had added a red cape and a magician hat to his ensemble and looked almost handsome. His eyes sparkled with enthusiasm.

I glanced at my watch and hurried to Bailey. "Has anybody heard from Maya?"

"I'm here!" Maya rasped as she raced into the shop carrying her black Burmese cat and what looked like a picnic basket. "Sorry I'm late. My blow dryer went on the fritz. My hair is a shambles. If I hadn't clipped it up, I would look like I'd been plugged into a light socket." She unloaded the basket, and the Burmese tried to scramble out of her arms. Coughing, Maya struggled to hold on to him while she pulled a bejeweled leash from her pocket. A tissue and a slip of paper flew out with the leash. She rushed to retrieve them, but the cat wouldn't comply. "Bootsie, hold still."

"I've got it." I picked up the fallen items. On the paper was scrawled the number for a Dr. Singh. As I handed the items back to her, I said, "Maya, are you okay?"

"My darned cold is worse. This doctor's concoction is

downright fabulous." She wrinkled her nose. "Okay, it's not *that* fabulous. It stinks to the high heavens, but it works. It's a real cleanser. He makes it in a gorgeous antique mortar and pestle. You've got to see him at work some time. Pure artistry." She wiped her nose, stuffed the tissue and paper back in her pocket, and bustled to the table we had set up for her and Tito. She secured her Burmese to a leg of the table and cooed for him to be a good boy. The cat didn't look pleased, but he settled down.

I spotted a group of costume-clad children and adults climbing out of a minivan and yelled, "Places, everyone. Aunt Vera, are you ready?"

Dressed in a burgundy caftan and turban, she looked like her old self, rested, restored, and ready to divine the future. She sat down at the vintage table and nodded.

When the crowd swelled to thirty people, Tito brandished his wand. "Welcome to all! For my first trick, I will require an assistant." He pointed to a towheaded tot who was avidly waving his hand. "Step up, young man." Tito went through the paces, asking the boy his name and where he was from. Next, he teased the boy, telling him someone must have taken the color from his hair. The boy blushed. With a wave of his hand, Tito produced a dark wig. He plopped it on the boy's head, stole the kid's nose, and promptly returned it. The audience laughed and applauded. Tito removed the wig, and the boy sprinted back to his mother. "For my next trick . . ."

Bailey sidled up to me. "Success." She bumped me with her hip. "Who knew Tito could be so adorable? He reminds me of someone."

"Who?"

"I don't know. Someone I met recently."

"Where?"

She frowned. "If I knew that, I'd probably remember who."

"Jorge?"

"Not likely."

"Any movement in that regard? Is he coming to his senses?"

She moaned, "Mothers," then waved me off: *end of discussion*. I felt bad for her, but what could I do? I wasn't Cupid. I didn't have a set of arrows at the ready.

Tito laid out three cups and one polished blue rock on the black cloth. Like a trained con man, he covered the rock and moved the cups around. This time, he asked a freckle-faced girl to help him. The girl hunkered down to make her eyes level with the top of the table, and she stared with deep concentration, as if she might be able to see between the black cloth and the rim of the cups. When asked by Tito, she guessed where the rock was: *Wrong*. She tried again: *Wrong*. She made a third guess: *Wrong*. The other children giggled. Someone called her *stupid*.

I hated that kind of talk and was ready to pull the plug on the magic tricks, but the girl shouted: "Sticks and stones may break my bones, but words will never hurt me." I applauded her spirit.

Tito quickly jumped in. "Okay, okay. Let me end your torture. You've done such a magnificent job, but I've tricked you." He revealed that the rock was not beneath any of the cups, and with deft hands, pulled the rock from the girl's ear.

The crowd went wild. The girl smiled, all better.

For another fifteen minutes, Tito regaled the growing crowd: losing a bunny and finding a lucky bunny's foot in its place, lighting up his fingertips, and determining the correct card pulled from a deck. When he was done, although the crowd shouted, "More!" he ceded the floor to Maya. Because he caught her in the middle of applying makeup to her red-chafed nose, he said, "You don't need makeup, my sweet. You are beautiful as you are." He hurried to her and magically conjured up the same set of silk flowers he had offered me earlier.

Maya shoved her makeup into her purse and stuck out her tongue. The exchange was so endearing, I wondered whether they had planned it.

"Hello, y'all." Maya crossed to the table and introduced herself for any that might not know her as she positioned pots of herbs, a beaker, and a cutting board in the center of the table. "Today, I'm going to show you how to make a love potion." The children erupted into titters; some of the parents covered their children's ears. Maya grinned. "C'mon. You didn't really think I was serious, did you? I'm going to teach you how to make a potion that will ward off colds and flus."

"But you have a cold," one astute kid blurted out.

"Aha. Good observation. Mine's on the way out because of this potion."

Or because she was going on her seventh day of having the cold, I mused. Most colds disappeared between seven and ten days. My doctor often told me to ride it out and shun medicine. I did my best.

Maya snipped herbs from the pots and chopped them on the cutting board. "Now, first, you want to start with a little myrtle and marjoram, both of which you can grow indoors."

As she proceeded, more people entered the shop. I was pleased to see many choose a few cookbooks and gift items before taking a seat. All took a raffle ticket for the giveaway basket we were offering.

Following the newcomers inside was Mrs. Davies, Pearl's housekeeper, wearing a black dress with white pinafore. Even clothed as she was, I couldn't shake how much she reminded me of Alfred Hitchcock. She was clutching the hands of two young girls, one on either side of her.

Out of nowhere, a stark-white dog, off the leash, raced to the front door and barked at the top of its lungs.

Maya snapped to attention. So did a lot of people.

A tremor of fear rippled through me. I knew the superstition about dogs barking at night. Their cry meant death was around the corner. What did the barking signify during the day?

Chapter 26

MRS. DAVIES SCUTTLED inside with the girls, then she
rushed to the door and closed it. "Hope you don't
mind," she said to the crowd. The dog paced outside as if
looking to find a way in. "Girls, are you all right?"

The girls, each dressed like Pippi Longstocking with
bright red braids, yellow and blue smock, and red panta-
loons, nodded.

Shaking off my fear, I moved to greet them. "Nice costumes, ladies. Mrs. Davies, are these your grandkids?"

"Heavens, no." The copious folds of her neck wobbled.
"I'm their new nanny."

"Nanny?"

"Trisha fired me. I had to find a job." She fingered her
white pinafore. "I've made myself out to be Mary Poppins
in no time at all. No magical umbrella, mind you, but we
sing songs and generally have fun, don't we, girls?"

"Yes," they answered on cue.

"Why did Trisha fire you?"

Mrs. Davies screwed up her mouth. Her hooked nose nearly connected with her lips. She released the girls and gave them each a gentle push. "Go sit, my little ones." Then she faced me. She lowered her voice and said, "Since the day I arrived from London, Trisha never liked me."

I thought of my terse exchange with Trisha last night. She had accused Mrs. Davies of being a thief. Supposedly she had swiped one of Pearl's brooches. Had she also taken the Thorntonite so she could pawn it and send the cash to her needy mother? Did Pearl find out? Would Mrs. Davies have killed Pearl to silence her? Choosing a roundabout way of getting to the truth, I said, "Trisha mentioned that you used to write a column in England."

Mrs. Davies stiffened. "I knew it! The little sneak saw the articles I kept. Yes, I did write a column. I was quite good. *Dear Mumsie*—that was the name of it. I was nearly a national treasure, one critic said. Much like your *Dear Abby*."

"Why did you give up a lucrative journalism career to move here? Were you off to see the world? Fleeing an abusive husband? Did you have a run-in with the law?" I winked, trying to soften my delivery.

"How would you—" She smashed her lips together. Her gaze grew steely. "Ahh, I get it. You were fishing. Fine. I might as well confess. Honesty is the best policy, after all." Through taut lips, she whispered, "Yes, I was in a bit of a bind. I had a penchant for betting the ponies. I was in debt and owed some bad people quite a lot of money. I met the missus in London, when her husband was doing a speaking tour. He was a revered geologist, you know. She took a liking to me, and I to her. During one of our lunches, I revealed that I was in a dicey situation. If I didn't leave England altogether, I could wind up swimming with the fishes, as your reporters like to say. The missus said everyone deserved a second chance, and she offered me a job. I didn't mind abandoning my position. I'd had enough of giving advice to sorry folks. My only regret was leaving my mother back there."

"I heard she's destitute."

"Mum? Heavens, no. Who told you—" Mrs. Davies *tsk*ed. "Don't tell me. Trisha. Wicked girl. Yes, I send money to my mother occasionally, but for the very reason I left England. I like to play the ponies. I never did lose that ghastly habit. Mum does rather well on my behalf."

"Did you—" How could I ask delicately? I couldn't. I plowed ahead. "Did you take something from Dr. Thornton to support your habit?"

"You're asking if I stole Dr. Thornton's brooch, aren't you?"

Not exactly. I was thinking more about the Thorntonite.

She sighed. "That Trisha has a filthy mouth. Her mother wanted so much for her." She shook her head. "Cross my heart, I would never steal from the missus. She was too good. An angel. I would wager Trisha was the culprit. She was always trying to blame others. She might be an A student, but she has an F personality." Mrs. Davies clicked her tongue. "Her mother will be sorely missed. Now, if you wouldn't mind, I should attend to my new wards. If that's all?"

What could I say: *You're under arrest?* For what? Confessing to a shady past?

As she walked away, I glanced outside for the offensive white dog; like a phantom, he had disappeared. I reopened the door to let in fresh air.

Bailey joined me. "What was that about?"

Before I could answer, Emma rushed past us without saying hello, her red sweater flying open, the tails of the scarf she wore around her neck fluttering with abandon. How had I missed seeing her in the parking lot? She was like a whirlwind of energy.

Bailey murmured, "Huh. How can she afford an Hermès scarf on her salary?"

Emma made a beeline to my aunt and pressed a hand to her chest as though she were out of air. She mouthed something. My aunt shook her head and reached out to her. They gripped hands for a long time. Emma released my aunt, bussed her on the cheek, and hurried back to Bailey and me. "Sorry for rudely running by, but that's the first time I've seen Vera since the car accident." She twisted the end of the scarf around a finger and released it. "The moment I heard, I went to urgent care, but she had checked out. After that, it's been like a nightmare at work. Over the last twenty-four hours, more than six dogs ate chocolate and were sicker than sick. Sometimes, I hate Halloween. Pet owners just don't pay enough attention. Wouldn't you agree?"

I couldn't answer. I was too busy gawking at the red, gold, and black Hermès scarf that Bailey had brought to my attention. On several occasions, Pearl had worn a scarf with the same design. She bragged about it being a gift from *him*. I had assumed she meant her husband. Looking back, I suppose the gift could have been from the man she had lusted over until my aunt temporarily won his heart—Greg Giuliani.

Bailey nudged me. "What's wrong?"

"Huh?" I sputtered. I glanced at Mrs. Davies. Trisha had accused Mrs. Davies of stealing Pearl's brooch, and Mrs. Davies had blamed Trisha. Were they both wrong? Was Emma the thief? Did Pearl find out and accuse Emma? Was the whole story about Emma being in love with Pearl a ruse to cover up her penchant for stealing?

"Jenna?" Emma said. "Are you okay?"

"The scarf you're wearing. Was it Pearl's?"

She fingered it gingerly. "Yes," she answered with no artifice. "She gave it to me as a gift for being her hand-maiden on the night . . . the night . . ." She pressed her lips together, unable to continue.

I felt my cheeks warm with embarrassment as I remembered the gold box Pearl had handed Emma right after inducting her into the Winsome Witches. Dumb me. Talk about jumping to conclusions. I was lethal. Lock me up and throw away the key.

Emma said, "Now, I wear it because . . ." She ran her teeth over her lip. "Well, I actually thought she gave it to me as a token of . . . you know."

How would anyone ever know? Pearl wasn't around to refute the story.

FOR DINNER I ate a fall salad heaped with grilled chicken, pumpkin seeds, and cheddar cheese. Then I decided to be brave and make a batch of double dark chocolate cupcakes—the recipe required ten ingredients, which I was able to manage. Yay, me. I didn't intend to eat them. I had made a promise to stay away from chocolate sweets after dusk, and I intended to keep that promise, but the aroma would calm me. After setting the cupcakes in the oven, I sat at the kitchen table and opened a new Coffeehouse Mystery by Cleo Coyle. I flipped to the back, as I was inclined to do, and counted the recipes. Over twenty.

"Wow," I whispered. "This is a cookbook. Here, Tigger. Up." I patted my lap.

Tigger, who was bounding after a sponge ball, skidded to a stop. He raised his bitty nose and eyed me, long and hard.

"Don't you want to snuggle?" I said.

He pawed the ball and resumed chasing it.

"Hmph," I muttered, and then recalled the day Maya dashed into the shop. Her cat had run off. Katie said that cats avoided owners when they were sick. "I didn't catch Aunt Vera's cold, Tig-Tig. I don't even have allergies."

He ignored me. I didn't dwell on his rejection. I had received plenty of love in the past week. I could have received more had I been open to Rhett's advances. I warmed thinking of his touch, his kiss.

You keep thinking like that, Jenna, and before you know it, you'll be making a phone call you'll regret. Read!

Would I really regret it? Rhett was entirely delicious. I could imagine long walks on the beach and scrumptious dinners at sunset—

Read!

I refocused on the mystery. Twenty minutes later, I pulled the cupcakes from the oven and drank in the rich scent. My mouth started salivating. It required all my willpower not to take a bite of one.

Knowing fruit would be a better choice for a snack, I fetched an orange from the refrigerator. I opened the drawer next to the stove to look for a serrated knife; I didn't keep one in the knife block. As I was pushing aside utensils, my hand brushed the flavor injector, and I flashed on the morning we'd found Pearl dead. She'd been injected with something. At the clandestine meeting in my storeroom with Cinnamon and Emma, I'd suggested poison. Cinnamon hadn't refuted me. I had never asked her what kind. Was the type of poison significant? Would Cinnamon tell me if I asked? She'd revealed that Pearl had been sedated with zolpidem.

I dialed the precinct. Cinnamon was responding to a breaking-and-entering call. The clerk said, "Why don't you speak with Deputy Appleby?"

Before I could say *no*, she patched me through. "Miss Hart," the deputy said. "How are you today?"

I bridled. Why did he always sound so arrogant? My aunt enjoyed him. Did I just bring out the worst in him?

"I'm fine, Deputy. I've been thinking—"

"Thinking." He cut me off. "That's nice. Thinking is always a good thing to practice."

I didn't laugh. I wouldn't give him the satisfaction. "Cinnamon—Chief Pritchett—told me that Pearl Thornton was sedated before she was poisoned."

"Did she?"

I didn't add that I had pried that tidbit out of her. I wanted Deputy Appleby to believe Cinnamon had willingly given me insider information. "I wondered if the coroner had determined the type of poison used."

"Why would you care? Oh, right." He chuckled. "Because you've been *thinking.*"

I pressed my lips together. *Play nice* ran like a litany through my mind. After a quiet beat to tamp down a come-back, I said, "Will you share?"

"It's the same poison used in Agatha Christie's *Appointment with Death.*"

"Digitoxin?"

"Aha, you're a reader."

"Deputy, I own a bookstore."

"A culinary bookstore."

"I've been an avid reader my whole life."

"Me, too."

Uh-uh. We were not taking a walk down memory lane to find out what we had in common. I didn't care that Aunt Vera said he might have feelings for me. I was so *not* interested.

"Isn't digitoxin found in foxglove?" I asked.

"Officially digitalis is a genus of about twenty herbaceous plants known as foxglove or *Digitalis purpurea*." He pronounced the words like a Latin expert. "The scientific name means fingerlike, as in the flower can be fitted over a fingertip. The term *digitalis* is also used for drug preps that contain glucosides or cardiac glucosides, particularly digoxin. Got it? Okay, bye."

He hung up, the creep.

But I didn't care. I had learned something. Foxglove, a pretty purple bell-shaped flower on a stalk, could be found along the coast. I had seen some on my hike with Rhett, which made me think of Edward Wright. He collected and photographed rocks. Did he do the same with flowers? Would he know the chemical properties of foxglove? What if he knew how to extract poison from the plant and revealed that method to Emma? I thought of Maya, who worked with herbs. She crushed them into potions. She had to know about foxglove's poisonous traits. And then I flashed on Trisha, who admitted she was studying plant physiology at college. I would bet she knew how to extract poisons, too. Granted, she had a verifiable alibi, but what if she or her boyfriend had rigged the cameras at the college to make it seem like she was in the lab at the time of her mother's murder?

Chapter 27

❧✖✖❧

I GLANCED AT Tigger, who was crouching beneath the kitchen table. He had trapped the sponge ball between his forepaws and was holding on with all his might. The poor ball was never escaping if he could help it, but then he lost control of it. The ball squirted away and rolled under the Ching cabinet. Out of sight. Tigger raced to the cabinet, hunkered down, and stared.

Seeing him in deep concentration made me recall a moment during Tito's magic act. The redheaded girl from the audience had crouched down so she could focus hard on the rock and the cups. *Sticks and stones may break my bones . . .*

"The stone!" I leaped up from the table. Yes, the method of poison mattered, but so did the missing Thorntonite. Someone had stolen it. Why? When?

"Storyboard this, Jenna," I said. "Start with the moment of finding Pearl dead." Storyboarding, first developed by the Walt Disney Studio during the 1930s, was a graphic way of organizing a sequence of events, frame by frame. I had used the technique often in my advertising career. The drawings weren't detailed, more like freehand cartoons.

I grabbed a piece of blank white paper and a pen and did a quick sketch of Pearl sprawled across the fire pit, arm extended, palm up.

Below that frame, I drew a second picture with a wider point of view. It encompassed the patio, the lounge chairs, and the garden. Pearl remained in the picture, across the fire pit.

Next, I roughed out a picture of Aunt Vera and all the others who visited the crime scene that first morning: Bingo, Maya, the police, Trisha, and the housekeeper.

Isolating Mrs. Davies, I drafted one picture of her talking to my aunt and me, not the morning when we found Pearl's body but a few days later, right after she discovered that a portion of Thorntonite was missing. She insinuated that Trisha had taken it. If Trisha hadn't taken the Thorntonite, then who did and why?

I glanced at my artwork. What if the sequence was out of order? What if the crimes happened in reverse? What if the killer stole the rock prior to Pearl's demise? What if Pearl found out about the theft and accused the thief? We only thought the two crimes were related because we found Pearl and then noticed the missing sapphire. For a brief moment, we all believed Pearl had been killed so someone could get his or her hands on the rock. The sapphire was worth millions. But then the sapphire was recovered. No harm, no foul. Had the killer put the sapphire in Trisha's backpack not only to frame her but also to divert attention from the missing Thorntonite?

I stood up and stretched. Did the order of the crimes matter at all? Were the two crimes related or just coincidental?

According to Trisha, Pearl wouldn't break up or sell her husband's mineral collection. Also, per Trisha, the collection was evil. She might have been right about that, if coveting a part of the collection had provoked murder. I thought of Maya's claim that Trisha was into alchemy. In addition to experimenting with acids and bases, Maya's friend said

Trisha ground down stones and buffed them. Trisha said she was doing nothing of the kind. Truth or lie? Was she curious about gemology, or was there something more to her activities? Perhaps she'd lied about doing experiments with rocks because she had wanted to keep her interest in them a secret.

I began adding new graphic drawings to my storyboard. When Rhett and I went hiking, Edward picked up a raw garnet. He said he was taking it for Emma, claiming she collected the stones in honor of her mother. So why, when I asked him about it, did he drop it like a hot potato? Guilt by association? I went a step further. Edward was a caver. He intended to visit all the caves in the world. Maybe, instead of continuing his career as a dentist, he craved a future as a geologist or as a collector. Perhaps he was amassing his own collection of rocks and gemstones. Was it a wild stab in the dark to think that he might be on the hunt for the original site where Dr. Thornton found his specimen of Thorntonite?

What was so special about Thorntonite other than its rareness? Per Emma, some people would pay handsomely to get their hands on shavings of sapphire; the stone had exquisite healing properties. Did Thorntonite have healing properties, as well? Could that make the Thorntonite much more valuable in the long run than the sapphire? I recalled Mrs. Davies saying that the *missus* claimed Thorntonite was packed with *sele*-something. Was that a mineral used in healing? Would owning an abundance of the mineral make someone like Edward Wright a fortune?

I opened my computer and entered *Thorntonite* into the browser. A number of articles emerged. The one that caught my eye, about sixth in the list, was written by a research scientist at UC Santa Cruz. Dr. Thomas Thornton had lent his Thorntonite specimen to the school the very week he had made the discovery. The scientist was surprised to find, in addition to quartz, silver, and copper, an entirely new mineral within Thorntonite, a mineral akin to selenium.

Selenium. That was the sele-something Mrs. Davies had been going for. According to the researcher, selenium was a trace mineral that aided in the healing of cancer. When used in conjunction with vitamins C and E, selenium could protect cells against the effects of free radicals. It could also prevent tumors from developing. The research scientist claimed that the new mineral found in Thorntonite would help treat cancer better than selenium, with very few side effects. Selenium in large doses was toxic.

I wondered again about Pearl's health. Had she been sicker than she'd let on? Cinnamon said Pearl's doctor confirmed that Pearl was suffering from type 2 diabetes. I had asked whether Pearl had cancer. Reflecting back, Cinnamon hadn't responded. Had Trisha, a budding chemist, learned about the special properties of Thorntonite and told her mother? Had Pearl taken the Thorntonite and ground down a portion so she could use it as a curative?

No, the more I pondered the idea, the more I was convinced Pearl didn't have cancer. She had none of the symptoms. Up until her death, she had vibrant skin and buoyant energy. My mother had grown so weak at the end due to the coughing and weight loss; her skin had turned jaundiced, her humor lackluster.

I resumed pacing, knowing I was on the wrong track. I stopped at the kitchen table and viewed my sketches again.

Pearl > rock; rock > Pearl.
Pearl > sedated > injected.

Who had Emma heard lurking in the house when she was there? Edward? Trisha? Mrs. Davies? Someone else?

I glanced at the second drawing of my storyboard and eyed Aunt Vera. Poor thing. Stress over the loss of her friend had weakened her immunities and saddled her with a miserable cold. Curiosity had nearly gotten her killed in that accident.

I halted and stared harder at the picture. I zeroed in on Maya. She had caught a cold, too. Hers was lingering. It was so bad that she had conjured up a potion to ward off colds and flus. What if she didn't have a cold? What if she had something much worse? Earlier in the week, she claimed her voice was hoarse from calling for her missing cat, but she was raspy days later. Cats ran from their owners when they were sick. Did they disappear for hours on end if the owner was dying? At the Winsome Witches luncheon, Emma had kidded Maya about using more makeup. Maya laughed and said she was considering becoming a cougar—a woman on the hunt for younger men. Later on in the ladies' lounge, I caught a sneak peek of Maya's pallid skin when she was reapplying makeup after rubbing it off with tissues for her cold. I didn't pay attention to her skin tone at the time because she smelled of marijuana. We chatted about her illegal crop. Was she using marijuana to ease the pain of a deadly illness—an illness that a dose of Thorntonite might heal?

I flashed on the note containing the holistic doctor's information that had fallen out of Maya's pocket. Singh was the name. Was the doctor using ground-down Thorntonite to treat her? I tried to visualize the telephone number. Was the last digit a nine or a six?

I glanced at the clock: 8:00 P.M. Would a doctor's office still be open? I dialed a telephone number, using a nine at the end, and reached a nursery school. Closed. I dialed the second number, using a six at the end.

A woman with an Indian-tinged accent answered. "Integrative Medicine. How may I help you?"

"You're open?"

"Only to schedule appointments."

"Is Dr. Singh there?"

"No. He's gone for the day. Might I take a message?"

"Can you tell me what integrative medicine is?"

The woman said, "We take the whole-person approach. IM, as we call it, is designed to treat not just the disease but the mind, body, and spirit. All of our products are herbal and naturopathic medicine."

"Does Dr. Singh use minerals in his healing?"

"Trace minerals."

"No other kinds?"

The woman cleared her throat. "I'm not sure what you are asking."

"Does the doctor grind down minerals like quartz or agate?"

The woman sputtered. "I'm sorry. What is the nature of this call? Do you wish an appointment?"

"Is your patient Maya Adaire suffering from cancer?" I blurted.

"What? How dare you." The woman couldn't have sounded more righteous if she were the queen of England. "Our patients' privacy is of utmost importance to us. Who is this? Are you an agent for an insurance company?"

I hung up, hoping she didn't have the recall feature on her phone so she could trace my number and hand it over to the police. Cinnamon would have my head. On the other hand, I didn't care if Cinnamon felt I was butting in. I wanted the truth. Pearl Thornton deserved justice. As my aunt, my father, and Rhett had advised me, perhaps it was my destiny to help those who couldn't help themselves. Maybe that was why I had returned to Crystal Cove.

While pacing the cottage, I considered Maya's motive for killing Pearl. If she was suffering from cancer or something equally horrific, at some point, she might have revealed her illness to Pearl, perhaps at a therapy session, if indeed she was a patient. Pearl, aware of the findings by the research scientist, would have mentioned the healing properties of Thorntonite. Maya, scared out of her wits to have the fatal disease, needed that mineral and set about getting her hands on a portion.

As friendly as Maya had acted throughout the evening of the haunted tour, I assumed she did not steal the rock before killing Pearl. Did she lie in wait until all the guests were gone? Emma thought she was alone with Pearl, and Trisha didn't mention seeing Maya, so Maya must have been hiding, or she had left and returned. The killer had come prepared with zolpidem and a syringe filled with digitoxin, which meant Pearl's murder wasn't done in the heat of the moment.

I envisioned the setup. Maya sneaked into the house, intent on stealing the rock. She overheard Emma professing her devotion and gleefully realized she had something to lord over Pearl. She wouldn't have to filch the rock after all; she would coerce Pearl to hand it over by threatening to expose Emma's secret. Pearl was too professional to allow a patient's secret to come to light. Maya waited until Emma left, and moments later, she appeared with drinks in hand, one of them laced with zolpidem. She toasted to a successful night. During the conversation, Maya told Pearl that her new holistic doctor could grind minerals into a curative potion. She appealed to Pearl's humanity and asked for a portion. I only knew Pearl to be a wonderful giving woman, but Trisha claimed her mother exhibited a cruel side. In the past week, Pearl's life had shifted drastically. She had been diagnosed with a life-changing disease. Did the ailment affect her personality? The night of the haunted tour, Pearl argued with Bingo and then quarreled with her daughter in front of all her friends. Did her anger carry over to Maya? When Maya explained her plight, did Pearl heartlessly deny her?

The scenario made sense, but I needed proof. Was there foxglove on the premises at The Enchanted Garden? If the police found it among the plants, would that give them enough evidence to prove Maya was the killer? I had toured the shop enough times to know that foxglove wasn't out in the open. Where might she hide it?

A notion niggled the edges of my mind, something that Rhett said to me last night about going out the door I came in. I thought back to the night of the haunted tour. A couple of teens were heading toward a door at the garden shop that looked like an exit. Maya raced to stop them and guided all of us out the same door we had come in. She said leaving that way was a Southern superstition. I hadn't thought anything odd about her request at the time, believing she was steering us away from that door because it led to her precious, temperature-controlled hothouse. Had she been adamant about us not going through that door to keep us from seeing what was inside? What if, along with her illegal marijuana and prized mushrooms, she was growing the lethal foxglove?

Chapter 28

I CALLED THE precinct and learned Cinnamon was still dealing with the breaking-and-entering case. According to the front desk clerk, masks and costumes were involved. Having no desire to go head-to-head with Deputy Appleby again, I decided that consulting my aunt was the best course of action. I hurried to her house and found her making candy. She loved handing out homemade goodies to the neighborhood trick-or-treaters. Most parents in Crystal Cove allowed their kids to bring home a treat that hadn't been store-bought.

I told Aunt Vera my theory about Maya.

Her eyes widened as I laid out every detail. "How could she have drugged me at Aunt Teek's? Bingo made the tea."

"But Maya admitted to starting to help Bingo before heading to the restroom."

"Why, then, would she follow me and try to get my attention by honking?"

"To make you drive erratically. She wanted you to crash."

Aunt Vera's voice dropped dramatically. "She wanted me to die."

"I'm afraid so. At the luncheon, you mentioned you were going to find Pearl's killer. The next day, Maya realized when the three of them arrived at Aunt Teek's that you were keeping true to your word. You were nosing around. Soon—"

"She felt certain I would remember something," my aunt said, finishing my thought. "I did happen to see inside her purse that night. She was pulling out a business card for one of the guests. Perhaps she believed I saw the hypodermic. Let's go."

"Where?"

"The Enchanted Garden is open late for the Halloween Eve sale." Aunt Vera spun around, looking for something. "I'll distract her while you find that foxglove."

"Me?"

"You're spryer than I am. You can slink around the place without getting caught. We'll need a sample of the plant to convince Cinnamon to take us seriously."

I shook my head. "Cinnamon will be furious if we confront Maya."

"Nonsense. She'll thank us."

I highly doubted that. I envisioned a future with my aunt and me sharing a cell with only water and bread as our diet. No more cupcakes or soup à la Katie. No more hugs from Tigger. "Aunt Vera, let's talk about this a bit longer."

"Where are they?"

"Where are what?"

Aunt Vera stopped moving and placed her hands on her hips. "Silly me. Of course."

"Of course *what*?"

"I have no car keys. My car is in the shop. We'll take your car." She propelled me out of the house while adding, "As if you'd let me drive anyway."

My resolve melted away. Had she worked a spell on me? No matter what, I knew there would be no arguing with her.

* * *

THE ENCHANTED GARDEN was bustling with customers, many in Halloween costumes. Fairies seemed to be this year's favorite little-girl costume; bloody monsters for the boys. The scent of pumpkin pie–spiced candles and freshly popped popcorn filled the air. Usually, I loved the aromas of autumn. Not tonight. Every fiber in me was tense. I could barely breathe, let alone smell.

Maya, in a long black satin gown and the witch hat with white flowers that she had worn all week, was near the cash register chatting with Pepper and a few of her beading friends, all of whom were wearing witch hats.

I gripped my aunt's arm to hold her back. "Pepper," I whispered, then diverted my aunt to the right. We waited until Pepper and her friends exited the shop, and then Aunt Vera approached Maya.

A consummate entertainer, my aunt pasted on a smile and reached forward with both hands. "Maya, don't you look glorious?"

"As do you, Vera. You must be on the mend."

Aunt Vera tapped her temple. "The brain is fully functioning, and the sensory perception is intact. What a crowd. Business looks good."

"Indeed. Many of them were at The Cookbook Nook earlier today. They loved my potions demonstration. Between you and me, some of the children look dead on their feet. It's way past their bedtime. But far be it for me to tell a parent how to raise a child. Besides, it's always good to expand one's clientele." Maya winked. "Feel free to put your business cards at the sales counter, and anything you find, tell the clerk to give you an extra ten percent off."

Maya started to leave, but Aunt Vera firmly grasped one of Maya's hands. "Darling, wait. I wanted to tell you about a new man in town." With her other hand, she waved me to get a move on.

My insides started fluttering wildly. My mind raced for

an excuse to explain why I wasn't staying and chatting with them. "Uh, I'm going to take a look at the gift items. I wanted to offer a prize at tomorrow's Halloween party. Maya, you have pumpkin vases, don't you?" I had seen them yesterday when I came in to ask about the identity of the secret admirer.

"We do. Small, medium, and large." She pointed.

As I headed away, I heard Aunt Vera say, "He came to me today for a reading. He's a bachelor. Just your type. A vegetarian. He has his own herb garden."

I stole to the door that Maya had steered us away from the other day. It was closed. Locked. I glanced at Maya and my aunt. They were turned away, their backs toward me. By the bobbing of her head, I could tell Aunt Vera was still talking. I ran my fingers along the top edge of the door, but I didn't find a key. I didn't spy a ring of keys hanging on the pegboard behind the counter, either. Dang. I swiveled toward the door and noticed a wrought-iron étagère to the right. Dozens of pots of herbs filled the upper and lower shelves. On the middle shelf stood a number of decorative bird feeders. One had a blue dome and a single drawer at the base. I recalled Maya whistling while fiddling with that drawer when I came to buy herbs last month. I slid open the drawer and found a single key. I slotted the key into the door's lock and twisted. The door opened.

My pulse kicked up a notch as I slipped inside.

The hothouse was expansive, about forty feet by twenty feet. The walls were opaque. Serrated-edged bushes—marijuana, planted in clay pots—were thriving along the left length of the hothouse. Down the middle were beds of tomatoes and mushrooms, the mushrooms blossoming blissfully out of chunks of wood. Along the right side of the hothouse, wooden shelving held dozens of pots of orchids, bromeliads, tropical vines, and African violets. At the far end stood a huge potting table fitted with two wide drawers. Pots, soil, garden tools, and a few vases of flowers sat on top of the table.

I tiptoed through the garden looking behind plants, but

I didn't see foxglove. Maya wasn't growing any. Was I wrong? Was she innocent? Did I need to reconsider theories about Emma, Trisha, or Edward being the killer?

As I was passing a section of orchids, I noticed a grouping of small dainty white flowers arranged along one side of a stalk. A marker named them: *Onvallaria majallis*. I drew up short. Weren't they commonly known as lily of the valley? I remembered doing an ad for Lily of the Valley perfume. One woman working on the campaign, a loudmouth with no inside voice, joked that the perfume should really be called Love Potion #9 because lily of the valley was poisonous. Was lily of the valley in the genus of flowers that could produce digitoxin or, as Deputy Appleby advised me, cardiac glucosides?

I flashed on Maya's satin witch hat, adorned with lily of the valley. Her business cards had a lily of the valley design on them as well. She was fixated with the flower because her mother had named her Maya Lily: *Maya* for May, when she was born, and *Lily* for her mother's favorite flower, lily of the valley, which bloomed in May. Growing the flowers indoors was the only way to cultivate them in October.

Pivoting, I surveyed the potting table holding garden tools and more. A beautiful blue porcelain vase, filled with stalks of lily of the valley, was perched on the far corner. Had Maya crushed the petals of the flower to create the poison, or were all parts of the plant poisonous? Would the water they stood in work as a poison?

I took a quick picture with my iPhone and started for the door, ready to relay my findings to the police, but I hesitated as I was passing the wild mushrooms. No, I didn't pause so I could admire them. I was recalling an occasion when I had flipped through a cookbook at the shop, on the hunt for a wild mushroom puff pastry recipe made with cream and Parmesan, heavy on the garlic. In the introduction, the author provided all sorts of photographs and instructions on how to grow wild mushrooms. Using a hypodermic needle, she had injected chunks of wood with mushroom spores.

Did Maya have syringes lying around? Did she fill a

mushroom syringe with deadly lily of the valley poison and inject Pearl after she sedated her with zolpidem?

If I could find the syringe, I would have more than enough evidence to take to Cinnamon. I hurried back to the potting table and scoured through the top drawer. I found plant tags, bags of seeds, green bamboo stakes, and bendable ties, but no syringe. I slid open the second drawer and gasped when I spotted an open package of cubensis syringes. Only three of the four were left, each with a clear pump and silver needle.

A waft of air cut up the back of my neck. Out of the corner of my eye, I caught sight of the door to the main shop opening. I bumped the drawer with my hip to close it and faced front.

Pepper rushed in. I tensed. What in the heck was she doing here?

"Aha," she said, full voice.

I whispered, "Shh."

"I knew it. You're up to something. I'm calling my daughter." She pulled a phone from her purse.

"I thought you left with your friends," I rasped.

"That was my intention. I saw you and your aunt slink into the shop, and all the hackles on my neck stood on end. I knew you were up to no good."

"Pepper, be quiet. Maya—"

"I will not be quiet. What are you doing back here anyway?" She scanned the hothouse. When her gaze landed on the marijuana, she gulped. "Is that what I think it is?"

I nodded.

"That's illegal." She started stabbing numbers on her cell phone.

Before she pressed four digits, Maya pushed through the marijuana plants wielding a machete, looking for all intents and purposes like a big-game hunter.

"Pepper," I yelled and pointed. Too late.

Swiftly, Maya slung an arm around Pepper's throat and said, "Jenna, don't move or I'll hurt her. Pepper, give me your phone."

Pepper handed over the cell phone. Maya flung it behind the marijuana. My heart sank. If only Pepper had been able to connect with Cinnamon.

Think, Jenna. What can you do? Throwing a pot wasn't going to disarm Maya, and I might clock Pepper in the process.

"How did you get in here?" I said, while glancing around the hothouse for some other weapon. Plants, stakes, wire, bags of dirt.

Maya grinned, but her gaze was feral. "Every building requires a second exit, sugar. Didn't you know that? Fire safety regulations. This one is hiding behind my stash. What are you doing in here, Jenna? Snooping?"

"What? No." I didn't sound very convincing. I peeked at the tools on the table. The garden spade looked snub-nosed and not hefty enough to battle a machete.

"Maya," Pepper said, her voice trembling with fear. "Why are you holding me captive?"

"Hush," Maya ordered and clucked her tongue. "Ah, Jenna, you and your aunt. Two peas in a pod."

"Where is she?"

"Looking for you. In the ladies' room. At least, that's where I told her you went. Then I locked her inside."

Swell. Aunt Vera was going to be heartsick that she hadn't foreseen where I really was. She was also going to be ticked off that she was trapped. Maybe she would pound on the door like she had when she'd gotten trapped in the bathroom at the back of The Cookbook Nook. What a load of noise she'd made.

"By the way, Jenna, you left the drawer of the bird feeder open an inch," Maya clucked her tongue. "Sloppy detective work, sugar. If you're going to keep up the practice of sleuthing, you've got to learn that's a dead giveaway of your intentions."

"Maya," Pepper tried again. "Let me go. Whatever your beef is with Jenna—"

"Maya killed Pearl," I cried. "She poisoned her with lily of the valley."

Maya smirked. "So you figured it out."

"Lily of the valley is your signature." I eyed the strand of vegetables down the middle of the hothouse. One of the logs holding the mushrooms might make a good weapon, unless it was rotten from the moisture. "The flower," I said, vamping. "Is it in the foxglove family? I imagine it has cardiac glucosides."

"Good guess," Maya said. "But why did I do it?"

"Because you're suffering from cancer. You needed the Thorntonite because it has similar properties to selenium."

Maya looked impressed. "Well, you are cleverer than I imagined."

"But Pearl said *no*. You couldn't have it."

"She was so selfish. I had a private conversation with her that night. After her argument with her daughter. She told me she didn't like being mean. I said, 'Prove it,' and I asked her for the rock. 'It's magical,' I said. 'It can save my life.'" Maya's face twisted with hate. "I trusted she would hand it over because she treasured being Pearl the Beneficent. She needed everyone to adore her. I told her with my miraculous recovery, she would get the credit for what her husband had discovered. After all, she was the one who told me what supernatural properties it possessed."

Magical. Supernatural. Maya was living in a dream world.

"But, lo and behold," Maya continued, "she refused me as she had so many times before."

"You'd asked her for help on previous occasions?"

"Three times to be exact."

"Why did she refuse?"

"Because she couldn't dream of touching her husband's precious collection, not for something as New Age as my treatment. She said I was crazy to even ask. Crazy. Me."

"So you went home and got the things you needed to kill her."

"Indeed, I did. I'd been considering doing her in for weeks, but that night I wanted to give her one more chance. I thought with all the good vibes going around during the

Winsome Witches events, she might reconsider. I was wrong. She was a vile, selfish fiend."

"You returned with zolpidem to lace her drink—"

"Isn't that a sleeping drug?" Pepper asked.

Maya ignored her, her gaze fully on me. "I needed her to be cooperative."

"So you could inject her with poison," I said. The word *inject* triggered a memory. Seconds ago, Maya said I hadn't fully closed the drawer of the bird feeder. I glanced over my shoulder at the potting table. As expected, the drawer was open an inch. Bless my bad habit! The empty syringes lay inside. Maybe I could nab one of them. A year out of college, I plunged an EpiPen into a friend who was in anaphylactic shock. She reported later that the pain I had exacted was excruciating. A syringe was no match for a machete, but I had to do something to neutralize Maya. Without turning my head, I walked my fingers down the inside of the drawer.

"When I came back, I saw Pearl lounging on the patio," Maya continued. "So I went to the kitchen to fetch some of that yummy Witchy Woman concoction. There was enough for two drinks left in a pitcher. I filled a pair of martini glasses and dosed one with ground-up zolpidem. The drug works faster with liquor."

Using my pinky, I drew the syringes forward. The plastic wrapping scraped the bottom of the drawer.

Pepper coughed loudly. Had she heard the sound? Was she covering for me? Was she finally on my side? If so, I really owed her a good batch of dark chocolate . . . if she would ever speak to me again after being taken captive.

"Then, thanks to this lovely *thing* I have"—Maya twirled her finger to signify the disease that had taken hold in her body—"before I approached Pearl on the patio, I needed the loo. I was in the bathroom when Emma showed up." She snickered. "So I finished my business, and I stole to another room to watch the whole event. I had a ringside seat. It was quite a show, Emma admitting her love to the dear doctor."

Pepper drilled me with a look. "Does everyone know?"

"I didn't tell anyone," I said.

"Neither did I," Maya said. "If I had, I would have been admitting my presence. Poor Emma. I do hope she can work it out with her husband. He's such a nice guy. A good dentist, too." Maya smiled. "Do you like how white my teeth are? Dr. Wright says a whiter smile makes people feel young again. If only I were a decade younger and didn't have this *thing*."

I pried one syringe from the packet. I wrapped my hand around the empty plunger.

"Anyway, while I was eavesdropping, Trisha showed up. She didn't see me. She, too, watched in secret as Emma threw her ring in the fire and Pearl reached to catch it. After Trisha and Emma departed, I realized my opportunity. If necessary, I could pin the murder on either of them. Two for the price of one. As store owners, ladies, you know the value of a good deal."

"What happened next?" Pepper said, as if caught up in the story, but I realized she was trying to draw Maya's attention away from me.

Kid you not, I was starting to like the woman. She had pluck.

Maya turned her face slightly. "As Pearl was dousing the fire, I appeared with cocktails."

"How did you explain your return?"

"I told her I'd left my cell phone behind, and then I let on that I'd overheard Emma's confession. I asked if she wanted to talk about it. She didn't. Even so, I offered her a drink."

"And she drank it, even though she'd been diagnosed with diabetes?"

"I convinced her it was okay. One cocktail wouldn't hurt. To celebrate. We talked about the party and the upcoming luncheon. After a few minutes, Pearl grew drowsy. That's when I attacked. I plunged the hypodermic into her arm. Instantly, she grew nauseated though she didn't vomit. As she lay dying, I promised her an antidote if she would tell me where to find the key to the mineral display case. She did. She begged to live. She sounded so pitiful that it almost broke my heart. But I didn't have an antidote. I'd lied. She died in minutes."

"You posed her over the cold fire pit to frame Emma," I said, finishing the saga. "You planted the sapphire in Trisha's backpack to draw the focus away from the Thorntonite you'd taken."

Maya grinned.

I said, "Is the Thorntonite working?"

"We don't know yet. These things take time."

"But you've run out of time," Pepper hissed, and like a karate pro, she jabbed Maya with her elbow. Maya, surprised as all get-out by Pepper's strength and determination, caved inward. Pepper grasped Maya's forearm and yanked downward. Maya was too weak to hold on. She spun away from Pepper. Desperately, she swung the machete, but she only hit marijuana plants. "Now, Jenna!" Pepper yelled.

I raced at Maya and thrust the empty syringe into her thigh. Maya fell forward. I stepped on the arm holding the machete and kneeled on her back. I didn't have many pounds on Maya, but empowered by Pepper's courage, I had grit.

The door from the shop flew open. Cinnamon hurried in, gun drawn.

I said, "How did you—"

"I dialed 911," Pepper blurted out.

Aunt Vera followed Cinnamon in. A clerk and a few customers clogged the doorway.

As Cinnamon cuffed Maya, I filled her in. On the lily of the valley poison. On Maya's sneak attack. On how Pepper saved the day with a little help from me. "I believe you'll find evidence of Maya being at the crime scene. Her fingerprints should be on the chaise. Marijuana leaves from this garden might be among the leaves gathered from the crime scene."

Aunt Vera said, "I knew something was bugging me about Pearl's patio. I'd noticed drag marks from the chaise to the fire pit, but they were gone by the time we returned."

"That won't be enough to convict me," Maya argued.

"I'll bet you coughed that night," I said. "You've been coughing for a long time. Your DNA will be in the area. Maybe even on Dr. Thornton's body." I looked to Cinnamon for confirmation.

She grinned. "Don't look at me. You're the expert."

Chapter 29

ᑲᴇ᙭᙭ᔎᔑ

ON HALLOWEEN DAY, I panicked and decided to hold my party at The Cookbook Nook instead of my cottage. Why? Because around noon, as I was answering question after question about Maya Adaire—yes, she was in custody and not being released on bail, and yes, she had been charged with murder—I had a *duh* moment. No way was I ever going to be able to cook everything for the party by myself in less than three hours after closing the shop. Sensing my distress, Katie offered to help. I wasn't stupid. I screamed *yes*.

On a break at 3:00 P.M., I flew home and picked up all the ingredients and my costume. When I returned, Katie was at the ready, arms extended. Popcorn balls—a snap. Wart-topped quesadillas with less than five ingredients—also a snap. In addition, Katie had borrowed a half-dozen cookbooks from the shop so she could whip up some adult desserts. All were divine. My favorite was a pumpkin cheesecake laced with maple syrup.

A half hour after we closed the store, I slipped into the

stockroom and donned my Dorothy from Oz costume, which was inspired by the Oz club ladies who had visited the store earlier—a sweet gingham dress, ruffled white shirt, short socks, and ballet slippers instead of Mary Janes. I weaved my hair into two pigtails. Next, I secured Tigger's witch hat to his head. To my surprise, he sat completely still. What the little scamp wouldn't do for a few oatmeal tuna treats. Finally, I dimmed the store's lights, and I toured the shop to light candles and tweak Halloween decorations.

"Nice pumpkin you carved," I said to Bailey. She had used a stencil of a witch riding an airborne bicycle.

"Thanks. I'm already practicing for next year's competition."

"What's that?" I said, pointing to a basket that was sitting by the register. It was filled with what looked like homemade caramel-dipped marshmallows. Wire-edged ribbon adorned the handle of the basket.

"What do you think?" Bailey held it up. "It's another token from your secret admirer."

At that moment, Deputy Appleby ambled into the shop, knocking on the door frame as he entered. "Hiya, heard there was a party." He was carrying a big bouquet of roses.

I did a double take on the flowers and the basket on the counter. Uh-oh. I felt warmth flood my cheeks. *Please tell me he isn't my secret admirer. Please, please, please.* I said, "You have to be in costume."

He grinned. "I am. I'm a floral delivery man." He pointed to a handwritten sticker on his shirt.

Tricky but not very imaginative, I mused. I snatched the basket out of Bailey's hand and brandished it at Appleby. "Is this from you?"

He shook his head. "Not I."

"Oh, really. Who are those flowers for?"

"Your aunt."

"My—" Not believing him on either account, I glowered at the note on the basket. If forced, I would attempt a handwriting analysis test. But then I laughed out loud. "Yoo-hoo, Bailey, did you read this?"

She shook her head.

"It's not for me, it's for you. It says, 'To my beautiful Bailey. Will you ever get the hint?' "

She snatched the basket back. "That's not Jorge's writing."

The front door opened and a warlock wearing a Zorro-style mask entered.

I said, "Say, isn't that the guy who played Pin the Bat on the Pumpkin at Vines the other night?" I stared harder. "Wait, a sec. Isn't the cape he's wearing the same one Tito wore as a magician?"

Bailey moaned. "Uh-oh. Remember how I said Tito's voice reminded me of someone? He sounds like the warlock at Vines, which means . . . it's him!"

Our intrepid reporter sauntered toward Bailey and reached gallantly for her hand. Before she could tug it away, he kissed it, and suddenly, thanks to a mental smack to the forehead, I realized that he—Tito—was the secret admirer. The tokens hadn't been for me. They were all for her. Simply because they sat in front of the store, I had assumed . . .

Well, we all know what happens when someone *assumes*.

I giggled. Wasn't it amazing how a guy could transform himself simply by donning a mask? Bruce Wayne became the Dark Knight. Superman added glasses and became Clark Kent. Tito, thanks to the power of the mask, was chatting freely, and Bailey seemed to be taking to him. *Magic.*

In less than an hour, The Cookbook Nook filled with family and friends. Katie, who had delegated the catering of the party to her staff, stood near the food table with her boyfriend, Keller. Both had dressed as zombies. Pepper was wearing a simple black dress with one of the prettiest witch hats I'd ever seen, adorned with lacy netting on the front, its brim sparkling with red beads. Before leaving The Enchanted Garden, she had hugged me and told me how thrilled she was that I'd picked up on her silent signals. We weren't best buddies quite yet, but earlier this morning she had warmed to me even more when I took her a dozen dark chocolates zinging with cayenne pepper, all made by Katie. Of course, Katie wouldn't take the credit. She assured me I would be able to make the candies in due time.

The door opened and Aunt Vera entered with my father and Lola, Bailey's mother. Aunt Vera was beaming. She wasn't wearing a costume—well, not a real costume. She had donned a spectacular purple caftan and turban, which clearly signified she felt her powers were restored. Deputy Appleby, true to his word, strode to her and handed her the roses. She blushed like a schoolgirl. What was it with her and younger men lately?

I hurried to my father and Lola, surprised to see my father wearing a costume. To my recollection, he had never worn one in his life, despite my mother's moans and groans. How had Lola talked him into it? I would bet she'd threatened that if he didn't wear something fun, she would show up nude. The two of them were dressed like Nick and Nora Charles. She wore a prim black dress with a white lacy collar and a perfectly coifed 1930s wig. My father—stop the presses!—wore a pinstriped suit. A phony black mustache finished the getup. Granted, the mustache looked sort of silly with his silver hair, but I wasn't going to mention it.

He hugged me and whispered, "You and I have to talk about what you did, dragging your aunt into a dangerous situation."

"Dad, she insisted."

He glowered at me. "We'll talk."

Lola hugged me and said, "Don't worry. I'll handle your father. Now, tell me everything. I just saw Emma and Edward Wright and Bingo and the Reverend walking down the boulevard. They seemed like old friends."

"Emma and Edward are putting their lives back on track. They're meeting with a marriage counselor starting tomorrow." Emma had rushed into the store first thing this morning to tell me the news. "She and Bingo are working hand in hand to make next year's Winsome Witches a huge success, in honor of Pearl. Edward has even agreed to attend."

"Wow."

"And Bingo has told the Reverend everything." The Reverend contacted the ex-fiancé. Money changed hands. The negatives were to arrive via express mail tomorrow. "Their wedding is a go."

"I know," Lola said. "They're having the night-before-the-wedding reception at The Pelican Brief."

My father, who seemed to have gotten over his initial peeve at me, said, "I heard the Reverend is quite a gourmet."

Lola rolled her eyes. "You should see the menu they've planned. Everything from fried eel to braised shark."

Speaking of gourmets, I scanned the party for Rhett. I wondered if, because I hadn't wanted to, you know, go *further* the other night at his place, I had scared him off. *Boo, I'm so scary.* Dang, but I could be self-sufficient.

Aunt Vera said, "I received a call from that sweet Mrs. Davies today. She's been keeping tabs on Trisha, despite Trisha's loathing of her. She feels she owes a debt to Pearl. Anyway, she wanted to give me an update on Trisha. It seems that UC Santa Cruz, given the extreme circumstances, has granted Trisha dispensation. Her boyfriend is not in trouble, and Trisha has been allowed back to classes, but she'll have to comply with weekly drug testing."

I was glad to hear that. The young woman would have enough to deal with in the coming years. Maybe knowing that she'd had her mother's love would help her mend, in time.

"Also," Aunt Vera continued, "it seems that Trisha has been in contact with a museum in San Francisco. With the approval of the estate trustee, she's going to donate the Thornton Collection. She wants no remuneration."

"Wow. How benevolent."

"Mrs. Davies clucked with pride, as if she herself had given Trisha the idea."

The door opened again and Cinnamon and Bucky arrived—on roller skates. She wore a carhop outfit that really showed off her muscular legs. Bucky had dressed as a fifties-style grease monkey, complete with a pack of cigarettes rolled into the sleeve of his oily T-shirt. Right behind them came a scarecrow. Full mask. Corn husks and hay jutting from every part of his costume. He punched Bucky on the arm, then walked with a bowlegged gait toward me.

"Hey, Dorothy," he said, then yukked.

"Rhett," I said, recognizing his eyes. "I'm so glad you showed up. I thought perhaps, after the other night, you might not—" I waved a hand. "It doesn't matter what I thought. Did you dress like that to match me?"

"Yup."

"How did you guess I was dressing as Dorothy?"

He tapped his temple. "I've actually got a brain."

"Cute. No, really?"

"Your aunt called me."

I eyed her. "I didn't tell her."

"Maybe she divined it."

I glanced at her again. Was she really psychic? All this time, I'd thought she was making up the fact that she had powers. To test out the theory, I willed her to turn in my direction. I would never know if she did or not because Rhett grabbed me in a dance hold and spun me around.

He stopped suddenly and said, "By the way, I wanted to talk to you about sticking your nose in where it doesn't belong."

"Uh-oh, what did I do now?" Had he and my father been chatting? Was I going to get a lecture?

"Cinnamon says she's going to reopen the investigation into the arson at The Grotto."

"Really? Yay!"

"Thank you."

He planted a kiss on my mouth that sent me reeling, and I was pretty sure I wouldn't put him off any longer.

Recipes

❦

From Aunt Vera:

*The very first year we held the Winsome Witches
luncheon, I was the one to come up with this recipe.
I'm not a big drinker, but I really love a sweet, fun
cocktail. A colorful drink in a martini glass brings out
the twenty-something girl in me. Invigorating when one
is well into her sixties. Serving the cocktail in a
sugar-rimmed martini glass makes the drink look ever
so festive.*

Witchy Woman Cocktail

(makes 4 to 6 drinks)

Sugar for martini glasses
4 ounces Midori Melon liqueur or Citronella liqueur
4 ounces dark rum
4 ounces light rum
8 ounces red cranberry juice
8 ounces apple juice
4 ounces simple syrup
8 tablespoons lemon juice
Melon balls for garnish

Prepare the martini glasses by wetting the rims and dipping the rims in the sugar. Set aside to let the sugar harden.

Meanwhile, pour the liquids into a pitcher and mix well. Set in a refrigerator to chill.

When ready to serve, pour 6 ounces of liquid into each martini glass. Garnish with a skewered melon ball.

Simple Syrup Recipe

1 cup water
2 cups granulated sugar

Bring the water to a boil in a 6-quart pot. Dissolve the sugar in the boiling water. Stir constantly. Once the sugar is dissolved, 3 to 5 minutes, remove the pot from the heat. Don't let the syrup boil too long or it will get thick.

From Katie:

I made this special chocolate as a favor for Jenna to give to Pepper. It did the trick. Pepper adored these chocolates. This recipe is an easy way to make your own homemade chocolate. You'll never buy store-bought again! Here's a little chocolate-making tip, however. Make sure that no water or liquid gets into the chocolate, as it can cause the texture of the chocolate to get grainy. Ick. Even be careful of wet hands or a drop of water when you pour the chocolate into the molds.

Dark Chocolate Laced with Cayenne Pepper

¼ cup coconut oil
½ cup natural cocoa powder
1 to 2 tablespoons raw honey or pure maple syrup
½ teaspoon vanilla extract
¼ teaspoon cayenne pepper
Pinch of sea salt

Melt the coconut oil in the microwave for 20 to 30 seconds until it is a clear liquid.

When the coconut oil is completely melted, add the cocoa powder, honey (the more honey, the sweeter the chocolate), vanilla extract, and cayenne pepper. Make sure all ingredients are well incorporated and smooth.

Using a candy pourer (found at specialty shops) or a pastry tube, pour the chocolate into candy molds. Let harden for several hours at room temperature. Then remove the candy from the molds. If the candy is not yet hard, stick it in the fridge to harden.

From Jenna:

I found a brittle recipe in a cookbook with the incredibly long title Ghoulish Goodies: Creature Feature Cupcakes, Monster Eyeballs, Bat Wings, Funny Bones, Witches' Knuckles, and Much More!, *but I didn't have all the ingredients, so I experimented and came up with this recipe. The author of the recipe mentioned that tons of recipes for candy brittle include a big baking soda addition, which can make the hot sugar puff up too much and get sort of cloudy looking. The puffiness looks cool, but the candy doesn't have the crispness that brittle-lovers crave. So, note that this recipe doesn't have a ton of baking soda. Also note, you need a candy thermometer. Luckily, I had one because my aunt was wise enough to furnish my little kitchen with one. She knew I had a sweet tooth. The recipe is easy. The candy flavor is divine.*

Sunflower Seed Brittle

1 cup granulated sugar
½ cup firmly packed brown sugar
1 cup water
⅓ cup light corn syrup
2 tablespoons butter
1 cup shelled sunflower seeds
¼ teaspoon baking soda
1 teaspoon vanilla extract

Grease a large rimmed baking sheet with butter. Put on oven mitts.

In a large, heavy saucepan, combine the granulated sugar, brown sugar, water, and corn syrup. Cook the mixture over medium heat, stirring constantly while the sugar dissolves. Cook until the mixture comes to a full boil. This will take 3 to 5 minutes.

Slip the candy thermometer along the side of the pan. Increase the heat to medium-high and continue to boil without stirring until the temperature reaches 260°F on the candy thermometer. This will take 10 to 12 minutes. (Note: the temperature gets to 200°F fast . . . but then be patient.)

Remove the pan from the heat, then stir in the butter and sunflower seeds with a wooden or heatproof spoon. (Don't use a plastic spoon; it could melt.) Return the pan to the heat and continue to cook the mixture, stirring constantly, until the temperature reaches 295°F on the candy thermometer. This will take about 5 minutes.

Remove the pan from the heat and quickly stir in the baking soda and vanilla extract. Be careful; the vanilla will spatter. Yipes!

Pour the mixture onto the prepared baking sheet. Spread it as thinly as possible, using the back of the wooden spoon or a spatula, and let the brittle stand until completely cool. Break the candy into serving pieces (I gently whack it with a mallet) and store the candy in a plastic ziplock bag. Remember to squeeze out the air before sealing. The candy holds for up to 2 weeks, if you can keep from eating it that long.

From Jenna:

I left the Winsome Witches luncheon with such a craving for this delectable cake. I told Katie about it, and she figured out how to make it. She said the trick was adding a dab of coffee or espresso. I have to admit it wasn't that hard to make. Chopping chocolate takes a bit of time and muscle, but that's it!

French Silk Fudge Cake

(à la Jenna, à la Katie)

(serves 4 to 8)

- 1 (3½-to-4-ounce) bittersweet chocolate bar, chopped
- 1½ (1-ounce) squares unsweetened chocolate, chopped
- 5 tablespoons unsalted butter
- 1 teaspoon ground cinnamon
- 1½ teaspoons brewed coffee
- 2 large eggs
- 1 large egg yolk
- ¾ cup granulated sugar
- ⅛ teaspoon salt
- 3 tablespoons flour (may use gluten-free flour plus ⅛ teaspoon xanthan gum)
- ½ of a 3½ to 4-ounce bittersweet chocolate bar, broken into ½-inch pieces
- Whipped cream or frosting, if desired

Note: I used Ghirardelli 72% dark chocolate instead of bittersweet chocolate.

Preheat the oven to 375°F. Grease four mini Bundt cake cups.

Place the chopped bittersweet chocolate, unsweetened chocolate, and butter in a microwave-safe bowl. Place the bowl in the microwave and cook on low power until the butter has melted and the chocolate is soft, 2 to 3 minutes. Stir often to avoid burning the mixture.

In a mixing bowl, whisk the cinnamon, coffee, eggs, egg yolk, sugar, and salt until combined. Stir in the flour. Mix in the chocolate mixture. Stir until smooth. Add the additional bittersweet chocolate pieces. Spoon the batter into the prepared Bundt cake cups. Fill about ¾ full.

Bake for 15 to 18 minutes, until a toothpick inserted in the center comes out with "streaks" of thick batter. The tops of the cakes will be nearly firm. Remove from the oven and cool in the pan for 5 to 10 minutes. Serve warm, or wait 20 minutes and serve at room temperature with whipped cream squirted into the center of the Bundt shape.

Note: If you want to frost this cake, consider baking it in cupcake tins. Bake 17 to 20 minutes. Or in a 9-inch springform pan lined with parchment paper. Bake for 30 to 35 minutes.

From Jenna:

*I know I've shared a bonbon recipe with you before, but
this one is really different and perfect for Halloween
because of the pumpkin. Now, mind you, the dipping
in hot chocolate was a challenge, but I did it! I'm
getting quite good at the fork trick.*

Pumpkin Pecan Chocolate Bonbons

1 12-ounce bag white chocolate chips
½ cup pumpkin purée
1 teaspoon ground cinnamon
¼ teaspoon ground ginger
¼ teaspoon ground cloves
Dash of nutmeg
1 cup ground pecans
1 12-ounce bag semisweet chocolate chips

In a small saucepan over low heat, warm the white chocolate
chips, pumpkin purée, cinnamon, cloves, ginger, and nutmeg. Stir until the mixture becomes smooth and silky.

Remove from the heat and pulverize the pecans by either
putting them in a ziplock bag and whacking with a mallet
or by blending the pecans in the blender. I personally like
the whacking method.

Now add the ground pecans to the white chocolate and
pumpkin mixture. Stir well. Set the mixture in the fridge
and let cool for a bit, about 20 minutes.

Line a 9-by-15-inch sheet pan with parchment paper and
scoop the pumpkin-pecan mixture by small spoonfuls (about
1 inch in size) onto the pan. Place the sweets in the freezer for
about 2 hours.

Two hours later: Slowly melt the semisweet chocolate chips in the top of a double boiler. You do not want this to go directly on the stove because the chocolate will get fudgy and thick.

Remove the pumpkin pecan balls from the freezer. Using two forks as tongs, carefully dip one ball at a time in the melted chocolate, covering the entire thing in chocolate. The technique requires *rolling* the ball between the forks.

Carefully slide the bonbon back onto the parchment paper. Repeat until all the bonbons are coated. If you need to, reheat the melted chocolate as needed.

Place the bonbons in an airtight container and set in the refrigerator to harden.

From Katie:

These are the easiest but possibly the messiest things in the world to make. They're a tad time-intensive because you have to cut up the marshmallows and caramel squares. You'll probably want a hot, wet knife when you're cutting. Also, be aware that when you are rolling these into balls, the gooey mixture is sticky and hot—not so hot as to burn, but be careful.

Katie's Caramel Popcorn Balls

¾ cup light corn syrup
¼ cup butter
2 teaspoons cold water
2¾ cups confectioners' sugar
1 cup marshmallows, cut into tiny pieces
12 caramel squares, cut into tiny pieces

8 cups plain popped popcorn
Safflower oil for molding

In a large saucepan over medium heat, combine the corn syrup, butter, cold water, confectioners' sugar, and diced marshmallows. Heat and stir until the mixture comes to a boil.

Remove from the heat and add the caramel squares and popcorn, carefully combining the hot mixture until the popcorn is coated on each kernel.

Grease your hands with safflower oil and quickly shape the popcorn into tiny balls before the mixture cools. Wrap the balls in cellophane or plastic wrap and tie them off with ribbon. Store at room temperature.

Note from Katie: If you want this recipe to be gluten-free, make sure to use gluten-free marshmallows.

From Bailey:

Okay, Jenna didn't mention this, but the recipe book that Katie took the recipe for Pumpkin Maple Syrup Cheesecake from is my mom's! Well, actually, it's The Pelican Brief Diner cookbook's. I introduced my mother to this fabulous cookbook publisher in San Francisco—she used to be a local in Crystal Cove—who couldn't wait to put the cookbook together. Mom adores sweets. I do, too. Especially cheesecake. I also adore breakfast, and there's nothing that says breakfast better than syrup. Pancakes and syrup. Waffles and syrup. Even scrambled eggs and syrup. Don't tell me you've never swirled your eggs into that last bit of syrup left after you've had a pancakes-with-all-the-trimmings breakfast. Anyway, put the two together, and this makes for a delicious and not-too-hard-to-make cheesecake. Follow the baking instructions. The wait time after the cake is baked is crucial.

Pumpkin Maple Syrup Cheesecake

1¼ cups graham cracker crumbs
¼ cup granulated sugar
¼ cup butter or margarine, melted
3 (8-ounce) packages cream cheese, softened
1 (14-ounce) can sweetened condensed milk
1 (15-ounce) can pumpkin purée (about 1½ cups)
3 large eggs
¼ cup pure maple syrup
1½ teaspoons ground cinnamon
1 teaspoon ground nutmeg
½ teaspoon ground ginger
½ teaspoon salt

Preheat the oven to 325°F.

In a small bowl, combine the graham cracker crumbs, sugar, and butter; press firmly on the bottom of a 9-inch springform pan. (Note: if you need to eat gluten-free, you can make this crust using crushed gluten-free sugar cookies.)

In a large bowl, beat the cream cheese and sweetened condensed milk until fluffy. Add the pumpkin, eggs, maple syrup, cinnamon, nutmeg, ginger, and salt, and mix well. Pour the mixture into the prepared springform pan.

Bake for 1 hour 15 minutes, or until the center appears nearly set when shaken. (Don't shake like crazy; a little nudge will do.) Turn off the oven and let the cake stand in the oven for 15 minutes. Remove from the oven and cool for 1 hour. Cover and chill in the refrigerator for at least 4 hours.

To serve, spoon some Maple Pecan Sauce over the cheesecake.

Maple Pecan Sauce

  1 cup whipping cream
  ¾ cup pure maple syrup
  ½ cup chopped pecans

In a medium saucepan, combine the whipping cream and maple syrup. Bring to a boil. Reduce the heat to medium-low and continue to boil for 10 to 12 minutes or until slightly thickened. Stir occasionally. (Note: this is a candy, so do not let the mixture go past the caramel color stage. If so, it will burn and you'll have to start over. So pay attention the last 5 minutes.)

Remove from the heat and stir in the chopped pecans.

Cover and chill the sauce until ready to serve. Stir once before serving. By the way, this sauce is fabulous over plain vanilla ice cream, too!

Dear Reader,

You may not know this, but I write two culinary mystery series under two names—my real name, Daryl Wood Gerber, and my pseudonym, Avery Aames. Avery writes The Cheese Shop mysteries. The sixth book in the series, As Gouda as Dead, debuts February 2015. I thought it would be fun for fans of The Cookbook Nook series to have a taste of cheese at the end of Stirring the Plot. Why not? So turn the page to read the first chapter of As Gouda as Dead.

If you're not familiar with the Cheese Shop mysteries, let me introduce you to Charlotte Bessette. Charlotte is the proprietor of Fromagerie Bessette—or, as it's more commonly known by the residents of small-town Providence, Ohio, The Cheese Shop. Charlotte loves offering samplings of bold cheeses and delicious wines, and for the pièce de résistance, solving a little crime. In As Gouda as Dead, love is in the air, but so is murder. When a beloved bar owner is discovered murdered on Charlotte's fiancé's farm, her betrothed— artisanal cheese farmer Jordan Pace—believes they should reschedule their upcoming wedding, given the dicey turn of events. Of course, Charlotte is torn up over the postponement. Could this put a wedge in their relationship? Even though the whole town is celebrating Valentine's Day with weeklong events, putting together lovers' baskets with heart-shaped cheeses at Fromagerie Bessette doesn't lift Charlotte's spirits. When a second murder occurs, and it's clear someone is not feeling the love, Charlotte is more determined than ever to smoke out the killer.

I hope you will join Charlotte and the cast of lovable characters as Charlotte once again seeks to right a wrong. Perhaps you'll even find a new cheese or a great recipe to share with friends.

For those of you who love *The Cookbook Nook* series, take heart. There will be more of those to come, too! The fourth installment will debut in 2015.

Savor the Mystery!
Daryl Wood Gerber

"WHERE ARE YOU taking me?" I asked. "And don't 'Hush, Charlotte' me again." I hate being blind-folded. Even as a girl, I despised it. I remembered one time when my oh-so-sly cousin coerced me into following him into a cave. We encountered shrieking bats and spiders and—*ick*—something creepy-crawly with a long tail that skittered across my foot.

"Hush, Charlotte," Delilah said. The moment I'd arrived home from work, she and Meredith, my other best friend, had hijacked me.

"It's Thursday night, for heaven's sake. I've got to open Fromagerie Bessette early tomorrow. We have so much to do to prepare for next week's Lover's Trail event before I—"

"We're going to a party."

"A bachelorette party," Meredith added.

"Yours." Delilah pushed me at the small of my back. "Now, move it."

"Look." I tried to dig in my heels, to no avail. "I'd be game for whatever you have up your sleeves if I didn't have things to do."

Tons of things: decorations to put up and gift baskets to create for the Lover's Trail event. Not to mention all the things I needed to do for my impending nuptials: a hem to stitch, boutonnieres to fashion. Did my sweet friends care? Not a whit. They were giggling too hard to care about anything.

A brisk gust of February wind attacked me. I shivered from the cold. "Where are we?" I demanded. Delilah had escorted me out of her car a minute ago; we were on foot. On cement. A sidewalk, I was pretty sure. I heard light traffic. I detected the faint smell of cinnamon and coffee. Were we near Café au Lait? I could use a cup of coffee. "At least take the blindfold off. It's tugging the back of my hair."

"No, ma'am," Delilah said.

"Ma'am," Meredith sniggered. "That's right. You're going to be a ma'am soon. Maybe we should continue to call you *Miss Charlotte* for a while longer." More giggles erupted from Meredith. How had Delilah talked her into this escapade? Meredith was usually the reliable and sane one. Sure, back in high school, she had been sneaky, but now? "Sounds like something right out of *Gone with the Wind*," she continued. *"Miss Charlotte.* Hmm. Which do you prefer, *Miss* Charlotte or *Mrs.* Jordan Pace?"

I didn't know who, where, or what was on the agenda for tonight, but in three days, on Sunday, I was moving forward with my life and marrying the man of my dreams—Jordan. A sizzle of desire shot through me just thinking about him. Prior to moving to Providence, Jordan had been the chef and owner of an Italian restaurant in upstate New York. One night outside the restaurant, he saw two thugs attack a third man. Without hesitating, Jordan, a former military man, sprang to the third man's defense. Days later, Jordan entered the WITSEC program to testify against the survivor, whose buddies had been the linchpins of a gambling ring. Entering WITSEC had landed him in Providence, Ohio. Lucky me.

"This way, Miss Charlotte." Delilah steered me to the right.

A door opened and I breathed easier. I recognized the jingle of the chime above the door. We were entering Fromagerie Bessette. The aroma of a potent Irish Cheddar cheese—our last sale of the day—hung in the air. I detected a hint of the quiche I'd made in the morning, too—apple bacon Gouda. It had been rich with a smoky, savory flavor.

"Let me go and tell me which way to head."

"Uh-uh," Delilah said.

"C'mon." I could navigate blindfolded through the shop without their help. I often dreamed about Fromagerie Bessette—or as the locals called it, The Cheese Shop—and its displays of cheeses, honey, mustards, and specialty crackers. Yes, I was a major cheese geek. Being a cheese shop proprietor was a dream job. I had inherited the shop from my grandparents, who had migrated from France to the States after World War II and had raised me to love the shop as much as they did.

Delilah joggled me. "Oops."

Although I would have been safe if I'd been allowed to grope along on my own, with Delilah as my guide, I instinctively reached out in front of me. Good thing I had. My foot hit something hard. "Ow." I grasped what had attacked me—a display barrel, the old oak cask kind with metal struts. "You did that on purpose."

"Did what?" Delilah guffawed.

"Shh," Meredith cooed. "Charlotte, just a few more feet."

Gingerly, I shuffled across the hardwood floor praying I wouldn't wind up with ten stubbed toes. At least I was wearing a pair of Uggs boots; they were padded and perfect for the winter. I still couldn't understand a girl wearing them in the summer, but I wasn't a fashion guru.

"Where are we headed?" I asked. "The annex?" The wine annex, which my cousin managed and stocked with some of the finest wines this side of the Rockies, was situated to the right through a stone archway. "Ooh, are we having a wine tasting?" I was always up for one of those.

"Sort of," Meredith said.

I had known Meredith and Delilah since I was in grade school. The two of them were like night and day. Meredith was blond and sun-kissed with freckles; she had a rosy disposition. In contrast, Delilah had dark curly hair, striking features, and a wicked sense of humor. Meredith was an elementary teacher and soon would run the Providence Liberal Arts College. She was married to my cousin, and stepmother to my preteen, twin nieces—I referred to them as my nieces; they were really my first cousins. Delilah ran The Country Kitchen diner across the street. She had returned to Providence after her career on Broadway stalled. Weekly on Monday, the three of us and a few other women went out for girls' night. I imagined tonight's bachelorette soirée was going to be an entirely different kind of event.

"What are we going to do at the party?" I said.

"It's a secret," Delilah answered.

"How many people?"

"Just a few of us."

"All girls?" I asked.

"No boys allowed," Delilah said.

"Well, almost no boys." Meredith snorted.

What had gotten into her?

A chilly wisp of air tickled my nose. Abruptly Delilah pivoted me and ushered me in the direction of the cold. Good thing I'd worn a cashmere sweater and heavy winter leggings. I knew where we were headed. Downstairs, into the cellar. My cousin and I, with Jordan's help, had installed a wine and cheese cellar. It was one of the best investments we had made. Even after cheese makers shipped wheels of cheese to us, we preferred to age some of them a tad longer.

I stepped down the stairs, drinking in the luscious perfume of cheese. The temperature in the cellar ranged from a cool fifty-five degrees to a toasty fifty-eight. Heat affected the speed with which wine and cheese aged. We had painted the cellar white and had fitted it with wood racks. In addition, we had commissioned a local artist to paint a faux window with a view of the rolling hills of Providence in the eight-foot, semiround alcove. Below the painting stood an oak buffet as well as a mosaic-inlaid table with chairs. Perfect for a small gathering.

My left foot touched the cellar floor. "C'mon, ladies, out with it. I smell something nutty with a hint of charcoal and fresh herbs. Are we having a cheese tasting party?"

I heard more tittering. Not from my guides. From other party members already in the cellar.

"Please say something," I pleaded. "Wait, do I also smell . . . suntan oil?"

Meredith brushed my arm with something furry.

I recoiled. "Ew, what is that?"

"It's a paintbrush, silly."

I moaned. "We're having an art party?" I'd heard about them. They were very *au courant*. "I'm not an artist. Isn't this supposed to be all about *me*?"

"No, you goon," Delilah said. "This party is about all of *us* giving you a fabulous send-off into married life. Get with the program."

"Don't worry," Meredith reassured me. "None of us are artists."

"You are, Meredith," Delilah chimed.

"I'm not sure about 'this kind of art.'" Meredith pinched me.

"What do you mean 'this kind of art'?" I cried, truly hating being in the dark . . . about anything. "Take off my blindfold. Now!"

"Don't get snippy." Delilah released my hand and moved behind me. She started to untie the scarf she had slung around my head. "One, two, voilà."

"Surprise," the other party guests yelled.

When my eyes adjusted to the light, I realized each was wearing a cream-colored artist's smock over warm winter clothing, and each held a glass of sparkling wine. A gorgeous spread of appetizers was laid out on a long table behind them: biscuits stuffed with ham, mini quiches, and one of my all-time favorites, a cranberry-crusted cheese torte.

"Turn around," the women said in unison.

When I did, I couldn't believe what I saw.

*Someone takes decorating for
Halloween to a deadly level…*

FROM NATIONAL BESTSELLING AUTHOR

B. B. HAYWOOD

TOWN IN A
PUMPKIN BASH

A Candy Holliday Murder Mystery

Halloween is on the way, and Cape Willington is busy
preparing for the annual Pumpkin Bash. Local blueberry
farmer Candy Holliday is running the haunted hayride
this year, hoping to make some extra cash. But her hopes
might be dashed when she discovers a dead body near
some fake tombstones. Now, as Candy uses her keen
eye for detail to unearth secrets, she'll discover that
not all skeletons hidden in this small town's closets are
Halloween decorations . . .

"A savory read, which brings the people
of coastal Maine to life."
—*Bangor (ME) Daily News*

INCLUDES DELICIOUS RECIPES!

hollidaysblueberryacres.com
facebook.com/HollidaysBlueberryAcres
facebook.com/TheCrimeSceneBooks
penguin.com

M1373T0913